CURIO CITIZEN

Katherine Forrister

Published by Inkshares, Inc., Oakland, California
www.inkshares.com

Edited by Ryan Quinn and Christine Ma
Cover design by Tim Barber
Interior design by Kevin G. Summers

ISBN 9781950301799
eISBN 9781950301805
LCCN 2024952942

First edition

Printed in the United States of America

For Johnny. I would have crossed the universe to find you, but luckily for us, you were the next town over.

CHAPTER ONE

SOME PEOPLE FEEL whole all their lives, or so I'm told.

When I was a kid, I would lie in bed and look down at my feet, and my legs would feel a mile long. I would wiggle my toes just to make sure they were mine. I would walk around on them each day and sometimes ponder, in a child's way, if my feet and I would ever feel like they fit.

As I grew, and my feet got farther and farther away from my brain, I still didn't feel whole. I wasn't sure if it was my feet, my brain, or everything in between that was at fault for the disconnect. Mamá had laughed once when I'd told her of those strange, private thoughts, years later at age eighteen. We'd been standing in front of a section of the Great Murals in Baja California, where ancient, painted giants hovered on stone over our heads.

"Maybe you came from one of them," she'd said, pointing at the largest of the featureless figures of red and black, "and you still remember what it was like to be so tall."

That was one of the last laughs we'd shared before an even greater piece of my disconnected soul blasted off in one huge chunk. A hollow cavity had grown deeper and deeper in its place ever after.

I guess that's why I was back at the Great Murals in the Sierra de San Francisco nearly ten years after that moment of gentle laughter with Mamá. I was trying to fill a hole that could never be filled.

I can still feel how dry my mouth was with ash that day. Every breath I took threatened to shrivel up my lungs in seconds. My protective goggles, respirator mask, and what little skin was exposed between were coated in gray, coagulating-with-my-sweat powder. I tried not to sway too much from the bungee cord suspending me twenty feet above the ground, while I brushed ash from the rock ceiling over my head with delicate flicks of my wrist.

"There you are," I said. "Thought I'd lost you."

A curve of red paint peeked through the natural rock shelter's coating of black soot. I recognized it as the right side of a painted human's head, twice the size of mine.

"Wasn't this one smiling before?" Crispin asked. He didn't sway at all from his bungee cord several feet away; one of his strong thighs tensed as he braced his big soot-coated hiking boot against the rock wall. He'd raised his goggles. Rings of ash encircled his eyes, the contrast like brown topaz sparkling amongst dull pebbles. Ash smudged his flat nose as well and coated the rounded apples of his dark brown cheeks, making it clear he was smiling, though his wide mouth and dimpled chin were covered by a respirator mask.

I huffed a small laugh as I glanced at the giant he was uncovering beside mine. He'd already exposed the entire red head and part of a black shoulder. Each of our ancient giants was divided vertically; half their bodies were red from crushed lava paint, the other half black from charcoal paint.

"No, and don't you dare paint a new one," I said. "This isn't a bar bathroom stall. And you better not be rushing this."

I steadied my worn boots against the rock and went back to brushing ash from the ceiling.

"Ah, that's right," Crispin said. "You're the one who used to smile."

I frowned at the ceiling. "What's that supposed to mean?"

"You've been on edge since we got here."

"Have you looked around?" I swung my arm in a grand gesture to our surroundings beyond the shade of the rock shelter.

Ash covered all. Wind whisked powder from the rocky ground so that it billowed and curled, an ominous threat to stir any lingering embers, but otherwise, there was no movement in sight. None.

What had once been a thriving, mountainous desert with verdant cacti, spiky agave, sprawling elephant trees, and sharp-crowned yucca trees was now a wasteland. Most of the plants would have been flowering this time of summer; we'd passed many blooms of all colors and sizes on our mule ride here before we'd reached the site of the recent blaze. Now the stunted trunks of cacti and blackened elephant trees emerged from the ash like fingertips of drowning people. The overpowering smell of smoke clung to the air and swirled like oil on water.

Here, coyotes had once trotted and prowled, kangaroo rats and rock squirrels had scurried, jackrabbits had loped, and small brush lizards had crawled. Their bones were now motionless, buried by the ash of their fellow dead until one of us workers scraped a boot across them mid-stride, scattering their small, charred remains.

The worst part was the oppressive silence, the otherworldly aura similar to that of wandering through a landscape of freshly fallen snow, but with a much heavier heart.

"Beyond that, I mean," Crispin said, waving away the view, though I knew it bothered him as much as it did the rest of our team. "This is your first time back here. After . . . you know."

My brushstrokes grew shorter, like my wrist was a string plucked by a musician in a quick, mindless rhythm.

"You haven't talked about it at all," Crispin said softly. His voice wasn't as muffled, but I didn't look to see if he'd taken off his mask.

"There's a reason for that, don't you think?" I said, squinting through my clouded goggles as I kept brushing.

"I'm not pressuring you, I'm just saying . . ."

"I'm fine."

"Carmen, you can argue all you want, but being here, Baja California, near—"

"I'm fine," I said, harsher this time.

"Okay," he said, though I could hear the skepticism and pity in his voice. My jaw tightened; my boots pressed harder against the rock.

The headdress of the ancient giant began to emerge, resembling two prongs of a jester's hat. Within the next hour of deliberate silence, I uncovered the figure's entire head. There were no eyes, and no smile. The ancients never painted themselves smiling, but were always stoic and expressionless silhouettes we archaeologists dubbed "monos." It had become one of my favorite aspects of prehistoric artwork, the lack of obvious emotion.

I felt a swell of comfort and relief that I had saved at least this painting's blank face from destruction. We were lucky that the wildfire's devastating flames had been limited in height by the low-lying desert scrub. If we'd been in a thick pine forest like some post-fire sites I'd visited, there was a chance that these seventy-five-hundred-year-old paintings, long protected by dry climate and isolation from humans, could have been wiped from existence in a single day.

I jolted as a loud bark broke through my concentration. I dropped my brush and grabbed my bungee cord to stop swaying as I looked down to see a medium-sized mutt sniffing my brush.

"Smita," I said with a smile. Smita yipped and pranced at my attention, wagging her bushy tail. She perked her ears, a quirky blend of pointed shepherd's and floppy hound dog's that gave her a perpetual lopsided, indecisive look. Her black and brown splotchy fur, speckled with white, was partially hidden by an orange vest with reflectors. She had a long pointed snout, but her mouth opened wide and her tongue lolled in a common expression that had earned her Hindi name: Smita. *Happy Face.*

Crispin laughed, full and rich, and gave a salute toward the ground. "Gaurav."

I looked past Smita to see Gaurav grinning up at us with the same childish anticipation as his dog. His balding scalp and the champagne frames of his glasses looked sleek and wet in the flashing sunlight, though their thick lenses were smudged with ash.

"Carmen! Crispin!" He raised his hand and bushy black eyebrows in greeting, revealing a yellowed pit stain under his white button-down shirt, with ash smeared across the tan scrollwork down its front. He wore it untucked, often claiming it hid his growing belly, which he blamed on his increased desk time after taking on a board position in our private consulting company, Wildfire Archaeology Response Services. He'd insisted on coming in person to this particular site, however, and from his excitement, I figured I'd soon know why.

Behind him, a pair of middle-aged colleagues I didn't know were in deep conversation in Spanish, with earnest eyes and sharp, ecstatic hand gestures. A gaggle of three college-age kids stood nearby, along with one of my coworkers, Pete Dockson.

"You're supposed to be wearing a helmet," Pete drawled, squinting his watery blue eyes up at me. Sunscreen was smeared across his pasty face; a big gob of it even clung to a strand of shining blond hair over his forehead.

I fought rolling my eyes. "You wanna come up here and do this?" I asked. He glared. "Didn't think so. Don't tell me how to do my job."

"He's right, Carmen," Gaurav said. "For next time. But you won't need it where we're going."

I frowned. "Going? Gaurav, I need to—"

"Trust me, guys, this is worth stopping for. It's about the site down the hill." He caught my eye. "We just got the lab results back. It's a lot older than we thought."

"Gaurav, you know that's not why I'm here this time," I said, glancing back up at the ancient painting.

"I know," he said, soft pity lurking in his gravelly voice. "But I need my best on this. And, Carmen, trust me, you don't want to miss it."

"So, the petroglyphs, right? How old are they?" Crispin asked, already rappelling down the rock. I did the same; I needed to get my brush from between Smita's prancing paws anyway. My toes were still a couple feet off the ground when I started fiddling with my carabiner, struggling a little with my ash-coated fingers.

"Fifteen thousand years old," Gaurav blurted out like a kid with a huge secret.

My carabiner snapped open. I slid down the rope, burning my palm before I could stop myself with a jerk. Smita jumped up on my thigh and made me sway. "Hey now! Baitho, Smita. Baitho."

Smita sat down at once, following my order in her only command-fluent language, Hindi. Even after Gaurav migrated to LA to teach at the university where I'd earned both my bachelor's and master's degrees, he hadn't bothered educating Smita to bilingual status. I'd always admired how obedient she was, which was the only reason Gaurav was able to bring her with him on post-wildfire sites like this one. Though, like him,

Smita had put on a few extra pounds after his switch to a board position. Knowing Smita, she was probably as bored as I would be if I had to glue myself to the confines of an eight-square-foot office.

I ruffled the thick fur between Smita's ears to steady myself.

Gaurav laughed. "I thought that might get your attention."

"Wait. Wait." I let go of the cord and found my feet. "If those petroglyphs are as huge and detailed as you said last week, they would have to correlate with a sedentary lifestyle. That would undermine everything we know about prehistoric life in this region."

"Gaurav, you're serious?" Crispin said. "That new art is *twice* as old as the murals?" He waved at the paintings over our heads and glided down his bungee cord with more finesse than I'd managed from such startling news.

Gaurav nodded, barely containing his broad grin behind his mustache and goatee. "We've found something big, guys. I want you in on it."

"Unless you want to keep piddling with those," Pete said with an almost-sneer. A woman beside him looked perturbed, but said nothing.

"Let me introduce you," Gaurav said, nodding to the strangers. I picked my way out of my harness and wiped my hands on my khaki shorts. Only ashy streaks resulted.

"I'd like to introduce you to Professor Luis Ramos Franco of the National School of Anthropology and History," Gaurav said with a genial smile at the man, whose short brown hair was ruffled and sweaty from his recent mule ride into the site. Our handshake was warm and damp. His leather-banded watch wiggled over his plastered arm hair; the gold-framed clock's face was too dusty for me to read the time.

"And ecologist for the Climate Change Impacts Project," Gaurav continued, "Señora Julieta Mendez Herrera."

"Julieta, por favor," the woman said as she extended her hand to me. Her white hair fluffed around her head in a messy bun, and though she wore sturdy khakis, her navy blouse was flowy and sophisticated, with a colorful collar of embroidered flowers. Her soft-looking skin was lined with venerable wrinkles.

"Luis, Julieta, this is Crispin Johnson and Carmen O'Dwyer," Gaurav said.

I smiled and shook Julieta's hand. Her four chunky silver rings had soaked in the warmth of the August day.

"Es un gusto conocerte. Gaurav has said great things about you both," she said. Her accent was coastal; she spoke so fast that her vowels were a blur in Spanish, though when she switched to English, she spoke slowly and took care with her pronunciation.

"Gracias. Nos da gusto estar aquí," I said. "I would hate to miss out on this; thank you."

She smiled wider, I hoped in approval of my confidence. I had a history of coming across as overeager. I'd tried to temper my enthusiasm over my career so that I wouldn't seem like a perpetual wide-eyed undergrad when, in truth, I was twenty-eight years old with a graduate degree and five years in the field under my belt.

"I was uncertain how many outsiders we should include in this discovery, but Gaurav assures me that you are both valuable assets. Your Spanish sounds Poblana," she added with a smile that reminded me of my abuela.

My smile faltered. "Sí. Mi madre venía de La Ciudad de Puebla."

My whole family was from Puebla on my mother's side, and it was easy to tell. My accent was markedly distinct, songlike and melodic, varying in pitch, particularly when asking a question. The Poblano accent was often referred to as "cantadito" by non-locals.

"¿Y tu padre—O'Dwyer—viene de Estados Unidos?" Julieta guessed. I nodded; my smile twitched into an awkward silence.

I didn't like to think about my father, Kevin Joel O'Dwyer, who had skipped town when I was eight, but he was responsible for Mamá's decision to emigrate from Mexico to the US when they married. Dad was of Irish descent born in Colorado, but Mamá, Lucia del Carmen Pérez Aguilar de O'Dwyer, was born in Puebla. My hair was thick and dark brown like hers, my skin the color of sand on a stormy beach but with Dad's freckles scattered across my cheeks and shoulders like seashells. My eyes were the same evergreen as Dad's mother's, Grandma Maisie (who I'd only met twice), but I'd inherited my mother's wide cheekbones and the gentle curve of her jaw, her angular nose, and full lips. My proportions were an echo of hers as well. Five feet six, thin-waisted, wide-hipped, and big-busted, though my career's penchant for taking me to rugged terrains gave me muscles she had never possessed.

Ethnic was often a word people used to describe me, especially white people. Fellow Latinx generally accepted me without comment, but some people would often ask, bluntly, what race I was. Ordering coffee—*Where are you from?*—as I stood with my hand outstretched for the cup in the barista's hand. Or filling up a gas tank—*I couldn't help but notice how unique you look!*—as I watched the digital numbers take too long. At a part-time job interview as an undergrad—*Tell me, what is your heritage?*—before I could even sit down, or worse—*Can I see your green card?*

"Pete's finished assessing safe zones," Gaurav said, rescuing me from sharing more details of my family, "so we can take a straight shot to the site."

Pete folded his arms across his chest. His chin was raised so high, his nod looked like a pigeon's head bob. I shoved my harness, tangled bungee cords, and jingling ring of carabiners into my backpack, which had been leaning in the shadow of the murals. I hesitated as I glanced at the painted giants over-head, still mostly covered in soot.

"My interns just finished La Natividad section of the murals," Luis said, gesturing to the three college kids. "They're my best. They'll take over from here."

I forced a smile. I knew it wasn't my right to be so posses-sive. Sure, I was half-Mexican, but I'd spent my entire life in the US. Those interns had more of a right to the Great Murals than I did, no matter how emotionally attached I might be. Still, I couldn't help but aim a subtle glare their way with a clear warning that they had better do a perfect job.

"All right, what are we waiting for?" Crispin said, rocking once on his heels. "Lead the way, Gaurav."

"Pete," Gaurav said, gesturing ahead. Pete smiled like a weasel and took the lead to navigate us through the stunted-tree-dotted landscape. The ground felt mostly firm and stable as we stayed within a path that Pete's team had marked off between double rows of wire stakes with hot-pink plastic ribbons tied to the tops.

I tried to resist looking back again at the murals up the slope, but I couldn't cut the string of longing from my heart or fill the guilty pit in my stomach, knowing I was leaving them to the hands of undergrads.

"I have to say, this is a unique situation," said Julieta as she fell in line beside me. "I've studied quite a few wildfire loca-tions in the past fifteen years, but none have turned into an archaeological site."

"Well, that's our specialty," I said. "Glad we can be here to help. You'd be surprised how often wildfires expose archaeolog-ical finds that we'd never know were there otherwise, buried under the topsoil."

She smiled with a ponderous nod. "They expose truths for my line of work as well. It's amazing to think about how much our climate has changed since these petroglyphs were made.

How much it's continuing to change. I've researched the causes of prolonged droughts and subsequent effects for years. I've studied the ecology so much, I haven't stopped to think about what the people were like back then. Being here is changing that." Her eyes twinkled with excitement. "Wait until you see the carvings. They're as detailed as any Aztec temples I've seen, but those temples are less than two thousand years old, yes?"

My heart beat faster. "That's right. If these new ones are fifteen thousand years old . . . well, if it gives you some perspective, the Great Murals were only painted around seventy-five hundred years ago. The only evidence we've got in all of the Americas of detailed stonework from before that are small sculptures and figurines. People lived a hunter-gatherer lifestyle back then; they were always on the move. The notion of stable civilization—cities, temples, walls, pyramids, traditional agriculture—didn't occur in Mexico until the Olmecs thirty-five hundred years ago."

I could have gone on for hours, but I doubted Julieta wanted a full history lesson. I'd learned through the years when to stop before people's eyes glazed over and to save details for my academic papers.

"Increíble," she said. "To think how far we've come. What our species could still do if given enough time. But . . ." She looked over the landscape, and a sad frown settled on her face. "Al que se aleja lo olvidan y al que se muere lo entierran."

Crispin lost his footing a few feet ahead, and I darted forward and caught his arm. He laughed and gave my hand a squeeze as he pulled his boot out of a small hole in the ground. A thin trail of smoke wheedled its way into the air from the hole, but it disappeared, nothing more than a remnant ember. Still, anger rumbled in my stomach.

"I thought you said this area was safe," I called ahead to Pete, who hadn't bothered looking back at Crispin's yell of surprise.

"It is," he sneered. "I've held my red card longer than you, remember?"

"Yeah," I said with a short laugh, "you'd think you'd be better at your job by now."

"Carmen," Gaurav said, sending me a subtle, stern frown. I forced my mouth to form a sober line when Julieta and Luis exchanged glances of worry as they walked past.

Crispin leaned in, bumping my shoulder with his. "Hey, 'the board loves Pete,' remember?"

I huffed at his echo of Gaurav's constant mantra on the subject, used whenever I bluntly pointed out Pete's inadequacies. Pete had been assigned the role of division supervisor for our most important projects for years. He'd screwed up more than once on other sites, leading to minor blazes and unsteady footing. I didn't think Gaurav was too fond of him, either, but he never said so. And now that Gaurav was on the board himself, he was even less likely to criticize.

"What did Julieta say a second ago?" Crispin asked.

"Oh, it's . . . similar to the phrase, 'out of sight, out of mind,' but like . . . those who go away are forgotten, and those who die are buried." I paused. "My mother used to say that. Mainly to remind me to chill out when I was upset. Put things out of sight, out of mind. Al que se aleja lo olvidan . . ."

I again swept my eyes over the landscape as we passed hollowed husks of tree trunks and stubs of cacti. Clearly, Julieta had used the phrase on a grander scale; humanity had turned a blind eye to the changing climate around us, kept the seemingly distant problems out of sight, out of mind. If we didn't do something to stop it, fires like this were only the start. We would be the ones dead and buried if we kept pushing our problems away.

One cactus nearby was still green and healthy on its top, but the trunk was cracked and burnt to a tan color, lined with blackened stubs of needles, its base reduced to charcoal. It made me sad, knowing that its lush green head would soon succumb to the ravages the fire had dealt; the cactus would fall and die, inevitable.

"It looks so different," I said. Why shouldn't the land be a mirror to how much my life had changed since the last time I was here?

"You sure you're okay?" Crispin put his hand on my shoulder. I stiffened. Strands of my ponytail lay pinned under his strong fingers. I'd often admired how similar they were in shade, both a rich walnut brown. My hair silky, his skin smooth, both warm and soft when tangled together on a cool pillowcase.

I rolled my shoulder. His hand fell to his side. The thin crow's-feet at his temples crinkled as he masked a wince with a smile.

"So, you excited?" I asked, slipping my hands into my pockets.

"Of course I am," he said. His eyes sparked, and his broad forehead lost all lines of concern as he grinned. "We dropped everything in New Mexico to come here, didn't we? I could have stayed there researching our dear old Jornada Mogollan."

"Like you would have."

He chuckled. "I was ready to chase the next fire anyway."

I knew how he felt. Chasing fires was what we lived for. Wildfire archaeology was a niche job, to be sure, but as wildfires became more frequent, so did the need for archaeologists when some park ranger would call us up wondering what to do with some ancient figurine or pottery sherds. For me, the possibility of brand-new discoveries and the drop-everything-at-a-moment's-notice lifestyle was exhilarating. We'd arrive as soon as the flames were suppressed by firefighters and bordered in flame-retardant powder, ready to comb the ashes for any newly exposed artifacts.

I had studied sites from all manner of different cultures and locations throughout my career, trying to answer the perpetual questions of *who* and *how* and *why*—questions that no anthropologists would ever truly know the answers to, yet we wanted to weigh in all the same. We fancied ourselves academics, but really, we each did it just to satisfy our own damn curiosity. What were people like so many years ago? How were they the same as us? How were they different? What on earth did they use this bizarre tool for?

Or, my job—what the hell were these artists thinking when they painted *this*?

The closer we got toward the fresh site that the devastating Baja California wildfire had unveiled, the more my excitement grew. I always felt guilty at times like these, when other people's and animals' sufferings yielded discoveries that dazzled my mind. The local rancheros had been the focus of the firefighters' protection during this wild blaze, so little was harmed as far as buildings and homes went, but the desert ecosystem was obliterated within days. The animals and vegetation people relied on were gone, and in some cases, their livelihood along with it. My guilt was even heavier now after my conversation with Julieta, who had reminded me that these wildfires were a sign that all of Earth's and humanity's well-being was at stake with our changing climate. Our ancestors had faced such drastic changes in the past and won by the skin of their teeth. Would we?

Yet, my guilt fled entirely when we arrived at the site of the new discovery.

I stared with wonder at a large sculpture standing in a shallow pit in the ground, surrounded by nothing but a wide expanse of ash. The rear half of the sculpture looked like a natural boulder, but the front-facing panel was chiseled into one of the most detailed bas-reliefs I had ever seen. The bas-relief was shaped like an arch, no less than fifteen feet wide and six feet high, though I suspected it was much taller because the lower half curved inward, suggesting it might be a full circle. For now, the beautiful carvings disappeared into the ash and soil at the boulder's base.

The wildfire had exposed the top of the stunning petroglyphs; it was up to us to dig them the rest of the way out. Pete's team had gotten a good start throughout the past week, regardless of my criticisms of his personal leadership style. The lower half of the art was off-color brown, showing the layer where they'd dug through the ash to hit the soil underneath.

"See? What did I tell ya?" said Gaurav.

I hopped the few feet down into the pit, feeling a familiar seed of awe budding in my chest and blossoming into my mind with heady elation. I could barely take all the artwork in; my eyes wandered in dizzying circles around the outer edge of the arched panel, which was carved with a series of geometric reliefs that resembled gemstones, as if a lapidary had abandoned the fine jewelry business and decided that dull limestone was a far more worthwhile medium.

Thin lines of obsidian were embedded in the grooves between each relief, so the boulder glimmered in the sunlight. The pale stone on either side was so flat and smooth, it didn't seem like millennia could have passed at all, but the lab's assessment of the obsidian and volcanic deposits couldn't lie.

Two thin arches were chiseled within the boundaries of the gem-style border, and they overlapped in the bas-relief's center like two petals around a flower pistil. A person's profile was carved from head to shoulders within the center of the abstract flower. The person was bald, but looked feminine. She held her chin high with her eyes raised upward. She had no eyebrows and her eyelids had no lashes; her nose was small and straight, and her ears were smaller than most people's. Her neck was long and slender, and though no other adornments were pictured, she wore some kind of mantel upon her shoulders that created an illusion of two rigid half disks standing upon them. Her thin lips wore an enigmatic Mona Lisa smile.

My eyes zinged like Ping-Pong balls from one side of the bas-relief to the other. A smaller bas-relief of a man holding an upright staff stood within one arch, while in the other, a woman supported a basket on her head. They each had long hair bound upon their heads; the man had a bushy beard.

None of the depictions of people were solid, monochromatic silhouettes like I was used to seeing on stone walls from fifteen thousand years ago, hell, even from thirty thousand years ago. Unlike the geometric border, the chiseled people were not stylized in any way, but were pieces of realism.

They were all smiling.

"Impossible," I whispered. "This would have taken years."

Running with my suspicions that this artwork continued underground, perhaps to form a complete circle, I couldn't help but compare it to the Aztec Sun Stone that Julieta had mentioned. The Sun Stone had been created with stone chisels like the bas-relief in front of me must have been, but the Sun Stone was made in the 1500s and had no doubt taken years to complete. The Aztecs were sedentary people, a huge, impressive civilization. If this new carving had taken even half as many years as the Sun Stone, it would mean that the ancient people, who we thought were hunter-gatherers in 13000 BCE, had been a sedentary civilization. Either that, or this project was deemed important enough that generations had revisited this same spot—a spiritual pilgrimage, perhaps—to continue their ancestors' work time and time again.

Regardless of how similar the shape and concentric circles were to many examples of Aztec calendar stones or sacrificial temalacatl stones, or meditative mandalas of Hindu and

Buddhism, they were different from any civilization's style that I had ever seen or heard about. Smoke lingering in the air conjured images of ancient campfires in my mind, but I found it harder than usual to imagine the people who could have created such a magnificent piece of art, no matter how vividly they were portrayed in stone.

I squinted as I saw faded scratches arranged in what looked like purposeful designs, etched in three rows above the ancient people as if watching over them.

"Is this . . . This can't be an inscription," I said. I looked over my shoulder at Gaurav and Luis. "Is it from a later date?"

"No, it's not," said Luis. "We have a top linguistic expert coming in this week."

"Didn't I tell you this was big, Carmen?" said Gaurav, patting Smita's head beside him. She popped to her feet and looked around at all of us with eager, bright eyes and an expectant perk of her ears.

Crispin crouched beside me. He gave a low whistle of admiration as his eyes roved the artwork and possible *writing* from thousands of years before we'd thought the written word had ever been invented.

"Pete's team has been digging all week so we can get a better look at the rest," Gaurav said. "I want you both to be there when they finish."

"Of course," I said. "You have a track hoe?"

"You should know by now that digging post-fire sites has to be done with care," Pete said, his large hooked nose wrinkling as he sniffed.

Of course I knew. The guy couldn't even pick up sarcasm.

Gaurav didn't lose his childish grin. "We pace ourselves, do this right, and we could be doing academic tours all over the world next year. Be patient, Carmen."

"Have you met her?" Crispin said. Gaurav chuckled.

Luis's handheld radio crackled, making me jump. I tuned out his half conversation in Spanish, but was forced to pay attention when he announced his boss from the National Institute had arrived and was waiting for us at the makeshift town of tents we'd set up a ways off, blocked from the fire zone by a massive table rock formation.

Though reluctant, I pushed myself off the ground and clapped dust from my hands. As much as I wanted to stick around, I knew that meeting the local boss would be necessary to put myself definitively on this project. I might have come to Baja California to pay homage to my mother by saving the Great Murals, but I couldn't help but latch onto this new discovery and follow the team toward camp. I was arguing with myself about whether Mamá would frown upon my actions or not when, thirty or so feet down the hill, my reluctant trudge scuffed to a halt. Crispin bumped into me with a grunt.

"You two coming?" Pete drawled from ahead, eyeing us like we were the laziest people he'd ever met.

I glanced at Gaurav, feeling an irritating flush of embarrassment, but straightened up.

"There's a little section of the Great Murals not far off the path," I said, nodding to our left. "Can I check on it? Won't be long."

Gaurav nodded, his smile sympathetic. "That's fine. You checked this whole area, Pete?"

"Of course I did," Pete replied. "All cooled off and solid as a rock."

"I'll stay with you," Crispin said. He lowered his voice. "I don't care how safe Pete says this area is."

I huffed a wry laugh and headed left, eyeing the departing group until they were out of sight. Crispin tagged along for fifty or so feet until we entered the shade of another rock shelter, dusted with soot. I remembered it from my visit years ago, a smaller section of the four hundred Great Murals in the regions of Baja California and Baja California Sur. Yet, this one was nearly unrecognizable now without the surrounding shrubs and cacti. An elephant tree had once lorded over the outcrop, the roots sprawling around the rock. Now the tree trunk was a severed hand; the gnarled roots clung to the rock like dead, charred fingers.

I looked at the ceiling of the rock outcrop. Amidst the ash, a few painted deer frolicked beside two featureless mono figures of humans. I let out a soft breath of relief. At least this mural hadn't been harmed.

I lowered my gaze from the ceiling and inspected the rock wall at the back of the natural shelter. The elephant tree's roots snaked down the jagged rock and coalesced into a blackened mesh on the ground. Through the mesh, any soil that might have once existed was burned away. The wildfire had exposed a hole.

"Crispin, look."

I pointed at the mesh near my boots. Despite Crispin's cautious, trained steps, ash puffed up as he joined me.

"What is it?" he asked. "Whoa. Is that—"

"More," I said. I crouched and brushed aside black, twisted bits of cacti and yanked at stubborn scrub roots, though the thicker elephant tree roots wouldn't budge. A black pyro beetle, seeking a place to lay its eggs in the heat of the receding wildfire, scuttled out of the way.

With Crispin's help, we cleared away enough of the charred roots to reveal a rocky hole about three feet across. Gem-style carvings like what we'd observed at the site behind us crawled down the stone into the narrow entrance of a cave.

"We've gotta go get everyone," Crispin said.

"No." I caught his leg. He swayed and playfully kicked my hand away. "Crispin, wait. Everyone else will descend on it like a flock of vultures."

"Respectful vultures."

"Yeah, but don't you want to see it first?"

I fished for my hard hat in my backpack and settled it on my head. The yellow beam of its lamp illuminated more of the cave's carved wall below, but I couldn't see the bottom. I grabbed a rock near to hand and dropped it into the black maw. It hit with a dry clatter in seconds.

"It isn't deep."

"Carmen, we should wait. It might be unstable."

"Pete said this area is safe."

"Yeah, and I thought we agreed Pete's a dumbass."

"Do you really want him to get ahold of this first? He'll take all the credit."

"We're all on the same team, Carmen," Crispin said, but I could hear a tilt in his voice; I just had to drop something heavy on my side to change his mind.

"Yeah, but it could be *our* names in the papers. You and me, Crispin. We weren't in on the first discovery. With this, our names will be in the academic journals, too. It's guaranteed."

His mouth shifted sideways as he thought it out. Crispin had a weak spot for any situation that could put our names on the same roster—whether it was in a company assignment or in a newspaper. Even better when it was side by side under the title of an article in a scientific journal. That had happened only once, but I could tell by the flicker of excitement in his eyes that he was imagining the possibility of us coauthoring a fresh article on a world-changing archaeological discovery.

"Ah, fine."

"Atta-boy."

I grinned and pulled my harness out of my backpack before digging around for a bungee cord with shaky fingers, but I couldn't find a single carabiner. I could hear them rattling, so I pored through the pockets and shook the pack a couple of times. I growled in frustration, and my heart started racing. Nausea rose in my stomach.

"Hey," Crispin said. His large hand came into view, holding a carabiner. I took it and sent him a quick, stiff smile. "Thanks."

"You don't have to go down there."

"Yes, I do. And I'm fine. Help me strap up."

I told myself I was being stupid. I'd spent the better half of my career delving into caves and wriggling between tight spaces of rock formations to reach some hidden panel of prehistoric art. But even after years of experience, I had an instinctual fear of going any place where walls could threaten to crush me.

Being here seemed to be exacerbating my panic more than usual. When I was eighteen years old, Mamá took me on a mother-daughter trip to see the Great Murals. On our way back to the US, we were driven off the road by a drunk driver, or maybe some shithead involved in the chaotic trifecta of cartels, Mexican government operatives trying to dispel them, and US border patrols, all of whom had taken over northern Baja California and made it hostile, even for passersby. Regardless of the cause, our car had rolled and crashed, mangled like a picked-at carcass. We were crushed by squeaking, groaning, grating, suffocating metal. I made it out.

Mamá didn't.

I didn't talk about that experience much, but I'd made the mistake of confiding in Crispin once; his deep brown eyes had held a tinge of pity for me ever since.

I closed my eyes. I pushed the sounds of screams, mine, Mamá's, out of my brain. I counted backward from ten, pulling on my years of developed coping mechanisms to force myself to stop focusing on the past, and instead focus on the next step toward the future.

I stood up. Crispin double-tied my bungee cords and locked carabiners, triple-checking every knot and hookup to make sure I wouldn't bust my ass. His movements were slower than I'd prefer, but his methodical approach did help me calm down.

"All right, you ready?" he asked.

I took steady breaths, one inhale through my nose, then out through pursed lips, in, out, in, out.

"Yes."

Crispin tugged hard on my harness once. Satisfied, he held the attached cord in both hands and stepped back from the edge of the cave pocket. I scooted to the edge, and he started lowering me down. I found footholds with care as I listened to my surroundings. Hopefully, the fire was recent enough that any animals hadn't had a chance to make the cave home.

As my rock test had predicted, the drop wasn't far, but the hazy clouds of ash hid the sunlight as soon as I was past the top ledge.

"You okay?" Crispin called.

"Yeah." My boots hit bottom with a thump. Heat swelled around me, trapped underground, not yet cooled by the wind above.

"I won't let go. I'll be right up here," he said, his pity laced with condescension.

"I know," I answered, sounding more bitter than I intended. "Thanks."

"You know I got you."

I turned around and looked up. My headlamp flashed off the ash-covered walls near the surface like blinding snow, but when I lowered my gaze from the glare, the rocky walls below were clean, and on every surface my headlamp illuminated, chiseled artwork shone.

My eyes widened as I turned in a slow circle.

"Jesus, Crispin. This is . . ."

Words failed. Multiple bas-reliefs covered the cave walls. Each individual carving was smaller than the magnificent chiseled boulder aboveground, but there were so many, they stretched at least twenty feet on either side of me. Each separate relief was defined by a circular, gem-style border, their grooves filled with obsidian shards. Inside each circle were two overlapping ovals. As I'd suspected when looking at the boulder on the surface, the carvings continued into a full circle.

And just like the sculpted boulder, the ovals in these new pieces contained realistic bas-reliefs of people's profiles, reminding me of an Alphonse Mucha Art Nouveau piece. But unlike the boulder, this cave didn't restrict people to the color of stone. The figures were invigorated with paint concocted from red crushed lava and yellow ochre, black charcoal, and white chalk. People in each center space were painted white and adorned with yellow swirls or slashes across their skin. The smaller people on either side of them were painted mostly in red and black.

Overall, these new bas-reliefs were even more detailed, more colorful, and gleamed with more obsidian than the sculpture above. This place felt like a sanctuary.

"Carmen? What's down there?" Crispin's voice sounded muffled by the ash swirling around.

"Tell you in a minute!" The slack from my bungee cord trailed behind me as I walked down the row of large art panels, my headlamp shining in frustrating spotlights that couldn't illuminate everything at once. I noticed that each bas-relief had two small yellow circles positioned along each overlapping oval, and from bas-relief to bas-relief, the circles appeared to travel along each oval's edge, growing closer together as the series of art went on. They were always parallel to one another, but they never touched.

In places, the stone artwork was weathered and speckled with "popcorn"—a nickname for bubbly calcite rock formations often found in caves. In another place, a stalactite had formed less than an inch from a wall, too close for a human hand to squeeze behind to chisel such detail. Stalactites took thousands of years to form, and this one nearly touched the floor. If the stalactite and the popcorn had time to grow on top of the artwork, that indicated the artwork was thousands of years old, possibly the same fifteen thousand years old as the carved boulder Gaurav and his colleagues had already dated.

My lips parted as I reached the end of the series, where a chorus of painted handprints decorated the wall.

I burst into a smile. This was not the first discovery of ancient painted hands around the world, not by far. It was a worldwide phenomenon that proved links between all cultures of humanity—similar ways of thought, even in the first inkling development of art. Many anthropologists argued that engagement in artistic expression was one of the first signs that made us *human.* The mental capacity for abstract thought, for symbolism and metaphors to describe our reality, that was what separated us from our primitive hominid forebears.

Unable to resist, I pressed my palm against a handprint at eye level, feeling the cold stone and smooth paint that a distant ancestor from fifteen thousand years ago had touched. An exhilarating thrill ran through me that raised goose bumps on my arms. I closed my eyes, soaking in the feeling of profound connection to that ancient person, long dead, yet still living on through this single painted handprint.

I opened my eyes, then tilted my head a little as I inspected the handprint. The width and height of the palm fit my hand, but the print had longer fingers. I slipped my hand away and realized that the disproportional length was due to an extra set of knuckles.

I looked over the other handprints. They all possessed four knuckles on every finger as opposed to my three. Why had these ancient people felt the need to exaggerate the length of their handprints? What did it symbolize?

I knew my questions would only increase as time went on, but perhaps with enough study, I'd find the answers. My heart thrummed as my mind raced through predictions of my future—weeks, months, spent down here and at other sites in this region, deciphering clues and finding answers.

I raised my gaze higher, above the reaching handprints, but frowned. Another bas-relief cast shallow shadows and glinted with obsidian, but its paint was smeared and messy, like a child had scribbled on the walls in the throes of a temper tantrum.

I had to get higher. My headlamp splashed light off the rough stone walls until I saw a natural rock staircase leading up to the art panel. I wiped sweat off my palms and heaved myself up the first of the haphazard stack.

"Carmen, what did you find?" Crispin's voice trickled in.

"Not sure yet," I grunted as I climbed up the next rock and made it to the top ledge.

My headlamp lit up the art panel in a burst. More bas-reliefs of profiled people, encircled by overlapping ovals, covered the panel.

"Carmen, come on. You have to say something!"

"It's amazing, Crispin! Bas-reliefs, painted handprints, and here . . ." I frowned and narrowed my eyes as I studied the new panel. A beautiful bas-relief lurked underneath smears of paint and jagged etchings of a far more primitive nature than most ancient art I had seen, definitely less sophisticated than the Great Murals. But there were still some distinguishable elements.

"Human figures," I called. "Like, traditional figures you'd expect . . . Stylized monos, silhouettes, spears, arrows, but no animals. Both petroglyphs and paintings. But why are the bas-reliefs so different? What made people regress?"

As I stared, I realized that the crude etchings and painted figures weren't the only messy aspects of this panel. The bas-relief underneath was marred and cracked in places, and huge chunks were missing. It looked like the bas-relief had been sliced and beaten with considerable, destructive force.

I had seen similar occurrences in rock art before, evidence that one image had been superimposed on top of an older image, sometimes destroying the old artwork in the process. Sometimes the reason was unknown, perhaps as simple as an update in style by the ancient dwellers, but other times, the cover-up had greater implications. *Cultural superimposition* was the technical term for "correcting" images wrought by previous generations because of a change in opinion toward the subject. I had all sorts of personal names for the practice that were far more insulting.

Was cultural superimposition what this ancient vandal had in mind? If so, their change in opinion was disturbing.

Painted spears fleeted across the bas-relief between etched stick figures of people. Some people were painted red or black; others were white and yellow. One red person was a pincushion for arrows, their prone body painted right over a fissure in the bas-relief of a yellow-and-white-painted face. Above, what appeared to be a white bird flew upward, but its wings were tattered and red ochre blood trailed behind it. A chalk and yellow ochre person lay *inside* the bird as if the creature had swallowed them. The person was either sleeping or dead.

I tensed when I heard a voice join Crispin's on the surface. They were arguing, and it didn't take me long to decipher Pete's obnoxious, nasal tone. My body heated with a flare of possessiveness over the amazing creation I'd just discovered.

I hoped Crispin might cover for me by saying I'd fallen and nothing was down here, but that hope fizzled when my headlamp flashed over Pete's lanky body scrambling down the cave pocket's entrance. He wore a hard hat with a headlamp, but our "safety expert" hadn't bothered to strap into a harness, and in lieu of a bungee cord, he was hanging on to a long, dangling tree root to lower himself down to my level.

I cursed and sidled down the rocky ledge as quickly as I could.

"What the hell are you doing here?" I asked.

"Could ask you the same thi—" Pete's curled lip slackened into awe as his wide bug-eyes surveyed the artwork all around us. Then he started laughing. "Oh, man, look at this. When I tell the board . . ."

"Knew you'd try to take all the credit," I said. "What are you even doing here?"

"Gaurav told me to come check on you," he said. "Doesn't trust you to be careful."

"More like he doesn't trust your word that this place is safe."

"Of course it's safe, you insubordinate sl—"

"You do *not* want to finish that sentence," I said, taking a step toward him. He jerked back a little, which would have given me a sense of satisfaction if his sudden movement hadn't tugged on the root he was using for stability. Soil and small rocks scattered to the cave floor. I eyed the ceiling—it wasn't all solid stone.

"Okay," I whispered, suddenly terrified that the smallest sound might cause a cave-in. "Okay, let's just go back up, and we'll figure this out from there."

"Pete, Carmen, come on!" Crispin called. "We'll get the rest of the team."

"Yeah," I agreed, my eyes on the root Pete still held. "Crispin, pull me up! We'll get a cord and harness down to you, Pete."

Pete snorted at me and pulled on the root again. Everything seemed to slow as the root unraveled from the mesh of roots, soil, and gravel overhead like a zipper on an old coat, catching in little jerks as it *zip-zip-zipped* from the cave ceiling.

Wind rushed in. Dormant embers, buried in the roots of trees and cacti all along the cave tunnel's ceiling, invisible until now, burst into flame.

Pete screamed. The charred trunk of the elephant tree cracked and fell through a gap in the ceiling. I ducked and covered my head as it crashed into the high-up bas-relief, the one superimposed with messy, painted depictions of ancient war. The bas-relief crumbled into chunks of rock and showers of dust. Sparks showered down, and through the orange spray, a pale-blue light shown from within the sundered rock like a lighthouse's beacon.

I squinted at the strange light through the chaos, but I felt a hard jerk on my harness. A burning scrub tumbled down from the surface, and I darted around it toward the cave's opening. I grabbed Pete, who was trying to scramble up the rock. My ash-dusted hands slipped on the rock face, but between my frantic climb and Crispin's pull, we made it to the top ledge.

A whoosh of flames ran through the cave as if lit by gasoline and burst to the surface.

Crispin heaved us away, and I collapsed into a shaking heap. Pete coughed, found his feet first, and ran without a second's glance for our safety.

I jumped to my feet as flames rushed toward us along the network of roots, spreading beyond the cave in a starburst. Fire flared up at the rock outcrop over the cave where the beautiful giants of the Great Murals looked down. We watched, at first as frozen and helpless as they were.

I exchanged a wide-eyed glance with Crispin, and we took off running down the hill.

The flames followed us.

CHAPTER TWO

I COUGHED A cloud of ash and dust, my lungs burning, and pushed myself off the ground in a daze. Someone extended a hand. I took it and met the eyes of one of the local workers from Pete's dig team who held a first aid kit. His black hair was as frazzled as his frayed nerves.

I looked around. We were at the bottom of the hill, a good distance away from the burning slope, which was crawling with firefighters. They seemed to have restrained the hungry flames from spreading more than twenty or so square feet.

"A root fire," I said, my voice shaky as I tried to calm my railing heartbeat. The beautiful bas-reliefs and painted figures in the cave swept into my mind, followed by the section of the Great Murals, positioned right above, flaring orange in the flames. Did the ancient murals I so cherished survive the blaze?

"If she had listened to me, this wouldn't have happened," I heard Pete's voice cut through my disorientation. "She had no right going off on her own, and—"

"It wasn't Carmen's fault," Crispin said. "She discovered—"

"Everyone, calm down," Gaurav said.

Calm down, my ass. I spun around, hunting for Pete. Anger burned in my chest as I pictured his misleading rows of little pink safety flags and his hands yanking on an unstable root that *anyone* could see wouldn't support him. I found him standing a few feet away near Gaurav, Crispin, and Luis. Pete's face was ruddy with anger, and everyone was speaking in harsh, clipped words to each other. Julieta's back was turned to them, her shoulders hunched.

I breezed past the worker who had helped me up and ran straight at Pete.

"Do you know what you did?" I asked, rage boiling in my stomach and shooting straight to my mouth like a geyser. "We found a site, an *important* site, and you destroyed it! And the Great Murals?" I squinted hot tears away. "Did you fuck them up, too?"

"Wasn't my fault it was wrecked, sweetheart," he sneered.

"Don't call me sweetheart."

"Fine. Bitch."

The building heat in my body flared into an inferno. Every beat of my pulse put pressure on my muscles, harder and tighter like my body was producing a diamond. My vision narrowed into a shrinking tunnel; I was on a speeding train with nothing but tracks ahead. I couldn't turn left or right or redirect any of my thoughts away from my fury's single focus.

The pressure was too high. The furnace exploded. The diamond shattered.

My fist collided with something. It took me a moment to realize it was Pete's face.

Pete sputtered blood from his mouth and nose as he staggered. My rage crackled like an empty plastic bottle, used up but satisfied as I rode the tight pain in my knuckles.

Someone grabbed my arm from behind. I jerked and reared my fist back.

"Carmen," Crispin said, grabbing my fist. "Stop."

My pulse thumped in fuzzy beats in my ears. Blood drained from my head and seeped into my toes as my overheated body cooled. Crispin released my fist. I lowered my hand and slowly turned around.

Everyone was staring.

"You're fired!" Pete said, his voice nasally and tight as he kept his hand over his nose. He looked at Gaurav. "She's fired, right?"

I looked from Pete to Gaurav. Gaurav's face was lined with deep disappointment.

Shit.

"Carmen," Gaurav said, striding forward. "Pete says he saw you down in a cave up the hill. He says that *you* caused the fire. If you hadn't jumped down there without alerting anyone, without thinking about the stability of those tunnels . . ."

"I . . . No." I shook my head back and forth. "This wasn't my fault. Pete said it was safe. I was being careful. *Pete* yanked on a root that brought the whole thing down!"

"No, Carmen," Gaurav said, more firmly than I'd ever heard him speak. "Maybe we can salvage what you found, but . . ." He sighed and tilted his head in frustration. "I'm sorry, Luis, Julieta. Truly. We'll do what we can to fix this." He looked over my head. "Crispin, you're not off the hook, either, but . . . I know Carmen can be persuasive. And now after this." He gestured to Pete's bloody nose and flung his hand as if waving the entire situation away. "Carmen . . . I'm sorry. You've gone too far. I can't have someone so reckless on my team. Not with something this important."

My stomach contorted into knots. This couldn't be happening. This wasn't my fault.

"No," I said, digging my heels into the ground. "I'm not going to—"

"Carmen," Gaurav said. My name sounded like he'd slammed a door in my face. My words balled up into a lump in my throat.

"Come on," Crispin said softly. He took my shoulder and guided me away. My feet felt like weights dangling on strings.

"I shouldn't have let you go down there," he said when we were out of earshot.

"It's not your fault."

"Still—"

"Just shut up."

He did. We walked with footsteps silenced by ash.

We were at the cluster of tents behind the crescent rock formation by the time I emerged from my daze. Lawn chairs grouped in little circles, and a large folding table with a scattering of tin cups and a stray plate stood off to one side for group dining. A heavy-duty trash bag hung from a rocky outcrop across the flat patch of dirt. We hadn't seen many animals returning to the burnt landscape, but we didn't want to invite any coyotes or a rare puma into camp with welcome arms.

Smita barked from inside one of the tents; Gaurav must have put her there during the fiery chaos. We headed for the two tents next to his.

"I'll speak up for you with the board," Crispin said. "I'll tell them it was Pete's fault."

"You'd just get dragged down with me. You're in enough trouble as it is."

"Carmen."

But he didn't argue.

"That jackass had it coming, though," he said. I caught the smile on his face as I trudged along. "Wish I'd taken a video."

I wiped away angry tears and forced a dry laugh. "Yeah. I've wanted to do that for years."

Crispin laughed and put his arm around my shoulders for a sideways hug. "You wanna talk about how we almost died back there?"

"Maybe that would have been better," I said, but I shook my head and shivered away the imaginings of what would have happened if we hadn't escaped the flames in time. It had all happened so fast, the danger didn't even feel real anymore. Besides, we'd lived through the fire. My job was what hadn't survived.

"How about opening that bottle of champagne Gaurav left us?" he said. "You look like you need it."

He released my shoulders and unzipped his two-person green tent, only a little bigger than my red one next door. He ducked inside and came out holding a green bottle. The gold foil on its cork shimmered under the hot sunlight, a glittering, happy shout of *congratulations!*

Crispin put his thumbs on the cork; I waited for the pop.

"Hold on," I said, imagining jinxing my entire future by opening celebratory champagne prematurely. If there was even a chance I could fix things, I couldn't gamble with fate. "I've got something stronger."

I headed for my tent and jerked on the zipper so hard that it caught. I finally got it open and crawled onto the nest of my disheveled sleeping bag. My laptop was closed in a corner, its screen usually filled with graphical analyses and a long row of browser tabs of scientific journal articles. It was cushioned by a jumble of clothing, handwritten scrawls on Post-it Notes, and crude drawings on scraps of paper towels. A handheld LED lantern sat beside the pile.

There wasn't much room for anything else, yet I'd managed to prop a six-square-inch canvas against the lantern. My chest clenched, harder than usual, as my eyes traced each textured stroke of paint on the canvas that formed a vibrant flower. Patterned details inside the center consisted of dots, lines, and neat curves in a style often used in Mexican folk art. The patterns were beautiful, yet contained.

The flower's outer rim wasn't a solid circle or arranged in neat petals in the traditional Mexican style, however. Instead, paint went wherever nature had decided to take it under

Mamá's paintbrush splatter, as wild and free as her laugh whenever I'd watch her paint in our drop-cloth-coated living room. All of her unique paintings embraced the neat decadency of her home country's artistic heritage but were fueled by the passionate chaos of the universe. Just like she was.

I shuffled over on my hands and knees and slumped in front of the painting. I'd first placed it at my bedside at age eighteen, the night I'd arrived back home in Denver from my flight—alone—from Baja California after Mamá didn't make it out of the hospital.

It was hard for me to picture all of her free-spirited paintings collecting dust in a storage unit, but that's where I'd put them after I'd been forced to sell the house to pay off my student loans. I stopped by the unit whenever I was back in town, but that was becoming rarer and rarer these days. Now I lived in and out of six-month apartment leases at the most. More often, I was in a trailer or hotel room or tent near job sites all around the world.

Maybe one day I'd have a house big enough to display all of Mamá's art like it deserved. A couple of local museums had made offers back in the day, vying for the praiseworthy work of Lucia del Carmen Pérez Aguilar de O'Dwyer, but Mamá had always said no, that she made her art for her family.

My globetrotting career choice, and lack of house by proxy, was Mamá's fault. When I'd realized that my talent as an artist was scritch-scratch compared to hers, I'd swapped my paintbrush for a textbook to fulfill the passion she had instilled in me. I had tried to focus on modern art several times after her death, but no matter what piece I looked at, all I could think about was my mother's.

Prehistoric art was different. None of the ancients had faces. Their two-dimensional stick-figure paintings or chiseled petroglyphs in stone made it easy to keep my emotions at a distance, as far as the thousands of years that separated me from their creators. The tools they used were different, and the paint was often so faded and the stone so eroded, it was hard to compare it with the vivid colors Mamá used. I studied the figures' stylized limbs in their rhythmic positions of dance, but I never tried to invent any music. I followed the fleets of hunters as they burst into their final run to spear their prey—bison, guar, deer, mammoths, a host of animals both extant and extinct—but I never felt the thrill of the hunt. I joined circles of families around vibrant hearths, smiled at the children and the round swell of mothers' bellies with a distant pride for my species, but I never made it personal. I never imagined my own family amongst them.

The artwork inspired my sense of awe for the past and my desire to link it to the present, my initiative to bind the entire world's cultures together through study and interpretation, to extrapolate the notion of a collective consciousness based on facts.

By studying art, I felt like Mamá was lighting my way, even after she was gone. My work could never replace her, but it was enough to keep me going.

Until now.

I dragged my eyes away from Mamá's painting and rummaged in the pile of clothes till I found a small bottle of tequila buried in my underwear. I backed out of the tent and jerked the zipper shut.

Crispin grinned when he saw the tequila. He grabbed two half-empty water bottles and dumped out the water.

* * *

I buried my face in my pillow to crush the headache railing inside my skull. I couldn't tell if I'd fallen asleep, or if I'd just sobered up from a drunken haze in a bad way. Moonlight shone through a thin, green tent wall that I realized wasn't mine. I grumbled and turned my head away from the light.

Crispin lay beside me. The tight spirals of his black hair were still perfect, and his face didn't look anywhere near as haggard as I was sure mine did. His arm sprawled across the top of the pillow we shared, his bare chest rising and falling in breaths of slumber.

"Right," I muttered.

It'd been years since Crispin and I had slept together. We'd started a friends-with-benefits arrangement in grad school. There was a time when he had expressed wanting to get serious, but I'd shot him down. He had accepted that without too much disappointment and seemed content to keep our relations casual, but I'd shot him down in that regard, too, once our careers started. Sleeping together as fellow students was one thing, but as coworkers? That was too risky. My career would always come first, I'd told him.

But I didn't have a career anymore, did I?

I kicked off the sleeping bag in a fit and rolled to the side before tossing the bag back over Crispin's naked body. I shivered. The temperature had dropped into nocturnal desert cold. I rummaged around for my clothes, wincing at the residual pain in my knuckles from their collision with Pete's face. I looked down to see a blotchy row of purple bruises.

I had donned one of Crispin's blue sweatshirts and was buttoning my khaki shorts when Crispin stirred in the sleeping bag and sat up. He looked a lot rougher now that he was awake—scruffy hair, bleary eyes; I could almost see the headache pulsing at his temples.

There was a little twinkle in his eyes, though, as he said, "What are you doing? It's cold. Come back to bed?" That twinkle was hope, and it made me cringe.

"I can't sleep," I said, "and you look like you need it." I slid on my boots and started tying them. "I'm going for a walk. I'll be back soon. Just need to clear my head."

"You want company?"

"I need to be alone."

He winced. "Carmen, I missed this. Us. I think you know how I've . . . That I never stopped . . ."

"I can't talk about this now."

He leaned over and brushed my hand. I hesitated. The smell of sex clung to us both, amplified by our close bodies. His eyes, the color of charcoal with an ever-present luster of embers, met mine of cypress-green.

"I'm not some petroglyph to be studied whenever you feel like it, Carmen. I'm not made of stone."

My heart squeezed, but my pulsing temple ticked nothing but irritation through my head.

"Well, maybe I am." I pulled my hand away.

He frowned and took a breath like he wanted to say more, but he just shook his head. I ruffled my hair and snatched his headlamp from the corner. I unzipped the tent door and crawled from the suffocating space.

I stood up in the cold night air, still thick with floating ash flakes and the oppressive smell of smoke. I glanced at Gaurav's dark tent next door. My stomach sank. He would confront me in the morning. Berate me some more about how I'd destroyed priceless artwork, priceless information about Mexico's prehistoric roots, a priceless avenue for the progression of my career.

When he should be yelling at Pete.

I skirted the outer perimeter of the tents, staying close to the looming, crescent-shaped rock formation that encircled us.

All was quiet, but I couldn't stand the idea that someone might be watching my lonely sojourn from a tent's screen window, that maybe Pete was watching, gloating. I shoved my hands in my pockets and switched on my headlamp as I headed farther away.

A whine squeaked like a metal swing set from somewhere ahead. I frowned and stopped. The whine came again, followed by a prolonged grumbling yelp.

"Smita?" I called. I peered into the dark. "Smita?"

I was familiar enough with Smita's various noises to know she wasn't in pain, but she was worried. Something was out there. But why was she out of Gaurav's tent?

I glanced back. There was no sound or movement from the camp. I considered running back for Crispin, but then I might lose track of Smita. I winced but looked back ahead toward the ashen wasteland through the opening in the rock formation.

Another high whine skimmed the air.

I hesitated, but then plunged toward the sound. Some animal might be near, a coyote, a puma, big enough to scare Smita and dangerous for me, but I couldn't let her face whatever beast it was alone. Besides, it might just be a rock squirrel or some rodent the dog had never seen before. It was hard to tell how grave a worry was with a dog as expressive as Smita.

I kept going, kicking up ash, my headlamp's glow splashing off hunks of rock in erratic waves, making stunted tree trunks dance like skeletons. Blackened cacti needles looked like the legs of countless dead insects stuck to the tan, cracked bases. As I got closer to the hillside where Pete's shitty safety assessment had started a fresh fire, the soft glow of residual embers made the remnants of spidery desert scrubs look like the Burning Bush of legend.

Smita's whines and grumbles kept getting farther away. I called her name a few times, but she wouldn't come.

Then I froze. My eyes were caught by an enormous object standing in the center of the flattened landscape at the base of the hill. The moon, in a waxing phase where you could almost see it as the sphere it was, shone light upon a huge egg-shaped sapphire, standing upright at double my height with a base as wide as a sedan. Wide facets glinted along its sides, smooth and methodical as if cut by an expert lapidary.

Smita growled at the alarming object from a few feet away. She crouched low, her tail whipping back and forth before she leapt backward and barked. She jumped sideways and crouched again, snarling. She snapped her jaws at the object, but then retreated with a yelp, like she couldn't decide if she should attack the strange menace or run.

The big egg didn't move or make any noise. I shot my eyes around the clearing. There was no sign of anyone nearby.

"Smita," I hissed. She whipped her head in my direction and froze. I sharply waved her over, but she leapt back around and recommenced her growling.

I exhaled through my nostrils. My heartbeat raced and I shivered as I looked around the area. I tapped my fingertips on my thigh in indecision, then licked my lips and said in a wavering voice, "Hello?"

I got no response other than Smita's continued growls. I cleared my throat and tried again, "Hello? Is anyone here?"

I spun in a slow circle, still catching no sight or sound of people. We were in the middle of the desert; we'd had to ride mules to get here. So how on Earth did something like this bizarre sapphire egg show up in the middle of the Sierra de San Francisco?

I scowled and looked back at Smita. I didn't know what that thing was, but I at least had to get her away. I took a deep, chilling breath and pried my boots off the ground to walk toward the giant jewel. I would grab Smita, drag her away, head straight back to camp, and get help.

I could feel heat through my boots as soft ash clouded at my feet all the way to about fifteen feet from the egg. But I frowned when my boot clomped on hard stone. I looked down, and my eyes widened in fascination.

All around the sapphire egg, the ash had been swept clean, exposing an expanse of flat rock. Under the yellow pool of my headlamp, low bas-reliefs were chiseled into the stone. They were cracked in many places, but the style was unmistakable—the same gem-like carvings that had surrounded the petroglyphs of ancient people, both on the exposed boulder and in the cave.

Instead of a portrait in the center of these gem-style carvings, there was the gem-like egg. Smita still barked and growled, but I was drawn to it, a deep curiosity building with every step. I didn't know what the egg was; I didn't know if it had anything to do with the unprecedented style of carvings and bas-reliefs in this region, but somehow, against my scientific mind's better judgement, I connected the two, tying them together in an irrevocable knot. And that knotted string yanked me straight to the egg.

Smita whined at me as I reached her. She darted in front of me and growled at the egg, then leapt behind my legs before jumping in front of me again. She kept up this dance between cowardice and bravery as I grew closer, while my own mind pitted curiosity against fear. I stopped an arm's length from the egg.

Curiosity won out.

Up close, the egg looked even more like a glimmering gem, cut into a mosaic of facets more intricate than I had ever seen in jewelry; step-cut ovals, brilliant circles, glinting roses, and shimmering teardrops all winked in the moonlight. They were arranged like puzzle pieces into perfect circles and straight lines, defined by gilding that shimmered like spun silver. Some circles were as big as a basketball, others as small as my thumbprint. They overlapped one another in some cases; in others they were concentric targets; still others were open and blank, their edges a single, impenetrable barrier.

They were as countless as stars with patterns as intricate as constellations.

"Hello?" I called again, tearing my eyes from the egg to search the darkness. No one answered. I swallowed, but took a bracing breath and started to circle the object, drinking in the magnificent artistic expression. My headlamp glanced off one of the broader facets. I winced and swung the light to the side so I could get a better look. The surface almost looked translucent, like the egg might be hollow. I raised my hand and, after a slow-motion moment of trepidation, pressed my palm against the surface.

The egg felt smooth, sleek, and hard as glass. I traced one finger along one of the silver-gilded grooves, which felt like glass as well. I continued my circle, Smita's whines fading in my ears as I became immersed in eerie beauty. I kept tracing my fingers along the silver gilding, running them in circles and following the lines while I walked.

"Applied at an upward angle," I mused. "Someone was creating this from a lower height. What kind of tool, though . . . ?"

I knew this artwork would be chiseled into the membrane behind my eyelids forever. The clean, poised lines connecting perfect circles felt noble and poetic, with a sense of order and peace I had never witnessed in any culture's art before. It was logical, mathematical, precise. The artist had been striving for perfection.

Then my fingers hit a section that was completely different.

Silver gilding erupted from the confines of the neat methodical grooves like ocean spray, swirling into a circle three feet across, positioned right at my eye level. Clearly, this circle was made by a far more passionate hand, an artist who applied the silver glass with wild strokes in multiple, textured layers that spiraled out like hurricane clouds. I had first suspected that the silvery veins all over the egg had been applied through slow direct methods, but this vibrant display revealed the process could be much faster and malleable, as easy to apply as paint to a canvas.

The piece was mesmerizing. The center of the circle was vacant and felt like a deep, hollowed pit, while the surrounding storm yearned for something out of reach with passionate desperation.

I didn't know why I felt the need to stare for as long as I did. Minutes? An hour? Or was it mere seconds that felt like an eternity?

I touched the silver glass, layered and sculpted like a Chihuly sculpture inspired by a spiral galaxy, twinkling with stars.

I jumped back when a blue glow blinked on under my touch. Smita barked.

Only a finger's width of blue light shone under the wild silver hurricane. The rest glowed along several short silver lines nearby, embedded neatly in grooves between the egg's sapphire-like facets.

My brow furrowed. The light was in the shape of a hand, precisely where mine had touched. I scanned the surrounding surface, and my eyes widened. I hadn't noticed a pattern before, but now I pieced together more short silver lines and small circles among them, nestled in the gem-cut grooves. Goose bumps frosted my skin.

Hands. Embedded between the jewel facets of the egg were outlines of hands, hidden in a mystifying connect-the-dots.

My heart thumped as I dared to touch my pinkie finger to the glowing thumb of my first handprint. Then I pressed my full hand against the adjoining silver veins. My hand nestled into the grooves as if it belonged there—except for one difference.

Both hands, now each glowing blue, appeared normal, save for the fact that their fingers had four knuckles rather than three, each defined by tiny silver circles. They echoed the bizarre, ancient handprints I'd discovered painted on the walls of the now-destroyed cave. And the light . . . I'd almost forgotten the beam of pale-blue light that had shone from the ancient bas-relief in the cave when the blackened tree trunk had busted through it. I'd had to escape the ensuing blaze before I could learn more, or even accept that it was real, but now I had no doubt that the shade of blue light in the cave matched the blue light on this huge egg perfectly.

"What?" I whispered. It didn't make any sense. The painted handprints had likely been thousands of years old, and the worn, gem-cut stone under my feet, cleared free of ash, looked ancient as well. Despite the eerie similarities, this mysterious egg-shaped object looked polished and new, and it certainly hadn't been here under the sunlight. As far as I knew, I was the first person to see it.

My palms were sweating, but I couldn't resist planting my hand on the next dormant constellation handprint like an impulsive child exploring a new toy. It, too, glowed blue. A smile grew on my face as I kept pressing my hand to the prints, forming a long chain of four-knuckled hands as I walked around the entire car-sized egg. I reached the spiraling hurricane circle again and stopped.

Smita was whining and barking in turns, still sounding indecisive about whether she trusted the object or not. But I . . . I was convinced that there was no way this object was dangerous. It was too beautiful and captivating to be a weapon.

I blew air through pursed lips and pressed my hand into the grooves that met with the wild circle's border. The last handprint, from what I could see.

The handprint glowed a vibrant blue like all the others, but was joined by a barely audible electronic hum. Then I heard a mechanical groan. The egg shuddered.

I scurried back, my eyes darting around the egg's surface. Smita snarled and collided with my legs in her race to get in front of me. I grabbed her faded red collar and jerked her back, but she struggled and kept snapping at the air as if she could bite the hard egg and rip it to pieces.

"Smita," I said, but my voice whined like a dying engine into silence. A wide, tall, rectangular section of the egg was outlined in bright white light. The section of blue glass fell outward and hit the carved stone ground, forming a ramp to a blinding opening.

"Carmen!"

I spun around. My fingers slipped off Smita's collar.

"Crispin!"

A sudden force hit me from all sides, pounding my lungs into submission and turning sounds to sludge. The invisible force wrenched me backward as if my entire body was plastered to flypaper. My heels dragged on the stone as I lost control of my feet.

Crispin ran toward me through a cloud of ash. His head-lamp flashed in strobe effect, making it hard to see his face. The force yanked me up the glass ramp and into the egg. My back slammed into a wall, and the force dropped me onto the floor with a splash. A warm liquid, reeking of iron and salt, surrounded my elbows and thighs and leaked into my boots. I had to close my eyes against the blinding light that surrounded me, but I heard Smita's growling turn to sharp yelps, and then her voice whimpered into silence as her soft body collided with mine.

"Carmen!" Crispin shouted, closer, but not close enough.

The door of the egg rose up from the ground and slammed shut. The white light around me was extinguished.

I scrambled to my feet, but stumbled against the wall in the dark. The rough leather of my boots began to dissolve as if the liquid were acid. My bare feet slipped on the floor, but no pain seared my skin.

"No," I said, my mind blanking as I tried to assess what was happening. I had to get out. *I had to get out.*

I sloshed my way through the liquid, which rose higher by the second. My outstretched hands hit glass. I banged on it and looked through, catching the faint light of Crispin's headlamp through the semitransparent surface of the egg.

"Crispin!" I banged on the glass again, so hard my hand hurt, but I didn't stop. "Crispin!"

The egg shuddered again. I fell to my knees. The liquid began to eat away my shorts and shirt. I sputtered foul-tasting fluid as I tried to find my feet, but I was knocked underwater when the egg propelled itself from the ground and shot high into the air. I kicked off the floor, but the liquid was now too high to stand and was raising me toward the ceiling. Smita had stopped whining.

I looked down through a wide facet of the egg. The black expanse of the ground was far below. Crispin's headlamp was refracted like a tiny star through the blue glass. It disappeared.

I looked up through the top of the egg. Moonlight shone brightly for a moment, but then the light was blocked by a looming darkness. The egg shot upward into the black. Below my feet, all lingering moonlight disappeared with a loud slamming sound as if my egg-shaped vessel had entered some larger enclosed space—a bigger egg? A hovering *vehicle*?

My observations ended when I was forced to take a final panicked breath. Liquid submerged my head. My hair floated in wild, thick waves around my face. I fought against the resistance of the liquid to hit the side of the egg in slow motion, a taunting nightmare of helplessness, but then I spun and stretched out my arms. Smita. I wanted Smita. I was going to die in here, I was sure of it. I needed to feel her warmth. I needed to not be alone.

I felt nothing but warm consuming liquid, but then my fingers found wet fur. Smita wasn't moving, but she was still warm. I felt for her head, finding her soft ears and cold nose. I wrapped my arms around her in a tight hug. My mind screamed as my head burst with oppressive, pounding dizziness. My lungs burned, and when I finally opened my mouth in instinct to breathe, liquid flooded my lungs, but it wasn't painful like I expected. It was just . . .

CHAPTER THREE

MY FINGERTIPS PULSED first, then my toes, as if my heart had stopped and I was experiencing newborn beats. My pulse quickened as blood lurched through my arms and legs like an old engine trying to start. Rust had crept into my extremities; my body was a hollowed cavity lined with the crust and acerbic smell of dried gasoline. I waited for the next pulse.

"Mamá . . ."

There it was—my heart. It beat once, strong and sure, like it was trying to tell me something important: *Now.*

I opened my eyes. And screamed.

A nightmare stared back at me. A splayed corpse on an autopsy table, its skin peeled back to display white and bloodied bones, pink muscles, and slick innards—worming intestines, thick dark liver, gurgling stomach, pale fleshy lungs, pumping heart.

The lungs expanded and contracted in fast breaths. The heart pulsated in quick bursts of each chamber. I met the body's wide eyes.

They were mine.

Tears blurred my vision, which in turn filled the body's green eyes. The tears spilled to the side and ran down both my and the body's temples. The body's long, dark hair spread out as if on a flat surface rather than falling to its shoulders from gravity.

As my other senses flooded in, I felt a cold, hard surface running along the entire back of my body. I was lying down, and that realization made me suspect that the image above me might be my twisted reflection, but how could that be?

My mind stuttered when the image changed. The edges of the body's flayed skin receded like grains of sand pulled by ocean waves. The muscle and bone dissolved until all that was left was a series of miniscule red strings entangled with one another to form a hollow cage in the shape of a body. Blood wormed its way through each string and coalesced into a pumping heart. The beats were fast and sharp, and the dewy organ pulsed harder and faster with each second.

My heart matched each staccato beat.

I was staring at my circulatory system—every single one of my veins, arteries, and capillaries floated above my head. Yet clearly my pounding heart was still in my chest.

I tore my eyes away from the disgusting, pumping ropes of blood in the reflection and twisted my neck a fraction to see the edge of my real shoulder and arm, covered in skin like they were supposed to be, but no longer shielded by Crispin's borrowed sweatshirt. My swallow of relief choked when I saw and felt a cold metal cuff around my wrist, bolting me to the surface I lay upon. I jerked against the restraint, but my hand was stuck palm-down beside my thigh.

I turned my head the other way and tried to yank my other wrist out of an identical cuff, but the restraint bit into my skin, and a brief struggle revealed that both of my ankles were also restrained. I looked down and saw the curve of my breasts and stretch of torso, past my hips and down to my feet. I was nude, my skin bright and vulnerable under a set of overhead spherical lights that blazed brighter when the image of pulsing veins above me disappeared.

I slammed my head back against the cold surface. Shadows lurked around the edges of the bright lights, the extreme contrast obscuring my surroundings. But my pause in panicked breaths and screams allowed other sounds to enter my ears.

A steady hum of machinery reminded me of the sound of the egg-shaped vessel's opening, but softer. I felt no movement as I had in the egg; my surroundings were still and grounded.

The humming became an irritating tinnitus in my ears as I struggled to notice any other clues of my whereabouts. My attention latched onto a new noise, a low, erratic hum, which rose and fell and stretched in muffled tones.

A voice.

"H-hello?" I said, my voice scratching the air. "Crispin?" It seemed not a moment ago, I had seen his terrified, desperate face staring up at me through the translucent egg, watching me disappear.

The muffled voice said something else in light alto tones, suggesting the speaker was a woman. Soft footfalls drew close from my left, and a hand slipped into sight. The woman was wearing a strange glove—paper-white, adorned with splashes of shimmering gold.

I flinched as she touched my chin and tilted my head toward her face.

Every question on my tongue fizzled. The woman's skin was white and pristine as marble. Glistening gold patterns dotted her face and arms like a calico cat. Her head was bald, but more gold covered her scalp like a painted crown, with golden tendrils curling to form hairless eyebrows and add definition to her round cheeks. Her ears were pressed flatter to her head than most people's, and her nose was pointed like a storybook pixie.

Her eyes were black and emotionless as stone. Two solid onyx jewels with no whites at all and only the faintest hint of a thin ginger iris embedded inside.

I jerked my chin from her hard fingers. She withdrew, and for a second, I couldn't pin down what else was wrong with her hand. Then my chest shuddered and my body tingled as goose bumps sprouted down my arms and legs.

Each of her fingers had four knuckles. Not three. Four.

"Artist," I whispered. My throat felt like razor blades had sliced my vocal cords.

The woman said some mild, yet stiff, words in a language I didn't recognize and in a tone that didn't expect a reply. A soft, blue glow flickered into the edge of my sight, illuminating the woman's face while she studied the light like it was a screen, but I couldn't see any details. Some kind of equipment hummed and dinged close by.

I licked my dry lips and cleared my throat.

"Where is this? Who are you? Please. Tell me." My voice still scoured the air, but rose in pitch and volume with every question. "What's going on? Smita. The dog. Where is she? What happened? Talk to me!"

The woman didn't answer. She walked toward the foot of the metal table to which I was locked, giving me my first full view of her body. She wore a long, cream-colored robe that swished as she walked, sleeveless and collared at the neck like a halter top. Her front was covered by flowing linen, but the garment left her upper back exposed. I stopped breathing when I saw her back and shoulders in the spotlight.

Her shoulders were tall arches like she had two boney, gold plates mounted on them. Her back was almost entirely gold, pushing the softer-looking white skin to the edges of her torso. The golden skin had a hard, scaly sheen, but as she hunched a little to inspect another blue-glowing display on a different boxy piece of equipment, the skin of her back split into five vertical lines. A third texture of skin lurked inside each slit, glossy pearl that reflected the light of the ceiling with a sudden flash.

The bright light shot red through my closed eyelids and beat into my skull in time with my throbbing pulse. My stomach turned a somersault. My entire body began to shake, and my skin felt clammy as nausea overwhelmed me. I groaned and opened my eyes, but the world around me was rolling and twisting.

More unfamiliar voices crackled in my ears like a broken speaker. Two new people hovered over me, both coated in white-and-gold skin. I felt the cuffs around my wrists and ankles loosen, but before I could move, hard hands clamped around my upper arms. An electric, triggering sensation pulsed from the hands into my skin. There was no pain, but my muscles loosened in a landslide from my arms down until my entire body went slack and my vision caved. I was vaguely aware of being lifted and carried out of the room before my stunned brain clicked out.

* * *

When I woke up, I wished my mysterious captors would knock me back out.

I wasn't strapped down to a table anymore or surrounded by low-key humming machinery. Instead, I was in a five-square-foot cubicle with a freezing white, glassy floor and four clear glass walls. My hope of freedom dwindled when I realized the glass was too strong to break and that I'd only been set loose from the restraining cuffs so that I could freely vomit into a shallow basin dug into the floor.

I lost track of time, but it felt like days, days in which all I could think about was surviving, but all I wanted to do was die. I could only judge the passage of time by the fact that the bruises on my knuckles from punching Pete had already disappeared, and by how much the reek of bodily fluids built up in my cage. The smells of sweat, piss, shit, vomit, and other byproducts of being human I had never considered before dwelled in my nostrils, when they weren't lined with thick snot. I coughed till I was hoarse, my chest swamped with mucus and painfully tight with every breath. My stomach and intestines were in constant pain, with so many variances—sharp stabs, deep cramps, moving bubbles, and loud growls. My head was fuzzy and hot, and my hands and feet were clammy. My mouth felt like I'd stuffed it with a dung-covered cotton ball. I gave up trying to move; whenever I did, my limbs trembled, and I'd collapse before I could make it to my knees.

Other times, I would wake up from an ill-timed slumber and everything would reset. My cubicle and body would be clean, and little red prickles appeared in my inner elbows. I always felt a little stronger after that and suspected my captors were administering some kind of nutrition and hydration while I slept.

I was still naked, and the thought of these monstrous people coming in and touching me and cleaning me while I was unconscious was unbearable. I told myself over and over that I would stay awake and bust out during one of their cleanings, but my escape plans couldn't make it past the vague dreaming stage before another swell of nausea would hit. I wanted to throw things and shout and scream, but all I could do was lie in a puddle of misery.

Everything beyond my sterile cage was a blur to my hot feverish eyes. I gathered the sense that my cubicle was inside a much larger room, lined with other glass cages on an opposing wall. Some cages were smaller and some far bigger, with blurred shapes and shadows moving within them. Animalistic roars, shrieks, and groans echoed in my ears, melding with nightmares crawling through my brain. I couldn't tell when I was asleep or awake, what was real and what was not.

At one lucid point, I was curled up in a corner, my entire body shaking, my skin itching from dehydration. I wanted to close my eyes, but the spinning in my head was worse without definition, so I kept them open.

I perked up a little at the sight of feet under a long hem of brown fabric. The feet were encased in dark brown sandals with straps shaped in half circles. The spaces between the straps revealed gold and white skin.

A sharp, high whine made me wince, followed by a scrabble of nails against hard floor. I looked up and saw one of my abductors pushing a creature into an empty cubicle next to mine. I wasn't sure if the smile in my heart made it to my mouth.

"Smita. You're alive."

Smita whined as the strange person pressed their hand on a smooth panel on the outer corner of her cubicle. A thin, white vapor swirled within the frame of the cubicle's opening. I watched in wonder as the gaseous substance turned solid in an instant. An unbreakable glass wall now blocked Smita's exit. She shoved her black nose against the wall, but then whined and backed away. She retched.

I looked away so I wouldn't do the same.

"Hey!" I called to the stranger, but they spared me no more than a glance and walked away. I focused on breathing for a moment so that I wouldn't pass out. Smita slumped on the floor of her cubicle, her flanks rising and falling in steady breaths. Her every exhale was a whine.

I dragged myself toward the clear wall of our adjoining cells. I pressed a weak hand to the wall.

"Hey, girl."

Smita didn't move, but her whiskers twitched, and her eyebrows rose a little.

"Hey, Smita. You okay?"

Smita rumbled a half growl, half whine. She rolled her big brown eyes in my direction. I thought I saw a flicker of recognition.

"I'm sorry," I said, my voice breaking. "You knew, didn't you? That the egg was dangerous. Why did you try to save me?" I rolled my forehead against the cool wall, but the relief from my burning skin was brief. "Humans are stupid, aren't we?"

Smita twitched her head off one of her limp paws. Her tail brushed the floor in a half wag, but she laid her head back down with another whine.

"Sick, too?" I sighed and rested my cheek on the floor. "Fuck this place," I mumbled.

Smita huffed in agreement and closed her eyes.

* * *

I opened my eyes to a wall of blurry green and dull tan. Then, individual blades of desert grasses came into focus. I felt their prickle against my cheek. I inhaled the smell of arid soil. I rolled onto my back and squinted in yellow sunlight.

A cloudy blue sky was overhead. The sun itself wasn't in view, but my skin glowed with warmth. Grayish-brown, fissured tree branches with spiky green leaves stretched into the edges of my sight. I turned my head to see several tall trunks descending to the ground.

The world had stopped spinning. My stomach wasn't sloshing or cramping with every small movement I made. My feverish, foggy brain felt clear.

I felt stronger than I had in days, and lighter, like a heavy weight had been lifted. I took a quick breath and pushed myself off the ground. I must have pushed harder than I intended because I launched into the air. I stumbled forward and caught myself on unsteady feet, putting a hand over my startled heart.

I looked around. Elephant trees, scattered with tiny buttercream flowers, shaded thriving desert scrub grass. Yucca trees reached for the sky with their towering clusters of white summer blossoms. The tree nearest me was a half-grown blue palm; broad, silvery-blue fronds draped like tattered curtains from its short trunk. To my left and right, blue sky stretched to the horizon, but a tall, wide rock wall blocked the view ahead. The wall was smooth except for a jutting outcrop that provided a deep patch of shade. The outcrop looked like it could have been plucked from the Great Mural rock shelters in Baja California, though from what I could see from a distance of twenty or so feet, any ancient painted figures were absent.

"I'm back." Relief flooded through my body in a cascade so powerful it almost forced me to the ground again.

I was in Mexico. Had it all been a horrific dream? The egg-shaped vessel with its puzzling art, the terrifying abduction, the awful sickness that nearly made me nauseous again just thinking about it . . .

But I was fine now. My skin felt fresh and free of sweat, my hair fluffy and washed. My fingernails were clean and freshly trimmed. But when I looked down, my eyebrows knit together. I was naked, just like I'd been in the sterile cubicle during my sickness. I looked around again, and this time, I took real, conscious note that not a single plant around me was burnt or blackened or dead. If I was back in Mexico, it wasn't the same site I'd come from.

A distant shriek made me jolt. Then came a loud roar, followed by a rush of sharp chattering. Heavy, thumping footsteps made the ground beneath my feet tremble. I fought to keep my balance as my toes left the earth like I'd been tossed onto a taut trampoline.

The unearthly shriek crawled up my spine again. I spun around, and my eyes widened as I saw the desert landscape give way to a clear wall, nearly invisible but for the sunlight glaring off its four corners. The wall stretched thirty or so feet high and ran a width of at least fifty feet. Darkness loomed beyond.

"Oh, god," I whispered as goose bumps raised the hair on my scalp.

Clearly, this was another prison, designed to look like the mountainous desert region of Sierra de San Francisco in Baja California. The trees and desert scrub were an elaborate ruse, but *why*?

I squeezed my eyes shut to stop tears and blinked them away. I needed to see what was beyond the wall, but I felt stuck to the grass and soil under my bare feet.

Always the next step, Carmen, I told myself, pulling on my coping mechanisms that I so relied upon following Mamá's death. But this step would have to be a running leap, or there was no way I'd keep my resolve.

I took a solid breath and ran toward the wall, stumbling on the way as my bouncy step caused one of my foot's toes to collide with my other heel. I caught myself on the hard wall, which felt like the walls of my cubicle in what I'd gathered was a medical facility—smooth and firm like glass, but as strong and unbreakable as diamond.

I hit it anyway for good measure, but only hurt my hand as a result. I winced and peered through the wall with heart-thumping trepidation. A large, wide room lurked outside. Its floor looked like dark gray stone, and though it was flat, lacking gem-cut facets, it was engraved with the same manner of artwork I'd studied on the egg-shaped vessel—perfect circles connected by straight lines, forming intricate patterns that looked mathematic in nature. The art continued up narrow columns along the walls and coated a high, arched ceiling.

Between the carved stone columns, the walls were enormous clear barriers like mine, but their interiors didn't look like Mexico. They didn't look like anywhere on Earth at all.

Directly across the large hall, a clear wall displayed a thick canopy of foreign trees. White sunlight glowed through small gaps between the trunks, illuminating vibrant, dark purple leaves with turquoise veins. The leaves clung to spindly branches, and the trunks were black and spotted with yellow fungal growths that bubbled and oozed.

I gasped when a big orange blur raced up a tree in a tornado spiral. When it stopped in the high branches, I saw it was a creature unlike any I had ever seen. Sharp bristles with bright red and yellow tips shielded a body that had the carriage of an elongated lemur but was large as a panther in size. The creature's wide, round mouth opened to reveal a womb of two rows of razor teeth. Its throat expanded, then contracted as it called out a shrill, piercing cry like I had heard moments ago.

It looked right at me. I met its wide, red-eyed stare.

It screeched and leapt toward me from its branch. I flinched as it smashed into the clear wall in front of it head-on. I snorted as it slid down the barrier in an ungainly position. The creature shook its head upon reaching the ground, which I noticed, with fascination, was blue and seemed sticky beneath the beast's pincer paws. It raced up the trunk of another tree and sprang out of sight, heading deeper into its otherworldly jungle home.

I shuddered and dared to look farther down the long hallway that curved out of sight in both directions. All along the walls were more exotic landscapes, each separated from each other by stone columns.

The environment next to the red and yellow creature's was enveloped by rose-hued fog, but I could make out large, blurred mushroom-shaped objects hovering inside. Then, a long, twisting, curling creature swam through the fog several feet above the ground. My skin crawled as I watched its worm-like movements, and I recoiled when a second one joined it. They pushed their way through a wisp of pink fog so I could get a full view. They looked identical, long and insectoid, but their bodies were translucent like wax paper; I could see pumping blue and red organs through their skin. Both ends of their bodies looked like faceless nubs. They didn't have wings of any kind, but they floated through the fog with ease, undulating around each other's bodies. Perhaps, whatever kind of gas made up the fog was light enough to carry them. Helium could be light enough, maybe, but helium didn't have a color.

I caught rustling movements from within several enclosures farther down the hall, but no other creatures were close enough for me to see in detail. I couldn't see anything on my side of the hall, either, but I heard a vigorous high-pitched chatter from my left, mixed with a continued host of unfamiliar and disturbing grunts, sharp chirps, and massive roars. They rioted in my ears as if the space beyond my wall was a hollow world rife with monsters.

A shadow fell over me. Across the room, to the right of the strange, bristled creature's jungle, was a huge aquarium. A mammoth fish groaned through the water, casting the entire room into twilight. My heart stood still as it swam overhead, making an eerie, low call. The rough skin on its forty-foot-long body resembled barnacles, its stubby head wide and unwieldy.

A school of small, sharp-headed creatures, which I wouldn't quite call fish, hurried past in a flurry of skeletal bioluminescence, somehow carving through the underwater ripples their larger friend had summoned.

The heavy groaning amplified as the leviathan moved on through its gargantuan tank, swimming around a curve in the hall and out of sight.

A low growl sounded right behind me.

I spun around, eyes wide, fists raised. Some beast lurked in the shadow of the rock shelter. I could see its low shadow coming closer and hear desert scrub rustle under the steps of more than two feet.

The growl grew louder, a warning knell.

The creature burst from the shadows in a full run. I screamed, my back hitting the wall. The terrifying animal jumped and collided into me.

It barked.

My eyebrows fled upward. "Smita!"

The dog yipped and pushed her paws against my chest. I wrapped my arms around her soft fur and let her comforting weight rest against my body.

"Jesus, Smita," I said, rubbing her sides as she yelped in happiness. "Could you have at least *tried* not to scare the shit out of me?"

She licked my face and hopped back to the ground, wiggling her entire body as if her tail couldn't possibly express everything she wanted to say.

I scratched behind her perky ears, but then knelt in front of her and slowed, hugging her again, pressing my face into her fur, which smelled as fresh and clean as my hair. I squeezed my eyes shut against tears, and then pulled back and smoothed the fur on her muzzle as I met her round eyes.

"What are we gonna do?" I asked. She butted her wet nose against my cheek. Then she sat down expectantly as if answering, *I don't know, you tell me.*

"I don't know where we are. I don't know what—they—are. Or how anyone will find me. Or you," I added, my voice lilting in apology.

Smita whined. A ragged groan escaped me. I ran my hands through my hair and grabbed fistfuls, pulling taut on my scalp. I tucked my knees against my chest and buried my face in them. I caved, finally letting my repressed tears flow. "Why am I so stupid? Crispin . . . he . . . Why? Fuck!"

My broken words dissolved into incoherent sobs. Smita leaned against me, her weight providing steady comfort. I cried till my tears and painful thoughts were spent and my body was wracked with exhaustion.

I rolled my forehead against my kneecaps and loosened my grasp on my hair. I sniffled and lifted my head. I wiped my tears away and stared into space for a while, until I let out a sigh of finality.

Crying wasn't going to do me any good, nor would feeling sorry for myself or wallowing in regret. I was drawn to that damn egg through my curiosity and intelligence and go-getter attitude that Gaurav so praised. I could use those traits to my advantage now, no matter how vulnerable I felt.

I had to get back. I had to find Crispin. I had to get Smita back to Gaurav, dammit. Tears filled my eyes again as I thought of how much he must be missing his dog. Funny how I almost felt worse for taking Smita from him than for being kidnapped myself.

"No, no, no," I muttered, almost descending into fear and despair again, but I forced myself to stand. Smita gave my fingers a little lick before she followed me to my feet.

It was time to find the next step forward.

First step—I had to figure out where I was, and I had to figure out if I was alone. I was surrounded by strange creatures—animals, they seemed, because I had heard nothing akin to a spoken language aside from that of my captors. But what if I wasn't the only human taken to this mysterious place? I considered the blue light shining from the ancient artwork in the cave, matching the blue light on the egg-shaped vessel that had captured me. Had the fire Pete started triggered some signal in the cave? What if his mistake had called in more eggs, more troops of kidnappers? I hoped nobody else was in danger, but a bigger part of me hoped desperately that I could see anyone who wasn't golden-skinned and hairless.

That thought led me to wonder again, who, and *what*, were my captors?

I looked around, reassessing our situation with a clearer head. My prison looked like Mexico, the plants transplanted here, maybe, to provide me with a familiar environment. The creature across the hall lived in its own habitat, different from mine—far different. Maybe our captors had taken the same approach with my other inmates.

The tall rock formation in my enclosure hemmed in the back wall, but the sides of my environment looked like open desert stretching to the horizon. It had to be an illusion, so what did it hide? Walls, maybe a hidden door?

Only one way to find out.

I walked to my right, stumbling a little. My step still felt lighter than usual, like I was walking along the taut skin of a drum, though the soil felt firm when I dug my heels in. I took a step, then another, paying careful attention to my heels, the balls of my feet, and my toes. Though my every step felt like I was walking along the floor of a swimming pool, the effect wasn't quite floaty enough to persuade me that I wasn't just imagining the difference.

I stretched out my arms as I neared the end of the clear wall. As I suspected, my hands soon collided with another solid wall that felt like glass, but was somehow disguised as a pristine desert skyline. I felt my way down the wall, tapping places, hitting others, looking for some kind of disguised door or weak spot. I jumped as high as I could, which I could have sworn felt higher than usual, but by the time I reached the rock formation that formed the back wall of my prison, I had found nothing.

The rock wall's face was far too smooth to climb, but I felt my way along until I reached the single outcrop of rock that resembled a natural shelter. The outcrop only shadowed a space of five or so square feet. A thin pile of broad palm fronds looked purposefully arranged into a sleeping pallet. On the other end of the shelter, a small hole lurked in the ground that, upon closer inspection, contained a slick pipe deep inside that led into darkness.

I wrinkled my face in disgust, but my hands started to shake. If a sleeping mat and toilet were deemed necessary by my captors, then how long were they planning to keep me here? Despite my new primitive, degrading surroundings, this setup had a much more permanent feel than my sterile cubicle in a medical ward.

Panic buzzed through me again like a swarm of wasps, but I focused on the shelter, the trees, the walls, assessing my options for some concrete step toward escape. I headed for the final wall that looked like an endless sky. I repeated my methods to search for a door, feeling and tapping the wall, looking as hard as I could for any subtle outlines of an opening, but I finally had to slump back in defeat.

Looking up, I still couldn't see the sun itself, but there was a faint grid between the tops of the trees and the lazy clouds above. Were they wires to an open-air cage? The walls of my prison seemed impenetrable, but that grid, that sky . . . That direction offered hope.

I walked to a nearby yucca tree that had one of the lowest boughs, the most branches, and the fewest saber leaves at its crown. The sturdiest branch was still several feet above my head, but I had to try.

I took a solid stance, bent my knees, and jumped. I gasped in midair as I saw the ground far below my toes, my stomach flipping like I had jumped in a descending elevator like I used to as a kid; Mamá had even jumped with me sometimes, laughing.

My fingertips scraped the rough bark of the limb, but I couldn't get a good hold. I landed with a slight bounce and splayed my fingers out wide for balance. There was no more denying my lighter steps. Something was *very* off.

I looked at Smita. Her bounds and excited leaps all seemed higher than usual as well, and only now did an insane idea slither into my head.

Gravity.

The egg-like vessel that had captured us had shot into the air in a way no aircraft I'd ever heard of could. When I'd looked up through the tinted, sapphire facets, a great shadow had suggested we'd entered a larger vessel before I'd blacked out.

What if the vessel hadn't stopped in the upper atmosphere? What if it had ascended higher . . . higher into space?

I almost laughed at the idea, but it would explain the bizarre inhuman people who had captured me. They didn't look to be from this Earth; if they were, where had they been hiding all this time, and why?

Somehow, the idea of them being . . . aliens . . . made way more sense. Was it possible that I was on a huge spaceship with some kind of artificial gravity in place? Or even on a different planet?

My panic renewed with almost unbearable force. I leaned on my thighs, blowing air in and out in controlled breaths, feeling dizzy as I processed the implications. Even if I could reach the sky and escape this prison, what lay outside? Would I be any safer?

Smita was staring at me, her expressive eyebrows crinkled in horizontal question marks. My heartbeat slowed a little, but another worry arose. Even if I did escape through the ceiling, I wouldn't be able to bring Smita with me. I couldn't leave her.

I shoved the thought away and stood straight. There would be time to think about that later, *after* I reached the top of this damned yucca tree. No matter what waited outside, huddling in here, scared and trapped, had to be worse.

I focused again on the lowest branch and concentrated on my muscles. I squatted lower this time, took a breath, and propelled myself off the ground. I grabbed onto the branch with both hands and laughed a little as I dangled from the creaking limb. Now I had to somehow pull myself up.

I had always been athletic. I'd been raised on softball and soccer, and as an adult, many of my journeys to remote areas of the world required rigorous hikes to reach an ancient ruin or isolated village. When in more connected regions, I'd often stop by a gym when I could.

Still, it was to my great surprise that with a single hoist, I popped up to sit upon the limb. If my tentative hypothesis was right—that I was, for whatever reason, in a different gravity field—then my muscles were used to a higher force of gravity. Here, they had less resistance. I was stronger.

I looked down at Smita, who was watching me with an anxious whine.

"It's okay, girl. Don't worry about me. I got this."

I looked at the limbs above me and stood up, rocking on the arches of my feet. The branches of wild yucca trees never looked like products of intelligent design. There was no symmetry, just wayward spider limbs with spikes on each branch's stubby top.

"I think," I muttered.

I heaved myself up the closest branch. My torso curved around the fissured bark, legs dangling while I shimmied upright. I kept climbing, experimenting with my newfound strength while ducking around as many spikes as possible. I still got some scratches and a couple of good pokes, but I let out a satisfied puff of air when I reached the highest limb that could still bear my weight. The mesh-like grid was only a few feet above my head, but worry gnawed at my gut. The clouds drifting across the blue sky looked closer than they should, and what I had hoped were the metal wires of an open-air cage looked suspiciously two-dimensional.

I glared at the sky and jumped. My fingertips stretched high . . .

And touched solid glass.

I landed on my branch and scrambled to grab the wood at the base of the spiky leaves. I steadied my pounding heart that had joined the lurch of my stomach at my sudden drop.

I gingerly plucked a leaf blade from the tree and threw it at the sky. It smacked the glass between a space in the cross-hatched grid before bouncing back and hitting me in the nose. Like the illusion of the walls, the sky was a solid ceiling.

I yelled and shook the tree in rage. There was no way out.

The treetop swayed, and my foot slipped. I caught my balance, but as I looked down, something new caught my eye.

A person was across the hallway, inside the red-and-yellow-bristled creature's habitat. One of *them*.

I hadn't gotten a good look at any of my captors aside from the woman I had first seen before my horrendous illness had taken over all powers of observation. The stranger across the hall had the golden and white complexion, bald head, and solid black eyes I had come to expect from those I'd seen in blurry passing.

But the woman's calico patterns, willowy frame, and soft features contrasted with the new stranger's sharper patterns and taller stature. The stranger's broad shoulders lacked the arched, boney shoulder ridges that the woman had possessed. Overall, the new person looked masculine in the same way human males look in comparison with females. I decided to run with my assumption that he was a man.

He was dressed in a long robe similar to the garment the woman had worn, but his clothing was made of stiffer, black fabric. Both styles had tight collars around the base of their necks, but unlike the woman's, the man's clothing covered his shoulders and extended to elbow-length sleeves. I stole a glimpse of his back as he walked with slow steps through the habitat. The top half of his robe looked like a backward vest. Strips of fabric on either side of his shoulder blades were cut in sharp angles and stuck out in a manner that made him look strong and severe.

All the skin down his back was golden, and five vertical slits were barely visible from his shoulders to his waist. The skin twitched a little around the edges as he moved, and I assumed they could open to reveal white, pearly skin underneath like the woman's had done.

I looked at his face, but his nose and mouth were covered by what looked like a breathing mask. He walked with cautious steps toward the wild, bristly creature perched on a low branch of a tree, all the while looking at the ground to avoid eye contact.

The man looked anything but submissive, though. Respectful, yet confident, he kept walking toward the beast. The creature appraised him but didn't seem fearful of or aggravated by its invader. It cocked its head as the man pulled a small, blue wafer from a black satchel at his side. He extended his hand in offering, still not making eye contact. The creature scrabbled on its branch and plucked the wafer with two delicate pincers. It stuffed the wafer into its mouth. The treat moved in visible increments down its gullet.

The man's eyes crinkled as if he were smiling. He gently stroked the back of the animal's paw, and its red and yellow bristles flattened down its body like dominoes. It shimmied down the tree trunk and poised its pincers on the bright blue ground, and I noticed the man wore cleats that suspended him on the sticky ground with the same tentative hold as the creature's paws.

The man pulled out another treat from his satchel and used it to coax the creature toward the clear wall at the front of the habitat. It followed him in an eager trot.

The man held the treat against the wall. The creature reached for it, but the man lifted it higher at the last moment, and the creature's paw hit the wall. It jerked back and looked at the invisible wall in surprise.

The man lowered the treat again, still pressed against the wall. This time, he kept it still as the creature pushed its paw against the treat and pinned it there. Then it snatched the treat and opened its round jaws. My eyes widened as I saw its double rows of teeth gnash the treat inside, though the creature's jaw itself didn't appear to move.

The man's eyes crinkled in a smile again. I watched him repeat his process, trying to teach the poor creature that the wall existed so that it wouldn't smash into it anymore.

I felt a pull of sympathy for the creature and an involuntary rise of tenderness as I watched the man's kind eyes and patient gestures.

Then he looked up at me.

I froze, high up in my tree. His golden eyebrows furrowed, concern fleeting into his eyes. He gave the creature beside him one last treat, and then stood up.

He didn't hesitate to meet my gaze; I assumed he knew or guessed that I wouldn't run headfirst into the wall like the bristled animal had the first time I'd made eye contact. That was encouraging, at least. For a moment, I felt like time slowed down as we stared at each other, and then he slowly raised his hand beside his head, palm out, as if sending me a single wave of greeting.

I raised my eyebrows and waved back. He blinked and stepped one foot back, his eyes crinkling again in a smile at my echo of his gesture.

"Hey," I said. "Hey, come here."

He lowered his hand but didn't answer. He looked back down at the strange creature beside him, who paid him no mind now that it had its treat. The man backed away and disappeared into the black-barked trees.

I tensed, ready to call out again, but then he reappeared outside the beast's enclosure in the outer hallway. He must have used a hidden exit, which was maddening—maybe my own prison had a similar door. I stayed, unmoving, in the relative safety of my tree and kept my hard gaze on him, waiting to see what he would do.

Smita startled me by barking at him. She hunkered low, hackles raised in a mohawk all down her back as she darted side to side with growls and barks, riled up more and more the closer he got. He stopped right outside the glass and removed the mask from his nose and mouth to let it dangle around his neck.

Smita yipped and sat down.

I frowned, trying to recall if I'd ever seen him before because Smita seemed to recognize him. He looked like a young adult by human standards, perhaps a year or two younger than me. His face was the shape of a chiseled diamond, with high cheekbones and hollowed cheeks, a straight boney nose, and a narrow jaw. His golden patterns looked like concentric tree rings, but many narrowed into sharp points or flowed like rivers, coaxing me to envision the polished inner slice of a geode instead. His shining black eyes were round as if he wished to encompass the entire universe within each glance. Right now, the entire universe seemed to harbor only me.

No, I'd never seen him before. I would have remembered a face like that.

With Smita pacified—whether that was a wise reaction of hers or not—the man spoke, and though his voice was muffled through the barrier, his single foreign word sounded compassionate.

Unlike the woman in the medical facility, this man seemed receptive; perhaps he would listen to me and answer my questions as best he could, even if we didn't speak the same languages. Maybe he would help.

My throat felt tight and my legs wobbly, but I focused on finding the strongest limbs and sturdiest handholds to climb down from the tree. The man frowned with concern as he watched, but when I was halfway down the trunk, I saw he was no longer alone.

A second man strode down the wide hallway. He wore a long brown robe, and his golden patterns dripped off his head as if someone had cracked an egg over his scalp. He was shorter than the first man and looked older, but he held his chin high and narrowed his beetle-black eyes as if trying too hard to impose authority. He reminded me of Pete.

He said something to the younger man, who gestured to me in response. The short man looked my way and analyzed me from head to toe. He reached out toward the clear wall of my prison, but then drew back his hand with a shudder from fingertips to shoulder. His subtle grimace of distaste accompanied a sentence and an odd rumbling sound in his throat; he looked at the other man with a conspiratorial smile, but the other man didn't look amused.

The short man retained his thin, close-lipped smile that had a slippery, reptilian feel to it. Goose bumps fled up my arms.

He turned away and volleyed what sounded like an order over his shoulder. The younger man answered in a defiant tone. The cadence of their language was lyrical; none of the consonants were harsh, and the vowels were smooth and never spread far apart. There was beauty in it, but I doubted I would find the meaning beautiful.

The man in charge said something else and gestured sharply down the hall. The young man looked back up at me with worry, but started to follow the boss away.

"No," I said, my shred of hope seizing. "Wait!"

I looked down at the many branches between me and the ground, where Smita looked up at me, whining and prancing on nervous paws.

I slid down onto the nearest branch, but the one below it was farther away and at an awkward angle. I stretched out one foot and found a solid place to step, and then pushed off the trunk. Swinging, I reached for the next handhold.

My right foot slipped out from under me, and I crashed against the hard branch and tumbled through scratching twigs and sharp leaves.

My head hit the base of the tree trunk with a loud and painful smack.

I heard fast footsteps and a hiss like steam as I waded through my pain and spinning vision. Smita snuffled my shoulder, and then I felt arms around me and heard a low, comforting voice. A gentle hand cradled my head. I cried out as another pulse of pain pounded through me, but two fingertips brushed my forehead, and my muscles relaxed in a soothing wave before everything went dark.

CHAPTER FOUR

I OPENED MY eyes to vibrant orange light obliterating the shade under a rocky outcrop. I rolled onto my side, rustling broad blue palm leaves underneath me. A headache pounded at the outskirts of my brain. I frowned and sat up.

I felt like I'd missed a step on a staircase; I was falling, but where to? Where from? Up or down?

Smita barked, jolting me out of my disorientation. I looked at her big round eyes and pointed snout and inquisitive, lopsided ears. Everything came back to me in a rapid flood.

"Smita," I puffed. She wagged her tail and started eating something off the floor. It looked like a dense, crumbly granola bar.

My stomach panged. I looked around in a daze and soon saw an indented ledge on the back wall of the shelter, high enough to be out of Smita's reach, where a tan, round, biscuit-like food waited.

I wasn't sure if I could trust my captors enough to eat their food, but they hadn't killed me yet, and my stomach reprimanded my hesitation with a growl. I climbed to my feet but cried out when I saw a smooth, shiny orange blob on my right forearm. Veins of red marbled through its flat surface; it pulsed like a three-inch-wide leech.

I smacked my arm, but the mass was stuck. I gritted my teeth, lifted the rubbery edge with two fingernails, and ripped it off. I flung it away; it landed on the floor near the toilet hole. I backed up, writhing amidst goose bumps, and bumped into Smita. She grunted and shook herself a little, but came around my legs to see what the fuss was about.

I eyed the slick orange thing, dormant on the ground. It continued to do nothing. I kept it in my peripheral vision and dared to inspect my arm in the morning light of the fake sun. My skin was yellow and blotchy where the orange patch had been, with a short line of hardened scab running through. I scrunched my eyebrows and poked the scab. A dull ache thrummed beneath.

I frowned in incredulity. The bruises and cut hadn't been there mere hours ago. Yet the wounds were nearly healed.

My fall from the tree the day before drummed painfully into my memory. As did the worried face of the man who had watched me from across the hall, his eyes round and captivated just before I fell.

Had it been his arms around me before I faded from consciousness? The soft words had been comforting, but a throb of my scalp brought a vague recollection of the medical ward with the cold table, bright lights, and humming equipment. I touched the back of my head, where another orange patch lurked amidst my hair. Had my captors taken me to medical to patch me up before returning me to my prison?

I had missed an opportunity to escape. Had I been awake, I would at least have seen a door in this seamless room, maybe even scouted out the medical facilities for a way out of the building.

I screamed in frustration and ignored the biscuit on the shelf, determined to inspect the walls again. I noticed another bright orange bandage on my ankle in passing, but a whine from Smita stole my attention. She had finished eating and was looking at the clear wall.

"What? Do you see something?" I saw nothing aside from the dim outer hall and the glow of the other habitats.

"Why don't you go check it out? Jao." Smita stood up to follow my order, but she snapped to attention as a terrible, piercing shriek rang against our eardrums.

Our neighbor across the hall was back in its tree, announcing the day like a rooster on steroids.

Smita cocked her head at me, bushy eyebrows raised.

"Okay, together then." I approached the wall, ignoring the tweaking pain in my ankle as best I could. Smita turned a circle and trotted at my side. I peered into the outer hallway, darting my eyes every direction, but nothing was different.

Smita's hackles raised, a suspicious growl revving like an engine in her throat. I placed my hand on the top of her head. She woofed and took a protective stance in front of me. I was grateful for her comfort, but I doubted a guard dog would do me any good in a place like this. Especially when I heard voices echoing from the left.

My chest felt tight and my breaths short as I trained my eyes down the hall. The voices were growing louder. Titters of excitement joined the calm musings of interested discussion, intertwined with high-pitched shouts, followed by the mild calls of more reasonable tones, all speaking in the babbling foreign language of my captors. Footsteps soon joined the fray.

It sounded like a *lot* of people.

I bolted back to my shelter, but sunlight poured in, whittling the shade down to a sliver. Smita stayed where she was, her growls unceasing and louder by the second. I pressed my back against the rock and froze when a scattered group of people came into view from around the hall's curve.

They were all sculpted marble statues, their gilded patterns as distinct as thumbprints. They wore robe-like garments with floor-length hems, the colors muted and subdued compared to their lustrous golden skin as if they were trying to tone themselves down.

As the group trickled along the hall, they paused in clumps in front of various false environments. Some inspected a habitat down my side of the hall that exploded into boisterous, monkey-like chatters. Others paused at the creepy worms in their rosy fog diagonal to my left, and some reached the red-and-yellow-bristled creature across the hall from my prison.

Not all the people were calm in their interest, however. Some were short and wiry in frame and darted around with unrestrained energy and big smiles on their faces. Their golden patterns were sparser and less organized, like a half-finished Pollock painting.

One short person pointed a gold-spotted finger right at me and shouted a high-pitched word. Taller people with more elegant golden patterns joined in a hubbub of interest as they followed the little one's scamper toward me. A gaggle of more little ones, all speckled with gold spots like gilded fawns, pressed their palms against my wall, skin smooshed flat, spreading their fingerprints wide.

I needed no interpretation of their language to guess the meaning of their thrilled words.

"*Look!*"

They were children. Not intimidating captors poking and prodding and stunning me into black unconsciousness. Tinier ones, clearly infants, clung to adult women's backs by clasping the shoulder ridges that seemed to be a female trait, revealing the boney projections' use. The babies were entirely white, with no gold on their skin at all, and their big black eyes stared at everything around them with an infant's wonder. Their heads were smaller in proportion to their bodies than any human infant's I had ever seen, and they had no trouble swiveling their necks as they stayed upright with ease.

Gangly youths, who must have been their pubescent siblings, all looked like they had a bad rash. The perky little dots of childhood spread into blotchy, failed attempts at ornate adult patterns. The youths looked bored, lurking behind their parents in sullen protest as if coming here was beneath their sense of burgeoning dignity.

Seeing the unexpected children made me consider that these beings, human or not, were not so very different from those I knew as family, as friends, as any people I had seen on my numerous travels.

Yet, they clearly saw me as something other, something lesser.

Smita barked, yanking me out of my analyzations and my heart away from the empathy I was starting to feel toward the humanizing children. I was naked, trapped here against my will, and was now being raked over by countless black eyes that fixed on different parts of my body as if inspecting some new, bizarre creature.

I sank to the ground in the dwindling shade of my shelter, tucking my knees under my chin and crossing my ankles to hide as much of my body as possible. Some of my viewers frowned in disappointment. They kept staring for a little while longer, but then they all drifted off to see the leviathan in the aquarium tank.

I let out a breath and peered down the left-hand hallway. It was empty, but I thought I heard more voices drifting my way.

I scurried out from under my shelter and snatched several large palm fronds from the ground. I twisted the stems and fronds together to tie them around my breasts and hips. The top and skirt weren't perfect, but the fronds at least served to hide my privates as a new group of people walked into the hallway.

Feeling a little less vulnerable, I decided it was time to meet these people head-on. My squirm of humiliation threatened to stop me, but I rolled back my shoulders and took slow steps toward the wall just as the first spectators arrived. They all looked intrigued, using similar expressions as humans did—raised eyebrows, light smiles—though subtler. If the children didn't wear such vibrant faces, I might have thought the adults' facial muscles weren't capable of exaggerated expressions. The adults spoke with their children often but rarely said anything to each other. They exchanged frequent glances, however, making me feel like I was back in elementary school getting the silent treatment from conspiratorial bullies.

I stopped a few feet from the wall, swallowing as I absorbed all the humiliating attention. Smita crouched low by my side, her tail swinging back and forth like she was on the hunt.

"My name is Carmen," I said, my voice trembling as I tried to be diplomatic. I patted my chest—"Carmen"—and pointed at them. "Who are you?"

A sweep of murmurs followed my words, but no one answered my question. They only spoke with each other or sent one another more conspiratorial looks. They all kept making a rumbling sound in their throats, and some clicked their tongues in a deliberate manner, but it didn't seem like an attempt to communicate with me.

"Where are we?" I asked, involuntary tears springing to my eyes despite my need to appear composed and intelligent. "Why are you holding me here? Please, talk to me!"

They kept talking to each other.

"Hey!" I banged my fist against the wall. Smita barked in echo.

A couple of the children jumped back. Their parents laid hands on their heads in comfort, but the adults didn't seem worried at all.

"Are you listening to me?" I asked, louder this time. I could hear them, so surely they could hear me. Yet still, they didn't respond. "Let me go! You can't hold me prisoner here. Take me back. To Mexico, to anywhere, just let me go!"

I got a few wary glances, but most of the mild smiles didn't fade as people started to move on to the habitat next to mine.

"No, no, don't go," I pleaded, but the stragglers ignored me, and the little children rushed off.

"Wait!" I shouted, but then snapped my head to my left when I heard more voices. More black eyes met mine, more white-and-gold fingers pointed, more wide mouths babbled.

As the sounds of their voices mingled with the shrieks, chatters, and roars of my neighboring creatures, I attempted to wrap my head around my new, increasingly obvious reality.

The only strangers I had seen before today had acted like staff members of this facility, but the children and adults who now stared did so with delight and casual interest rather than an attitude of study or medical attention. I was only familiar with one kind of place where people came to view creatures unlike themselves for fun.

A zoo.

I was in a *zoo*.

"What the hell?" I looked from one face to another of my current visitors as if they were all stupid. "I'm not an animal."

They didn't react to my words, perhaps treating them as background noise like I did with all of the bestial noises surrounding us. But how could they not understand that I was speaking a complicated language, not grunting or howling like the animals in this place? How could they not see the similarities between us, that we were both bipedal hominids at the least?

"I'm a person," I said. "I'm a human, an intelligent being, *not* an animal. Do you understand?"

I searched for sympathy, but they only looked at me with various levels of curiosity before walking away, their interest satisfied.

My breaths picked up speed, stealing my ability to call after them. I leaned against the wall to keep myself standing. Normally, this level of panic only came when memories of the car wreck in Baja California blasted into my brain.

Take the next step.

I closed my eyes and counted backward from ten, forcing my breaths to slow. My heartbeat rattled in its cage, but it calmed with each new recited number, each new breath, until it was content to merely pace back and forth, beat by beat, step by step. *Take the next step. Move on.*

I opened my eyes and pushed myself from the wall just when a fresh group of people approached my *zoo* habitat.

They stopped in front of my wall, gibbering and rumbling. This time, one of them thrust their finger in the direction of the orange bandage around my ankle. A chorus of cooing noises and clucks of tongues followed. Judging by their round eyes and indulgent smiles, it became clear they thought I was cute.

I looked down at my ankle. Images of kittens in casts and coned dogs popped into my mind.

I began to shake with rage. I resisted the urge to tuck my ankle behind the other, and the more compelling urge to run back into the shelter.

"What is *wrong* with you?" I yelled. "Look at me!"

They were looking, but they weren't seeing. A group of young ones pointed at my hair and pulled invisible strings from their bald heads. One of the adults grinned at the children's antics and joined indulgently in their behavior.

I snapped. The same feeling of outrage that had prompted me to punch reckless, sneering Pete now triggered my every muscle. I flashed my eyes around, looking for something to throw. I found a rock the size of my fist and snatched it off the ground.

With a wrenching yell, I hurled the rock at the wall. It struck with a clanging bang and bounced off onto the grass.

The children screamed and jumped back. Their parents consoled them, holding them close. Some lifted them into their arms and stroked their foreheads in what appeared to be a soothing gesture.

Encouraged by their reactions, I found more scattered rocks to throw and shouted a string of curses that seemed to be the only vocabulary left to me in my horrific conditions. Smita joined me in a loyal display of fierce aggression, barking and growling threats in a way that would terrify me if she'd been off leash and I'd been on the other end. I threw rock after rock, imagining them smashing into people's faces, but they only ricocheted off the wall and clattered to the ground.

When I ran out of rocks, I bent over and dragged my fingers into the earth, feeling dirt push under my fingernails. I balled up my hands, and bombs of dirt exploded in the spectators' faces as I threw fist after fist. Soon, the ground beneath me was nothing but torn tufts of grass and roots upended at my feet.

A singular expression of wide-eyed surprise flowed through the group like an encroaching tide, taking hold of everyone at once. Grimaces of nausea followed as if a virus had spread in seconds. A few of the children still looked more curious than scared, but most wore frowns that didn't smooth.

I slowed my tirade, my chest heaving, my throat sore from yelling. The adults I could ignore and despise, but I looked from one child's face to another, to another, to another.

"Oh, god," I said. My knees hit the ground like I was hit by a hammer. I scooted forward on the prickly grass. I pressed my hand against the cold, glassy wall in fervent apology. "I'm sorry."

The nearest child flinched, and their mother scooped them into her arms with a frown of intense suspicion that every adult around her echoed.

"No, wait," I said, then flicked my eyes around the group of kids. "I didn't mean to scare you. I'm . . ."

A single child protested and looked back at me with longing as their mother coaxed them away, but within seconds, the entire group had fled.

Temper, mijita.

My mother's voice brushed my mind in a gentle chide. She'd said it enough times when I was young that my mind replayed the exact tone of her voice and warning kindle in her eyes. Her phrase had annoyed me too many times to count growing up. Now it was a grain of hope.

I had flown into fits of rage before, despite her attempts to teach me patience and understanding. But I had never, not *once*, aimed my anger at anyone who didn't deserve it. I had never, and would never, lash out at children.

Yet, I just had. They were kids. They were just kids.

Those children probably wouldn't forget my tantrum for as long as they lived. My stomach clenched and turned sour as guilt surged in. I rolled my forehead against the glass, suppressing a groan.

Another shriek echoed from my neighbor across the hall. I watched the large, spindly beast swirl its way up a tree. It shrieked again at a group of visitors clustered around its enclosure.

Someone must have made eye contact. The creature leapt off its tree right toward the watching group and smacked into the transparent wall. It slid down in the flattened, ungainly position that was just as comical as I had witnessed before.

Hitting the sticky, blue ground of its habitat, it shook its head and crept into the background to sulk.

I swayed back as if I had been hit in the chest with a battering ram. That's how I looked to them. A stupid animal, too dumb to know that the dirt I'd thrown at the wall wouldn't hit my audience. Too wild to be a civilized being.

I wondered if the poor creature across the hall was as aware of its degradation as me. Perhaps it was, but for all the similarities of our conditions, even in our reactions to our captivity, there was a striking difference between us. Every time the creature was aggravated, it would leap at the wall, and every time, it was shocked when it collided with a solid surface. The creature was not intelligent enough to remember that the wall existed.

Why these people couldn't see that I was more intelligent than the creature, I didn't know, but hurling rocks and shouting obscenities was not going to convince them. So, what would?

I stood and walked back to my rock shelter to ponder my dilemma. I laid a hand on the overhanging rock's jagged edge, warmed by the sun. The back wall of the shelter glowed, a blank canvas for the ancient artwork that the shelter's real counterpart in Baja California bore. I imagined the vivid art—enormous red and black figures of humans, some hunting ancient deer, sheep, or mountain lions, others standing next to whales, sea lions, and birds in flight. I looked down at the pallet of palm leaves my captors had made for me, and I imagined my ancient ancestors taking shelter here, sitting around warm fires on cold desert nights.

My brain struck flint to cause a dazzling mental spark. I spun around.

Climbing trees hadn't offered salvation the night before, but maybe I could put them to a different use. I scoured the prison, snapping some low-hanging limbs off elephant trees and gathering fallen sticks from the ground. I tested each stick's flexibility and tensile strength, snapping them and digging my thumbnail into the softer meat inside.

"Perfect," I praised when one of the largest and flattest branches accepted an indent from my fingernail. I took a nervous breath as my heart pattered with hope. I found a sharp rock and started pecking at the branch. It was slow going, but after a while, I had created a quarter-sized hole in the middle.

I hunted for smaller sticks next and pulled up tufts of scrubby grass. I gathered palm fronds and twisted fibers together to make a short rope. Smita followed me around with keen interest for at least an hour, and she wasn't the only one watching. I could feel the pressure of many eyes, growing in number as people lingered outside.

"Keep staring," I muttered. I wanted a large audience.

When all was ready, I brought my supplies to an open space in front of the clear wall. I laid one large branch on the ground and covered it with the branch with the quarter-sized hole. I then picked up a long, slightly bowed stick and lashed my makeshift fiber rope to both ends in tight knots. I looped an eight-inch-long stick into the middle of the rope until the rope felt taut like a bowstring. I turned the short stick upright and notched it into the hole in the top branch on the ground. I placed a final chunk of wood on top of the short stick to create a handhold.

I took a breath, and then put my right knee on the ground and my left foot on top of the branch. I gripped the handhold and pushed my shin heavily on my wrist. I drew back my other hand and began to rapidly run the bow back and forth across the stick. The stick twirled in the hole. I breathed steadily, in and out, in and out, as I put all my energy into creating friction.

A wisp of smoke issued from the hole, and I heard sounds of approval and curiosity from my watchers. I stopped drilling and set my implements aside. The hole was charred black at the edges.

My fire safety courses to get my certified "red card" hadn't only taught me how to stop fires, but also this priceless, rudimentary skill of starting them. While my current need for a bow drill was far different from what I had ever anticipated, I could only hope it would do me some good now.

I gently lifted the branch to see the flatter one beneath. Black powder fed a thin stream of smoke into my nostrils. My anxious hope drove me to hurry, but I forced myself to work with slow and steady hands to lift the newborn coal and pour it into my bundle of grass tinder.

The coal hit the grass with a tiny crackle. I pursed my lips and blew a stream of air into its heart, and my chest swelled in elation as a spark flared. I lifted the tinder packet by its edges and tilted it so the little flame could spread.

Gasps reached my ears. I looked up and smiled at my audience, nodding and pointing to the blaze.

"See?" I said. I sidled to a nearby tripod of wood I had prepared and nestled the burning tinder inside. More leaves and twigs caught flame. Soon I had a small campfire crackling away.

I stood and placed a firm hand on my chest. I pointed at the fire.

Humans made fire. It was, in an ancient sense, what separated us from beasts.

A wave of collective smiles greeted my action, but my audience's enthusiasm was laced with rumbling in their throats that I suspected expressed humor, and many clucked their tongues again in a sound of endearment.

"What is wrong with you people?" I waved my arms from them, to me, to the fire, but no one was listening. The show was over, and people began to drift off to see what antics my beastly neighbors were up to.

"No!" I shouted, running to the wall until my palms collided with it. "No, come back! Look what I did! I made this!" I gestured again to the fire. Then I pounded my fists against the barrier, desperate to get the attention of those who remained, but my renewed aggression bored them, and they were gone.

"No," I said, stumbling back. "How can they—I'm not . . ."

I stared at my fire, hopeless.

A crack of thunder jolted a buzz down my spine. Smita gave a startled bark and ran for the shelter with her bushy tail tucked between her legs.

Rain poured down from the ceiling. Though the clouds seemed like an illusion, the water was real enough, and cold. My fire sputtered out. I was soaked within seconds. I trudged to my shelter and slumped to the dirt floor, the edges of which were bubbling as they seeped into mud. I bowed my head and stared at a blurred leaf near my big toe.

I didn't know how long I sat there, ignoring my train of audience members, but eventually, the lights outside dimmed. The rain continued falling from false clouds that weren't even gray. I was alone.

Then the short employee who had reminded me of Pete the night before, who I assumed was the boss of this establishment, strode into view outside my prison.

Like humans, these foreign people seemed to smile for a wide array of reasons. While baring of teeth are signs of aggression in primates, close-lipped grins are signs of submission. Many anthropologists believe that human smiles are based on that same instinct. Smiles are our way of submitting to each other, in a sense, to set each other at ease. Smiles can be an expression of pure happiness at times, yes, but a politician's false smile when posing for a photograph, or this inhuman boss's cocky sneer now, was not of a purely happy nature.

Whatever the reasons for us evolving in a similar way, I held a degree of confidence that I could at least communicate with these people through facial expressions, if not words.

I sent the man a cold glare and gave him the finger for good measure.

He spoke and gestured to me, to the enclosure, to the exposed hole I assumed was a toilet—which I had forgone eating and drinking that day to avoid using in front of strangers—and to the deluge of rain.

Although I could not understand a word of his language, his condescending meaning was perfectly clear:

This is what you get for misbehaving.

My lips twitched and my nostrils flared. I scrambled out into the open, grabbed a fistful of sloppy mud, and hurled it at his face. It smacked into the wall and slid down. His throat rumbled with amusement and his lip curled in disgust before he sauntered away, leaving me to my misery.

I stumbled back and fell onto the palm fronds in my shelter. I curled up on my side, hugging my knees as cold raindrops dripped from my hair down my face. I watched streams of water pouring from the top of the rocky outcrop and splatting on the mud, and the falling uniform rain beyond.

I squeezed tears out of my eyes with a fierce squint. My last sight of Crispin hit me, his worried face and frantic shouts as he ran through billowing ash to save me from the mysterious trap stealing me away.

He loved me, I knew. He'd tried to hide it, but his feelings slipped through his façade like he couldn't control them. Had I denied my feelings for him? Or was my memory flawed now because of my utter, devastating loneliness?

I wanted Mamá. I wanted her warm arms around me and her assurances that it was going to be all right. I didn't even have her cherished painting with me to give me comfort.

More tears came and turned to heaving sobs. I had traveled the world and rarely felt homesick, and my one moment of true heartache was ten years past. This shuddering pain was so consuming, I knew I was suffering from both in droves.

Eventually, my chest stopped heaving, and my heart slowed. I felt spent, and I curled into myself and clutched a fistful of hair like an infant grasping its mother's finger. Smita snuffled over and licked a tear off my cheek. She huffed and curved her warm, soft body around me, resting her head on my shoulder. The strong smell of wet dog hit my nostrils, but I was glad for her closeness. A song swam into my ears, an old lullaby Mamá used to sing.

CHAPTER FIVE

IT GREW DARK during my retreat from reality. Beyond the edge of the rock shelter, I could see a few stars peeking through the clouds. I peered up at the tiny lights, trying to piece together familiar groupings, but they all looked foreign and offset. Did they even contain the warriors of protection—Orion, Perseus, or Hercules—or the ever-watchful beasts—Ursa Major, Canes Venatici, or Pegasus? If I kept staring, would I find my own horoscope constellation, Aries? I had never taken much stock in astrology, but at this point, I would welcome any guidance I could get.

The moon never made an appearance. I waited for it in a daze until pink dawn from an invisible sun lightened my habitat. I finally emerged from the shelter. The tall rock wall that formed the entire back of my prison sparkled. Rainwater rolled down its face in little streams, clinging to the edge of the shelter's outcrop for seconds before falling as teardrops to the grass. The paths of water on the rock wove in and out of each other in artistic fractals of nature, yet looked purposeful, like some invisible hand had ordained where they should go.

Of course.

How had I not seen it before? Freshman year, my first class with Gaurav. Prehistoric Art 101:

The ability to create art of a symbolic nature is believed to be a defining characteristic of humanity, a cornerstone of the first evidence of complex cognition, a bridge between Homo sapiens *and those species who came before. With symbolic art came the ability to develop language, to share technology, and to work together to expand across the globe. Art is what makes us human.*

I dashed through the rain to my dormant fire. Charred sticks sat in a sad, wet pile. I found one that looked solid enough to not break under pressure. I touched the tip; black charcoal smeared on my fingertips.

I walked on mud-caked feet to the smooth rock wall. My audience was gone, but maybe I was being recorded in some way. Maybe someone was watching.

I lifted the stick and took a breath. Studying art was my vocation, but creating art had never been my specialty. Fortunately, the basic strokes of the constellation-like artwork on the egg-shaped vessel that had captured me were fairly simple. I could make a passable imitation, at least. I had to pray it would be enough.

I drew a black horizontal line across the stone. I twisted and turned the stick to make a large dot, and then started a new line emerging at an angle from that point. I swiveled another dot into place and drew more lines and more dots until I had created a four-knuckled hand. I drew another line, another dot, and more and more until I had connected two more four-knuckled hands to the first. I drew faster and faster as I stared at the hands, so similar, yet *so* different from mine. I imagined those hands touching me, stunning me into unconsciousness, pointing at me through a terrarium wall like I was some animal to be ridiculed and mistreated. I drove charcoal into the stone with greater force with each new line. A crack splintered down the length of my stick, but I couldn't stop; I had to keep going. They had to see. They *had* to.

No longer capable of the restraint needed to compose lines, I ran my hand in circle after circle in the same spot as if I could drill my way out of this nightmare. Smeared black streaks of charcoal escaped as galaxy spirals, hurricane arms, an expression of the storm inside me, screaming to get out.

I did scream. I screamed at the rock wall and at my charcoal circle of rage. My broken, splintered stick was now nothing but a crumbled, worn-down nub.

Smita barked loudly. I whipped around and froze.

A gold-patterned man stood inside my enclosure.

I grabbed a new stick within reach and raised it in a position halfway between a baseball bat and a spear.

The man held out a pacifying hand to Smita, who stopped growling and woofed a greeting. She recognized him as much as I did. He was the young man we'd seen in the enclosure opposite ours the night before, with the same sliced-geode patterns on his skin and wearing the same black robe of utilitarian fabric, a glossy black satchel at his side.

But the sweet confidence he'd shown the creature across the hall and the gentle wonder he had aimed at me were gone. His attention was fixed on my charcoal circle that I wouldn't even call "art" anymore. Just a madwoman's rage in another form.

He took a single step toward the rock wall as if he were both terrified and mesmerized, a moth batting frantic wings against its urge to dive-bomb into a burning fire. His eyes glittered over my attempts at the constellation-like artwork, his lips parting with wonder, but his gaze was dragged back to the circle—my subconscious, dark, vengeful imitation of the enthralling hurricane artwork, so different from the rest, that had ensnared me into this nightmarish hell.

He took slow breaths, the black fabric over his chest trembling with each inhale. He reached out and touched the drawing of the wild circle, coating his long fingertips in charcoal.

Then he pressed his marble-white lips together and turned toward me. I clung to my raised stick as if it were a rope that would keep me from falling.

The man absorbed every aspect of my face, my wet hair plastered to my skin, raindrops blending with tears. He twitched his head at Smita, who now lay close by, watching him, then he looked back at me. His metamorphizing expression looked like some closed door was slowly cracking open in his mind. He locked into my gaze; his eyes grew round and full.

"Selis." A single, soft word. His hairless eyebrows raised the smallest amount. He was waiting.

Not a single person had spoken to me that way since I'd arrived. No one had ever expected an answer.

"Selis," he said again. "Iri Eis. Eis."

I tightened my sweaty grip on my stick, my tense arms shaking as I tried to fathom the emotions in his solid black eyes. This man was different; even his facial expressions were far more vivid and powerful than any of his peers. He wanted to connect with me. He saw *me*.

I let out a slow breath and loosened my hold on the stick. I took a chance and lowered it.

"Yes. I'm like you," I said, my voice hoarse with nerves as I tested my words like my tweaked ankle. I pointed to the constellation-like artwork, and then to myself. "See? I can do that, just like you. Your . . . people."

His people. Hatred dug a pit in my gut, but if I was to convince this man of our similarities, then I had to focus.

"We're both hominids, right? Close enough anyway. We both have opposable thumbs." I lifted my hand to show him. His gaze sharpened, and his frown deepened. "We're bipedal. We make tools. We *think* beyond the here and now."

As I pleaded, I made out dim amber irises embedded inside the darkness of his eyes, like viewing a solar eclipse through tinted glasses. They made him look more human.

"Please," I whispered. "You have to let me go. You"—I pointed at him, then me—"*we* are the same. We are."

It was my turn to wait. He looked again at the artwork, and then at me. He said something indistinguishable, but in a tone of affirmation. His eyes narrowed, his mouth formed a line of determination, and his shoulders squared as he stood straighter. He looked around the habitat with a glower of building anger.

Was I finally getting through?

"Please," I said, "get me out." I pointed at the clear wall, realizing with sudden despair that I hadn't seen how he had entered my enclosure in the first place. "Get me home."

He watched my mouth as I spoke.

"Yes. Yes! I speak," I touched my lips with a frantic tap of my fingers. "Eis," I repeated, hoping I had chosen an appropriate word in his language to echo. When he'd said it, it sounded somewhere between *ace* and *ice*. I could only hope my pronunciation was good enough for him to understand.

He took a quick breath, and his eyes lit up. He flicked his right wrist so that his palm faced the fake blue sky. A circular projection of white-blue light flashed from a thin metal ring around his middle finger. The circle hovered flat above his palm, and he raised his left hand and started tapping the light with his fingers. Whatever the device was made of, it was solid to the touch. He kept tapping his fingers and running them in circles around the edge as if it were some kind of a translucent tablet screen. What looked like a foreign alphabet appeared; I could see symmetrical symbols through the back, visible between his fingers.

When he stopped, the symbols disappeared. All the translucent tablet displayed were a few empty circles bordered with white light.

He said something and pointed to my mouth. He then pointed to his mouth, said something else, and pointed at my mouth again.

"Yes, I can talk," I said, my heartbeat quickening with a surge of hope. The man nodded with vigor and offered me his empty palm as if giving me the floor.

"Why are you the only one who's noticed? It's not like I'm growling or chattering. I know some animals can make pretty complex sounds, but—I'm smart, believe me."

I paused as I caught the tail end of a flash of yellow on the tablet screen.

"What are you doing?" I asked, watching the tablet. More splashes of yellow crossed the screen within one of the circles; they corresponded in peaks and valleys with the cadence of my voice.

"Yes! I can speak like you, a complicated language that means more than just the basics of hunger, of aggression, of fear . . . Ha!" He jolted in surprise. "I can speak two! ¿No oyes lo que hago? ¡Fíjate en lo que hace un animal!"

A jarring clang sounded from the tablet. The man frowned and concentrated on it for a moment.

"¿Pues que no te gusta el español?" I sent the tablet a mocking smile for not finding Spanish agreeable. "How about English again?"

The tablet clanged again with a confused splotch of red overlaying the yellow, but the man wasn't watching the screen anymore. He was watching me.

"So, you don't need technology to tell your ears what they hear. I was beginning to think you should be the one in the cage."

I started talking faster about anything that came to mind, offering constant translations of my speech as I switched from one language to the next. Confused splotches of red and yellow continued, but then flashes of white light appeared that seemed to match patterns between both languages as if struggling to combine the two, perhaps analyzing grammar structures. I grew more exhilarated by the moment, but when I was in the middle of an increasingly speedy tirade in Spanish—which had something to do with complaints about this place's boss—he held up a hand to stop me.

"¡Todavía no termino!" I barked. "Yo——"

He stiffened his hand, emphasizing his motion.

I silenced with a last annoyed, "Tch."

He flicked his wrist down, and the projected screen shot back into his silver ring with a flash. He reached into his satchel and pulled out a bar of food that looked like Smita's breakfast. She shuffled her front paws, her tail whipping water drops off the scruffy desert grass. She glanced at me with questioning eyes as if asking my permission, and then whined with a lick of her chops and looked back at the man. At least she trusted me more than the stranger.

"Fine," I said, twitching a nod. The man made the rumbling sound in his throat that I'd heard others make, accompanied by a close-lipped smile and eyes crinkled with delight. Smita darted to him, sniffing the satchel and the man with unceasing fervor. He handed her the treat in his flattened palm. She snatched it up and bolted to my side, where she plopped down on the grass, holding it between her front paws as she gnawed, immersed in her mindless activity.

The man looked at me with searching eyes and pulled a new item from his satchel—a biscuit-like food like what had been waiting for me in the shelter. He extended his hand.

I stared at it for a few seconds, and then laughed, long and a bit delirious. I sputtered rain from my lips and wiped drops from my eyes as I tried to recover.

"Are you serious?" I asked, looking back up. "You think I can be pacified with a fucking biscuit?"

The man was wide-eyed again, and he lowered the biscuit. His next words were quiet, careful, *caring*. His intrigue was now accompanied by a pensive frown, rather than the excited dazzle akin to what I always felt when encountering new artwork on a dig site.

The implications of that idea usurped my tentative hopes. He was intrigued by this new find, this human. I had thought he might be here to help, but was he only analyzing me? Had I been brought here to be studied? For what purpose?

He used the biscuit to gesture to the little ledge in the wall of my shelter, where the other untouched biscuit lurked. He said something, his tone containing a respectful request. I could guess the meaning well enough: *Please, eat.*

I glared, suddenly determined to do just the opposite and ignore all food as I'd been doing.

His frown deepened, and his head twitched as if he were frustrated by my silent answer. But he argued no further and rose to his feet.

"Wait!" I jumped up so fast and high that I stumbled when I landed. I regained my balance and faced him with a solid stance. Smita barked.

He tensed at my command. His posture straightened, his strong shoulders widened, his chin raised, and he became instantly, unquestionably dominant.

No doubt it worked on the animals.

I stood straighter and locked eyes with him, refusing to back down. For a moment, we were at a standoff.

The man relaxed his muscles and stepped back. He wasn't submitting to me, I could see that plain as day, but he was accepting my refusal to bow down. At first, my pride kept me from dropping my strong demeanor, but then I relented, stepping back as he had done.

His eyes lingered on my face for a moment, analyzing me with some silent, rhetorical question. Then he backed farther away. He gestured to himself, and then to me and the surrounding enclosure as if telling me he was going to come back. I drew a breath, ready to tear after him and push my way out of this prison or die trying, but then I heard a low hum. The sound rose and fell in pitch, slow and calm, soothing.

My lips parted. He was humming my mother's lullaby. I didn't know I'd been humming aloud earlier, I'd been so consumed by grief. Had he been watching me? Listening to me?

I felt a swelling in my chest and took a shaky breath. He met my tear-filled eyes with an uncertain expression, but he'd reached the sky-blue wall. He brushed his palm against the wall, and with a hiss, a tall arched doorway appeared, turning the section of blue wall to white vapor in three seconds' time. The vapor thinned into translucent mist that swirled in the doorway as if trapped within the frame.

How was I supposed to know how to open a door like that? This could be my only chance to escape. If this man left, would he keep, or be able to keep, his promise to return? Should I trust his expertise in this insane place, be patient, and wait?

No. Fuck that.

I ran for the door with a burst of adrenaline. The lower gravity level boosted my legs to thrilling speed.

"Aao, Smita!" I called. Smita barked and, in a single canine bound, reached the door at the same time I did. The man didn't have time to react. I shoved him through the misty doorway and darted past. Smita was already ahead, running for the sheer fun of it, it seemed.

The man shouted something and grabbed my arm. I felt a small tingling of whatever power the handlers had used to stun me into unconsciousness and experienced a flash of panic, but the tingling fleeted away as if the man had changed his mind. I yanked my arm away and dashed after Smita down a long, gray-walled hallway with an arched ceiling. Clearly an employees-only area, as it lacked the elaborate atmospheric decor of the hall filled with visitors.

I whipped my head back and forth with every step, looking for doors. Realizing they might all be invisible misty matter-shifters like the one in my enclosure, I started trailing my hands along the walls, bouncing back and forth from one side to the other, knowing it was slowing me down, but what else could I do?

A sharp curve forced me to go right. I hoped it led to an exit, but fears bombarded me as I wondered what awaited outside. I thought I heard heavy footsteps behind me. Or was that my drumming heart? *Focus.*

My eyes widened as I saw a gray stone archway at the end of the hall, and under the arch—a door. A true, solid, visible door.

Smita skidded to a stop at the door, but I slammed into its black, glassy surface and barreled through when it caved open.

Searing white light consumed me. My eyes felt like they'd been punched and stabbed at the same time, and I cried out and raised an arm to shield them. I closed my eyes so tightly, pulsing purple and deep red drove in painful beats into my skull. My raised arm itched, and then burned as if enveloped by flames. I screamed and stumbled back into the darkness of the hallway, clutching my blistering arm to my chest. Smita whined behind me, but her yelp cut off. Two firm hands grabbed my biceps and yanked me backward. I opened my eyes for the briefest of seconds in which I could stand the pain and saw the blurred, watery faces of the two handlers who had stunned me in medical before.

"No," I said, my voice tight with pain. I felt shuddering power pulse from the handlers' hands and through my muscles, and I knew what was coming.

I blacked out. This time, I almost welcomed it.

CHAPTER SIX

MY EYES BURNED the second I opened them. The world was blurred and full of unknown, looming threats. Hands touched me out of nowhere; voices were far off one moment and right in my ear the next. My arm spasmed in throes of searing pain, and then something covered my eyes so all was darkness. I crawled inside of myself, too shaken by the sensory assaults around me, unable to process, to fight back, to move. I stayed that way, huddled in a dark, safe corner of my mind, praying it would all stop and that I could one day emerge, wondering if I'd ever be safe in the outside world again.

I didn't know how long I stayed in my small space, shutting the world out. But at some point, I opened my eyes to a new world, one that wasn't blurry or confusing anymore. My eyes didn't burn, and my arm only throbbed as a distant subliminal pain, allowing for coherent thought again. I grounded myself in the objects around me, the table I lay upon, the thin blanket covering me, I assumed for warmth rather than privacy. The white walls and floor suggested I was in the medical facility.

My arm was wrapped in a rubbery orange- and red-marbled bandage; raw mottled blisters showed through the translucent material. The thought of scars or even life-ending infection crossed my mind. I forced the next thought away, that maybe that would be an easier escape.

I exhaled a trembling breath and looked further around the small room. I was alone with a variety of boxy medical equipment, absent of any glowing, projected images. No blinding lights shone down from the ceiling.

Instead, dim light filtered through a *window*.

I raised my head as best I could, given my restraints. The glass of the small, round window was tinted dark, but I could see through well enough.

My breath stopped. There was a ten-foot stone wall outside, which was disappointing. But beyond, there were buildings. I had seen no sign of buildings in any visible habitats lining the hallway outside mine. The habitat outside the window wasn't built for animals. It couldn't be false.

It was the real world.

My limited window view showed the edges of two buildings not far from the wall, and the gap between them revealed another one farther away. They were each tall in layered, pagoda-style stories, but I had to look down before I could reach the roofs. Despite the tint of the window, sunlight glanced off the buildings in bright flashes.

Was that what had caused my arm's sudden, blistering burns during my escape attempt? Pure sunlight?

Sunlight on Earth would never have hurt me so fast.

I looked down at the steel-gray cuffs on my wrists. They looked solid and seamless, but so was my resolve. I took a breath and strained hard against them, my abs burning with the effort to lift myself off the table.

The cuffs buckled. *Yes, yes, yes,* my mind shouted as I pulled harder. My right wrist's cuff creaked and loosened from the table a fraction, but then it stopped. I gritted my teeth to keep from yelling as I kept pulling as hard as I could. My wrists burned with pain as the cuffs' edges bit into my skin, deeper and deeper.

Finally, I had to stop, gasping and cringing. Blood seeped around my wrists, and the orange bandage on my arm was wrinkled so that it rubbed against my blisters with searing pain.

I took heavy breaths. Even with my extra strength, the cuffs were too tight.

A soft whooshing sound made me jolt. An arched section in the wall to my left turned from solid white to thin fog. I raised my eyebrows when the vapor cleared. The young man who had listened to me and spoken to me in my habitat stood in the doorway. He was dressed in black again, but in addition to his small satchel, he carried a large black bag. His eyes were wide with worry, but then deep lines furrowed his face as he took three quick strides to reach me. The vapor in the doorway hissed and turned solid behind him.

He dropped his cloth bag on the floor, and his eyes darted over my red wrists and ankles and bandaged arm. He turned away and walked out of sight, but returned in seconds carrying small squares of white cloth.

"Hey," I said, finding my voice. He met my eyes for a brief moment, but then focused on tucking squares of cloth into each of my restraining cuffs to soak up the blood. I flinched each time, but once they were all padded, I struggled again.

I stopped when the man hovered his first and second fingers together over my face. After a moment's hesitation, he pressed them as one against my forehead. I stiffened, but then closed my eyes in surprise.

A subtle pulse of energy emanated from his fingers, and the muscles of my forehead smoothed. The pulse continued in a low, comforting wave of euphoria. I blinked a few times as I waded through the soothing experience.

He removed his hand and gave me one of the most tender smiles I'd ever seen.

"Get me out," I said, flicking my eyes to the window and back again. "Please. Help me."

He lowered his gaze and gave a nod to the floor as if confirming a decision. He then headed for the window and glanced outside before placing his hand on the pane. It transitioned from tinted glass to opaque white. He crossed the room to the place the door had been and pressed his palm against its solid surface.

It shuddered as if settling into immovable place.

"Why aren't you opening it?" I asked.

His shoulders twitched in response, and the five vertical slits in the golden skin of his back opened to reveal the sheen of pearly skin underneath. He straightened and took a long breath. The slits closed, and his back returned to nearly seamless gold. He strode to the medical equipment near my bed.

Anxiety pulsed at his temple, but he pressed a few places on the boxy equipment and brought up several glowing, pale-blue projected screens. Symbols scrolled and flashed on the screens, lighting up white under his touch.

I frowned as a machine projected an image of my head into the air above me. The left side of my skull was open to expose the insides of my brain.

"What are you doing?" I tugged at my restraints. The man said something, but it was snipped and distracted. He studied all the images and diagrams on the screens with fastidious interest; I got a worrisome impression that he was looking at something he had never seen before.

He stooped and retrieved a small, silver, crescent-shaped object from his bag. Several short strings dangled from its flat, delicate curve. My face twisted when the strings started to wiggle like tiny tentacles.

The man looked down at me. I did not like the uncertainty on his face.

"What the hell is that?" I asked, my voice rising in pitch as he stepped toward me. He said a few soothing words, but nothing he could say would take my attention from the wriggling metal device in his fingers.

"No. Don't—"

He pressed two forefingers together as one on my forehead. Again, I felt the strange pulse of energy from his touch, forcing my muscles to relax in a wave of soft euphoria. The light overhead gleamed brighter, and I cringed and closed my eyes. The man swept his hand through my hair and tilted my head to the right.

Something hard and cold pressed against the skin behind my left ear below my hairline. I gasped as numbness tingled the entire patch of skin, followed by a jarring digging sensation. It wasn't painful, but I suspected the numbing of my skin had happened for a reason.

I shrieked, but the man's strong hands held my head down as I struggled.

"What are you—" My words caught in my throat. My tongue and jaw twitched in uncontrollable stutters. I clenched my teeth to make it stop.

The man winced and looked at the projected diagrams. I jerked my head, but he wove his other hand into my hair and stroked my temples with his thumbs. He clicked his tongue a little and hummed a soft, deep knell in an unfamiliar, but comforting, sound.

I whimpered as the burrowing sensation subsided and my muscles smoothed beneath his thumbs, easing a headache that threatened to push through. He watched my face, particularly my mouth, and then tilted my head to look behind my ear again.

He released me. I rolled my head against the cold table to stretch out my tense neck. I wanted to reach up to touch whatever he had put in my head, but the restraining cuffs wouldn't budge.

He flicked his wrist, and his circular tablet screen projected from his ring and glowed over his right palm. He reached into his satchel with his free hand and pulled out a thin, circular board. He pressed the board against the glowing projection, and when he pulled it away, the screen came with it, separating from his hand to become a separate device.

He dove into his satchel again and took out a transparent cord with tiny dots of blue light inside. After a moment of fumbling, he connected one glowing end of the cord to his tablet with a quick buzz. He set the tablet by my thigh and brought the loose end of the cord to my head.

"What is th—" I was cut off by another spasm of my mouth and jaw. I closed my lips and looked up at him with fear.

He hummed another low knell and brought the cord to the silver crescent device behind my ear. He placed one steady hand on my forehead to hold me still, and I heard a small buzz. Then he released me and stepped back. The cord stayed attached, linking *me* to his tablet.

He picked up his tablet and brought up the same program as when he'd assessed my speech, but the glowing circles weren't blank now in my silence. Yellow and red peaks were dancing and flashing white as they had before when I'd guessed they were matching English and Spanish similarities. Now a third chart also existed below the first two, flashing white to match up with the others. Was it a third language?

The man said something and pointed to my mouth, encouraging me to speak again.

I swallowed, nervous about my twitching jaw, but said, "What are you doing to—"

My mouth spasmed again through my speech—my tongue flipped, and my lips expanded to say different vowels than what were needed to pronounce *you*, *doing*, and *to*, yet I'd heard myself say the words as if I'd spoken them uninhibited.

I looked up at the man with wide eyes. His were just as round, but instead of fear, his were alight with excitement. He squeezed the tablet hard.

"Need . . . you . . . I . . . por favor," he said.

The majority of his sentence was in his language, but bits and pieces were English and Spanish words.

"What?" I asked. I tensed as yet another twitch of my mouth failed to match my words. "¿Pero qué estás—doing?"

"You . . . are . . . speech," he said. I watched his mouth carefully. Every time he said a Spanish or English word, his mouth didn't match what I was hearing. But when he said words in his language, his mouth lined up perfectly with the sounds he made.

"¡Ay, Señor!" I said. "This is some kind of translator, isn't it? What you put in me."

The man smiled wide enough for me to see his two sets of glinting canines. His eyes raced over me with an intense expression of wonder.

"I knew you could speak!" he said.

None of his words matched his lips as if I were watching a poorly dubbed foreign film. But I could understand every word.

"This is—" A wave of shuddering tingles raced from the back of my neck down to my toes. I wiggled my body to make sure I could still move. The translation device had to be messing with my brain and nervous system to cause that reaction.

"Regrets," he said. "Your body . . . adjusting."

"Am I speaking your language?" Every word failed to match my mouth.

"Yes," he said. "I wasn't . . ." More foreign words kept interrupting the flow of his sentences. "You were intelligent enough . . . you can!"

"Intelligent enough? Of course I'm intelligent enough!" I winced at a prickle of pain behind my ear. The anesthetic seemed to be wearing off.

He frowned and touched the skin behind my ear with light fingers. After a quick inspection, he drew away, but wasn't fast enough to hide the drops of blood on his fingertips. My blood.

"I followed the instructions." He glanced at the projected screens beside me. "Simplistic enough . . . It looks . . . diagrams . . ." He looked back at me with an anxious frown. "Hurt?"

"Not anymore," I said, licking my lips after my mouth stretched to form another unfamiliar vowel.

"The translator is syncing . . . speech . . . brain," he explained. "If . . . should be hearing your language but speaking *my* language. I think . . . still unused to the words, so . . . having trouble pronouncing several . . . That should . . . time."

I frowned, trying to decipher what he was saying through his jumbled sentences that were still half-foreign. But the magnitude of what was happening sank in. He could understand me. I could understand him.

"Some words won't translate," he continued, more and more of his language becoming understandable as he spoke, "if there's no . . . one of the languages." He expelled a short huff. "It's hard to . . . But the more sounds I heard you make, the more I was convinced. You speak an intelligent language."

"Yeah, I think we've covered that." I jerked at my restraints again. "Now, help me."

"Not yet," he said. He looked at his tablet again. The charts were dipping and peaking in constant motion, flashes of white matching the three languages together. Was it analyzing grammar structures? Comparing roots of words, perhaps? I had heard countless conversations spoken in my captors' language since my imprisonment. Could the technology of the translator pick up on that and bring their meaning and pronunciation to my conscious state? It was attached to my brain, after all. Maybe it was delving into the speech center and dissecting information, utilizing every delivery route it could to implant the foreign language into my mind.

My hypotheses were wild and many, but whatever high-tech method the translator was using, its success increased with every passing second. The entire process seemed to be veering toward English, which I used more often than Spanish. Was it somehow able to comprehend that English was my dominant language?

"It's still syncing, and we can't leave the museum until I have enough proof," the man said.

"Museum? Is that what this prison is supposed to be?"

"Prison?" He jerked his gaze from the diagrams. "No, I . . ."

"Where's Smita?" I asked, remembering her sharp yelp when the handlers had stopped our escape. "The dog?"

Smita and *dog* formed as Hindi and English words in my mouth.

"My friend," I said, fighting back tears as I watched the man's blank expression. "The animal who came with me."

His sleek, golden eyebrows raised. "Thirty-three? She's well. She's back in your display. Smita. Is that what you call her?"

"Yes. And I'm Carmen. My name is Carmen O'Dwyer. Who are you?"

"You have a name?" he said, his eyes round with ever-increasing fascination. "You have a *name*. I never imagined you'd know the concept, that you would—"

"What *are* you?" I shouted. I strained against my metal cuffs, but fell back, my strength still useless. My throat felt thick and full. "Who are you? What is *your* name?"

"My regrets, you"—his voice dropped to nearly a whisper—"you must be . . . so confused. I . . ." He looked down and tapped his fingertips on his satchel as if regrouping his thoughts.

"Carmen," he said, looking back up. His mouth matched the word, which seemed to place weight on my name; it must not have had an equivalent translation in his language. "My name is Inquieto."

"What?"

"My name is Inquieto. That's what you can call me. If you want."

"Inquieto?"

His name was a Spanish word. I tried to find a way around my adjusting translator. "Your name . . . it means 'restless'?"

I paused in surprise, a pause he filled with a confused statement.

"My name *is* Inquieto."

My eyes flicked downward as I tried to process what was happening. His name sounded Spanish to my ears. Yet, when I asked him if his name *meant* "restless," the word had translated to English in my head, but the motions of my mouth told me I had actually spoken the word in his foreign language, a fact emphasized by his statement.

As jumbled as the words were in my head, to him, it all sounded the same.

"Is something wrong with your translator?" he asked, glancing from my ear to the medical monitors with a swift frown.

"It doesn't matter right now," I said, pushing away fresh worries that he had fucked up my brain. "Just get me out of here. I mean it."

"Carmen," Inquieto said. "Stop struggling. Please. You're injured—you're fortunate that most of your skin stayed in the shade. You have questions. I will answer the ones I can."

I flinched. I had to get out of the cuffs or I was going to go crazy. I was so close to getting free. What if something happened to prevent it beforehand? Inquieto seemed resolute, though, and I did need answers.

"Okay," I said; the word came out English. I paused. "All right," I said instead. That word seemed to have a better match in Inquieto's language as my mouth formed a foreign word.

"Where are we?" My voice sounded small. "Not this 'museum' . . . beyond that."

Inquieto hesitated. Then he looked steadily into my eyes.

"Carmen, I do not wish to frighten you any more than you already are . . . more than I already have, but . . . Do you know what a planet is?"

My chest clenched. "Yes."

"Do you have an understanding of solar systems?"

I nodded, unable to speak, despite my new translator.

"Good," he said, like a teacher would to a child who gave a surprisingly accurate answer in class. My translator was doing a good job of estimating tone and inflection between our languages, and his voice sounded natural no matter what language he was speaking.

"You are in a different solar system than the one you came from," he said. "You are on a different planet than your own."

I was ensnared in a web of silence, struggling to free myself from the immobilizing venom of truth and fly back to a world that made sense.

I had suspected I was on a different planet. I'd been captured by a flying vehicle of an unheard-of technology. I was under the effects of a difference in gravity. I was surrounded by strange, inhuman people and bizarre creatures. I had started to become sure there was no way I was still on Earth, but now that I knew for certain, my mind bucked against reality.

I scoffed. "You're an alien."

"We're from two different planets, yes," he said, and my skeptical humor fizzled. His voice turned breathy with awe. "We're two different *intelligent* species."

For a moment, we locked eyes in silence. A heavy weight sat on my chest, pressing me into the cold table. Then my stomach curdled as I pictured the spacecraft that had captured me hurtling through the stars.

"Wait. If I'm in a different solar system . . . how long did it take me to get here?"

I recalled the iron-flavored fluid that had surrounded me and Smita when we were inside the egg-shaped vessel. Was it possible that we had been frozen in time somehow, some cryogenic-like process to keep us from dying during the thousands of years it would take to reach an interstellar destination?

"Less than half a Paz revolution," Inquieto answered, blinking as if coming out of a trance. "Not long."

"Does that mean Earth is the same as when I left? No one I know has died of old age; centuries haven't passed?"

A thin vertical crease formed through one of the sharpened tree-ring patterns on his forehead. "Given your estimated lifespan, others of your species who were alive when you left . . . Earth . . . are likely still alive now."

"Oh, thank god," I said, *god* tasting English on my tongue. "So, when you get me back to Earth, they'll be waiting for me?"

Inquieto drew a breath and almost spoke, but he gave a slow nod instead.

"You *are* going to get me back to Earth?"

"Yes." He swallowed. "Regrets, Carmen. This was never supposed to happen. The Curio Project is only meant for non-intelligent life. To bring back a . . ." He twitched his head at me. "None of the curio pods' programming has ever failed in this way since the project's creation two generations ago. We had no reason to suspect that you were not of significantly lower intelligence than us or that you were even much more intelligent than the . . . Smita you arrived with."

"You couldn't see *right* away that I was different?"

"It wasn't obvious at first, no," he said, his voice hushed in a pointed tone as he glanced at the door. "We've encountered other species, a few even on our own planet, that share our body type, but none of them have the same size ratio of our brains in proportion to our bodies. Everyone assumed you were a similar case, but I started to see glimpses of more. When you climbed a tree trying to reach the sky, risking injury to learn more about your habitat . . . that's when I knew you were different. And then you made fire. Several known species can spark flame, but always with an inherent physical feature. The salset has a rough coating on its tail that will create a spark when struck against its back claw so that it can create fire for warmth. The takoa's muscles can move so quickly that causing friction between two sticks is simple and hardly requires any thought, with a purpose to lure prey to the light."

His eyes grew rounder. "But you! No one else *wanted* to notice," he said, his voice a little rough, "but you used tools in a far more complex manner than any species in the museum. You made the implements you needed to enhance your ability to create adequate friction, and to create such a fine balance of tinder and kindling—simple technology, yes, but the thought process behind it, the progression of logic, was so *paz*. And when I saw . . . When I saw the artwork . . ." His eyes became earnest and soft, his lips parted with boyish admiration. "You made artwork."

"I copied what I found on the pod, but yeah . . ."

"No. You made artwork. The passion you showed . . . and what you made, it was like . . . Carmen . . ."

"Stop," I said. His intensity was giving me goose bumps.

"Regrets, only . . . I never thought I would see another intelligent species. Ever."

"Well, I 'regret' to ruin your excitement," I said, my jaw trembling, "but *I* never thought I'd be kidnapped by aliens and taken to another planet to be stared at as some . . . curio? Is that the term you used? Something to be collected?"

"Yes," he said, the magnitude of my accusation seeming to finally hit him as his wiry energy abated.

"Why?"

The harshness of my word made him startle a bit, and then his eyes shifted as he struggled for an answer. He opened his mouth, then closed it again. I suspected he had never had to explain to a curio why it was here against its will.

"Procurer ships go out into the galaxy and explore other worlds," he said, his voice taking on a wistful quality. "They are programmed to assess which planets are safe to approach and which are likely to harbor animal or plant species or unique minerals. They send down pods to collect samples to bring to Paz. It's our connection to the universe. The findings are placed in museums for scientific study and"—he sighed—"entertainment. You were picked up with a few other curios from neighboring systems."

"Neighboring systems? Inquieto. Am I the only human here?"

"You call yourself humans? Your species?"

"Yes. Answer my question."

"Yes, Carmen. You are the only human. I'm sorry."

"You're sorry?" I whispered, noting that my translator seemed to have picked up on the English colloquialism of *sorry* versus his language's *regret*. "Why does it matter that *you're* sorry? Do you have any power here? You can't even get these cuffs off me!" I banged the back of my head against the table.

"Carmen, no," he said, placing two of his fingers against my forehead again. My muscles loosened, forcing my body to calm. I nudged his hand away.

"Do you want my help?" he asked.

I glared. "Yes."

A smile twitched at his lips. I scowled.

I held my breath as he tilted my head and disconnected the cord from my translator. He unhooked the other end of the cord from his tablet, and the glowing screen flickered and shot from the thin circular board back into the ring on his middle finger. He stuffed the cord and board into his satchel and pulled out a black triangular object the size of a shirt button. He lowered it to one of my cuffed wrists.

"Will you trust me?" he asked. I focused on the halo irises lurking in the shadows of his eyes. "I'm going to take you someplace new, but you won't be hurt. I promise. Will you stay calm?"

I nodded. Anything to get me out of these cuffs.

He touched the small triangle to the cuff. It popped open. I yanked my injured arm up and pressed it against my chest in instinctual protection. He kept his eye on me but moved down to my left ankle. I tried to remain calm and patient as he opened each of my cuffs. As soon as I was free, I sat up, clutching my blanket to my body.

Inquieto reached into the large bag on the floor, the curve of his spine bending farther and more fluidly than mine ever could. He pulled out a bundle of beige fabric and shook it. It unfurled into a long robe like what the alien women wore. The fabric appeared tightly knit, but lightweight, likely from a plant source similar to cotton or flax. The robe was a single layer, lacked sleeves, and was trimmed with a satin-smooth fabric of a green shade that matched my eyes. I looked up at him in surprise.

"You covered your body with leaves in your display," he said. "Would you like to use something different? I brought this for you."

I stared at the robe and slid off the table to find my feet.

He held the clothing out—real, proper clothing—but then drew it back as if he was unsure if I'd know what to do with it.

"I know what that is," I said with faint exasperation. I snatched the robe from his hand. "Turn around."

His face shifted into a look of realization; maybe he'd only just now gathered that I'd covered myself not only for protection from the elements, but due to the higher concept of privacy. I didn't know if his people held the same views for their own clothing or not, but at least I was demonstrating my own capabilities of higher-level thought.

He turned around at once. His muscles were tense, and I realized how brave he was to turn his back on an unknown species. I wasn't sure if I would have been able to do the same.

I hurried to inspect the robe. There was a silver clasp on the back of the collar, and another clasp on each side of the waist. I dropped my blanket and wrapped the collar around the base of my neck and the robe around my body, fastening each silver clasp. My front was fully covered, but my shoulders and back were left exposed for shoulder ridges and back slits that I didn't possess. The robe was a little tight, especially around the bust and hips, but I teared up as I looked down at myself. I had never imagined how much simple clothing meant to my sense of dignity until I'd had to go without.

I swallowed the lump in my throat and squared my shoulders. "I'm ready."

Inquieto turned around and looked me over with a thrilled smile. "Carmen! You—"

"How do we get out?"

He clicked his tongue and blinked like a human saying "oh!" He crouched by his black bag and pulled out two long strips of beige fabric and a pair of brown sandals. The sandals' interwoven straps formed crescent patterns and looked to be constructed from the same material as his satchel. Both looked like leather, but weren't quite porous enough and showed no signs of patina. Perhaps the material was plant-based as well.

"Do you consent?" He looked at my feet in front of him.

"Consent? Oh! Uh . . . yes. That's okay."

He sent me a tentative smile. I braced one hand on the table as he lifted my foot. I jerked it back and fought an involuntary laugh.

"I'm sorry," he said. "I won't hurt you."

"I know; it just tickled. Go ahead."

His brow creased in confusion, but he seemed to accept that I wasn't afraid of him. I surprised myself when I realized I wasn't.

I did my best to hold still as he wrapped each foot with the strips of fabric like improvised socks, and then slid both sandals on my feet. His hands were firmer than mine, especially the palms, which were almost entirely gold, yet his touch was smooth and assuring. His four-knuckled fingers were bizarre, but I was fascinated by their dexterity as I watched him clasp the sandals into place.

He stood and shouldered the bag, which was still bulky.

"Are you ready?" he asked.

"Yes. What about Smita?"

"We have to focus on you first, Carmen. She's well, don't worry."

I hesitated, but nodded. There was only so much I could do in this situation. I could only hope my escape would lead to Smita's eventual release as well.

Inquieto gave me a quick smile and walked to the faint outline of the door, which, now that my tricked eyes knew it was there, was the slightest bit visible. He placed his palm against it, and the surface dissolved into vapor to reveal a long, narrow hallway with plain gray walls.

"Where are we going?" I asked as he led me down the empty hall in quick, cautious steps. He held one hand in front of him the whole time as if feeling for an invisible wall.

"We're leaving the museum," he answered, his voice low. I had the feeling we were sneaking out, which only heightened my nerves and made me question his assurance that I wouldn't be hurt wherever we were going. "But we're not free of this yet, Carmen. The High Council wishes to see you. They are the leaders of Paz. I need you to stay calm to help convince them that you are intelligent. Can you do that, Carmen?"

"Paz? Is that the city we're in?"

"It's the name of our planet. We also refer to our species as paz."

"Oh," I said, my stomach fluttering as I realized I was about to meet the leaders of an entire *planet*—a planet and people that were so inaptly named considering their treatment of me. *Paz* was the Spanish word for *peace*.

"What should I say to them?" I asked. "How can I be sure to convince them?"

"They should be viewing my preliminary evidence now. When we get there, I ask that you stay silent until they ask you a question. And stay calm," he beseeched. "That's imperative."

"Okay. I get it. I'll stay calm."

He eyed me with dubious appraisal. I took a breath.

"I promise," I said. "If it helps me get out of here."

"Thank you."

I nodded. I didn't need to be an anthropologist to understand that navigating a different culture without a guide could lead to serious consequences. Laws had to be followed, etiquette performed with care, lest a seemingly small slight escalate into profound insult or even criminality. It seemed every year some news story would circulate about an individual being detained in a foreign country for something that was legal in their country of origin. That person was then subject to foreign laws, sometimes trapped in harsh, awful conditions due to nothing but their own ignorance.

I wasn't going to let that happen to me.

We reached a sudden curve in the hallway. Inquieto jerked his extended hand back and froze. I kept walking before I realized that he'd somehow known to stop for a reason.

The short, unpleasant man who I'd assumed was Inquieto's boss was striding down the hallway. A spherical white light fixture on the ceiling made the dripping patterns on his bald head gleam like yolk oozing out of an egg. He blustered to a halt when he saw me. Inquieto hurried to my side.

"What is it doing out of its display?" the boss asked, but then he eased his stiff posture, cracking an incredulous smile.

"Clothes, Inquieto?" he said. His rumble of humor sounded like tires on gravel. "I gave you extra time to fix this one's behavior, but this is absurd. It's eating again and not injuring itself, tearing apart its shelter, or slinging mud at people; that's all I care about." His right eye flinched at me before he focused again on Inquieto. "I need you to look at the axbor. It's scraping its wings against the barrier again; they're down to the bone. The lifeist says it's psychological."

"Pensadora would be saved a lot of trouble if we tended to psychological ailments first instead of as a last resort, Justo," Inquieto replied, and although his tone and stance were calm, his jaw clenched.

Justo. I huffed a laugh at the boss's real name, at least my translator's version. It was a Spanish word with a meaning far different from the truth of his disposition—*just*.

"No need to get emotional, Inquieto," Justo sneered. "I see that Curator Alegre was right to warn me about you before his retirement. He said you extrapolate the extent of lesser species' consciousnesses. You project your own emotions onto them. I suppose it makes sense, given your—"

"I am not a lesser species!" I said.

Inquieto smiled. "Am I projecting my words into her mouth, Justo?" he asked, his voice calm and cool, despite Justo's low blow.

Justo gaped. When he managed to speak, all of his ploys at dominance vanished.

"It—it's dangerous," he said, backing away as if I'd threatened him at knifepoint. "I'll call the handlers."

"Like hell, you will!"

"She *will* remain conscious," Inquieto said, his voice harsh as he stood taller, a full head over Justo. "Now, move."

Justo pressed his back against the wall, revealing a black, glassy door less than twenty feet away. Inquieto led me onward, keeping me on the opposite side of the hallway.

As we passed, I looked Justo right in the eyes. He startled back, and it was my turn to send him a condescending smirk before I turned my gaze ahead and didn't look back.

We stopped in front of the door. I glanced back to see if Justo had followed us, but he had escaped the hallway entirely.

"We have to hurry," Inquieto said. "I don't know who he'll tell."

"I thought you said the High Council is expecting me," I hissed.

"I said they were reviewing evidence for your case," he answered as he dug through his bag and fished out another piece of lightweight beige fabric. "Not that they're expecting you."

His hands were shaking a little as he draped the fabric over my head; I was too anxious to protest. The cloth tumbled down my shoulders and back as a loose shawl, covering the skin that my robe left exposed. He brought one edge of the shawl over my mouth and nose and met my eyes as he fastened it with a clip over my ear.

He then took a short strip of black fabric from his bag. I winced as he placed it over my eyes, but my fear that it was a blindfold subsided. His face was still visible as he analyzed my disguise, but everything had grown darker like I was looking through a pair of sunglasses. He withdrew his hands, and the fabric conformed to my face and adhered to my skin on its own. I felt like an attendee at a masquerade ball or a bandit. Inquieto ventured a hand into his bag again.

"You get that bag from Mary Poppins?"

"What?"

"Never mind."

"Lift your arm, please."

I did as he requested. He started wrapping a long strip of more beige fabric around my right arm from shoulder to wrist.

"Are those for me, too?" I nodded at a brown glove curled over the edge of the bag.

"Yes." He gently tucked the strip of fabric into place around my wrist, taking care to avoid aggravating my raw skin. I grabbed the glove and tugged it onto my fingers while he proceeded to wrap my other arm in fabric.

"Inquieto," I said, growing more nervous with each added layer. The door was just like the one I had plunged through during my escape attempt, only to have my arm burnt to a crisp. "Is it safe out there?"

He took great care around the orange-bandaged section of my arm as he finished wrapping. He handed me a second glove.

"Yes," he said, his eyes flicking from one of mine to the other. "I won't let any harm come to you, Carmen. I promise."

He pushed open the door. I winced in a flash of bright light, despite my eyes' shield, but I managed to adjust with a couple of blinks.

I took a bracing breath and stepped through the doorway into the open air of Paz.

CHAPTER SEVEN

A BLAST OF heat hit me. My skin felt like all the moisture was sucked out of it on impact. Everything that met my mask-shielded eyes was off white, sandy beige, or deep black. Our long, dark shadows climbed a white stone wall in front of us, but they were blurred at the edges as if I were seeing double. A few scrubby, brown plants peeked through dusty stone flags at our feet. A breeze ruffled my linen shawl and tugged a strand of hair free to billow around my face like a loose spider thread.

An oblong vehicle sat in the middle of the small paved area surrounded by the wall. Sunlight glinted off the vehicle's glassy sides, which alternated between obsidian and tinted gray windows. It stood with perfect balance upon four narrow, curved stilts, which were locked into metal grooves that stretched along the pavement like single-rail train tracks. Four identical stilts were mounted on top of the vehicle, but their sharp points weren't connected to anything but the hot, dry air.

My eyes darted everywhere—the vehicle ahead, every corner of the courtyard, the roofs of buildings peeking over the wall. The wall was a good ten feet tall, but my steps felt just as buoyant and my muscles just as coiled as when I'd been trapped in my habitat. That proved it—this planet really did have less gravity than Earth. Could I jump over the wall if I had to?

When I glanced behind us, I gasped. The museum was sapphire blue, towering over us like an Egyptian pyramid with its apex sliced off. Its sloped, gem-cut walls were crawling with silver lines and circles, replicas of the artwork on the egg-shaped pod that had captured me on Earth.

But it wasn't the building that held me in such awe.

"It's huge," I said, stepping back. The sun beamed above the museum; its enormous orb shot white beams in every direction that stretched across a field of blue sky and thin, wispy cirrus clouds. I was enamored as I traced the beams to the horizon, but within seconds, I had to look away, even with the sun mask over my eyes.

I jumped when Inquieto grabbed my arm to coax me into a brisk walk toward the vehicle, reminding me of our furtive plan to escape. I winced when the slits in his back opened and the pearly skin inside reflected the harsh sun off his body in a brilliant flash.

"The procurer data indicated that your planet was farther away from its single star," he said, his words as rushed as his stride. "It looked smaller to you. Is that true?"

"Yes," I said. "Yours is almost half a sun bigger."

"Perhaps that one looks closer in size to yours?" Inquieto said, nodding toward the city skyline. My eyes widened as I saw a second yellow-white orb hovering between obsidian pagoda-style crowns of the towering beige buildings.

"You have two!" My stomach felt queasy as I looked back and forth between the two suns on opposite sides of the sky.

Despite my freedom from the museum, and the openness of the shining city and glimpses of treeless land beyond leading to a flat horizon, I felt more claustrophobic than I ever had. I didn't know what Paz looked like from space—I had no idea if it had large oceans like Earth, how many continents there were, if any of them were lush green or if they all looked like the desert biome around me; I had no idea if I'd see white clouds swathing a beautiful, lonely, blue marble. I was on a rock in the middle of the vast vacuum of space, a rock that was not *my* rock, and I felt more trapped than if I'd never left my zoo-like prison.

My chest constricted, and I felt fused to the ground for a second while Inquieto pressed his palm upon a small gray panel on the vehicle's side. I nearly shrieked at the sounds of a mechanical grunt and hiss, and I backed up as the entire side of the vehicle facing us extended outward into a ramp.

"We call this a cell," Inquieto said, gently gesturing me inside. "It travels along these tracks and can hook up to the main artery system throughout the city." He pointed to the pattern of tracks on the pavement, which looked like they'd been drawn with a spirograph. "It will transport us to the Egalitarian much faster than walking."

"I gathered that."

"Yes?" he responded, his eyes bright with ever-mounting excitement.

I ignored his enthusiasm and gathered the courage to walk up the low ramp. Inquieto followed me out of the direct sunlight. The vertical slits in his back closed again into a smooth layer of gold.

The ramp rose to re-form the side of the cell and trap us inside. I forced myself to maintain steady breaths as I looked around.

The interior was white and made of the smooth glassy texture of the walls and floors in the medical facility and back hallways of the museum. It was lined with a perimeter of beige cloth-cushioned benches. I saw no driver, but there was a panel with red, yellow, and blue buttons and the sound of humming machinery on one end. Panes of tinted windows along the sides and on the roof and floor showed views of the outside world, for which I was grateful. Leaving one enclosed space only to step into another was not my idea of escape.

Inquieto prompted me to sit down on one of the benches. He pushed several buttons on the humming panel and sat opposite me. He glanced through the tinted windows as if someone might be watching, then gave me a thin smile. I instinctively twitched a nervous smile back, feeling like we were partners in crime.

I curled in on myself when the cell began to move along the tracks. The vehicle crawled beside the wall until a large gate came into view made of thick, crisscrossed beams that looked like burnished steel. As we approached, the beams shot outward into slots in the wall. Our cell passed through the opening, and as I looked behind us, the beams shot back into solid, crisscrossed place. A tiny length of tension unraveled in my chest, but what if we were caught? What if the High Council at the Egalitarian wouldn't help like Inquieto thought they would?

I was distracted when a breathtaking view consumed the windows. The city was a lustrous, ornamental wonder filled with towering buildings that made up a broad skyline and surrounded us on all sides. Each building of varying heights was stacked with layer upon layer of stories, each story defined by extravagant overhanging roofs like broad pagodas. Some of the layered roofs formed smooth U's, while others were stacked as V-shaped daggers. The upward strokes of their architecture made them appear upside down like their foundations were in the thin clouds.

The pale-blue sky was crisscrossed by bridges formed by extensions of the pagoda roofs, connecting neighboring buildings at myriad levels so that a sprawling, entrapping net spread across the city; the sight reminded me of the illusion of a wired cage in the ceiling of my zoo habitat. A multitude of blurred double shadows added another layer to everything in sight, cast by the light of two warring suns.

The bridges low enough to see were embellished with the same gem-cut style as the spacecraft that had captured me, but lacked silvery artwork embellishments. Most were crafted from glass-like material of clean beige or dark hues, but every so often, the glint of a rainbow would peek through a sliver of clear prismatic glass like an accidental leak in the muted color scheme.

Countless paz walked across the network of bridges, which seemed to be for pedestrian use only. While many of the pagoda roofs were sleek and empty, there were others that held crowded, but orderly, rows of what appeared to be storefronts or other places of business. I couldn't hear or smell anything outside of our cell, but I saw puffs of smoke or steam coming from some like street food sizzling.

The harsh sunlight glinting off the bridges and glassy sides of buildings kept me from staring long, and the ground level wasn't much better. Far fewer people walked the streets; most were only making the short trek from a parked cell to a building entrance. Sunlight still had time to flash off the pearly inner skin of their backs, however, forcing me to look away, half-blind and on edge. Attack could come from anywhere.

I forced myself to focus on the vehicles to calm my rampant thoughts. There were some like ours—individual cells—but more common were long trains of cells hooked together. They traveled at a slow march like glossy ants. Short tracks fed off the main ones to individual docking stations along the sides of streets. I saw no drivers amongst any of them—it appeared that all the vehicles were automated, programmed to never deviate from their perfectly structured existence.

I startled when a flock of sleek birds swooped over our cell and flew low through the street before they whooshed up the side of a building and found a roost in a shaded corner under a low bridge. As we passed under their clawed feet, I saw that their black folded wings were hard like a beetle's shell, and their round heads and scrunched faces, with long fleshy proboscises rather than beaks, were scaly blue.

"This is unbelievable," I said.

"Those are mikrals," Inquieto replied. "And this is Raíz, the capital of Paz and the largest city on the planet. And this is only half of it."

I frowned at the twinkle in his eyes, and suddenly the world went dark.

I inhaled as our cell tilted and sped down a steep hill as fast as a roller coaster. Blackness consumed us, but then lights dazzled and revealed the end of our track ahead—with nothing but empty space beyond.

"Inquieto!"

I squeaked in surprise when our cell leapt off the track but somehow kept going. I looked up through the tinted sunroof and saw we were now hanging from a track above us, suspended in the air by the stilts on the roof. I looked down through the clear floor, and my eyes widened.

"Oh, my god."

We were in another city. But this one was underground, surrounded by a goliath natural cavern. The city's flat paved foundation was far, *far* below us. A curling network of dark-hued streets wove between buildings, but only pedestrians traveled them.

Cells zoomed along the ceiling, weaving in and out of magnificent natural stalactites that were all chiseled with elegant, abstract designs to fuse with their innate beauty. It was no wonder Inquieto had referred to the transportation system as an artery; it sprawled throughout the entire endless cavern in every direction, including vertically, with cells docking on hanging platforms and moving down rods like elevators to lower stories of buildings or for pedestrians to disembark onto the streets.

The buildings were the most awe-inspiring of all. They were an *exact* mirror to the city above. Stacks of multi-storied, pagoda-style arches or upside-down V's shot down from the cavern ceiling and didn't stop until they reached the floor many stories below. They were roots to the buildings aboveground, adorned with just as many windows, though many were clear rather than tinted. I could see countless people milling inside.

Some buildings were different. Long cylinders or huge bowls clung to the ceiling like the stalactites between them, most with large extravagant windows that glittered with lights. Some included the stalactites in their architecture, using them as anchors and sculptured adornments.

Lights illuminated the cavern from every facet of the city as if the paz were trying to imitate the bright suns above, but my impression altered as I imbibed them all. These lights were more like smoldering embers and twinkling stars. Yellow, red, and blue shone from windows and spherical streetlamps. Lights winked along the entire ceiling-based train system and glowed like constellations from the rocky ceiling. I was grateful to have a reprieve from the disturbing sight of double shadows cast by two suns; here, city lights cast shadows in all directions, just like I'd find in any human city. The effect was enchanting, but the lights couldn't fully illuminate the lurking background darkness of the cavern, as if we were surrounded by the deep vastness of space.

"How long did it take to build this?" I asked.

"These caverns have been used for tens of thousands of years, at least," Inquieto answered. "Even when we use the surface now, we're always building and rebuilding down here. All of these structures are no more than one hundred years old at most."

I followed his nod toward the left window and saw a black maw in a distant section of the cavern's stone walls.

Half-finished structures of glass, stone, and metal filled it like broken pixels, and mobile platforms of scaffolding crawled up the rock like mechanical spiders carrying workers and supplies. Large vehicles drummed up rock and earth, and I heard a low grumble from within the hole like a deep tunnel was being drilled.

A wide, white banner hung over the construction site. It displayed a prominent black symbol—a lower half of a circle topped with a horizontal line, which extended past the circle's edges on either side.

"They destroy the old buildings?" I said. "There's nothing preserved from before?"

"Why would there be? Those buildings were outdated and less functional."

"For history's sake. To remember the past."

Inquieto sent me a look of piqued curiosity. "Paz don't need buildings to remember the past. Although . . ." He looked down a moment, and a small smile touched his lips. "Do you think there's value in history, Carmen?"

"Yes. My job is based on the value of history. On Earth. Human history." I frowned at the reminder of my uncertain future. Did my career on Earth matter anymore?

"Humans must have advanced civilizations to have the luxury of a career focused solely on history," he said, sitting straighter and humming with childlike energy. "The notion of . . . That's really what you pursue?"

I nodded and looked through the clear floor again, grateful to find more distraction in the sights below. Most of the cavern's stalagmites must have been paved over during the countless bouts of construction and reconstruction, but there were still a few here and there jutting up from the rocky floor. A group of children climbed on one cluster of different shapes and sizes like a playground. Other formations had been carved into abstract sculptures, though it was hard to see details from our height. I wondered if at least those had some longevity to them, but after Inquieto's description, I suspected that they might have been sculpted and resculpted over the years.

Our cell sped up and passed through another tight tunnel of darkness. I took a deep breath when we emerged, but my chest felt constricted, and a trace smell of burnt matches didn't bring the calming wave of oxygen I needed.

Inquieto clicked his tongue. "I'm sorry," he said. He fished in his Mary Poppins bag and pulled out a breathing mask like he'd worn when I'd first laid eyes on him, but this mask was small enough to only cover a person's mouth, with two little tubes to align with the wearer's nostrils.

"This will monitor your oxygen levels," he said. "Wear it around your neck, and when you feel like a natural breath isn't helping, bring it to your mouth and inhale. Paz atmosphere contains enough oxygen for you to breathe, but underground, air doesn't circulate as well, and the constant construction and crowded city life doesn't help. Paz can handle the increased carbon dioxide, sulfur dioxide, and lower oxygen without harm, but you can't. Inside buildings, the concentrator may not be as necessary, but if you walk around down here"—he nodded at the pedestrians far below and on a hanging bridge across the cavern—"you'll need this with you."

"Oh," I said. I took the oxygen concentrator from him and hesitated. Its black strap almost looked like a dog collar, and after living in a zoo, that was not a welcome notion. But my breaths were coming short, and that shot panic through me. I squirmed the mask over my head and around my neck, and then lowered the linen shield from my mouth and nose. I brought the breathing mask to my lips and aligned the two holes at the top to my nostrils. I took a tentative breath.

Oxygen rushed into my lungs, and I took deeper, hungry breaths until I was satisfied. The mask wasn't attached to any kind of oxygen tank, so I assumed it filtered pure oxygen from the air. Though I felt better, the need for it made me feel even more vulnerable than I already had.

Our cell slowed as we neared one of the buildings that hung from the ceiling like a bowl. The structure was faceted with large, crystal-cut windows divided by webs of gold. Its stately appearance made me suspect it was the Egalitarian.

Cells docked on a platform suspended underneath the building, delivering passengers or taking more to reconnect with the main artery system. I tensed as our cell approached the rear of the building. No one was around on this side of the platform, like it was a back alley. Inquieto pressed a button on the vehicle's control panel, his every muscle tense like he was ready to spring into action at a moment's notice. But no one showed up as our cell docked on the edge of the platform with a small shudder.

He pressed another button, and the side of our cell that was connected to the platform began to lower into a ramp. The smell of burnt matches grew stronger, and I sneezed before I followed Inquieto to his feet. Guessing that the sulfur dioxide he'd mentioned was responsible, I inhaled another breath through my oxygen concentrator, hoping that tight breaths and minor irritations would be the worst of my problems.

We walked in quick steps down the ramp and across the platform toward a black glass door in the side of the curved building. Inquieto pressed his palm against it, and its solid surface dissolved into vapor. A small flight of stairs led into the inverted dome, narrow and gloomy. I got the feeling it was a back entrance.

Inquieto hurried me inside, but once we were in the shadows, he stopped and extended his hand into the dim hallway, palm out.

"What are you doing?" I whispered.

"Making sure there are no people around."

"With your hand?"

"Electrical pulses. Electroreception, electrolocation. I can sense if any life-forms are in the area by detecting the electricity they emit."

"Bioelectricity," I said. "Paz can use bioelectricity." I frowned with a twist in my stomach. "Is that also why you can stun me like an electric eel?"

"I never stunned you," he said with swift force, stopping to look me in the eyes.

I blinked. "No. You never did." But the handlers in the museum had. Though unlike an electric eel, their stunning hadn't hurt.

Inquieto wore a deep frown, but he aimed it at the floor.

"When you touched my forehead," I then realized, "I felt like my muscles relaxed. Soothed."

He nodded, seeming to break free from an ensnaring thought. "That was an electrical pulse, yes," he said. "I didn't want you to feel upset. Was that all right?"

I shifted my shoulders. "Maybe," I said, not sure how I felt about it. His intentions may have been good, but he'd still touched me without my permission before he'd had the ability to ask for my consent. No matter how kind he had been, or how much compassion he showed to Smita and the other animals, Inquieto still worked for the curio museum. He was complicit.

Yet his earnest question inspired my instincts to flourish—that he had my best interests at heart, at least for now.

He smiled and nodded toward a short, narrow staircase. "This way."

I was quiet for a moment as we resumed our clandestine walk. I had read about electrotherapy on Earth, the use of painless electricity to treat different ailments such as nerve pain and muscular atrophy. Humans might not possess whatever organs or systems were necessary to produce bioelectricity, but we did function on electricity. Our nervous system used electricity to send signals throughout our bodies; electrical pulses in the heart caused the heart muscle to contract with precise timing. Electricity was everywhere, crucial—and paz had the natural ability to control those processes in other people with a single touch.

There was nothing I could do to stop them from manipulating my muscles and nerves however they wished. Even Inquieto could use that power against me if he wanted.

Inquieto kept his hand out at all times as we turned a corner and walked down a hallway with a higher ceiling until we reached a wide, spiral ramp that made me dizzy as we climbed in circle after circle. Every time we passed an arched doorway, I hoped it would be our exit, but we ascended several stories before we finally stopped at a plain gray door at the top of the ramp.

Inquieto stepped to the side, his lips pressed thin.

"Is this where . . . ?" I asked.

He nodded.

"How can you be sure this will work?"

"I'm not the only one on your side," he said. He touched my face, making me jump. I held still when I realized he was only unpeeling my protective sun mask from my eyes. He lowered the linen shawl from my hair, letting it pool around my shoulders. His dark eyes traced my features for a moment, and instead of looking aside, I found myself doing the same to his foreign face.

"It will be all right," he whispered.

"Tell me that when I'm on a ship home," I said, though my stomach flipped at the notion of space travel. I turned to the door. Whatever was on the other side had to be better than the fucking zoo. That's what I tried to convince myself as Inquieto pressed his hand against the door's surface.

The door dissolved into swirling vapor, revealing an elegant, sepia-hued tableau, a striking difference from the plain gray hallways. It appeared that we were on the top floor of a domed structure aboveground, an exact mirror to the hanging bowl-shaped building underground. The entire structure was a sphere, separated in two halves by the cavern's rocky ceiling and the ground above.

Sunshine filtered through narrow, spear-point crystal windows that curved from the polished stone floor to the domed ceiling, tinted enough to assuage my sensitive eyes. The sepia walls were carved with countless small symbols that looked like writing, and a large, glossy obsidian symbol dominated one wall. It was the same symbol I'd seen hanging over the construction site outside—a long, horizontal line topping the bottom half of a circle, not unlike the bowl-shaped underground half of this very building.

Our door was small, but a much larger door of gem-cut obsidian under a high stone arch loomed across the round room. No doubt it was the main entrance for anyone except a paz prisoner, perhaps, because the entire space had the feeling of an elaborate courtroom.

Instead of one judge, ten paz sat behind simple obsidian desks arranged in a circle, though an eleventh desk was vacant. Each person looked official and important in matching cream-colored robes with dark brown strips of fabric running down their chests. The only differences in their ensembles were small symbols on the center of each of their robe collars. I glanced at Inquieto. His robe also had a symbol on its collar, made of the same kind of supple, satin-like fabric that trimmed my robe's hem. His symbol was a silver diamond with three lines inside that reached up from the bottom like tree branches. I grazed my collar with my fingertip and felt the same symbol on mine. In retrospect, I realized that every paz's robes I had seen so far had a symbol on their collars, of all different colors and shapes.

We lingered outside the doorway, unnoticed yet. All attention was on a woman standing in the center of the circle. A white, baseball-sized sphere hovered around the room like a drone, a pinpoint blue light on its surface aimed her way. I suspected it was some kind of recording device, which made my stomach squirm.

"You may remember that prior to my seat on the High Council, I was employed as an artist," the woman in the circle said.

She looked familiar somehow, but I couldn't put my finger on why. Her white skin sparkled like snow in the filtered sunlight of the room, her golden patterns blossomed like orchid petals. She was tall and stood with poise that seemed too perfect, like she'd had to practice it in years of etiquette classes. Her face was heart-shaped, as well as her glimmering golden shoulder ridges, adding to her graceful beauty. Her keen eyes, although pleasantly round in the centers, sharpened into abrupt, narrow points at each corner.

"Yes, we are quite aware of your past credentials, Counselor Reúnen," said a man, seated with his back to me. Though I couldn't see his face, his voice held a sneer.

The woman, Counselor Reúnen, gave him a stiff nod, but didn't visibly return his disdain.

A different man, thin-faced and elderly, interjected, "Counselor Reúnen, you are responsible for much of the artwork at the Curio Life Museum, are you not?"

My chest hollowed.

"Yes, Counselor Guían," Counselor Reúnen said. "I created much of the artwork within both curio museums in Raíz, as well as the curio pods, in the past fifteen years. The pod that brought Curio 0924 to Paz showed evidence that it was damaged upon its landing on Planet 0916. Its log shows that several scans for appropriate life-forms were made, but its internal opening mechanism was broken. Therefore, the door must have been opened from the outside."

"Your work is very intricate," Guían said. "I have visited the museums on a few occasions, and what detail!" He leaned forward. "There is a code to open each pod embedded into your artwork, yes? A mechanism too sophisticated for an animal to perform?"

The woman smiled. "Yes, Counselor."

"How, then, was it opened?"

"As we saw from the visual recordings that Citizen Inquieto Reúnen supplied, Curio 0924 has paz-like hands," she explained. "Outlines of hands are hidden within the art, and they must be touched in a precise order to open the pod. Curio 0924 could have placed her hands on the appropriate sectors to open it. The pod's scanning program would then have been activated, and at least her fellow curio, Curio 0033, was deemed a beneficial specimen to collect. Whether 0924 was processed correctly, being a potential species of higher intelligence, is up to us."

"You are telling me that this creature," said the critical man with his back to us, "used its crude imitation of our hands," he lifted one of his four-knuckled fingers, "to decipher the exact order of your code?"

"I am, Counselor Fortalecen," she answered.

"We don't know how long the curio took to open the pod," said a woman with cheekbones that could sharpen stone. "It could have been banging on the surface for days before it struck upon the proper sequence by accident."

I huffed air through my nose and clenched my fist. Inquieto had warned me to hold my tongue till he said otherwise, but it was getting difficult. He must have noticed my tension because he chose that moment to guide me into the room.

All eleven aliens jolted and shot their eyes to me as if I'd shouted my arrival and run at them full speed. Then they all took a deep breath, eerily synchronized, and their expressions began to vary from their joint surprise, though remained subtler than I was used to seeing with humans. I might have had trouble reading them if I wasn't on such high alert, but my adrenaline spurred me to pick up every little cue.

The angular-faced woman tittered with the derisive mutter, "Clothes." Others appraised me with far more serious expressions of concern. Many darted their eyes from Inquieto to me and back again as if he was the only thing keeping me from attacking them. I was lucky they didn't demand I be restrained or stunned.

I glanced at the man who'd had his back to us, Counselor Fortalecen, as we passed. He stared at me with such hard black eyes, I had to look away, but not before I saw his lips move and heard the softest utterance.

"It is an aberration."

"Citizen Reúnen, welcome," said Counselor Reúnen with a polite nod to Inquieto, though her eyes sparkled with what appeared to be deeper friendship. Her robe collar bore the same silver diamond symbol as his.

Reúnen. If surnames worked the same way as in my cultures, then it seemed Inquieto and Counselor Reúnen might be related.

"Thank you, Counselor," Inquieto said, locking eyes with her for a brief moment when we reached the center of the circle. The woman's smile turned sweeter and more assuring. She stepped aside.

"You were aware of his coming?" said Fortalecen; his voice held an underlying hiss. This time, I gave him a good once-over. His hard eyes were deep-set, his forehead slightly sloped back, with a square jaw that he held high. Even sitting, I could tell he was tall. His shoulders were smooth and broad, with long arms that ended in long-fingered hands, which he linked with poise on his desk. The patterns on his skin were a dark, distinctive bronze and followed each line of his elegant bone structure—his cheekbones and jaw, the bridge of his nose, his collarbones—as if his body had no tolerance for error. His hands looked like those of a bronze skeleton.

I was struck by how much younger he looked compared to every counselor aside from Counselor Reúnen, who, like him, couldn't have been more than forty by human standards.

"This is unexpected, Counselor Reúnen," agreed a new woman with fine, dignified wrinkles on her face who sat directly facing me. Her golden patterns graced her skin like interwoven fleurs-de-lis. Her voice was rich and soothing, yet held unquestionable authority.

"I believe this entire situation is unexpected, Counselors," answered Counselor Reúnen. She gave Inquieto an encouraging nod, though her eyes only flicked to me in one nervous twitch. "Perhaps you can give your additional evidence now, Inquieto?" she said softly.

"Yes, Prístina," he whispered, sounding grateful for her presence, and then turned to the rest of the council. Counselor Prístina Reúnen strode with light, smooth steps to the single empty desk and sat down. The white hovering sphere aimed its little blue light at us, recording, no doubt. I tried to avoid looking at it.

"Counselor Levantan," Inquieto said with a small bow of his head to the wrinkled woman. "Counselors." He nodded to the circle as a whole.

"Extraordinary," said Counselor Guían with a smile. "We can see why she is such a popular curio. The mimicry of the paz form—"

"Is an affront to our species, Counselor Guían," Fortalecen said. I analyzed him with a deep frown. Other aliens had made it clear how strange I was in their eyes, but their tones and expressions had been of either curiosity or mockery. This man's tone was pure, calculated disgust.

"You have given us much to address, Citizen Reúnen," Fortalecen continued. "We have viewed the visual recordings and annotated assessment you submitted. We have no reason to agree with your unsupported logic that Curio 0924 is a sub-level intelligent species, and—"

"She is a human, Counselor Fortalecen," Inquieto boldly interrupted. Fortalecen narrowed his eyes. "She is a human from a planet she calls Earth, where humans are the dominant intelligent species much like paz are on our planet. She has a name." His voice dropped to a low key of defiance. "May I present Carmen O'Dwyer to the High Council?"

The angular-faced woman who had scoffed at my clothing did so again. The rest of the counselors shifted with uncomfortable frowns.

"I don't know which subject is more appalling," Fortalecen said. "Your unspeakable belief that this creature is of any notable intelligence, or your unfathomable choice to bring this dangerous beast here, without permission, unrestrained—"

"I am not an animal!" I said, standing tall and facing them down. The entire council froze into silence.

"As you can see, Carmen can speak for herself," Inquieto said, though his voice shook a little as he eyed the counselors. "She is using a specialized translation device."

I stole a glance at Fortalecen and almost wished I hadn't. A vacant, haunted hole opened in his eyes for a half second, so fast I might have imagined it, before his face hardened into a cold mask.

"This technology is clearly a ruse," Fortalecen said, swiftest to recover, "and to release this creature, a subversive offense—"

"This is an unprecedented situation," said Prístina, sending a subtle glare to Fortalecen. "Inquieto has performed no deviances."

"We must speak as a council," said Counselor Levantan, extending her hands wide in a pacifying gesture. "We have many conditions to consider. A translator is . . . surprising. But its confiscation would directly affect our ability to judge this case. However, no matter the circumstances, your chosen route was . . . disappointing, Citizen Reúnen. Tell me, why did you go through such lengths to avoid the proper, lawful channels?"

"I had no reason to believe the proper channels would lead to Carmen's release," Inquieto said. His voice was controlled, but his contempt was obvious and sounded personal.

Levantan paused.

"Such disrespect," said a pudgy man who hadn't spoken before. He squinted his small beetle eyes at Inquieto.

"It is time for us to witness more for ourselves," Levantan said. "Curio 0924, which I will say for the record." She eyed her peers with emphasis before turning to me. "Carmen." My cheeks flushed with hope. "My name is Memoria Levantan. We know you must be confused, but we are here to discuss your future. Do you understand what I'm telling you?"

My whole body felt like one big stutter before I could reply.

"Yes," I said. Breaths of awe, murmurs, and grumbles swept around the circle. "I understand everything. I understand that you took me from my home."

I wanted to say more, to unleash the storm raging inside me, but I kept up a wall and only said what mattered most.

"Will you send me back?"

Some counselors exchanged apprehensive grimaces; others were immobilized as if caught in a time loop of incredulous dismay.

"This is a delicate situation," said the pudgy man, but his small eyes weren't as squinty as before. He sounded petrified.

"Sending her back would risk further interaction with her . . . kind," said a woman with heavy-lidded eyes. Her low voice shook like she was deeply afraid.

"Counselors," Fortalecen said, his voice as soft and foreboding as a dying man's pulse. "It was only a matter of time until some travesty like this occurred. I needn't remind you that my grandfather strove against the movement to create the dangerous Curio Project eighty years ago, and I've tried to persuade you of its extreme flaws since. But there were others of his generation who insisted that *exploration* was more important than civil safety.

"We have no reason to believe that this creature is sapient. Rudimentary speech and opening an entrapment pod by pure chance are not enough evidence. However, enough of the public has seen its paz-like body type for there to be . . . talk. Given the current political climate . . ." He paused. "The matter is exhuming topics that need not be discussed. Even discussions that are too lurid to speak of regarding *another* intelligent species . . ."

Visible shudders and frowns of consternation passed around the circle. Whatever third species he was talking about, his mention of it had an impact that he must have been counting on.

"Sending it back could appear to be a dangerous confirmation of people's misled suspicions," he continued. "It belongs in containment for the good of our people."

"Returning her to her home planet is of improbable success, regardless of our considerations," said another counselor, a woman with golden patterns that swirled like whirlpools. "Isn't it, Citizen Reúnen?"

I frowned at Inquieto. He kept his eyes on the council.

"I believe it is possible, Counselor Invierten," he said, "if we address the problem with enough resources."

"Problem?" I said. "What's the problem?"

Inquieto turned to me, his face lined with deep regret. "I should have told you before. Your pod was—"

"Address the council, Citizen Reúnen," said Fortalecen. "We cannot *hear* you."

Inquieto looked away from me. His jaw tightened like he was clenching his teeth to the point of cracking them. Prístina leaned on her desk like she was about to rise from her chair.

"There's no need for that, Dignidad," Counselor Levantan said softly, but she looked at Inquieto with a sympathetic frown. Prístina eased back, but looked perturbed.

"Carmen's pod suffered more damage than simply being unable to open on its own," Inquieto said in a high volume aimed straight at Fortalecen before he lowered his voice to a more appropriate level. "I also discovered that the coordinates recorded for her home planet were incorrect. Planet 0916 appears habitable for some form of life, yes, but there is no possibility that either Carmen or Smita—Curio 0033—could have survived under Planet 0916's conditions. The atmosphere would make it impossible for them to breathe, and the tectonic plates and volcanic activity are too unstable to harbor advanced life at this stage of the planet's evolution. In addition, Planet 0916's rotation and revolution do not match the assessment the procurer ship made in its physical approach to Carmen's planet. When the damaged pod linked to the ship's system, it must have impaired the information. It is obvious that the coordinates in the system are wrong."

He met my eyes. "I am sorry, Carmen. We don't know where your planet—your Earth—is."

My chest squeezed in sudden harsh pain. Inquieto looked back at the council.

"But we will find out," he said.

My mind spiraled into a tornado of images from the Hubble telescope, documentaries, and my own imaginings of galaxies and stars and the vast, empty void of space, followed by the single photo of that "pale-blue dot" captured from the outer fringes of our solar system by Voyager 1 when the space probe was four billion miles from Earth. How far away was I now? From where I stood, would I see no dot at all?

My hands started to shake. I wasn't sure if my physical body or my swimming brain was causing my black-spotted vision, but I felt an overwhelming need to sit down. Inquieto must have noticed. He took my arm and braced me upright.

"Counselor Reúnen," said Counselor Invierten, turning to Prístina, "is it possible to find 0924 and 0033's planet in the curio database?"

"Yes, Counselor." Prístina sat straighter and spoke with confidence, almost like she had rehearsed this conversation. "We have a vast collection of possible inhabitable planets for procurement purposes, but it would take at least a season to sift through all the data to find one that would match this species."

"And since it's clear the processing program is *less* than effective, paz eyes would be necessary," criticized the angular-faced woman. "That would take even longer, and who do you suggest we divert from their usual tasks to perform such an exorbitant endeavor?"

"We have a host of knowledgeable experts in this city," Levantan said, "and none of us doubt paz ingenuity." I watched her assuring face and felt a desperate pique of hope.

"Yes, but Counselor Invierten is correct," said the pig-faced man. "Paz time and resources would be better spent elsewhere. Especially considering the timing of this problem."

"I agree; it's not worth the effort," Fortalecen said. "Did you not see the depraved behavior it displayed in the recordings? It *is* an animal, Counselors. It has shown destructive and *violent* behavior."

"Stop!" I said. The counselors all looked at me, stiffening in their chairs.

"Please." I forced my voice's volume to lower. "Please. You took me from my home and put me in a *zoo*." I could tell that the last word came out in English when my mouth matched the phonetics. I flinched in frustration. "You imprisoned me. You degraded me. How was I supposed to react?"

"No civilized species would react how you did," Fortalecen bit out.

"We were wrong to bring her here," Inquieto said, his voice shaky, but forceful. His grip on my arm tightened as if Fortalecen might reach over his desk and snatch me away. The entire room felt like it could explode at any moment. "Carmen *is* an intelligent species. Her differences do not make her less of a person. She deserves to be treated like one. We had the technology to find her planet and procure her; we should have no trouble in using that same technology to send her home if given sufficient time and a team of experts."

Guilt lined the faces around the circle. It was the first hint of anything close to compassion I had seen from them.

"Counselors," said Levantan in a tone that would accept no interruption. Yet instead of speaking, she extended her hands to Counselors Guían and Invierten on either side of her. They each clasped their hands around her forearms, and she wrapped her fingers around their forearms in turn. Guían and Invierten then both extended their free hands toward the counselors next in line. Soon, all eleven council members were linked arm in arm.

They all looked down in silence as if praying.

"What are they doing?" I mouthed to Inquieto. He took a slow breath, wearing a pensive frown.

"Wait," he whispered.

I watched the sunlight and shadows creep across Counselor Levantan's bowed head. My heartbeat ticked faster the longer we waited, but it didn't speed up the passing seconds' relentless march. I was on the verge of bolting to find some other solution that I might have more control over when the counselors each released one another's forearms and placed their hands upon their desks.

"Citizen Reúnen," said Counselor Levantan, "we agree to delegate a team to search for the accurate coordinates for the home planet of Curios 0924 and 0033. For Citizen Reúnen's benefit, would all counselors who approved this decision raise their hands?"

One by one, all the counselors raised their hands, save one. I eyed Fortalecen, and his cold eyes met mine. I believed he thought I would look away; he certainly looked irritated when I didn't. His hands stayed locked together on his desk.

Inquieto let out a quiet sigh of relief. Counselor Levantan's expression softened.

"Carmen, we offer a profound apology for our actions against you. Had we known you were of any level of sapient intelligence, we would never have brought you here and taken your freedom. Regardless of the delicacy of this situation, we can all agree," she eyed her fellow counselors, "that we have made a grave mistake. One which we *will* remedy."

A lump tightened my throat as tears stung my eyes. "I don't need an apology," I said, unable to sweeten the bitterness in my tone. "I need to be home."

Levantan gave a solemn nod, her wrinkles deepening for a moment before she smoothed her features with a refreshing breath.

"And the dog," I said.

"What?" she asked, looking to Inquieto.

"Curio 0033," he said. "She calls it a dog. They are symbiotes, I believe. I placed them together for that reason."

"Thought you were trying to prove I'm *not* an animal, Inquieto," I muttered. He glanced at me, his eyebrows crinkling.

"And the dog, Carmen," Levantan said. I couldn't ignore the fresh tone of condescension in her voice. Symbiotes. As if I weren't capable of a true emotional bond.

"Where will we intern her until we find the coordinates?" the heavy-lidded woman asked. "The therapeutic center or the museum?"

I opened my mouth, but Inquieto spoke first, his voice low and simmering. "Would you place an innocent paz in a therapeutic center or a curio exhibit?"

The woman scoffed, and several others rumbled in their throats at the notion that I could be comparable to a paz.

"Inquieto," Levantan said, her tone suddenly parental, but then corrected herself. "Citizen Reúnen, you are one of the leading experts of your unique vocation. Your observations of Carmen's behavior and analyses of her motives are substantiated by your education and experience in curio-specific behavior. No one on this council can ignore the validity of your testimony. As such, you are more suited than anyone to maintain Carmen's good behavior."

"My council members," said Counselor Fortalecen as his shadowed eyes sliced the room, "There is no question that this creature needs to be contained and out of public view."

"She doesn't need to be in a museum or therapeutic center to be kept out of the public's eyes," said Guían, who looked at me with a cocked head and a smile in his eyes. "Citizen Reúnen, you reside with Counselor Reúnen, do you not?"

"Inquieto and I would be happy to have Carmen stay in our home," Prístina said. "We will take full responsibility for her."

"Then I propose that Carmen stays in Citizen Reúnen's care until we have made more formal progress in assessing her case," said Guían.

"Those who disagree with the proposal?" asked the angular-faced woman. She, the pig-faced man, the woman with heavy eyelids, and, of course, Fortalecen, raised their hands.

"The Council approves," stated Levantan, eliciting nods from the seven who had implicitly voted in my favor.

"I thank the council," said Inquieto, his sentence a puff of relief.

"Take her home, Citizen," said Memoria Levantan. "Know that you are to be held personally responsible for her behavior on Paz. Her actions are your actions. Do you understand? We shall contact you when we decide what further action to take on this matter."

"I understand," he said. "I look forward to your words."

They nodded as one.

I spun around when two paz in matching white robes walked through the large ornate door across the room. They stood at attention and looked at the council as if they'd been called in, though I hadn't seen or heard anyone do so.

"Citizen Sirven," Fortalecen said, "escort Citizen Reúnen and his . . . charge . . . to the dock."

"It's all right, Carmen," Inquieto said, though his shoulder twitched. "They're disciplinarians. They're here to help."

I tensed as the white-robed man and woman walked closer with authoritative strides. I gathered from the name and uniform they must be akin to police officers.

"Come with us," said the man, Citizen Sirven. His forehead was wrinkled with precisely three straight lines as if they'd been chiseled there by a constant weathering of stern warnings and hard decisions. He looked at me with sharp suspicion, but his fellow disciplinarian seemed to want to look everywhere *but* at me.

Inquieto released my arm, and somehow I found the power to walk with him. The eyes of the High Council followed me as we exited the room. Though their discussion of resources had been maddeningly calculative, both sympathy and fear seemed to have seeded their final decision. I wondered what emotion would take root in them and thrive. They were both there, waiting to be watered.

The disciplinarians escorted us down the spiral ramp, heading back underground. Sirven took the lead when we reached the back door. He made certain no one was in the back alley to witness the exotic curio in their midst before ushering Inquieto and me into a waiting cell. Sirven and his partner aimed for a different cell behind ours on the same ceiling-based track.

I sat on the cell bench as the ramp refolded into the vehicle's side. Inquieto trembled a little as he took his seat, and he twitched once, the slits in his back flashing open. Then he stilled his body and gave himself an almost imperceptible nod. He flicked his eyes to me.

"That went well," he said.

I huffed a wry laugh. Our cell shuddered and started gliding down the track. The track's blinking amber and blue lights illuminated a growing sparkle in Inquieto's dark eyes.

"What?" I asked.

"There's so much I want to show you."

I leaned back, floored that he could be excited in a time like this, after everything we'd just heard, all the terrible news I'd just received. But as we passed by the looming Egalitarian and whooshed across the bright, cavernous alien city of Raíz, I finally felt like I had space to breathe. I wasn't in cuffs or in a cage. I wasn't free, but I was out. And for the first time in weeks, I had concrete hope that I could return home to Earth. That was enough for me to keep putting one foot in front of the other and focus on the next steps ahead.

CHAPTER EIGHT

"WHY DIDN'T YOU tell me you couldn't get me home right away when I asked in the medical ward?" I asked Inquieto as our cell aimed for a sunlit tunnel.

"I'm sorry, Carmen," Inquieto said. "You were already upset; I didn't wish to heighten your anxiety. Not until I had words from the council on the possibilities for your future here. I was hoping good news would make your worries less . . . acute." His face tiptoed on the edge of a wince as if I were an unruly child about to pitch a temper tantrum.

"What, you think I'm violent like they do? Like I'm going to go wild, act out?"

"No, not like that," he said. "You are unpredictable, though."

I huffed at the renewed scholarly light in his eyes.

"Well, you're not the first to label me as unpredictable," I admitted. Gaurav. Crispin. Mamá. "But what would you have done if they wanted to lock me up again?" I avoided looking back at the disciplinarians in the cell behind us, but I hadn't forgotten for a single second that they were following. "You told the council that you didn't think the 'proper channels' would lead to my release. Why help me escape and then shove me into the government's hands?"

"Counselor Prístina Reúnen is my older sister. She helped me plan this, and I trusted she would be able to sway the council away from the opposition. I knew finding the coordinates for Earth would take some time . . . If there was any chance I could free you and have you treated as an equal during your stay here, I had to take it."

"You still should have told me about the lost coordinates. I . . ." I looked him in the eyes, fighting the trembling in my chest. "I need someone I can trust here. Can I trust you?"

"Yes," he answered right away. He leaned forward, locking eyes with mine. "I want nothing more than to protect you, Carmen. I want you to feel as safe here as any paz. I will do everything I can to prove that to you."

Usually, dousing my temper felt like a shock of cold water, but Inquieto's earnest words reduced my anger to a low simmer like he'd turned down a stove burner.

"I guess you're off to a good start," I said, lowering my gaze. "Getting me out of the museum. Putting this in me, as weird as it is." I touched the slim silver crescent embedded behind my ear.

Our cell jumped as we hooked to an adjoining track. When my stomach settled, I asked, "So, the opposition—you mean that guy, Fortalecen? Some of the others didn't like me, either, but he was . . . cruel."

Inquieto sighed. "Dignidad Fortalecen is deeply embedded into Gnosia, even more so than most. I knew swaying the council would be difficult with him in the room, but . . ."

"Gnosia?"

Inquieto twitched; the lights of the track reflected off the pearly skin of his back and bounced back in a flash at the window before his slits closed again. The artificial lights alone weren't bright enough to elicit such a strong reaction. It looked more like a nervous spasm.

"Gnosia is a deep connection that paz share," he said, seeming to be gathering his thoughts, "a collective mindset, communal information and memories . . ."

"I don't follow," I said.

He paused, his eyes shifting as if trying to find something through dense, murky waters.

"Paz have the ability to communicate in ways no other species we've found can," he said in measured words. "We have uses for verbal speech, yes, but paz also have the ability to communicate with one another through biologically produced microwave emissions."

"Say, what now?" I took a breath through my oxygen concentrator. My body still rushed with adrenaline from the High Council meeting, and hearing about an alien species that could communicate through microwaves was not helping my sense of isolation from all things familiar.

"Do you know what microwave radiation is?"

"Yeah, to a point. Humans use them for telecommunication, radar, some medical procedures. Plus in machines that cook our food."

Inquieto sent me a quixotic smile before continuing.

"Our bones are high in metal," he said. "Our nerves are conducted through them and can therefore detect a useable level of electromagnetic radiation. Our electro-organs produce that same level of electromagnetic radiation."

"So, you can produce and receive information? You communicate with microwaves like telecommunication towers?" My eyes widened. "You're basically telepathic!"

Inquieto looked to be processing my revelation, and I realized with delay that *telecommunication* and *telepathic* had come out English, but he seemed to have gleaned most of my meaning. His enthusiasm didn't match mine, however. He continued as if he were reading from a textbook, which felt odd considering how personal and expressive he was with other topics.

"We refer to this entire mental and biological process of communication as Gnosia. Information can be sent and received through multiple frequencies. The closer one paz is to another, the faster the high frequencies can travel through the atmosphere."

"So when the council did that praying thing where they held forearms, they all agreed to your petition after that. Is that what they were doing?" I asked.

"Yes. The fastest way to communicate is to touch one another as the council did. Messages take far longer over large distances, so we use technological devices to produce farther-reaching bandwidths to communicate globally."

"Like we do. The internet, TV, radio."

"Humans communicate globally?" Inquieto perked up.

"Yes. Through technology, like you said. So, can you read each other's minds? You mentioned sharing *memories*?"

He closed one hand into a fist, opened it wide, and then squeezed his knee.

"Communication through Gnosia is more immersive and complete than words could ever express," he said. "Messages are accompanied by images, impressions, memories, experiencing what it's like to *be* one another, joining minds. It's . . . difficult to explain."

"Can you control what information you send to others, or does it just come out willy-nilly?"

"People can control what information they send, though not what they receive. Much like verbal communication. Though one can't just cover their ears to shut out a microwave message, so paz use different wave frequencies to hold private conversations. There are numerous public frequencies used to spread information to crowds. It's a sophisticated system."

"So you couldn't listen to what the council was saying telepathically? They were on a different frequency?"

"I've never had to explain this to anyone before," he said. He gave me a quick smile, but his eyes' sparkle dimmed as if thick, nighttime clouds had darkened his thoughts.

A wash of sunlight consumed the cell. I held on to my bench and gasped as the vehicle raced uphill and broke into the surface city. The windows of the cell were tinted, but my eyes still dazzled with multicolored stars.

"Here," Inquieto said, and I felt his hands placing the sun mask on my face. He lowered the oxygen concentrator from my mouth and nose and replaced it with the shawl of fabric to cloak my face from the intense Paz suns.

"I don't like this," I said, my voice muffled by the cloth as I looked down at my wrapped arms and gloved hands. Stupid tears welled in my eyes again. I was tired of crying.

"Carmen," he said, my name an apology.

I stared through the tinted window in silence. I wondered if Inquieto's eyes had no whites because of the suns, solid black shielding his amber irises like sunglasses. I didn't bother asking, though. Discussions of paz versus human biology were a fascinating distraction, but it was also terrifying, realizing how different we really were.

"The curio pod scanned your environment and took flora samples for us to replicate," Inquieto said. "Were we accurate? Is that what your planet is like?"

I sniffed and fought to clear my head. "Part of it. Just one small part. There are all sorts of other biomes—mountains, forests, marshes, jungles, tundra—some I suppose aren't much different than this. Total desert."

The upper level of the city flew by our window. Though the landscape was dusty and arid, it was unlike Baja California or any other desert I'd visited. In patches of unpaved dirt amongst the buildings, there wasn't a cactus in sight, and the scrubby plants didn't have any leaves at all, only black spikes or shining, refractive burrs. Though I couldn't see far beyond the city, I spied some distant rock formations in glimpses, but the rock was white and riddled with deep purple-and-black strata in swirled patterns unlike any I'd seen on Earth.

"Jungles and forests, marshes? Some of the other curios come from places like that . . ." Inquieto sounded dreamy, but his wistful smile fell. "Paz's climate doesn't vary much from this, aside from shallow oceans and the equatorial regions, which are hotter. Only a few underground outposts dwell there. Raíz is in the southern hemisphere."

"Which was built first?" I asked as I watched Raíz's pagoda buildings flash by. "The underground section or the aboveground section?"

"The underground. We informally call it Provenance District, and the aboveground Mirror District, since it was built to reflect the original underground structures."

"What are other Paz cities like?"

"They're similar," he said, "though they tend to follow a more uniform plan. Raíz is one of our oldest cities so our layout is less organized, more sprawling. No other cities are as large as Raíz, either."

I thought of my overhead view of Provenance District, the streets curling like snakes rather than an organized grid. Up here, the streets I could see did the same, and the buildings were arranged at different levels and terraces as if built to reflect the uneven cavern ceiling below.

"You'd think you'd be expanding more of Mirror District, then," I said, "but there's that huge construction site underground that we passed on our way to the Egalitarian."

Inquieto nodded. "Fortalecen's Legacy District. He threw in massive political and financial support for underground expansion. He wants us to return to our traditions, our roots, by reminding us of the virtues of living underground. We've populated the surface for thousands of years. Fortalecen wants us to go backward. He claims we don't have a choice."

"Why would he say that?"

Inquieto again seemed to be measuring his words. "He believes that Gnosia is connected to our planet, that Gnosia wouldn't function elsewhere. That without our ties to Paz, we would all . . ." His sentence languished into soft longing but ended in a frown of resignation.

Gnosia. The English term was so specific, it was a wonder my translator had harnessed an appropriate term at all. The word could be both medical and spiritual; it described the ability of a person to recognize the form and nature of people and things, the faculty of perceiving, but a derivative term, *gnosis*, referred to mystical knowledge of spiritual truths, of humanity's link to divinity.

"So, living underground is symbolic for being closer to the planet?" I asked. "It's like a religion. The belief that the planet has some sway over your culture and personal lives."

He frowned. "I don't think anyone thinks of our planet that way. That's quite a primitive notion."

"Is it? And you all are so evolved that you can't stomach the fact that there might be an inkling of spirituality involved?"

"It's theoretical science, Carmen. If the magnetic fields are different on different planets, Gnosia may not be attuned to it. But, your thoughts are interesting. Truly."

I looked ahead through the window when a surprising, wide parting of skyscrapers ahead made way for a vast, foggy landscape. Two artery system tracks disappeared into the depths of fog; cells ahead of us were consumed by it, and cells coming the opposite direction emerged like ghosts.

"What?" I murmured as we sped toward the white, billowing wall. Gray clouds rolled over the sunroof from the sky high overhead, unconnected to the low-lying mist, though my mind imagined the gray masses had conspired to close in on us as easy prey. I pressed my hands against the window as we plunged into the fog.

"Is that steam?" I asked in dismay. We were crossing a vast lake; the water below us was barely visible through swirling, wafting clouds.

"Yes," Inquieto said, looking down through his own window. I felt a lurch in my stomach as I imagined crashing into the lake. I tried to convince myself it would feel like a hot tub rather than a boiling vat to keep myself together until we reached the other shore.

I released my tight grip on my knees, but tapped my heel on the floor as I saw the disciplinarians' cell behind us emerge through the obscuring steam.

The elaborate system of single-railed train tracks continued outside the central city, but we left the high-rises behind to bake in the heat waves. The streets widened, and open spaces of plant-dotted dirt separated shorter buildings, still built with stacked, pagoda-style roofs in upward curves or angled V's, but only three stories at most. I wondered if they, too, had an underground mirror to their architecture.

It looked like I was about to find out. Our cell slowed and pulled off on a long, narrow trail that traveled through a flat expanse of scrubby, dead-looking grass. The disciplinarians didn't follow us, seeming content to loiter on the street. I had no doubt they'd be staying there for a good long while.

I watched the surrounding landscape, speckled with squat bristly plants that reflected all light with thin spiky fibers. Other plants were as tall as trees, twisted black spires reaching for the scorching sun. Yet clouds were gathering and turning dark so fast it was like someone had squeezed an ink drop into them. Inquieto frowned at the sky, but I turned my attention toward a three-story pagoda that came into view, surrounded by a low stone wall.

The building was far more ornate than most of the buildings I'd seen in passing, though nowhere near as grand as the spherical Egalitarian or the pyramidal Curio Life Museum. The straight square walls looked like dark glossy jade. Gray stone columns, which tapered in the middle like joined stalactites and stalagmites in a cave, anchored each corner. Each of the three pagoda awnings were gentle curves of speckled granite, and the highest of them rose into a peaked roof like a teardrop.

The entire structure was carved with intricate circles, triangles, squares, and straight lines arranged within gem-cut facets like puzzle pieces; I suspected Prístina was responsible for the poetic, precise, sophisticated artwork of this house that she and Inquieto shared. My skin crawled, despite the beauty, as I pictured the egg-shaped curio pod she'd also designed.

Our cell followed its track toward the front of the house, turning parallel as it slowed. I sat straighter, prepared to exit, but Inquieto was still eyeing the clouds with a concerned frown.

"What is it?" I asked.

"It's about to rain."

"And?"

He looked back at me with a forced smile. "It's all right. Just please, do as I instruct when we arrive."

I jumped when a flash of lightning beat against the clouds like a prisoner trying to bust through their thick walls. Our cell stopped in sync with a deafening crack of thunder.

Inquieto pushed a button on the cell's control panel, and one side began to unfold into a ramp.

"As soon as the ramp's down, run toward the awning," he said.

"I don't mind getting a little wet, Inquieto." I rose from my bench, but stiffened when a big, fat raindrop hit the window.

It sizzled.

I watched the drop stream down the glass. It evaporated within seconds.

"Carmen, go."

I froze for a second longer, but more raindrops started to fall. I pinned my shawl to my hair and face with both gloved hands and dashed outside. A drop fell and sizzled away at my feet. One hit the bottom edge of my sun mask and seeped down through a tiny space between the shawl and my cheek.

"Ow!" I clapped my glove to my cheek as my skin burned. The ground started swirling with white puffs of scalding steam that threatened to soak through the cloth wrappings around my feet. I cried out and arced over the steam in two high bounds to reach the shelter of the stone awning.

Raindrops cascaded from the sky and beat the awning. Steam curled along the stone flags toward my feet. I backed away until I hit the jade wall of the house.

Inquieto winced as he reached cover. Faint pink dots speckled his skin where the rain had hit, but they faded within seconds. I felt like the one drop on my cheek would sting for days.

"Come inside," he said, reaching for a thin, straight handle of a black glassy door. I was surprised that it was a true door, not the thin, dissolvable doors that I'd come to despise. He pulled the handle sideways, and the door slid into a slot in the jade wall.

I hurried into the refuge. The automated cell hummed away down the track outside; I wondered if any vehicles were privately owned in Raíz, or if they were all run by a government transportation division.

"This is my home," Inquieto said, his voice tight and shy. He guided me through a short entryway that resembled a tunnel; curved, dark brown walls blended seamlessly with a dark brown floor. The tunnel opened into a large, round room with similar walls, pocketed with six open archways leading to the recesses of the house.

The environment felt very much like a dim cave, lit by an amber orb on the domed ceiling. Tall, vertical ridges ran from ceiling to floor every few feet like ribs.

"You'll be staying this way," Inquieto said. "With me."

Though his voice was kind and welcoming, I couldn't set aside my bitter unease, knowing that my new living arrangement was mandated by the High Council. There was no doubt about it—I was still a prisoner, and now Inquieto was my warden.

I followed him through an archway to our left and down another tunnel-like hallway. My chest tightened, and I peeled off my sun mask in a sudden panic so I could escape the swallowing darkness. Fortunately, the hallway soon opened up into another round room, though smaller than the first.

I lowered my shawl from my face and hair and walked to the center of the room. Five round, navy-blue cushions nestled into shallow craters in the floor, arranged in a circle, each large enough for one person to sit upon. Each seat had a low backrest that was fused to the floor and looked like it would make my back stiff after five minutes.

A set of black, glassy doors made up the entire wall beyond, the only completely straight wall in the room. Each door was beveled like a single, rectangular-cut gemstone. The tall, twisted-spire plants in the garden were silhouetted through them like a Van Gogh painting, and a miniature version stood in a stone pot on a little shelf beside the doors. A defined square of transparent glass in one door allowed natural light to shine upon the little sapling.

A rumble of thunder filled the silence in the room as I turned my attention to the left-hand wall, which contained a series of glass shelves displaying various objects. There was a long turquoise feather, though it looked harder than the soft wisps of Earth birds. A lizard-shaped husk sat beside it like the shed exoskeleton of a cicada. I recognized a sharp red-and-yellow-tipped spine, no doubt dropped from the creature across the hall from my habitat in the museum. I recalled how all the creature's spines had smoothed when Inquieto had stroked its paw after he'd given it a treat.

"From the lluthian," Inquieto said. "She's been in the museum for as long as I've worked there."

The shelf above the lluthian creature's spine housed an enormous, sharp tooth, nearly a foot long. I raised my eyebrows, gaining another level of respect for Inquieto if he'd been brave enough to enter the enclosure of such a mighty beast. All the objects were clearly shed from animals—curios, no doubt. None looked to be deliberately taken from the creatures.

Overall, the space was comparable to a living room, but it was so sparse and free of clutter, it didn't look like Inquieto did much living here. I wondered how much time he spent at the museum.

"I'm not sure what you're used to," Inquieto said, hanging back in the doorway. "I didn't have much time to prepare—getting you out of the museum was most important."

All his confidence seemed to have deflated like a balloon. I supposed jail-breaking an alien and facing down the government of an entire planet might have been a huge step out of his comfort zone.

"Do you need anything?" he asked, tilting his head. "Are you hungry?"

"Not for more curio kibble," I said, fighting a smile in the face of his awkward uncertainty. I remembered his show of dominance toward me in my habitat, no doubt a stance and attitude he'd perfected when interacting with the most dangerous animals under his charge. Now that I was a person, the animal behaviorist didn't know how to behave.

"If you want to rest," he said, "or . . . or if you'd like to bathe . . ."

"Do I smell that bad?" I asked, though I already knew the answer. My captors might have washed me the last time I was unconscious, but I'd had plenty of reasons to stress-sweat since.

"No, you don't," Inquieto said, sounding genuine. "Maybe it will help you relax, though?"

As soon as he said it, I couldn't help but agree, especially when I realized that a bath would mean I could be *alone*, a luxury I hadn't experienced since leaving Earth.

He smiled. "The hygiene room is this way." He led me to the left, where we passed by a brown column that tapered in the middle like a merged stalactite and stalagmite, with small amber spheres of light around its top.

The faint outline of an archway was on the brown wall behind the column. It was the telltale sign of a nearly invisible, matter-shifting door.

Inquieto raised his palm toward the door, but then he twitched his head and pressed his palm on a gray hand-sized panel beside the door instead. The panel glowed blue for a moment, and then went dormant.

"You try," he said with a smile. "You'll have to take off your glove first. I set the door to a lower level of electroreception to suit your level of electrical conduction."

That was why I couldn't open the matter-shifting doors. The knowledge that my own body's limitations were what had kept me a prisoner for so long was maddening. I couldn't do anything to change my body's electrical conduction, meaning the paz would always have the power to lock me into whatever place they wanted.

Yet Inquieto was giving me the power to open a door.

I removed my glove and pressed my bare palm against the door. It dissolved within seconds; I fluttered my fingers through the mist.

It was the first door I had opened since I was stolen from Earth. The simple action brought tears to my eyes.

I blinked them away and stepped into a small but well-lit room. Indented shelving in the brown walls looked like an imitation of natural weathering in a cave. White cylindrical containers of various sizes sat on the shelves, containing who knew what.

"Here's where you can clean yourself," Inquieto said, walking to a round, shallow crater in the floor, big enough for a person to recline in. There was no water faucet in sight, but a three-feet-wide, rectangular tank was mounted on the wall above. The tank looked like it was filled with crimson sand.

Inquieto opened a thin slit at the bottom of the tank. Red grains poured out and started to form little dunes inside the crater-like bathtub.

"What is that?" I asked.

"It's an exfoliant. Each grain releases a small amount of cleansing oil as it dissolves. It should work for your . . ." He eyed my hair.

"You don't use water?"

He shook his head. "This is better. But scrub gently; your skin is softer than ours, so this could be abrasive if you're not careful." He pointed to a small cylindrical bottle sitting on the tub's edge. "Take a sip to clean your mouth." He walked to an indented cabinet, nearly as tall as me, that had a clear door with a little handle.

"Hang your clothes on this rail and close the door," he explained. "They'll be clean by the time you're done bathing."

He walked back to the tank of red sand and closed the slot, ceasing the flow into the half-full tub.

"Does all that make sense?" he asked, then hesitated. "Do you need help?"

My gut twisted into knots, while heat prickled up my neck and into my cheeks with resurging humiliation. "No, I don't. If your fellow employees at the museum would have given me the chance, I would have done it without them—touching—me. When I wasn't even awake. When I couldn't—" I let out a ragged breath. "Can I bathe? Now? Please."

"Yes," Inquieto said, soaking in my words with a surprised, helpless expression. "I . . ."

But he didn't leave. Instead, his face softened into a frown. He walked to the shelf of white canisters. When he returned, he held a collection of rubbery orange bandages and a small bottle that sloshed as he set it down on the edge of the bathtub.

"May I look at your arm first?" he asked.

I hesitated. I had never been able to fully ignore the throbbing, prickling pain of my second-degree sunburned arm, but at least under its current bandage it was as out of mind as it could be.

Inquieto sat down with a coaxing expression. I winced, but nodded. I started unwinding the long strip of fabric from around my arm and sat down across from him. I unveiled the large orange bandage and peeled it off, inhaling through my nose to stave off the brief nausea the pain and sight conspired to bring on.

I laid the rubbery bandage on the floor, trying to ignore the gross crust of dried blood and dead skin shed from the blisters. My arm itself looked even worse, but I grabbed the small bottle of liquid from the edge of the tub.

"I'll do it," I said.

"It's going to sting," Inquieto said, but he didn't interfere. I braced myself for more pain as I poised the bottle over my arm.

I hesitated, feeling Inquieto's eyes on me. I glanced up and caught a tender, worried frown on his marble lips, with tiny crinkles at the edges of his eyes, like not helping me pained him. I felt like a baby, being afraid to doctor my own wound, but I was just too tired to put myself through any more stress. Despite my fierce need to not be touched by any more paz, Inquieto wasn't going to do it without my permission. My next heartbeat was a little lighter as I acknowledged that *that* made all the difference.

"Okay, you do it," I said, not looking at him as I held out the bottle and my tense arm.

I inhaled a quiet breath as he took my arm in a gentle hold. I didn't think he used any electricity on me, but my skin tingled all the same. He sprinkled a few drops of clear liquid onto my blisters. I gasped sharply and formed a fist. I distracted myself by focusing on the difference in textures between the golden skin of his palm and the white skin on the outskirts. The gold skin was hard and supple like scales, but it wasn't layered as scales were, just one flat surface. The white skin felt like a smooth riverstone, only a little more yielding.

The astringent liquid washed dried blood away, sending pink rivulets down my arm to drip onto the floor. Inquieto took a square of cloth from his pile of medical supplies and started dabbing blood away in slow, soft presses.

"Please, don't try to run again," he murmured. His request didn't sound controlling in the least, only deeply concerned.

"I had to escape." I swallowed, my voice quivering. "I didn't know anyone was on my side."

His brow furrowed, and his words came out a little hoarse. "I'm on all the curios' sides. I'm sorry I couldn't help you sooner."

It was hard not to believe him. His bowed head and tense shoulders matched the flicker of anger in his face, and his breaths were quicker than usual. Yet, his touch remained gentle as he pressed a fresh bandage onto my arm. He turned his attention to my wrists, still pink and raw from struggling in the hard cuffs.

I bit my lip as he finished applying the last bandage around my wrist, but managed to whisper, "Thank you."

He smiled and collected his supplies.

"I'll be in the common space," he said, standing. "With the seats."

"Okay," I said, itching to be alone. He stepped through the door, and it solidified into an opaque brown wall behind him.

As meaningful as the clothes on my body were, I hurried to remove them and hung them up in the washing cabinet. I slid the transparent door closed, and a rush of steam and blowing air fluttered the fabric. I watched it for a moment with curiosity before turning my attention to my much-needed bath.

I poked a toe into the red sand. It was soft, and I sighed when I sank both feet into the tub and the grains enveloped them like I was on a warm beach in the Caribbean. I knelt and filtered some of the sand through my fingers. It didn't stick to my skin at all and ran into the tub in crumbly streams, reminding me of kinetic play sand that I used to mold shapes with as a kid. When I rubbed my fingers together, the grains scrubbed my skin with mild warmth and dissolved into a smooth oil with a scent similar to rosebuds. The oil felt comparable to noncomedogenic sunscreen, soaking into my skin without leaving any greasy residue. I hoped that was a good sign that I wouldn't wake up with a slew of acne.

The sand was so soft and warm, I abandoned my previous wish for water and started massaging my upper arms, enjoying the sensations of the sand and oil. I hesitated over my bandages, not wanting to undo all the work Inquieto had just spent applying them with his gentle hands. I did my best to clean around them.

The soothing sand eased dirt and sweat away, but the more I scrubbed, the more it didn't feel like enough. I had spent long days in rough conditions before; my travels to wild, open country had prepared me for my recent stint in captivity, yet I had never felt so disgusting or degraded.

My heart crunched and collapsed like snow under a boot. Memories of Earthly travels coursed through my head—hiking up India's Kaimur Hills to study ancient rock paintings, analyzing petroglyphs at Creswell Crags in England, and my life-changing venture into the realm of painted animals in France's Lascaux cave.

Then, images of my childhood ranch-style house in suburban Denver swept in. Early memories of Dad propping his feet up on the coffee table, his laptop shining blue light into his eyes, and Mamá stirring her own recipe of hot chocolate on the stove, humming along with Christmas carols garbling from the radio. All my relatives from Mexico laughed and hugged me tight. Gaurav smiled with pride from the audience at my college graduation ceremony, while Crispin tipped his square cap and sent me a wink from his seat a few rows ahead.

I slumped down into the tub with a groan and leaned my head back on the edge.

"I'm going home," I told myself over and over. The High Council had promised they would find the coordinates for Earth. I couldn't believe how irresponsible these people were, to not only steal foreign species from their home planets to stick in a fucking zoo, but to *also* lose my coordinates through a malfunctioning spaceship. Yet their ability to travel through vast distances of space within a short time proved how intelligent they were. If the paz were that high-tech, and if they were as resentful and afraid of me as they seemed to be—for reasons I couldn't quite fathom—then surely they would get me the hell off their planet, even if they were afraid of "further interaction with my *kind*."

I felt a sudden jarring tingle from scalp to fingertips and sat up.

"Wait," I whispered, images flickering through my head like a scratched film reel. The gem-cut style of artwork on the curio pod, the four-knuckled handprints embedded between the facets like silver constellations, weren't the only examples of paz art I'd seen before my abduction. The prehistoric artwork I'd found on Earth in the cave tunnel also featured long-fingered handprints painted on stone—with four knuckles. They had been side by side with bas-reliefs that featured gem-cut facets of limestone and obsidian.

Now I knew why the bas-reliefs of the ancient, mysterious Baja Californians had no eyelashes or eyebrows, why their ears were small, and their necks a little too long. I understood why some had strange curving arches on their shoulders, which I had thought were aspects of elaborate clothing.

The people carved in profile weren't human at all. The handprints were not pressed upon the stone walls by human hands.

They were paz.

My "kind" *had* interacted with paz before. Humans and paz had done the impossible—found one another like two miniscule grains of salt in the vast ocean of space, which meant at some point, ancient paz had known Earth's coordinates.

I didn't know why present-day paz weren't aware of meeting humans in the past, but the fact that the curio pod landed near the ancient artwork on Earth couldn't be a coincidence. I recalled the ethereal blue light in the cave tunnel after Pete had unleashed the wild flames. Maybe in the modern pod's malfunction, it followed some ancient paz signal from the cave, and I was unlucky enough to be there when it did. The idea sounded far-fetched, even to me, but my entire life had become one big far-fetched mess.

It was hard to believe paz would have possessed the technology for space travel when humans were still using stone tools, but I couldn't think of any other explanation for the ancient artwork. If paz were so sophisticated fifteen thousand Earth years ago, surely they would have kept written records. Maybe those records survived. Records might exist somewhere here on Paz, right *now*, that contained coordinates for planets they visited in the past.

Maybe looking at history could reveal my path home.

But my tentative hope melded with unease. Would telling my abductors about their previous contact with humans be wise? For some reason, ancient paz visitors had chosen to approach Earth. Sure, it could have been a harmless exploratory mission, but what if they'd been after something in particular, a resource, perhaps? If I told Inquieto, or anyone, about the ancient artwork on Earth, where would it lead? What would be the repercussions? What if my news provoked a reason for present-day paz to visit Earth in numbers?

I felt a crushing weight of responsibility and sank down to my shoulders in the tub. I wanted to get home so badly, but could I live with myself if I ended up being responsible for conflict between humans and paz on any scale? Could a single conversation with Inquieto bring on a war?

I took a breath, trying to reel myself back from spiraling. Maybe my return home could be more discreet, I assured myself, but regardless, what would happen when I got there? Crispin had seen the curio pod take off with me inside. Who had he told? Gaurav and our team, my extended family, probably. But who else? Such a bizarre form of kidnapping would perplex the police, and since the pod had skyrocketed into the air and entered a bigger, presumably cloaked procurer ship, had the Mexican military noticed? Or the US or Russia or China? Did anyone guess the truth—that I had been abducted by a UFO, that aliens truly existed?

If so, a lot of people would want information. I curled my toes under the red sand as I imagined interrogation rooms and a medical quarantine that might follow my return. But once the initial processing was over, I might find myself working with top-level academia to dissect my unparalleled observations of this alien culture. Even if any involved governments made me swear secrecy, it would still be a giant leap in my career. Pete Dockson, anyone who had doubted me, would regret it.

Crispin's wry voice slipped into my head as if he were right beside me. I knew what his words to me would be: *You are an idiot if you don't take advantage of this opportunity, Carmen.*

I glanced at the bathroom door. Clearly, Inquieto was thrilled to meet someone of a different species; his excitement constantly bubbled under the surface, only receding when his quiet, yet intense, anger or worry would dominate in brief spells. His enthusiasm rankled my nerves at times, but now it gave me a little courage. I could take advantage of his avid curiosity to learn more about him, about Paz. I could gather observations to bring home to Earth. I'd already gotten a good head start. My natural curiosity had prompted me to ask constant questions since Inquieto had installed my translator.

I didn't know if I could trust Inquieto enough to tell him about the paz artwork on Earth or ask him to help me find Earth's coordinates through history records. It was too early to understand the consequences that might occur if he or any of his kind found out about the past. But given enough time, I could find out.

With time, I could decide whether or not I could trust Inquieto.

I latched onto my newfound purpose like a lioness to her prey. I could treat Paz like any Earth location I'd visited. I'd experienced plenty of foreign cultures where the customs were different, the architecture was different, the food was different, the people looked different. Sure, this place had two suns and less gravity and aliens who could use bioelectricity for their every whim, but . . . details. I forced my worries away with a blasé wave. Those were just details.

I would focus on my work like I always had, and by the time I had the information I needed, either the High Council would know how to send me home, or I would figure it out for myself. Time would pass by in a flash.

It had to.

I forced myself to solidify that view by ceasing my dwelling thoughts and moving on with my sand bath. I wiped my face free of tears, scrubbed my cheeks, and ran my hands through my hair. I was worried the oil would drag it down, but the substance was so light that it left my locks as soft and fresh as if I'd used two-in-one shampoo and conditioner.

My translator alerted me that the paz didn't even have a word for hair. I wondered how, in all their explorations throughout the galaxy, modern-day paz had never encountered creatures with hair or fur before. One of Earth's unique quirks, it seemed.

I reached for the little bottle Inquieto had pointed out as mouthwash. I fiddled with the cap until it slid to the side like a travel mug's lid. A burst of sweet perfume overwhelmed my senses, similar to a mix between cherry blossoms and peaches. I smiled a little at the pleasing, almost familiar smell, and my anxieties drifted further away. I took a sip and swished the sweet-tasting liquid around my mouth. It startled me by fizzing strongly, scrubbing my teeth and tongue all on its own.

When every part of me was refreshed, including my mental state, I felt like I could move forward with freer steps and at least an illusion of normalcy. I climbed out of the tub and walked to the clothes-washing cabinet. As Inquieto had promised, my beige, green-trimmed robe was clean and dry. I dressed, grateful that I didn't have to bother with all the mummy-style wraps, the gloves, the shawl, or the sun mask. I gave myself a short nod as I prepared to reenter Inquieto's presence and pressed my palm against the smooth door. It dissolved into vapor. A knot in my chest loosened. Logically, I knew there was no reason for Inquieto to lock me in the bathroom, but I was so accustomed to closed or invisible doors that I couldn't shed all my fear.

I stepped through the lukewarm mist and peered around the column into the living room. Inquieto was sitting cross-legged on the edge of one of the cushions, picking at a place on the floor in front of him. He lifted something between two fingers with a bemused expression. I looked closer and realized he had found a stray hair I must have shed.

My cheeks warmed with a twist of embarrassment, but I shoved it away and knocked on the column. Inquieto startled and tried to discard the strand of hair, but it clung to his finger-tips. He shook his hand, and the hair must have dropped free because he stood with a look of innocence as if trying to cover a up a crime.

A chuckle welled within me, but a residual twinge of bit-terness and nerves kept it from escaping. A small smile did emerge, however, one that made Inquieto's eyes light up.

"How are you?" he asked.

"I'm okay."

I shifted out from behind the column. Inquieto didn't seem to know where to place his eyes; they roamed around my face and the room and back to my face again. I knew how he felt. I ended up latching onto the tinted black doors across the room.

Boiling rain still steamed down, but a parting in the clouds made little rainbow dots cling to the glass before the drops evaporated. I imagined there must be an epic rainbow outside, with two bright suns beaming down.

"When will it get dark?" I asked, craving some reprieve from the sunlight.

"The suns are setting now if you'd like to watch," he said, though he gave me an apologetic half smile. "We simulated Earth's rotation in your environment. Our nights are much shorter and have been getting shorter for years now as the suns' separate orbits bring them closer together. I'll make sure you have plenty of time to sleep undisturbed, though, Carmen. You need more than we do."

His mention of sleep hit me like I'd popped a sleeping pill. I'd been running on adrenaline all day, and between my warm bath and feeling like I was in the first location of relative safety since Mexico, my body started to give out.

Still, my curiosity wouldn't let me give in to sleep quite yet. I shuffled to the doors. The sky was a wash of orange and pink, with a hint of lavender twilight above. A single yellow orb, slightly smaller than my sun, sank toward the horizon. The sight looked almost normal, and I felt like home was pulling me by a string, the knot on my end tied painfully tight around my heart.

"We can only see the more distant sun, Oscuro, from this angle," Inquieto said. "Luz sets in the opposite direction to the south."

"Do you have any moons?" I asked, searching the twilight.

"No. The other three planets in our system do. They're all gas giants, uninhabitable. Their terrestrial moons are in even worse condition than Paz in climate."

I lowered my gaze to the orange-bathed landscape behind the house. The flat, dusty expanse was similar to the front, but with a shorter distance to another street where black silhouettes of houses stood. I tensed when I saw two disciplinarians lurking in a vehicle in the long, double shadows.

I took a step back with an uneasy twist of my stomach and swayed.

"Carmen?"

"I'm fine, I just need . . ." I looked around, feeling heavy. I rubbed the heels of my hands against my eyes. "Sleep."

"Your personal room is this way," Inquieto said with a gesture to the left, his hands slightly poised to catch me if I swayed again. I trudged beside him, past another tapered stalagmite column, and stopped in front of two faintly outlined brown doors, side by side.

Inquieto pressed a gray panel beside the door on the right until it glowed blue, changing the setting so I could open it like the bathroom. I was too dazed to bother, though, so he opened the door for me to reveal a short, narrow flight of stairs leading upward. My chest clenched as I hesitated to enter the claustrophobic space, but my exhaustion propelled me onward. I climbed three steps up and crouched around a corner, where two more steps ascended into a room with a low ceiling that made me bow my head.

It definitely wasn't the most comfortable of spaces, but I turned around and saw Inquieto slip around the corner and up the stairs with ease as if his joints were rubber. Even though he was taller, his bowed neck didn't look strained at all. His ability to slink around in tight places explained why paz had a similar physique to humans despite Paz's lack of trees. If paz liked living underground so much, it made sense that their long limbs would have developed for climbing through cave tunnels just like humans' evolutionary ancestors used long limbs with opposable thumbs to climb trees.

Regardless of the room's tight dimensions, I felt a surge of relief that it was *mine*. No one would be watching me through glass or stealing inside while I slept. There was a small glass window, but it was tinted dark and cut like a gem, looking like a glittering mineral in the brown wall under the amber glow of a spherical light fixture.

The middle of the room had a person-sized, oval-shaped crater in the floor. A dark blue blanket nestled inside, and a partial dome of matching blue fabric was cinched like an accordion over one half, suggesting it could be spread out to encase the entire bed like an eggshell. It struck me as funny that all of the furniture in Inquieto's apartment was built into the architecture as if the designer couldn't fathom that any person might want a different layout.

There were a few empty shelves built into one wall, and a tall, arched cutout in another wall showed an empty metal rack inside.

"I'll provide you with more clothes, soon," Inquieto said, following my gaze. "Your . . . proportions are different from most paz women."

I caught him looking at my breasts and hips. I flushed.

"No doubt," I said, clipped. The paz women I'd seen had such flat chests, I wondered if they had breasts at all. He averted his eyes at my tone, and faint pink colored his cheeks around the edges of his golden patterns.

"My personal room is the door next to yours," he said, plowing through our awkward tension. "If you need me. For anything, Carmen. Anything at all."

I looked at the bed, my heart hurting as I imagined sleeping without Smita's warm body curled around me. "You think Smita will be okay? She'll wonder where I went."

"I'll visit her in the morning," Inquieto said with soft compassion. "She's safe in the museum."

"I don't know how you can work there after what they did to us."

"The other curios aren't at fault," he said.

"So, why do you condone it?" I turned to face him. "Do you think animals should be locked up any more than I was? That it's fine to steal them from their home planets?"

"I make sure they're cared for," he said, evading the question. "And happy. I like working with them."

"So your happiness overrides theirs?"

"Of course not. I didn't start the Curio Project." His tone sounded defensive, and his shoulders twitched, his back reflecting the amber light from the ceiling. But his frown softened, and he looked down. "But since it does exist, I can't *not* be involved. To meet creatures from other worlds, to learn about them and the places they came from—would you be able to resist that draw? If they weren't here . . . I'd miss them. If they were gone. The curios are everything to me."

"Maybe you should find something else." I closed my stinging eyes, then opened them with an irritable shake of my head. "I don't get why you can't understand how horrible that place is."

"You miss Smita. How is that any different?"

"I treat Smita as a friend. I don't lock her up. I didn't steal her from her home on purpose."

"And I didn't personally steal the curios," he said, his voice rising. He was tense, and I realized I'd struck some kind of chord. "I didn't steal *you*."

I huffed and glanced around the bedroom, different from my habitat at the museum, yet still a prison in its own way. "Didn't you?"

He sighed hard and looked toward the window. His shoulders slumped and his eyes clouded. A strange dysphoria seemed to settle upon him.

"When I look into a curio's eyes," he said, "or connect with them in whatever sensory way they can—not all of them have eyes"—his mouth curved in a gentle smile—"I see more than an animal, more than what other people seem to see. I see . . . a fellow being, living a life they didn't . . . Perhaps a life they never thought would be theirs to live. I see someone who's lost and needs comfort. Someone who needs a friend, someone they can rely upon. And I . . . I *feel* that there's a person inside of them. They're just unable to communicate with us in ways we understand, but that *doesn't* mean they don't have volumes to say. It doesn't mean they don't have a voice. I try to understand them. That's all."

"I guess it helps that I'm a curio who can talk, then, huh?"

I heard a small rumble in his throat. "Yes. It's unlike anything I've ever known. You're different from the other curios, obviously." He met my eyes, and I saw deep, yearning melancholy within his of such strength, it took me off guard. "You're more like . . . me. You're . . . you."

I looked aside, nibbling on the inside of my bottom lip. He'd countered my accusations, no matter how righteous, with such deep honesty that I didn't know what to say. My eyes roved the room while I searched for an answer, but my mouth went dry before I could respond.

I stood, frozen, staring at a piece of artwork hanging on the wall facing the foot of the bed—a spiraling circle of silver and clear glass, formed by passionate strokes in erratic layers.

The art piece wasn't a perfect copy, which made it somehow more perfect in its raw expression, but it was unquestionably crafted by the same person who had made the wild hurricane circle on the curio pod that had stolen me from Earth. Prístina had said she was responsible for the artwork on the pod in the council meeting, and I felt a sudden lurch of bitter anger.

"Is this Prístina's? Did *she* make it?"

Inquieto made an awkward clicking sound. "No. I did. I know I'm not a good artist. I can take it down if you want."

"You made this?"

"Yes." He sounded cautious of my reaction, lingering behind me.

I felt like he'd knocked the breath out of me. I had suspected there was a second artist, an artist who thought differently from the artist who'd made the rest, an artist who desperately yearned for something just out of reach.

Now I knew who it was.

"So did you," he whispered.

"What?" I looked his way. "Oh, the charcoal in the museum. No, I was imitating yours, trying to get someone to understand what I was capable of. Mine was nothing compared with . . ." Tears came to my eyes.

Inquieto sighed and walked to the artwork. He must have misinterpreted my tears because he reached up like he was going to take it down.

"No!" I said, lurching forward to stop him. I stumbled and he spun around and caught me.

"Carmen, please, you need sleep. Let me help you."

I looked around his arm, my eyes following the passionate glass circle, round and round. I finally gave in to my wobbling legs and went limp. Inquieto half-walked, half-carried me to bed and laid me down, but I stayed propped up on my elbows when he drew away. He brushed the spherical amber light on the ceiling with his fingertips. The light dimmed, but I could still see the glinting glass spiral in the twilight from the window.

"Rest well, Carmen," he said, his voice tender.

"Good night," I murmured, unable to look away from the artwork, and now a bit frightened to look at him. He left down the tight, twisting staircase. I heard the hissing of the door turning to vapor, then back to solid wall again.

Only now, unfathomable light-years from home, did I understand why Inquieto's art spoke to me with such intensity: I no longer had my small, cherished painting of Mamá's, but I didn't need it on canvas to see the round flower with chaotic petals, or to see how vividly it matched the wild, far-reaching galaxy on Inquieto's wall.

I sat up and clutched my knees to my chest. I rested my chin on them and stared at the artwork, seeking comfort like I always had from Mamá's painting when I needed her most.

CHAPTER NINE

LIGHT PUSHED AGAINST my eyelids, sending starbursts into my receding dreams. I blinked and felt, more than saw, the impression of high-noon sunlight filtering into my tent.

"Dammit," I said, a jarring sensation in my chest. I'd over-slept. Gaurav would be pissed.

I sat up. Static crackled between my hair and the tent ceiling. I looked up, and a heavy weight dropped into my stomach. I squeezed my blanket and hunched over.

"Ten, nine, eight," I whispered, trying to slow down the pace with each number. When I reached one, I would feel better. "Seven, six, five, four . . ." A deep breath, fighting to reach the surface, forcing my lungs to expand before they'd collapse and I'd crumple on the mattress.

For the third time in this single, barely there Paz night, I'd woken up to sunlight in utter disorientation, only to realize that I wasn't in a tent on a dig site, but under the fabric accordion dome of the bed in the room Inquieto had given me.

I wasn't on Earth. I wasn't safe.

"Three . . . two . . . one."

But I'd conquered my body, and that was enough for now. *Exhale. Sit up.*

I lowered my blanket and pressed it to the bed with calm, deliberate force. I gathered my hair into a low ponytail and slowly dragged my fist down to smooth the strands, pulling hard enough to prickle my scalp so I could wake up and surface from the mire of fear. I let go when I reached the tips of my split ends.

I unfolded the fabric dome from the bed. Light shone bright through the tinted window, illuminating the spiraling glass of Inquieto's artwork on the wall.

My heart clenched, and I looked away. The art had brought immeasurable comfort in darkness, but now it was confusing to see something so familiar, knowing the person who created it was a complete stranger. No matter how much Inquieto had risked on my account, or how much he had promised to protect me, I still didn't know him at all. Forging a bridge between his artwork and Mamá's probably wasn't the wisest idea, even if it had kept me sane last night.

I shook out my anxieties through my hands and climbed out of bed. I ducked under the low ceiling and squeezed down the tight staircase as best I could, but my neck and shoulders felt locked into place and rusted from my constant tension. I opened the bedroom's vaporous door and tried stretching my aching neck to the side, but I stopped at the sight of a shallow bowl on the floor that held a single spherical fruit—a pop of bright pink and mottled orange—along with a clear glass of blue liquid. Beside both was a flickering, circular screen similar to Inquieto's tablet, but the projection came from a little white cube instead of the ring he wore. A clear mask that resembled my sun mask sat in the screen's glow.

On the projected screen, Inquieto's face was smiling. His lips moved, but I couldn't hear his voice. I crouched down and poked the screen, the projected light somehow solid like glass and charged with warmth. As soon as I touched it, his voice became audible. It seemed to be a recorded message, since his sentence started halfway through.

". . . you're doing well. I've gone to the museum to see Smita, but I will be back soon. I hope you enjoy the pashil and solur juice, but if you don't like the food, we'll have the andalim meal as soon as I return. There will be more options."

I chuckled at his nervous babbling and shy smile. I'd take any food at this point to ease the tight cramp in my stomach. I realized between what must have been something like a liquid IV diet in the medical ward and my self-imposed fast in my habitat, I hadn't had solid food in days, maybe weeks. The pashil fruit smelled like a cherry blossom and a peach fused into one scent, the same aroma as my mouthwash the day before.

"This device will give you access to pubcom, so you won't get bored, I hope," Inquieto continued.

I eyed the white cube and listened to his next instructions, which involved pushing numerous buttons and wearing the mask sitting nearby. Then his message started to repeat.

I downed the blue solur juice in one go, too thirsty to risk not liking it. It left a strange, bittersweet aftertaste on my tongue, but it wasn't too bad. I then picked up the pashil and took a bite. I sighed and closed my eyes, savoring the burst of juicy, sweet flavor and soft texture, the thin fibers tickling my tongue. I stuck the fruit in my mouth like a roasted pig with an apple and put the clear face mask over my eyes. I picked up the white cube and walked into the living room, munching on my fruit as I went.

I pushed a couple of buttons and gasped in surprise as sights and sounds filled the living room. I felt a thrill as I realized that the cube and mask were an augmented reality system, giving me a chance to watch aspects of Paz and its people as if I were seeing them in person.

A life-size, virtual paz man cooked virtual food on a round stove that leapt with short flames, while he gave step-by-step instructions of his progress. Paz landscapes—rocky rhubarb-hued mountains, cracked deserts, a vast ocean dotted with barren islands, underground lakes in caverns that glowed with stacks of purple fungi on the walls—all appeared through the tinted doors, looking as real as the true neighborhood hidden beyond.

Later, a small, three-dimensional scene played out before the semicircle of seat cushions. Several miniature paz raced through the sky, leaping off dinner-plate-sized disks like sky-high stepping stones. As soon as their feet left one disk, they would toss a coin-sized object into the air ahead of them, which would expand into a new disk with a pop for them to land on. A ball of light zoomed around like a caffeinated firefly. Clearly, it was a sport of some kind. I smiled, wishing I had paper and pen to take notes.

After a while, an enlightening version of the news sparked into being, with life-size reporters and images all around. I didn't know if it was a recording or live stream; all I knew was that it felt *real*. The reporters were all far more expressive than paz behaved in person. After Inquieto's revelation about collective Gnosia, it made sense. If paz could communicate with one another mentally, there was less need for obvious facial cues. Yet through technological broadcasting, Gnosia was useless.

The reporters' expressive faces made them seem more human, and I found myself hesitating to change the channel to anything else. I didn't understand the context of most of their reports, but they were fascinating, nonetheless: *"Delegates from each of the Thousand Regions will be sending their regions' Wills to the High Council regarding the magnetic shielding initiative, particularly over the smaller cities . . ."*

"The rains on the plains of Lekron have caused dangerous erosion and scalded crops in the past few days . . ."

"As rising temperatures lead to prolonged underground living, children and the elderly are at risk of nutrient deficiency from lack of sunlight. Researchers are studying methods to enhance the vitamin absorption rate of skin without inhibiting the solar absorption of adjacent gold chitin . . ."

However, my admiration and wonder fell off a cliff when the reporters were replaced by a young woman with thick brunette hair, dark sandy skin, and green eyes, who walked across the living room beside a tall young man with white skin that flashed with sharp, tree-ring gold patterns, a smooth bald head, and fire-agate eyes. Together, they climbed into a cell in the back alley of the Egalitarian, heading to Prístina Reúnen's house where I now sat, open-mouthed with a squirming stomach.

"Curio 0924 was established on Paz nearly fifty days ago and placed in a popular exhibit in Raíz's Curio Life Museum," a news anchor said. He was then joined by Justo Muestran, and I choked back bile at the sight of the zookeeper's sneering face.

"The fresh exhibit drew massive crowds," Justo said. *"However, the creature began to exhibit extreme behavioral problems."*

More images of me popped into the living room. My primitive palm-frond clothing shook around my half-naked body while I was in a complete rage, throwing rocks at spectators, at children, and then the real me jumped as a projected rock leapt from the recording toward my face, but dissolved as soon as it got there.

"We called in the museum's curio life behaviorist," continued Justo. *"However, he has displayed past discrepancies in behavior himself, forcing us to greatly doubt his assessment of the animal."*

"The curio life behaviorist, Inquieto Reúnen, believes Curio 0924 is of above-animal intelligence and has brought his opinion to the High Council," the news anchor continued. *"We have no*

further knowledge of what the High Council's determination of Curio 0924 will be, but it appears they are taking time to consider Inquieto Reúnen's petition for the curio to not only be considered a species of intelligence, but whether we should expend valuable resources to send it back to the distant planet it came from."

The derision in the news anchor's voice was subtle but undeniably there. His visage was replaced by a still image of Inquieto.

"*While the case is under assessment, the High Council has decreed that the curio be placed in Inquieto Reúnen's custody. From the visual recordings we have acquired, it is clear he has taken the curio into his own home, a home shared by his elder sister, High Counselor Prístina Reúnen.*

"*Counselor Reúnen has been a long-time advocate of the Curio Project and proponent for the Migrationist movement. We plan to contact her as soon—*"

"Carmen."

I jumped as the real Inquieto turned the corner from the hallway and swept into the living room. I'd been so engrossed, I hadn't heard him coming. I peeled off my augmented reality mask and threw it on a cushion.

"Did you see—"

"Yes, but you don't need to worry," Inquieto assured, but his tone was tinged with anxiety and he looked a little harried.

"How did the story go public?"

"Prístina thinks Fortalecen is behind it," he said with a visible effort to calm his demeanor, flexing his fists and taking long breaths, "which is surprising. Fortalecen much prefers in-person, Gnosia-infused speeches to the public rather than pubcom broadcasts; he can influence people more easily that way. He's also always been a strict follower of the council's decisions. If he is responsible for that negative message, I worry that he has sacrificed his conscience for his Isolationist views."

I stiffened. "Fortalecen? But he wanted me locked away from everyone; he made that clear. Why would he get me on the news?"

Inquieto's mouth became a critical line. "Gnosia makes it difficult to keep secrets. After the council entrusted you into my care, he knew that you remaining a secret was improbable. I think he's changed tactics to try to use your presence here to his advantage. Unfortunately, broadcasting to the entire planet is a strong start."

"The entire planet saw that?" I asked, my stomach sinking.

"The public communications system is linked planet-wide," Inquieto said. "But don't worry. Prístina is coming home soon for andalim. She's certain to have word from the council."

I took several shaky breaths, but each was shallow, and my heart sped up to a rapid patter.

"Carmen," Inquieto said. I felt like I was about to crawl into a tight dark cave, but the bracing way Inquieto said my name provided a lifeline. He stepped close and looked me over, but he didn't touch me or make any pitying assurances like Crispin would have. My next breath felt stronger. I ran a hand through my hair as I exhaled.

"So . . . what do we do now?" I asked.

"Are you hungry? Would you like to help me cook before Prístina arrives?"

I scoffed, ready to call him out once again for offering me nothing but food. I stopped when I caught a mischievous sparkle in his eyes and the tug of a smile on his lips.

I collapsed into a fit of giggles that way overshot Inquieto's simple tease, but it was as if a floodgate of delirium had opened, and I couldn't stop.

"Carmen?" he said, a low, purring rumble under his word. "That sound, it means you're amused, doesn't it?'

"What, laughing?" I said, recovering. "Yeah, most of the time. Same as your, um, cat purr?"

"What?"

"The sound you make instead of laughing—in place of it, I think. It sounds a little like an animal we have on Earth. They look kind of like Smita, only . . ." I shifted my shoulders and arms with feline flexibility without really thinking about it, which made Inquieto rumble louder.

"You must have fascinating creatures on your world," he said. "I wish I could see them all."

"You've seen plenty from other worlds," I said, eyeing the shelf filled with his collection of teeth, feathers, claws, scales, and more. My time in the museum crawled back in. I shuddered. "Was Smita okay today?"

"She misses you," Inquieto said with a gentle smile. "You'll see her soon, I—"

"Promise, I know." I shook my head and sighed. "Well, what the hell, let's go cook."

The corner of Inquieto's mouth twitched in a smile. I was aware that *hell* had come out English, but he seemed delighted by every foreign phrase I used.

We left his little wing of the house and reentered the round foyer surrounded by open arches. We took an arch to the left and descended a flight of stairs, turning a corner into a wide room that provided only an inch of space between Inquieto's smooth head and the brown, earthy ceiling. I rubbed my robe between my fingers as I followed him into the cramped space.

The kitchen looked at once modern and old-world, blending a gastronomic workspace and a root cellar all in one. It was lit by a cozy strip of bubbly, amber lights around the top of the walls. A low glass table and four legless chairs with curved backrests sat on the right side of the room. An indented shelf behind the table was decked with sleek containers of different shapes and sizes. Myriad items hung from the ceiling—strings of bean pods, bunches of firm oval fruits, a thin cylinder full of red liquid.

We approached a round cooking stove in the center of the room, its surface engulfed in soft, red flames that hovered in short, controlled peaks like I'd seen on pubcom. Two wide, shallow bowls that looked to be made of stone hung from the ceiling on short cords over the flames.

"I bought a lot of new things for you to try," Inquieto said with a fresh twinkle in his eye and bounce in his step as he walked to a door in the corner. He slid the door open to reveal a small pantry. Cool air trickled from inside, continuing the root-cellar ambiance. He retrieved a couple of containers and set them on a waist-high metal workspace beside the stove.

"Your analysis revealed you have most of the same nutritional needs as us," he said, "but you will need an iron supplement, and your body requires twenty-six percent more protein than the average paz. We didn't detect any obvious potential allergens, but I suggest you don't eat too many vegetables of this shade." He batted the tips of a bundle of dark purple bean pods that dangled from the ceiling, making them sway. "Your digestive system won't process them well."

"Got it," I said, but my stomach did a small somersault. "So . . . the *analysis* . . . Was that why I got so sick when I first . . ."

"We had to ensure you wouldn't succumb to paz illnesses," Inquieto said softly. "Your body is so much like ours, inoculation was necessary . . . But yes, we also assessed your biology so we would know how to care for you."

I huffed through my nose and had to bite my tongue to stop from bringing up his role in the goings-on in the vile museum again, no matter how earnest and kind his motives seemed to be after his explanation last night. Yet he was the only person there who had seen me as a person and who had tried to help me. I couldn't discount that. So, I closed my eyes and tried to harness the feeling of light ease I'd just shared with him through laughter. I couldn't quite get there, but I managed to clear my head and lessen my frown.

"I get it," I said stiffly. "So. What first?"

"We can start with usil." He grabbed a container full of coarse white powder. I watched him mix an eyeballed amount with water so that it formed a paste. He rolled a bit of paste between his palms like a kid making a Play-Doh snake. "Would you like to try?"

I followed his lead and started rolling gummy paste into noodles. When we'd finished rolling, Inquieto turned off the red flames and laid the noodles on the stove's flat surface with a sizzle. After, he unwrapped a sleeve of paper he'd taken from the pantry, revealing several long, squiggly brown root vegetables inside. Then he pulled something down from a high shelf.

Every tendon of my body went taut. A sharp, silver knife flashed in his hand. If any aliens tried to stun me again, a knife like that might give me a fighting chance.

Inquieto paused. I wrested my eyes from the knife and caught a look of wary caution flick through his eyes as he looked between me and the knife, but I was surprised when a look of lost confusion took its place.

"So this andalim thing, what's it about?" I asked, hoping he'd go along with the change in subject.

"Andalim is the biggest meal of each day; everyone stops working when the suns are highest," he answered. His movements were a little slower, but he dove into his cooking again as if he hadn't noticed my reaction to the simple kitchen knife.

I watched the blade glimmer as he sliced up the root vegetables with confident precision. Each light tap on the cutting board jabbed shame into my gut for making him feel nervous in his own kitchen. He had promised he wouldn't hurt me. But did he trust that I wouldn't hurt him? Was I just another predator from the museum he so loved?

I looked away and sought a distraction—something positive, however small, that could give me hope. I'd done that a lot after Mamá's death. When the next step in life wasn't clear, or was halted by a deep ravine of despair, I'd find something positive to hold on to—something that could lay the first plank of a bridge to help me cross.

The sizzling usil noodles started to smell savory and comforting. I inhaled the smell, and it offered the small stepping stone I needed to keep moving forward. I summoned the strength of will to start with a simple task—helping Inquieto dust the vegetable strips with a powdered spice that smelled a little like nutmeg, while he sifted through a bowl of dark, leafy greens with his dexterous, four-knuckled fingers.

"What's that called?" I asked as he drizzled the leafy greens with tangy-smelling oil.

"Lesh," he answered. "One of our most common foods. It's the most prevalent crop in this hemisphere, though you wouldn't know it if you passed by the fields during the day; the leaves only open at night to avoid the suns. It's also inexpensive, since we don't have to import it like we do these." He pointed to a bowl full of orange peas that may have actually been tiny roots; it was hard to tell.

I nodded with interest, allowing curiosity to lay a new plank on my bridge of positivity forward. I'd found that paying attention to a people's food was an open window into their culture. The variety of ingredients could reveal agricultural practices and trade relations. Mealtimes could showcase societal structures by watching who cooks what, or how and where each person sits or stands while eating. Inquieto had filled in some of those blanks without my prompting, which brought a small smile to my face.

"And those are?" I asked.

"Kinos. They grow on the base of the kinosha plant, only this time of year."

"Ah, fungi, then."

"That's right." He handed me a raw kinos to try. I plucked it from his fingers and enjoyed its earthy, nutty flavor. He dumped the rest into a dish filled with a green jelly-looking substance, stirred it all together, and gathered a stack of thin sticks that looked like they might be edible. He started rolling the sticks in the jelly-surrounded kinos. When he picked one stick up, the kinos stuck to it in a row like a kebab. He laid it on a wooden board, and with my help, we soon had all the rest lined up in a neat row.

"You enjoy this, don't you?" I asked. "Do you cook often?"

"Sometimes. I've never had a reason to cook such a variety of dishes before."

"Is it just you and Prístina here?"

"Yes."

"Have you ever wanted to get your own place? Or is it normal for adult family members to live together beyond childhood?"

He hesitated. "Most adults live in their own homes with their House partners and children. Living with Prístina is . . . well, it's easier." He gave me a quick smile, but it didn't reach his eyes and dropped altogether as he scooped up the fried usil with a wide crosshatched implement. "There are some utensils on the far end of the shelf. May I ask you to retrieve them?"

I wanted to ask why living with his sister was easier, especially since something about my line of questioning seemed to bother him, but I allowed the interruption and walked to the shelf. Some of the containers bore labels written in the Paz language. The lettering was delicate and strong at the same time, full of straight lines and perfect curves, topped with precise dots in various arrangements. It comforted me that they had a written alphabet like so many human cultures at home, but it was also nerve-wracking that I couldn't read it.

I found the utensils sticking out of a cannister, long white sticks with tips that resembled elongated spoons. Their scoops were so shallow, they didn't look like they would hold much. I brought the cannister to Inquieto, who was dishing out food into several wide, shallow serving bowls.

"Do you eat meat?" I asked. None of the dishes we'd made looked remotely fleshy.

His serving utensil stopped in midair.

"Ah . . . no. No, we don't." His eyes turned aside. "Is that . . . something you normally consume?"

"Yes. Humans are omnivores. Didn't your thorough physical analyses figure that out?"

He frowned at my sarcastic tone. "Given the amount of protein your body requires, I suspected that might be the case. I did hope . . ." He paused with a sigh through his nostrils. The lines on his face became surprisingly firm. "Carmen, you will not eat meat on Paz. Ever."

I raised my eyebrows. "No one does?"

"No one," he answered with an exasperated sigh. The slits in his back opened a little, flashing in the light. "It's an act of violence. No civilized person would—" He twitched his head and pressed his lips together. He leaned both hands on the counter. The slits in his back closed.

"So, I'm uncivilized?" I said, my tone flat and combative. "Like Fortalecen said?"

"I'm sorry. I shouldn't get so . . . emotional." The last word was barely audible. "To you, eating meat is natural. You just seem so . . . paz . . . I thought you might be . . . That you would have overcome that *primal* need to . . ."

"I'm sorry to disappoint you," I said, not meaning it one bit.

He was silent for a moment. Then he resumed dipping lesh into a bowl.

"We have plenty of other options to meet your nutritional needs. I hope this satisfies you."

"Maybe I should be grateful no one on Paz eats meat," I said, crossing my arms. "Some people still think I'm an animal."

"They shouldn't." Inquieto frowned and looked down, subdued. "I know we're different. But I want to learn more about you. I hope you'll try with me."

His last sentence sounded so earnest that it suppressed the biting comments I had in mind. I had encountered other cultures that didn't eat meat, of course, but it was hard to imagine that an entire planet would share the same eating habits, and it was his judgement that had stung.

I looked down at the bowls, filled with the variety of foods I had helped him cook. He *was* trying.

"Well, while I'm stuck here," I said, but then met his eyes and gave him a soft, wry smile. "Curiosity is what keeps us going, anyway, isn't it? If paz and humans weren't so curious, we wouldn't have survived for so long. Question by question, moment to moment, moves us forward."

He smiled. "That's a good point. Boredom would make us complacent. Curiosity makes life interesting. Worth living."

"Exactly," I said, my smile widening. It was rare someone outside of my academic circles seemed to not only genuinely enjoy my musings, but participated. "So, to that end, how do other paz cultures compare? What's the most outlandish food you can think of?"

His glossy black eyes shifted in thought. "When I was in training school for animal behavior in Lekron, a smaller city just north of Raíz, there was a trend to use lesh as a filling in an usil pouch."

"That doesn't sound very different. What about other cultures, far from here?"

He frowned. "Everyone on the planet eats the same foods, perhaps minor variations." He raised his eyebrows and clicked his tongue. "Humans all eat different foods, don't they? You aren't connected by Gnosia; you don't have sweeping global trends."

"I suppose one could say we're headed that way. We don't have Gnosia, but we do use technology, social media. But billions of people, practically half the planet, still don't have or want access."

"Earth has billions of humans?"

"Yeah. What's Paz's population?"

"Around eight hundred million. It's a small planet, and we share it with many animal species, all of which need access to underground spaces. There's only so much life a planet like ours, in our position, can support."

"That's hard to imagine. Humans have thousands of different cultures, 195 different countries. They all have their own foods. And languages and religions, artwork, architectural styles, music, and . . . Well, everything."

Inquieto looked spellbound. "To have differences, to be able to—and *you*, you are—your voice!"

"Pardon?"

"Your voice, when I was analyzing your ability to speak cognizant language. It sounded like you were speaking in two completely different manners. Do you speak more than one language?"

"Yes, and my translator seems pretty confused by that, by the way. Paz names are coming out in one language and all the rest is translated into the other. Maybe because your names are all regular, singular words, I don't know. English is the most common language of the country I'm from, the United States of America. But my mother was from Mexico, a country to the south. Her native language was Spanish, and I was raised speaking both. I come from two different countries, two different races, two different cultures. Does Paz really not have that?"

Inquieto's face fell. "Paz, we . . . We don't have differences. If we're all the same, conflict can't arise. Gnosia mitigates diversity."

"Wait, just because you're all connected in this telepathic hive mind doesn't mean you won't disagree, right? Our internet culture is rampant with conflict."

His frown grew pensive. "Gnosia is like tides, tugged between moons. Paz are too connected with one another to decipher where any idea originates, but once an idea becomes known, it spreads and is either eliminated through collective decline or spurred on by collective intellect. If there are opposing opinions, Gnosia allows people to understand others' views on an intimate level, so it facilitates swift compromise, and Gnosia returns to a unified state. The waves of ideas and culture naturally ebb and flow until they settle into one calm ocean. Do you understand?"

"If every idea is approved or declined by Gnosia so fast, how do you stop mob mentality from causing chaos? Don't people's emotional reactions flood the system?"

"Extreme emotions are not tolerated," he said, his brow furrowing deeply, and his hand closed into a fist before opening again. He swallowed and took a deep breath before continuing in a flattened tone. "Paz pacify each other through Gnosia before emotions escalate, along with planet-wide societal and governmental rules."

My heartbeat slowed as all his words washed over me, clicking into place.

"You're all peaceful?" I asked. "Everywhere? The whole planet?"

"Yes, of course," he said. His voice was full of such innocence and certainty, I had a hard time believing he was simply naïve of the darker elements of his own culture. He was a grown man, after all, and I had to admit, even the conflict I had seen over my existence here had been handled in peaceful, emotionally restrained conversations.

Could the paz have really developed a culture that allowed for boundless peace? Inquieto spoke of killing animals for meat in the abstract, as a primitive and abhorrent act, let alone imagining the idea of humans killing each other.

Without warning, an onslaught of videos and photographs, hell, even the painting of George Washington crossing the goddamned Delaware flooded my mind. Bombs being dropped from the black-and-white airplanes of World War II, the mushroom clouds of Hiroshima and Nagasaki. 9/11 on live TV; I was sick at home that morning, sitting in my PJs when I was eight years old. Mindless mass shootings that never seemed to end. A new one every week.

Paz didn't have war.

"I guess your culture's peace doesn't extend to me, though," I whispered.

"It could," he said. "It only takes a few people to start the wave of an idea, Carmen. Now that you're here . . . maybe we can plant a new idea."

The sound of footsteps on the stairs made me spin around, fists raised. A lithe young man leaned his shoulder against the doorframe.

"Look who's had a bath!" he said with a cheeky grin.

Inquieto's eyebrows knit, but he recovered and clicked his tongue in annoyance. "Cálido. Manners?"

Cálido smirked, and then eyed me up and down. I returned an expression that echoed Inquieto's word.

"Well, it—she does look cleaner," Cálido said. "Though that scowl is the same."

"Maybe if you—"

"Carmen," Inquieto interrupted the insult he no doubt sensed forming on my tongue. "This is my brother, Cálido. Cálido, this is Carmen. And yes, she is in much better condition than when you saw her last, now that she is recognized as a person."

Fantastic. His brother had seen me before. One of my many visitors while I was half-naked and degraded. I swallowed my humiliation and gave a short nod. "It's nice to meet you, Cálido."

"Ah, she *can* talk," he said with a rumble in his throat. He ambled into the room, his chin raised as he scanned the spread of dishes, his eyes flicking from one to the next with increasing sparkle. He was shorter than Inquieto and looked a few years younger, but there was a definite resemblance. They both had high cheekbones and nicely shaped lips with just the right fullness. Cálido's golden patterns formed similar sliced-geode layers as Inquieto's, but Cálido's were speckled like stardust. He was dressed in similarly cut black robes, but he'd draped a coral sash across his chest, trimmed with fine threads of gold. I spotted the same silver diamond symbol woven into his robe collar as mine and Inquieto's.

"I didn't know you would be here," Inquieto said. "Didn't Prístina tell you—"

"Did you think I would miss meeting Carmen? You know me better than that." Cálido settled on the jelly-coated kinos kebabs and grabbed two sticks, one in each hand.

"You didn't come with Pare—"

"Be well, brother," Cálido said, taking a big chomp of one kinos stick. After a quick swallow, he said, "Carmen, how are my inventions suiting you?"

"Inventions?"

"The sun-filtering mask and oxygen concentrator," Inquieto said, "and your translator. Cálido tinkers in his spare time. You can understand us because of him."

"Tinkers?" I said, incredulous.

"It's nice to work on something light when not at school," Cálido said with a smile.

"Cálido attends the highest-level engineering school in Raíz," Inquieto explained. "Though you wouldn't know it from conversation with him."

Cálido smirked and said nothing to his older brother's good-natured jibes. I couldn't help but smile.

"Cálido," Inquieto said, more serious. "Carmen said there is something wrong with her translator. She speaks more than one language, and it's having trouble adapting."

"Truly?" Cálido said, his eyebrows creased with blatant confusion. "Well, I can take it out and inspect—"

"No!" I said, backing up and slapping my hand over the silver crescent behind my ear as if he'd threatened to stun me and rip it from my head.

"Carmen," Inquieto said with worry.

"I'm sorry; I'm fine. I just . . . I'd like to keep it in. In case it stops working. I can manage fine how it is."

I didn't even want to think about what would happen to me if I couldn't speak the Paz language anymore. Half the council thought me an unintelligent beast as it was.

Cálido offered me his spare kinos stick as if it would pacify me. When I failed to take it, he tilted his head and popped it between his teeth before grabbing the entire board of them off the table.

"More in storage?" he asked around the kinos stick, nodding at the pantry. Inquieto nodded, and Cálido grabbed two more dishes that must have been prepared earlier, balancing them on one long arm.

"Let's go downstairs," he said. He left the room with a jaunty step.

"Don't worry about Cálido," Inquieto said as he scooped the dish of lesh off the table with one hand. "He's—"

"Blunt?"

"This is a new situation," Inquieto said. "Try to be understanding."

He reached for the platter of usil, but I ducked under his arm and grabbed it, suddenly needing to feel useful. In delay, I realized *useful* meant *equal* under my current circumstances.

"Thank you," Inquieto said with a soft smile. I nodded in reply and headed up the stairs to reenter the round foyer. Cálido waited in the shadow of one of the arches across from us.

I paused when I saw a large banner hanging on the wall between two archways that I hadn't noticed before. Its white glossy fabric was woven with shimmering silver thread that formed the same symbol as the smaller versions on Inquieto's, Prístina's, Cálido's, and my robe collars—a vertical diamond shape, with three lines inside that reached upward like the branches of a barren tree.

"What does this symbol mean?" I asked.

"It's the emblem of Reúnen House," Inquieto said.

"The symbol of your family."

"Yes, but also of all the Reúnens around the world. It reinforces the global connection between us, even over great distances. Every House has a different emblem."

"Tenaz might wear it soon," Cálido said, a lilt in his voice.

"Tenaz?" Inquieto said, raising his eyebrows. "I didn't know you were so close."

Cálido merely slipped us a mischievous smile and sauntered down the hall.

"What is he talking about?" I asked as we followed down a flight of stairs. Cálido turned a corner at the bottom.

"If two people want to join with each other as partners, they submit a request for a House change," Inquieto explained. "Tenaz is in House Entienden. If what Cálido says is true, he and Tenaz will submit a request to the government to assess the balance of each of their Houses around the planet. If Reúnen House is found to have a higher population than Entienden, Cálido will become an Entienden. Under opposite conditions, Tenaz will become a Reúnen."

Marriage. He was talking about the paz form of marriage. I wondered if the union entailed the same concepts as human marriages usually did, but I didn't have time to ask. Cálido popped back around the corner so fast, I stumbled into Inquieto behind me, almost dropping the platter of usil. Inquieto grabbed my shoulder to steady me, but he hadn't have needed; his body was solid as a rock. Metal bones, he'd said, but his muscles felt like they were made of titanium.

"He's here, though," Cálido said, "so don't mention anything about the Houses."

"Tenaz is here?" Inquieto said, his soft breath brushing my hair. I took a step forward, but he leaned in, speaking over my shoulder to Cálido with sudden hushed intensity. "Cálido, I don't know Tenaz."

Cálido looked hurt. "Yes, but I do. He's on our side, Inquieto."

"Our side?" Inquieto repeated, leaning back again and exhaling through his nostrils in an attempt at patience.

Cálido turned cautious. "Inquieto?"

"I was unaware that Prístina was going to turn this into a social event," Inquieto said with stiff acquiescence. He opened and closed his fist like he was holding an invisible stress ball. If I hadn't been holding the usil platter with both hands, I might have done the same. The prospect of meeting yet another person than expected brought sticky sweat to my palms.

We turned the corner, where a short hallway opened into a wide oval room. Amber orb lights lined the dark brown walls, set in between stone columns that bowed toward the ceiling like ribs. I shuddered as I recognized, yet again, the same precise circles and lines that Prístina had etched on the curio pod adorning each column. Would I never escape them?

A long table was surrounded by curvy, legless chairs, an arrangement that was fused to the floor like all other furniture I'd seen in the house. The table was set with various empty bowls and cups, and no one was seated yet, but two individuals were standing near the closest end. They were eyeing each other with mild interest, but they weren't speaking. One I recognized as Prístina. The other was a short man, around my height, with stocky muscles, a square face with sleek Cubist-style gold patterns, and a winning smile.

"Carmen's here!" announced Cálido.

"She's been here," Inquieto said. He looked at Prístina with a pointed stare. "Adjusting."

"Carmen," Prístina said with the same intense fervor she'd used in the council meeting, though not without compassion in her dark eyes. "It is an honor to meet you. When we heard what happened, we were devastated. What a terrible misunderstanding."

She seemed to be speaking with the magnanimous royal "we"; I realized in retrospect that the entire council had often done so. She no longer wore the long brown lapel-esque sash of her council uniform, and without it, her cream robe looked so identical to my own that I suspected I might be borrowing one of hers. The gold, orchid-blossom patterns around her scalp and cheeks were almost too perfect, and I noticed a subtle change in texture along the edges. She was wearing some kind of makeup to perfect her appearance.

Again, I wished I could take cultural notes like I'd yearned to do while watching pubcom, but that thought reminded me of the horrible news segment. I shifted the dish of usil in my hands and gave her a simple nod in response. I edged around her to set the dish on the table.

"Tenaz, I assume?" Inquieto said. I turned around to see the stocky man approaching him. Cálido sent a sleek glance of flirtation his lover's way.

Tenaz smiled a roguish grin. "Cálido says many good things about you." He extended his hand to Inquieto, but then drew it back with a sideways flick through his eyes as if he'd just remembered something. He offered his hand to me instead.

"It is an honor to meet you as well, Carmen," he said. My name swirled in his mouth like caramel, bringing a blush to my cheeks. "Are we pronouncing that correctly?" His shoulder shifted the smallest amount toward Cálido, who it seemed he was including in "we," though Cálido hadn't seemed to care if he was pronouncing my name correctly when we first met.

"Yes." I gave Tenaz's hand a couple of good shakes. "It's nice to meet you, Tenaz."

He raised his eyebrows with an amused smile. "An Earth greeting, perhaps?"

I slipped my hand away with a tug of embarrassment. "What was it you were expecting me to do?"

He smiled wider and took my forearm in his grasp, pressing his arm against mine and wrapping his fingers around my elbow. It was the same gesture the High Council had used during their silent Gnosia session as they decided my fate. I took the hint and grasped his forearm as well.

"Whoa," I said as a soothing wave of electricity lapped down my arm.

"Quite different from someone with no bioelectricity," he said, glancing at the group. He released my arm, and I twisted my wrist to work out the weird feeling.

When I glanced up at Inquieto, he was staring at my arm with a nearly anguished expression, but it was so fleeting, I wasn't sure if I'd misinterpreted.

"You've been cooking, Inquieto?" said Prístina with a soft smile. "It's been so long since you've done that. Why don't we sit and eat?"

Inquieto and Cálido deposited their dishes on the table. Prístina started pouring pale-blue solur juice into skinny glasses.

"Can she have . . . We have water if—"

She and everyone else turned to the door in a sudden, unanimous twitch. I frowned, not knowing what they were reacting to, but then I saw the shapes of two people emerging from the dark hallway.

"It's true," came a woman's voice as she stepped into the light, her attention locked on me. She wore a robe the color of twilight fog, with a silver shawl draped over her head and shoulders. She lowered the shawl from her bald golden head as she scanned the gathering with keen eyes that matched Prístina's in shape. Her golden patterns were similar orchid blossoms, but the tips of her petals were sharp as thorns.

The man was a little shorter than Inquieto and Cálido. His eyes were farther apart than theirs, with golden eyebrows that slanted downward and out as if he were perpetually sympathetic. His golden patterns ran down his skin like rain. Yet, the diamond shape of his face matched Inquieto's to a fault.

"Parents," Prístina said. She walked toward the man and woman, her hands extended for a formal greeting. They each took her forearms with such synchronicity, it was like they were a single organism rather than two separate people. "We were not expecting you."

Shit. Time to meet the parents—and they did not look happy.

CHAPTER TEN

INQUIETO'S POSTURE WAS as stiff as his voice.

"Parents," he said. "May I introduce you to Carmen? Carmen, this is my mother, Marea, and my father, Oyente."

Oyente nodded, but his eyes lingered on Marea as if accustomed to giving her the reins to their social interactions.

Marea scavenged my appearance. Her eyes narrowed as she collected my squishy skin, my prominent breasts, and my un-ridged shoulders for her personal store of reasons to detest me.

"What is that smell?" she said, her nostrils flaring. "It's like a half-sunned skim pond."

Inquieto sighed and sniffed his shoulder.

"That's not Carmen, Mother, it's the axbor. I was tending it all morning. I didn't have time to bathe. Carmen's welfare came first; I'm sure you understand."

A smile twitched at my lips, both from his rebuttal to his mother, and in his endearing acknowledgement of his own aroma. I recalled Justo mentioning the axbor scraping its wings against the wall of its habitat at the museum. The creature's scent wasn't particularly offensive to me, but it was strong, like freshly cut grass. I wondered how the poor beast was faring under Inquieto's behavioral therapy sessions. I recalled how compassionate he'd been with the lluthian across from my own habitat in the museum. He did seem to care for the curios, the same as any zookeeper on Earth might. Maybe I was being too hard on him for choosing his career. Maybe he was doing the best he could to help the curios within the confines of a broken system. Maybe, with some coaxing, he would be willing to fix it.

Marea ignored him. Her lip curled as she inspected my green eyes as if viewing a painting on a wall rather than trying to establish a connection. Her dissection finished on my hair.

"It's much more disheveled than I expected."

"You're much ruder than I expected," I said.

Her eyes widened a slight amount. I wasn't sure whether it was due to my ability to speak or my insolence.

"Prístina," she said in a polite tone that was iced around the edges, "perhaps you should set a place for it downstairs."

I drew a breath.

"She is a guest, Mother," Inquieto answered. His words were careful and precise as if he had practiced ahead of time for this conversation.

"You wouldn't place an ochassa at the table, would you?" she countered.

I almost unleashed a torrent of insults, but Inquieto spoke first.

"She is a person, Mother." His voice was soft, but his tone simmered with a tension that threatened to boil everyone in the room alive were he provoked one more time.

Oyente's downturned eyebrows were masterful at expressing worry. "Perhaps we can indulge him this time," he said to his wife. Marea sent him a cold glare that suggested he had tread upon a well-beaten topic.

"This is not something to *indulge*," Inquieto said with force. "It is Carmen's right to sit at this table. She deserves a place as much as anyone here. I expected disdain, but I didn't expect you to be so—"

"Inquieto," Marea said sharply. Inquieto flinched.

Everyone looked wary, but their caution was not of Marea, but of Inquieto. He was clearly worked up, but under a restraint that I never would have upheld. His family, however, eyed him like he was a ticking time bomb. A wave of mistrust seemed to spread outward from Marea to everyone else's faces as they turned their eyes toward me.

Oyente looked away first. "Marea, let's eat. It appears the meal is ready."

Marea nodded but gave her eldest son a long hard look before she lowered herself into a seat.

"Marea," Tenaz said in a smooth, jovial manner. He came round to the seat opposite her. "How is work going at the Understand?"

She nodded in greeting but failed to smile as he tried to harness her into a conversation; indeed, she looked at him as if he were a viper. Prístina hurried to her side with a placating look, though she seemed to show Marea a great deal of respect.

"Would you like to sit, Carmen?" Inquieto asked, not looking at me or his mother as he gestured to a seat as far from Marea as possible.

My body felt like it was on fire, and I crossed my arms to stop my muscles from quivering from my urge to hit something. But I wrenched my gaze from Marea and did as Inquieto asked. He took a quiet seat beside me. His teeth were clenched, but otherwise, he appeared like nothing had gone amiss.

There seemed to be no set seating arrangement from what I could tell. Oyente did not sit at the head of the table as patriarch of the family; it seemed that Marea would be the head of the family, if I had to judge, but her seating choice also seemed arbitrary. From an anthropological perspective, such casual seating suggested trust and familiarity with one another, lacking a need for hierarchy to maintain order. With the harmony of Gnosia, it made sense.

My appetite had dampened, but I crossed my legs and accepted the shallow bowl Inquieto fixed for me. Cálido took a seat on my other side, and I eyed his utensil as he dove into his meal with relish. Even though the lesh looked leafy and light, the oil helped the leaves stick to his long utensil's shallow scoop like glue.

As I started to explore my bowl, I found that most of the dishes were cohesive enough to cling to the spoon, though it still required delicate movements to keep each bite balanced. Fortunately, I had used utensils with a higher learning curve amongst various human cultures, the notable chopsticks, as well as the crab forks and crackers I had once struggled to use during a trip to New England.

Every flavor that I succeeded in bringing to my mouth was strong, which was fortunately enough of a distraction to keep me from launching into Marea with many a *How dare you?* and *Who the hell do you think you are?*

A few dishes were overwhelming—too sweet, too tart, too salty—but as I got used to them, I started to enjoy most. I thought about the powerful fruit-scented mouthwash and Marea's comment about the axbor scent and wondered if the paz had a diminished sense of taste and smell compared with humans.

"Which do you like best?" Inquieto asked. Everyone but Marea awaited my answer with interest.

I perused the array. I pointed to a hearty grain mixed with herbs and sundry vegetables, one of the dishes Inquieto must have made ahead of time. The spice had warmed my tongue and burned inside my nose like I'd inhaled a whiff of smoke around a campfire.

"This one," I said. "It reminds me of something my mother used to make."

I quieted and took a bite of a pink pudding to cover my surge of grief and homesickness.

"We'll make it again sometime," Inquieto said, subdued.

"Sounds good," I replied, "but not this one."

He made a short rumble at my grimace. "No? Melsa is nearly everyone's favorite."

"Not mine," I said. Empalagoso was the only single word I could think of to describe how sickly sweet melsa was.

Inquieto flashed another smile; I could practically *see* the excitement tingling off him. It was enough to make a girl self-conscious. I took a swallow of a smoky tea he'd called yesau to wash the sticky pink mush from my mouth, but the tea was practically still boiling.

"Feces!" I said, covering my mouth while I sucked in air, trying to cool off my tongue. I almost choked when I realized what I'd said. Cálido glanced under my chair, I assumed to see if I'd taken a dump. Marea slowly pushed her bowl as far away from her as possible.

I swallowed and laughed. "Intercourse, I'm sorry," I said, then groaned in frustration as everyone exchanged extremely uncomfortable glances. "It's my translator, it's—those were supposed to be slang, not literal translations." I leaned my forehead on the heel of my hand. "Jesus. Okay, that one worked."

The Lord might not like His name taken in vain, but given the circumstances, I chose to believe that any existent deity would grant me amnesty. I had never been devout in a particular religion in any case. My expansive knowledge of world religions prompted me to view them as a cultural phenomenon, a powerful psychological force that had shaped, and would no doubt continue to shape, the species of humanity.

I stopped my attempted expletives and let out a short, deliberate breath, trying to suppress my hard blush.

"Carmen," Prístina said, obviously trying to soothe the tension, "what do you think of Paz?"

I squeezed my elongated spoon between three fingers as my humiliation took a darker turn. "I haven't seen much," I muttered.

"Tell us about your planet, then," said Tenaz. Marea's eyes slanted to the side, and Oyente stiffened.

God. How could I even begin? Basic words tumbled out of my mouth, all surface-level descriptions that I could manage without the lump in my throat swelling too large to speak.

"Earth only has one sun, but it's yellow and bright like both of yours. We have deep, huge oceans and green forests, snow . . ." I noticed that *snow* came out English and moved on. "We have different countries, all sorts of people and cultures . . ."

"Humans don't have Gnosia," Inquieto murmured.

Marea's frown deepened, and her next look my way was laden with suspicion. Then she looked at Inquieto, and I thought I saw subtle fear in her eyes.

"How do you communicate?" Cálido asked.

"Well, we speak like you do," I said.

"The Talking Curio!" He smirked and took a bite of yet another gooey kinos stick. The stardust patterns on the back of his hand were a little spottier than all of the adult paz's I had seen. I decided to forgive his rudeness due to youth.

"What else?" Tenaz asked me, while sending a smile of endearment at Cálido.

"Um . . . Our facial expressions are usually more exaggerated than what you all use. And we use our hands and bodies to emphasize certain points, as I'm sure you've noticed I've been doing." I had always been one to talk with my hands, particularly when I was excited by some academic topic. Crispin had called me out on it on many occasions.

"We communicate through touch, too," I said, softer.

I hadn't been hugged since my last night with Crispin. I had never been a touchy-feely person, but now I suddenly became desperate for touch, like I'd taken a sip of water after days without a drop and only just realized how thirsty I was. "We hold hands," I clasped my hands together to demonstrate, pushing back tears, "or hold each other for comfort or to express affection. We'll pat each other on the back or shoulder to congratulate or cheer each other up."

"How obscene," Marea said.

"At least we're kind to each other," I snapped.

Marea was far more elegant in demeanor than my dad had ever been, but her criticisms reminded me of him, in the few memories I had from my childhood. She was so different from Mamá, but as I looked around the table, surrounded by Inquieto's family and having a big family dinner, I couldn't ignore the miraculous similarities between us. Humanity was not completely unique in this universe. Paz existed.

"Look," I said, leaning my elbows on the table. "When it comes down to it, the people of Earth are very much like paz."

"The probability is nearly impossible," said Prístina, "yet here you are. A vivid example of what the universe holds. Imagine what else we could find."

"Tell me," Marea said, light and thin as she completely ignored her daughter, "how is your species like paz?"

I took a quiet breath and floated my gaze across the table. Marea's heavy black eyes studied me, while she lightly clutched a delicate glass, her full lips curled in a false, aristocratic smile.

"Where is it you work again?" I asked, not doing a very good job of tempering my tone that implied her stupidity. She acted like I was as different from her as a single-celled amoeba.

"The Understand," Marea said, not hiding her impatience.

"And you're *good* at what you do?"

Inquieto made an odd sound that I realized was his attempt to suppress a rumble in his throat. Marea's eyes narrowed.

Her disdainful expression was taunting me to cause a scene, but I caught Inquieto looking at me as if I'd performed some nigh-impossible feat, one that pulled a small smile of admiration, and a touch of conspiratorial mischief, from within his restrained demeanor.

"Earth sounds like a wonderful planet," Prístina said. "You see what could happen if we ever encounter—"

"I doubt Carmen wishes to keep thinking about Earth right now," Inquieto said, his smile disappearing as the slits in his back flashed open to reflect the light, a reaction I'd seen enough times by now to decide it was definitely a sign that he was agitated. "How would you feel if you were stuck on a planet far from home?"

"We can't know how humans feel, can we, Inquieto?" said Marea. "They are a different species. You would do well to keep your focus on ours. Prístina, to accept all this talk in your own home, and to let a creature like this in, with an *egg* in the house—it's dangerous beyond measure."

"The egg is well, Marea," said Oyente, "I assessed it before dinner; there's nothing to worry about."

"Now that the beast is here, we should all be worried." Marea stood. "Come, Oyente, it's time to leave these *out-thinkers* to themselves."

Inquieto's back flashed brighter. Everyone was quiet.

Marea's voice lowered. "Inquieto. I . . ."

She bowed her head, her jaw tight as she replaced her silver shawl over her head. She strode to the door; Oyente followed close behind. He sent Inquieto, and then the group as a whole—glossing over me—an apologetic smile before he disappeared.

"Inquieto, we're sorry," Prístina said. "She shouldn't have said that. Apologies, Tenaz."

"Ah, do not fret, Prístina," Tenaz replied. "We're certain she and others will be swayed to the cause in time." He took a sip of solur juice, and the group settled back into their meal.

I shoved my bowl away. Inquieto's utensil sat dormant on the table.

The others were all silent, though I saw a few flickers of eye contact here and there. My stomach turned as I began to suspect what they were doing. Sitting right next to each other at a dinner table was no doubt close enough to have a quick, silent conversation through nigh-telepathic microwave emissions with ease.

"Isn't anyone going to apologize to me?" I asked. Cálido dropped his utensil with a light clatter against the edge of his bowl.

"Yes, Carmen," Prístina said, her low intensity back. She set her bowl aside and linked her long fingers together on the table. "We all apologize, not only for Mother's words, but for bringing you to Paz without your consent. It was a mistake. Yet . . ." Her eyes kindled with fervor. "Your timing could not have been more ideal."

"Prístina, *your* choice of timing for this conversation could not be less considerate," Inquieto said.

"No, no, I wanna hear this," I said, glaring at Prístina in challenge. "Continue."

Prístina leaned forward. "Did Inquieto explain our binary star system?"

"Not in detail."

"Did he tell you the problems it's causing?"

I glanced at Inquieto. "No."

"Our stars each follow their own elliptical orbit, but around a central external point," Prístina said. She raised both hands, curled her fingers into two ovals, and drew them together in a shape like a Venn diagram. "Their orbits overlap, and the stars orbit in parallel. Paz orbits Luz alone, but about every twenty thousand years, Oscuro and Luz draw as close to one another as their orbits allow." She used another finger to point to the link in the Venn diagram's center. "Luz is only a little bigger than Oscuro, so when they are close together, Paz becomes trapped between their gravity wells. Paz's orbit around Luz stagnates for three thousand years as it's tugged on by both stars. During that time, Paz's surface becomes temporarily uninhabitable." She took a deep breath. "It's about to happen again."

"What? Now?" I said.

"Soon. Within the next eight years."

"That's about five Earth years," said Inquieto.

Prístina looked pained. "Paz's surface will receive double the ultraviolet radiation and experience twice the amount of solar weather than usual, which over the long term will lead to an overheated climate. We'll all be forced underground until Oscuro moves away and Paz finally breaks free to continue its orbit around Luz.

"The last time this happened, twenty thousand years ago, our ancestors were nearly as advanced as we are now. They had populated the surface, developed space travel, everything. But when the stars drew close, the climate forcing them underground wasn't the only catastrophe. Gnosia was . . . cut off. We understand now that the increased solar storms were what disrupted Paz's magnetic field, which Gnosia relies upon to function. Our ancestors lost the grand picture that Gnosia provides, the unifying force that ties us all together and keeps us working toward common goals. Worse, our collective, long-term memories were erased. Our entire civilization was reset."

"Wow," I said. "That's like . . . a magnet erasing an old hard drive. Does nothing remain?"

"A rare few are skilled enough to align themselves with the weak remnant knowledge that remains," she said. "But for most of us, the past is an empty hole. Like trying to comprehend existence before birth. Carmen, I am telling you all this because what happened before could do so again. Now. Without swift, decisive action, we are setting ourselves up for failure. If we don't escape now while we have the technology for space travel, we may never be able to leave Paz again. Or if we ever can, it could be ages from now when our descendants finally reach that level of technology all over again. We don't . . . I don't want that for our children. Our future."

"I'm sorry to hear that," I said as if I were at an acquaintance's funeral, fidgeting. I struggled to overcome my sudden claustrophobia, realizing I was stuck on a planet that could force me to stay trapped, underground, for the rest of my life. I let out a long, slow breath. I wouldn't be here when that happened. The council's appointed team would find Earth's coordinates far sooner than five years' time.

"Some of our population think we should delve farther underground and live like primitive animals as our ancestors did," Prístina pressed. "But many of us view that solution as too risky. Our civilization has come too far to regress back into caves. We want to broaden our collective mind to new solutions, even if that means leaving Paz. Even if it means changing who we are."

"We could become something new," Inquieto murmured, an undercurrent of longing in his voice.

Prístina nodded. "Whether we leave now or not, we cannot stay on Paz forever. Mere millions of years from now, this planet will die. You saw the boiling rain and lake water yesterday. Our shallow oceans are slowly, but inexorably, evaporating. Our suns cause ultraviolet radiation to break up the molecules of water vapor so that hydrogen escapes into space. One day, when no water remains on Paz's surface, carbon dioxide will build up in the atmosphere, and our planet will trap too much heat for any life to survive."

"Venus. Your planet will turn into Venus."

"Venus?"

"A planet in my solar system, close to mine. I read that scientists think that ancient Venus used to be habitable with shallow oceans, but the planet's closer to the sun, like yours. The buildup of carbon dioxide caused a runaway greenhouse effect and . . . it's hell now. That planet is the hottest in our solar system—sulfuric rain, volcanoes, heavy carbon dioxide and methane gases in the atmosphere . . . Jesus, is that really what will happen to Paz?"

Prístina was very quiet, her frown immeasurably sad.

"Yes," she said after a moment. "That will happen. That problem is far less pressing than the matter at present, but they are ultimately intertwined. Millions of years is a long time, but too short if you take a step back. Millions of years ago, life existed on this planet. Different life, yes, but life. Millions of years from now, there will be no life. To know there is an end, a finite end, without a single doubt, and there's nothing we can do to stop it . . ."

"Except leave," I said, the gravity of the conversation hitting me hard.

"Except leave," Prístina echoed, staring at the table as if it might hold answers. Tenaz tilted his head a tiny amount in her direction; Cálido did the same. Prístina took a breath and nodded to them as if extending gratitude for some invisible gift.

"You, Carmen, are in many ways like us. I can see that already," she said, seeming to have recovered from her melancholy. "Humans clearly have a penchant for peace."

"You're not thinking about interacting with humans?" I said, my stomach flipping. "Trying to migrate to Earth? I mean, most humans doubt extraterrestrial life even exists. We've barely scraped the surface of space travel. We've visited our moon, studied our solar system through probes—"

"Humans go into space?" Inquieto asked, his voice hushed yet exhilarated.

"A little, yeah, but that's it. If people, the governments, found out that there was an alien species that could travel to Earth in a short amount of time? God, I don't know what would happen."

Suddenly all my plans to record paz culture and present my findings to governments when I got home to win academic renown felt absurd. What was I thinking?

"Earth has its own problems with global warming, anyway," I continued in a rush. "We're not as close to our sun, so it wouldn't be exactly the same, but we're headed to a bad place and fast. *We* might have to migrate if we don't change course in how we treat our planet. If we can develop the technology. I don't think humans or Earth can offer salvation. I'm sorry."

"We aren't trying to impose on Earth, Carmen," Prístina assured. "Regardless of what we are learning of humans, finding intelligent life-forms is something we are trying to avoid."

A shudder passed through her body and cascaded through everyone around the table. Inquieto was still, but his frown hardened.

Prístina continued in measured words. "Eighty years ago, a wave of nearly half the population of Paz supported the notion of exploring the galaxy to look for alternate planets where we could live. However, there were, and still are, many who disagree."

"So, the compromise was to bring back curios," I said, recalling Fortalecen's comment about his grandfather denouncing the founding of the Curio Project.

"Yes, to ease people into the idea—in an educational and entertaining way—to indulge their curiosities. The High Council's consensus forbade us from approaching planets that showed any signs—radio waves, satellites, anything—of intelligence.

"Though we keep this information to ourselves, we are using the Curio Project to investigate potential habitable planets with the ultimate goal of relocating our people. But the fear we have of encountering other intelligent species is still one of our greatest obstacles."

"So, enter me," I muttered.

"As I said, your timing couldn't be better," she said with a small, apologetic wince. "We're hoping to have made progress by the time the High Council's appointed data-searching team finds your planet's coordinates."

"Progress?"

"Yes," she said with a smile. "Your presence on Paz could help secure our people's decision to leave this dying planet behind. If you can help prove that not all intelligent species are dangerous—"

"I will not be a poster child for your political movement."

"Carmen," Inquieto said, sounding uneasy. "Let's hear what she has to say."

I frowned at his sudden change. I shifted in my chair. "What would you want me to do?"

Prístina's eyes lit up. "Our people need to see that you can be trusted. From what Inquieto has described, and from what we've seen here tonight, we think you can be trusted, Carmen. If we can persuade the High Council to allow you to appear in public, now that you can speak our language, are clothed, and docile—"

"Like some zoo animal again? No." I slammed my hands on the table and stood up. "Why should I help you, after what you and your people did to me?"

"We only wish to help you," Prístina said.

"You can help me by getting me home. That is the only help I need, the only thing I want from anyone. And instead of finding curios and stealing them from their homes to sate your own damn curiosity and further your politics, maybe you should think about letting them all go back to their planets, too, and leave everybody else alone!"

Everyone leaned back in their chairs; fear raced around the table like a flash flood. I paused, taken aback by their strong reaction. Was I out of line? I didn't think I'd gone too far.

"We would like to focus on you rather than the other curios," Prístina said, exchanging uncertain looks with Cálido and Tenaz. She then nodded like they'd all had a discussion on the matter and she was relieved to have group support. It looked like the paz always tread in choppy waters whenever they had a single isolated thought. "Yes, the curios will stay where they are."

"Maybe they shouldn't have to," Inquieto said quietly, though his heavy frown made it seem like his heart wasn't completely dedicated to the idea. Still, it was a start in the right direction. He'd stood up to Justo when getting me out of the museum. Maybe if I worked on him a little, he could use that strength to persuade his people to let the curios go back to their home planets, too, even if he would miss them.

"Prístina, we will consider your proposal," he said.

"What?" I asked. "What, are you in on this, too? You want me to listen to this bull-feces—"

"Carmen." He brushed his fingers against my forehead to calm me. I drew away from the soothing sensation and scowled. He exhaled through his nostrils and looked aside.

"I will speak with the High Council," Prístina said. "I believe they can be swayed to allow Carmen more freedom on Paz. With your presence, Inquieto—I am certain that will be a requirement."

"Of course it will," I said with an exasperated wave of my hands. "Why are paz so mistrustful of foreign intelligent species, anyway? Fortalecen mentioned a different species in the council meeting. Does that have to do with this?"

An extreme domino shudder overwhelmed the table. No one looked at each other or me; they didn't even look like they were speaking with one another through microwaves.

"Andalim is almost over," Inquieto said. "I'll explain it to her."

The entire room's atmosphere sighed with relief. There were lots of smiles and clearing of dishes as people rose. Cálido and Tenaz said their goodbyes, spouting that they had to return to school and work for the remainder of the day. Prístina made excuses about having a council meeting at the Egalitarian. I frowned at the suddenness of it all.

"I'll make you something for your head, Carmen," Cálido said from the doorway, ruffling invisible hair on his head. "We don't want you looking 'disheveled.'"

I might have laughed at his cheeky tone if his lopsided grin wasn't a little twitchy like the rest of them.

As soon as they were all gone, I spun to Inquieto. "What is going on?"

"Please, sit back down."

"I'll stand, thank you."

Inquieto's back slits twitched. "They're just trying to help, Carmen."

"Is that what you're doing? Trying to help? Or are you just trying to help yourself? Why did you really rescue me from that museum, Inquieto?"

"I rescued you because I care about you," he said in a rush. "I couldn't bear to see you hurting and trapped and treated like an animal when you are clearly *no* such thing." He struggled to lower his voice. "I agree with the Migrationist sentiment, but I had no idea what they were planning today. I promise you, Carmen."

"But you think I should accept their offer? Why?"

He winced and looked aside. His eyes moved as if he were picking through frazzled knots of thought.

"Inquieto. What do you need to explain to me? Why did some people on the council—why did Fortalecen—look at me how they did?" My voice dropped. "Why does he hate me so much?"

Inquieto's eyes grew deep and serious, the soft amber irises barely visible for all the black that shadowed them.

"Carmen, you're the first intelligent species to interact with paz in thousands of years. But you're not the first known in our history."

"Really? What happened?"

"As Prístina said, there are a few rare paz in the world who have the skill to decipher knowledge from the remnants of the past. They are the most deeply embedded in Gnosia, forming a select conclave called the Sumergida. Most paz only use Gnosia for current communication that is relevant to the here and now, but the Sumergida value the past, and they remember, vaguely, what happened . . . before."

"Before the last erasure of Gnosia? Twenty thousand years ago?"

Inquieto nodded, pacing a few steps as he gathered his thoughts. "Our ancestors knew ahead of time that a disaster was on the horizon—just as we do now. The details of what happened are vague, but the Sumergida have agreed that a small group of our people traversed to a different planet in hope of finding a safe place to live, but that some catastrophe must have occurred there. Perhaps . . . a war. Our ancestors were as peaceful as we are; they hoped to establish a positive relationship with any intelligent species they encountered and share a planet in peace. They would have brought few, if any, defensive weapons on their journey. But their opponents might have had weapons and . . ." He shivered, but managed to continue.

"Afterward, the explorers returned to Paz but brought their immense emotional trauma with them. It infected Gnosia and spread like a virus throughout the entire planet. Oscuro then orbited too close as expected. Solar storms disrupted Gnosia and separated my ancestors from one another in mind, but their emotional trauma, the pain, the horror of other intelligent species . . . remained. It was too ingrained in each and every individual to be erased. My ancestors were forced underground for three thousand years with nothing but fear and agony from an unprecedented conflict to keep them company in the dark, while they scraped survival from the rocks.

"When Oscuro withdrew, paz were able to join through Gnosia again. Rather than heal, their trauma grew, and it still remains, now, ancient and embedded into the collective psyche."

He surfaced from his dark maze of thought and met my eyes.

"Carmen, I told you the truth when I said all paz are peaceful. The only time we engaged in war in remaining memory, the *only* time, was when we interacted with another species." His voice turned hoarse. "A species separate from Gnosia. We call the people of the foreign planet los cortados. On the rare occasions that anyone speaks of them at all."

Los cortados. Spanish. *The severed ones.*

Inquieto raised his palm and sent a pulse of electrolocation at the room's shadowed entrance. Satisfied no one was listening, he continued. His hand shook a little.

"Carmen. I know you—humans—are nothing like los cortados. But the mistrust paz have for other species based on that ancient fear . . . Nearly half the council was reluctant to consider looking for Earth's coordinates, and Fortalecen's pubcom ploy today might only be the start of his efforts to sway the rest. If we can't convince my people that you are peaceful, that you are like *us*, then, Carmen, there's a high probability the council won't risk sending you home."

My meal seemed to evaporate in my stomach. I looked from one of Inquieto's eyes to the other.

"That's why you're open to Prístina's plan," I whispered. My bottom lip trembled. "Because that's my only way home?"

"I'm sorry."

"And if the council judges me and decides I'm some violent being, will they do anything worse to me?"

"I won't let them," he said. "But I ask that you trust me, and I think we have to trust in Prístina."

"I can't believe all this is happening," I said. "Why me? Why did this have to happen to me, Inquieto?"

"Perhaps because you seem strong enough to bear it," he said. "Maybe another human couldn't have."

"You don't know any other humans."

"I'm happy I get to start with you," he said. His fire-agate eyes glittered with admiration, but he blinked, and a gentle longing seemed to supplant it. "Are you all right?"

I shrugged one shoulder and looked down, rolling my eyes at the entire situation. Yet his assurances kindled the ember of hope inside me that had nearly snuffed out.

Silence fell upon us; I sank beneath its fog.

"Would you like to rest?" he asked after a moment.

"Do you have to go back to work?" I mumbled.

"People rest when the suns are highest," he said. "The others only left early because . . ." He shook his head. "It doesn't matter. I'd rather stay with you."

CHAPTER ELEVEN

I COULDN'T SLEEP.

Insomnia had never been one of my impediments. I was always fall-into-bed, lights-out Carmen. Even when caught in the thralls of an intense research project, I could pass out so fast, people were envious. Crispin was.

Ever since my abduction from Earth, I didn't just count sheep; I hunted them. I prowled among my consciousness as a wolf, trying to pick them off one by one so I could just. Fall. Asleep.

My schedule was so off from Paz's shortened day-night cycle, I felt like I was in a continuous state of jetlag. I'd hoped to fall asleep early so I could wake up when Inquieto did the next morning, but that seemed like an impossible outcome now.

I sat up in bed, the blanket slipping down my chest into my lap. My eyes latched onto Inquieto's spiraling galaxy artwork on the wall. A strong surge of nostalgia hit, and I scowled and ran a hand through my hair. I debated whether I should leave the room for about two seconds before deciding my restlessness would never be cured by holing up.

I stood and straightened the short, black shift I was wearing as pajamas. The closet nook held only a few options, but

I was pleased by this one, as smooth as silk sheets. I tiptoed down the stairs and was surprised to see Inquieto's bedroom door was open, vapor swirling in its frame. I peeked my head inside. His room didn't have a narrow staircase like mine, so I could see straight into the dim stillness.

Inquieto lay on his bed, quiet with slumber. His long limbs sprawled out in perfect, idle relaxation, so different from his usual tension. The blanket was tangled around his waist and legs, and one foot stuck out, the golden sole shimmering a little. I smiled and took a small step into the room.

I lifted my gaze up his bare torso, which was mostly white. His abs and pectorals were indeed as muscular as they'd felt when I'd bumped into him before, defined by slivers of gold. His belly button was a pinched line of a scar. He had no nipples at all, confirming my suspicion that the flat-chested female paz probably didn't have milk-producing breasts.

I looked down at my body for the briefest of moments before my cheeks burned, and I felt a violent, writhing squirm in my gut. I conjured Marea's face as she'd judged my appearance.

What must I look like to them? The paz were so elegant and sleek, with their pearly skin, shimmering like gilded statues.

In contrast, I was soft and hairy with green eyes that seemed . . . off. So unnecessarily complicated and messy in comparison with the paz's onyx orbs. My cheeks were speckled with uneven freckles, not beautiful smooth gold. My lips were fuller and pink, my breasts and hips larger and superfluous. My hands were stubbier, with weak-looking lines in my palms and dull nails that were so different from the polished gold or white nails of the paz, which all looked like they had gotten fresh manicures.

No wonder they viewed me as a beast.

I had never been embarrassed of my body. I knew its flaws; I knew its attractive qualities. I had always enjoyed it and been comfortable in my own skin, even when eyed with confusion from someone trying to discern what race I was, or worse, the glares from those who looked down upon me because of my brown skin and dark hair, a sentiment that had become even more brazen in recent years, a terrifying prospect. But to me, and many, I was considered pretty.

Here, I felt ugly. I felt ashamed. I felt a drive to look different than I did.

And I hated that feeling.

Inquieto mumbled something, drawing me out of my spiraling thoughts. I watched his marble lips move in light half words before they went slack again. He tucked his chin against his gold-laced collarbone. His eyelids fluttered.

What did paz dream about? I wondered. Did they project their dreams into collective Gnosia; could they share them with others while they slept? A smile tugged the corner of my mouth at that notion, wishing I could step into his head, just for a moment.

I wanted to linger, to keep watching his gentle breaths and listen for more endearing, mumbled words. Realizing how creepy that would look if he woke up, not to mention how ridiculous I now felt, I backed away and headed for the hallway.

I wasn't sure what Pristina would do if she caught me wandering alone unsupervised, but I didn't want to find out. I needed to be alone, find somewhere to think. Luckily, the round foyer offered many options. I chose a dark archway I hadn't yet explored, but halfway down the long hallway, a door emitted a soft red glow. I hesitated.

"Carmen?"

I jumped like a thief in the night and looked inside the red-glowing room. Pristina sat in a low chair near the center, but it was the object beside her that stole my attention. A red light shone down upon a waist-high pedestal, where an orange egg the size of a grapefruit glowed like a setting sun. I could feel the heat from the doorway, like a comforting fireplace on a winter's night.

My lips parted. I took an involuntary step closer before my eyes jumped to Prístina. But she only smiled.

"Would you like to come in?"

"Is that . . . ?"

"My child. We know the egg is healthy; Father assessed it earlier, but I can't help but watch over it. Come in," she insisted, beckoning me inside with her four-knuckled fingers.

I looked between her and the glowing egg. Inquieto's words—*los cortados*—slunk through my mind. Prístina's open-minded trust to allow an alien like me near her unborn child was encouraging. Shying away from her offer of friendship probably wouldn't be wise.

I slipped her a small smile as I approached the egg. My skin grew warmer the closer I got, but chills raced up my arms and raised the hairs on the back of my neck.

The egg was stunning. The red light from above penetrated the translucent shell, revealing the gentle curl of a tiny fetus floating inside, like a fossil suspended in amber. As I witnessed the beginning of a new life, powerful images swept into my mind, more vivid with each step I took.

Mamá singing me to sleep as I curled up with my favorite blanket and my stuffed polar bear, Popsicle, that never left my arms. Running through the house in her high heels, clomping on the hardwood floors while she laughed and Dad yelled at me to stop scuffing them up; he was trying to watch the game. Mamá dusting Maseca off her hands as she tied a toddler-sized apron around my waist, embroidered with tiny flowers and *Carmen* on its front—Abuela had made it for me for my third birthday. The smell of tamales, right out of the steamer, the first warm bite melting in my mouth as I grinned and Mamá wiped crumbs from my face.

Those were some of my earliest memories, and they flooded into me so fast, tears blurred the already-fuzzy outlines of the developing paz child nestled in the safety of its eggshell.

Prístina stood and came beside me. "Would you like to touch it?"

I blinked tears away and shook my head.

"I'd better not."

"Try," she said. "That shell is stronger than nano-glass. You won't hurt it. Never mind what Mother said at andalim."

I swallowed. I'd almost forgotten Marea's biting comment about me being dangerous with an egg in the house. That made me want to touch the egg out of spite, but as I laid my hand upon the warm shell, all negative emotions fled. The shell was supple and rubbery, the orange hue marbled with red. I glanced down at the bandage on my arm.

"The stem cells of discarded shells aid healing," Prístina said, noticing. "Inquieto said you're so close to paz DNA, they work on you, too."

"I'm still in shock that's possible. That we can be so similar."

My attention flashed back to the egg when it jolted under my hand. The fetus twitched and kicked its shell with one tiny foot. It wiggled its toes.

"When will it . . . hatch?" I asked, mesmerized as the fetus stilled again, floating in its amniotic fluid in sweet repose. I envied it, so cozy and oblivious to the chaotic world.

"Not until next winter. The egg will be around the size of your head then." Prístina rumbled a little and sat back down in her chair, folding her legs to the side and clasping her sandaled ankles together. She gestured to a nearby seat in welcome, and I took it.

"How big was it when you . . . laid it?"

"Around the size of a kinos."

"That small?" I pictured the pea-sized, orange fungi that Inquieto and I had prepared for andalim. "So, it didn't hurt at all?"

"No." She frowned. "Does it hurt when humans lay eggs?"

I cleared my throat. "We . . . we don't. Lay eggs. Once our eggs are fertilized, we carry babies in our uterus for nine—um, nine of Earth's moon cycles, so instead of hatching, they just come out fully developed without a shell. And yeah, it hurts a lot. I've never experienced it, but . . ." I shrugged.

Despite the fact that many of my old high school friends were posting baby photos all over social media, motherhood was still a far-off idea in my head. I couldn't think about having my own kid without being dragged into thoughts of Mamá . . . how she would never be around to see her grandchild. I'd pushed the thought away countless times. I did so again.

Prístina's eyes were round, reminding me of Inquieto's. "That's quite . . ."

"I'm sorry. Does that disturb you?"

"It's different," she said in a tone of practiced diplomacy, but her next words sounded genuine. "I can see why Inquieto is fascinated by you. It's good to see him . . ."

"To see him what?"

"Invested. In a person, rather than just animals. We've never seen him care for anyone the way he has for you in mere days. And standing up to Mother like that . . ."

"What's her deal? Marea?"

Prístina's face was unreadable. After a moment, she spoke with care. "Inquieto's . . . a little different from the rest of us."

"I've noticed."

She looked aside, a tender smile on her lips. "I don't think less of my little brother, even if he doesn't realize it. And Mother, she feels the same way. She wants what's best for him. She doesn't know how to show it other than being overbearing."

I failed to agree with Prístina's generous interpretation of Marea's behavior, but I swallowed my comment.

"Where's your House partner?" I asked instead, nodding at the egg. "He wasn't here today."

"I don't have one. I chose artificial insemination. Many do, since House partnerships are based on forging a stronger connection to Gnosia rather than a need for procreation. Though, many still use traditional means to conceive. I'm dedicated to our people on a grander scale at the moment. I haven't found anyone to deepen my connection to Gnosia, rather than being a distraction."

"A politician has to have a deep connection to Gnosia? Can some people broadcast, or receive, or whatever, more powerfully than others?"

"That's correct," she answered. "Many politicians are born with a closer connection than most to Gnosia; they can understand the needs and desires of others as fluidly as they understand their own. Many are recognized as likely candidates from an early age and are trained to decipher wisdom from impulse. They learn to guide their people through delicate, compassionate persuasion. It is not a legal requirement, but those who perform well are chosen officially by the Will of the people."

"Inquieto mentioned a conclave. The Sumergida? He said they're the paz who have the deepest connection to Gnosia, but they aren't politicians, right?"

"The Sumergida," Prístina echoed, her eyebrows raised slightly. I couldn't tell if her tone was impressed or skeptical. "They are keepers of knowledge, choosing to study rather than lead. They delve into realms of Gnosia that may be of interest to some, but aren't suited for practical applications. It is rare they are consulted by anyone. They are the most isolated among us, with only a few underground outposts around the planet's equator, but there are enough of them to share the task of their internal explorations without impairment."

"Sounds pretty esoteric," I said.

Prístina gazed at her egg, wearing a gentle frown.

"I wasn't raised to be a politician, Carmen. Not like Fortalecen or the others. I was only an artist, but when I decided to become a mother, I couldn't imagine raising a child in darkness, underground. Maybe I shouldn't have brought this little one into the world, considering the state of things, but . . ." She shook her head, and the usual intensity in her eyes returned. "My supporters don't view my lack of experience as prohibitive. They are awakening to new ideals, so much so, they chose me to represent them as the youngest high counselor on record, even younger than Fortalecen was when he was elected. He held that record before me. His unique bond with Gnosia aided his political ascent—his connection is deeper and more pervasive than any paz in generations. Whatever combination of genes—his bioelectricity, his mental capacity . . . Well, suffice it to say he was born that way."

"Does Fortalecen resent you because you moved faster but took an unconventional path to do it?" I asked.

"Not resentment. Dignidad Fortalecen doesn't think in terms of emotions. It makes him a formidable opponent. He thinks I won't perform well since I haven't taken the necessary steps to reach the position of counselor like he has, and more importantly, that I'm not as deeply connected to Gnosia as he. He is determined to win this conflict of ideas, not for personal gain, but for the good of Paz. Extremely determined."

"No kidding."

She gave a small nod, and then leaned forward.

"Carmen, we didn't mean to overwhelm you at andalim. We can see how much of a person you are. How paz-like you are. Fortalecen's pubcom segment showed you at your worst in captivity. We can show you at your best, as the intelligent, *equal* species that you are in a refined setting in which your personhood cannot be ignored. The council has decreed that you may attend an upcoming event, one that could be a good test of your behavior in a large public setting, yet still in a contained environment."

"Oh, really?" I said with a skeptical frown.

"It was Counselor Fortalecen's idea," Prístina said. "He denied responsibility for the pubcom segment, and I was as surprised as anyone when he invited you to his Legacy District's preview event. He's been planning it for nearly a year now, and *many* guests will attend."

"That sounds suspicious."

She gave me a reluctant nod. "It does. But I have to admit that without his agreement, I may not have been able to coax the council to allow you to interact with the public at all, especially since the event is only four days away."

"Four days? Prístina."

"We'll prepare you, Carmen. Don't worry."

"What is this event about?"

"The Legacy District is intended to provide our people with an 'improved' state of living underground. This event is a preview of a completed section, where Fortalecen and his supporters will demonstrate the fresh luxuries he claims his district can offer. But I think we can use the event to our advantage. We will have many supporters there, and most people are far more curious about you now that you are *not* a curio. I've secured a tailor to make clothes for you to wear during your stay here. Why don't we commission one Earth-style outfit? We need to show everyone not just you, but your *culture*. We need a stunning image that will imprint a mark on Gnosia. Won't you consider it?"

I twisted my fingers together as I listened. I had just spent what felt like weeks in a cage being stared at by spectators in a zoo. The last thing I wanted was to parade in front of more people like a dancing monkey.

"Carmen, if you can help other people see your value, then maybe, even after you've returned to your home, paz can learn to welcome viewpoints from citizens who've had experiences outside the norm. Inquieto could be included for the first time in his life." She looked at her egg with a sad frown. "And anyone else different who may come along."

Her lips pressed together, but she looked back at me with a kind smile. I unraveled my fingers and squeezed my knees.

"I'll sleep on it," I said. I stood, shaking out the borderline painful tension in my hands. "I'm not sure if . . . But I'll think about it, Prístina."

My eyes rose once more to her glowing egg. I sent its mother a nod of goodbye and fled the room.

CHAPTER TWELVE

I THOUGHT ABOUT it. Now I wished I'd come to a different conclusion.

"Does it look *that* bad?" I asked, staring up at Cálido's grimace as we stood in Inquieto's living room, alone.

Cálido tried to rearrange his face into a smile as he looked at my bright red lips, made possible by a paste I'd commissioned of him when Inquieto had revealed that this Legacy District event was going to be a fancy occasion.

"Is it supposed to look like you're bleeding?" Cálido asked.

"No!" I covered my mouth and flipped the lid closed on the small container full of red paste. "It's just on my lips, right?" I lowered my hand. "It didn't go everywhere?"

"It's only on your lips," he said, his cheeky smile returning. "I made it just how you asked. Edible, though I can't guarantee it tastes good, but it will stay on all night without rubbing off on anything."

"I'm not going to eat it. I just meant it needs to be safe to put on my lips." I groaned and rubbed a finger hard along my bottom lip. As Cálido promised, none came off.

"Carmen?" Inquieto called, his footsteps approaching from down the hallway.

"Feces," I said, pressing my lips together. Cálido grinned. I wondered if *feces* was going to catch on as the new slang in his youthful social circles.

"How do I get it off, Cálido?"

"I made a liquid solution that will remove it, but I don't have it with me."

"What?" Embarrassment flooded me harder than I expected as I waited for Inquieto to round the corner.

Inquieto had been bouncing back and forth between work and home with the kinetic energy of a Ping-Pong ball. As much as I wanted to demand he stay home to make sure the disciplinarians at the end of the street didn't decide to kidnap me, I was also starting to realize how truly dependent he was upon his curios. Though he lingered a little in the mornings, hesitant to leave me, he always came back cheered, chatting about his day and the animals under his care. After seeing his tension around his mother and realizing how out of place he felt around his family, I started to understand why he was reluctant to consider sending the curios away from Paz, away from him. As he'd said, he would miss them. Maybe I'd underestimated how much he really would. And especially since Smita was still in the museum, it was hard for me to build up a grudge.

Inquieto needed an escape. So did I. My job was light-years behind me. In its absence, my momentum toward the future was arrested. The ever-present hole in my heart had deepened and widened, crumbling at the edges. I couldn't scramble fast enough to outrun the expanding pit and stay on solid ground; I was backsliding into the realm of darkness and hopelessness that had nearly swallowed me after Mamá's death.

I envied Inquieto's coming and going, his rapid race through each day that left no time for anxious thoughts. I needed a more important focus than the upcoming Legacy District event to distract me, but that was all I had. So, I had plunged into preparations, all while looking forward to Inquieto's return for midday andalims or in the evenings.

Today, I wished he'd stayed at work a little longer.

"Hello, brother," Inquieto said with a smile. "Carmen! Are you hurt?"

He dashed toward me, inspecting my lips with wide eyes.

"I'm fine," I said, covering my mouth again so my voice came out muffled. "It's something for the Legacy event."

Inquieto raised his eyebrows and looked at Cálido, who tilted his head and shrugged one shoulder.

"You're the behavioral expert on other species," he rumbled, and headed for the door. "I'll get that solution for you, Carmen."

He sauntered down the hall, leaving me alone with Inquieto. My stomach squirmed, and I kept my hand over my mouth.

"Carmen, may I see? I was only worried. I hope I didn't offend you."

I sighed and lowered my hand. His round eyes were drawn straight to my bright red lips. He tilted his head, then looked over my entire face with a growing smile.

"I like it," he said when his smile had become a full-on grin.

I crossed my arms and eyed my current outfit. "It doesn't match what I'm wearing now. It probably looks stupid."

Prístina's tailor had altered several different paz-style robes for me, which I was grateful covered my shoulders, back, and arms so I wouldn't have to wrap up like a mummy every time I stepped outside, though I hadn't yet been allowed to give their sunblock abilities a test run. They were all of varying shades of cream, with trims of pastel green, pale blue, or brown. The one I wore now was dark khaki, with pearl trim along the sleeves and the floor-length hem. The tailor had also managed to fashion me some closed-toe boots, made of the same firm brown material as paz sandals, though in the comfort of the house, I wasn't wearing them.

"Is your clothing for the event finished?" Inquieto asked. "May I see?"

I curled my bare toes on the cold floor. "No. It's a surprise."

He frowned, looking wary. "A surprise?"

"Yeah. Like, a good one."

"A good surprise?"

I laughed. "Yes. You don't surprise each other sometimes for fun?"

He scrunched his eyebrows. "Why would we?"

"The anticipation. Knowing you're about to make someone else happy when they least expect it. Humans do it all the time."

"That's so unique!"

I laughed again. "Oh, now it *has* to be a surprise."

His smile turned warm, but I lowered my gaze to the floor, suddenly feeling self-conscious again. "Not sure everyone else will think of it as a good surprise. Do you really think this will work?"

"Be yourself," he said, "and it will."

His eyes and voice were reassuring and sweet, but the next evening, when I held my commissioned dress up to my body and looked at my projected reflection in the bathroom, I didn't just have second thoughts about the event less than an hour away. I had third thoughts, fourth thoughts, fifth thoughts, all the way to infinity.

My original vision of the dress had stemmed from nothing but a pure lash of anger and spite. If everyone was going to stare at me as some alien freak, I might as well give them brilliant fodder. But when Inquieto had expressed such interest and curiosity, I'd found myself more concentrated on what *his* reaction would be; the anticipation had plagued me all night and into the day.

Now all thoughts of other people's reactions, including Inquieto's, fled. I was about to put on human clothing.

I crushed the bright red, silky fabric to my face and inhaled its scent as if it might carry a piece of Earth with it, but there was nothing but the growing familiarity of the cedar-like scent of Paz fabric and the warm, earthy scent of Inquieto's house.

My hands trembled as I pulled on the dress. I hadn't met the tailor in person, only sent off my measurements with Prístina, but they must have been the best damn tailor in Raíz. They'd ordered special dye to make the fabric so red, and went above and beyond to ensure the dress was worthy of a red-carpet gala. The garment was nothing like the loose, stoic robes I'd worn thus far. The fabric hugged and emphasized my every curve, starting with shorter straps than paz women's shoulder ridges could ever allow, leading into deep cleavage that they didn't possess. The dress then cinched around my thin waist before slinking outward to define my wide hips and flow gracefully to the floor.

The tailor's most impressive feat was crafting sparkling red stiletto heels. I slipped them on, and they peeked through thin slits on either side of the dress, propelling me three inches off the floor. I had already dusted my eyelids with shimmering gold paint, which Prístina used to embellish the golden patterns of her face, and lined them in subtle black, which she similarly used to enhance her black eyes. I'd braided two sections of my hair on either side of my head and twirled them together into a knot on the base of my neck, allowing the rest to unravel as a dark, elegant waterfall down my right shoulder.

I was unable to part with my oxygen concentrator, which hung around my neck like a bulky necklace. The party was going to be underground, and much of it in the open streets of the Legacy District rather than inside buildings with good air circulation. My outfit could withstand the flaw in its aesthetic just fine.

Although I had debated whether or not to use the lip paste Cálido and Inquieto had both remarked looked like blood, I'd decided to return to my idea that, if I was going to show off my culture, I might as well go all the way.

Once I was dressed, I took a slow breath, knowing Inquieto was outside, waiting. I stared into the reflection of my green eyes and coached myself to buck up. I tightened my fists and unclenched them in quick succession, and then opened the vaporous door. I peered my head around the temporary shield of the stalagmite column.

Inquieto stood in the living room, wearing a robe made of black fabric that was much finer than his usual, worn work clothes. Two wide strips of glossy black cloth ran down his front like long lapels. His golden back was exposed between the stiff, sharp-cut style of his backward-vest top, so I could see every small flex and subtle roll of his muscles as he stretched out his arms. I raised my eyebrows as I saw an extra set of bones between his neck and the inner curves of his shoulder blades. If the bones were raised higher, they could create the distinct shoulder ridges of paz women, a hormonal development in girls at puberty, perhaps.

He finished his stretch and tilted his neck, trying to work out a knot. Such human gestures. Yet, most paz couldn't see the similarities.

I tried to gain courage to enter the room as I watched him straighten his elbow-length sleeve so that its seam aligned with the crease of his elbow. Then he stopped, still gripping his sleeve between thumb and forefinger. He stared at some empty place past his hands, experiencing some thought too absorbing to allow multitasking. The slits in his golden back twitched open; the pearly skin inside flashed in the light.

I took a big breath and stepped out from behind the column. He jerked his head my way. I raised my chin, waiting for him to comment on how ridiculous I looked, that he couldn't possibly take me to the party looking like this, but he only stared. His lips parted, and his black eyes shifted over every aspect of my appearance, growing increasingly bright with every small sight. Then he stepped back, as if five feet away was not enough space to take in the full effect.

"I've never seen any . . ." He cleared his throat to get a better handle on his hoarse voice. "Carmen, this is a *very* good surprise."

My breath finally escaped in a laugh. I felt a sweet smile spread on my face as my cheeks warmed. I looked aside, then flashed my eyes back up to him.

"You don't look bad, yourself," I said.

Clearly, I wasn't the only one who'd sent off my measurements to a tailor. His robes defined his broad shoulders and sleek chest, and I could see the subtle triangle of his sharp hip bones before the fabric flowed loosely down to the floor. He stood straighter than usual, and his height and long arms displayed an elegance that he often hid in tight, nervous hunches or quick bouts of energy, but subtle pink bloomed under the pale skin of his cheeks, and I realized he was fighting a blush as much as I was.

"Time to go?" I said. Inquieto's admiration lifted a weight off my shoulders for the night ahead. I figured I'd better act on it before I changed my mind.

He nodded. "A cell is waiting downstairs."

I followed him through the maze of the house, down through three underground stories. I felt like my stilettos were precarious stilts in Paz's lesser gravity, but I mostly got the hang of walking straight by the time we exited onto a private docking station within Provenance District. The underground reflections of the surface houses spread out around us, sparser than the downtown skyscrapers. As we began traveling in our cell, we passed several stretches of glowing purple fields of fungi like I'd seen on pubcom.

"Is this what you always wear on Earth?" Inquieto asked. I drew my eyes away from the windows.

"I've never worn anything like this in my life," I said with a dry, nervous laugh. "But it's what a human woman would wear to an event like this. I've worn simpler dresses, though, and makeup and heels." I wiggled my foot. His eyes traveled down my body until he reached my shoes, peeking through the slits in my dress.

He gave a purring rumble. "You can walk in those?"

"Well enough."

"Does their height have significance?"

"Significance? Well, typically, only grown women wear them," I said, naturally donning my anthropologist's voice, even when describing my own culture. "They emphasize her legs and, well . . . They're supposed to make her sexually attractive." I shrugged, my unbiased tone retreating in the wake of an unexpected bout of demure eyelash-batting.

"You want to appear attractive in front of . . . everyone?" His eyes flicked from one of mine to the other with avid interest, though he seemed a little shocked. "Is that something humans normally do?"

"Well . . . I mean, yes? Do paz not try to look attractive in public?"

"Paz express attraction in private frequencies of Gnosia. No one else is supposed to know, if they're subtle enough." He swallowed, looking aside.

"I see." I fiddled with my dress's shoulder strap to make sure it was secure. "I guess that's just another animalistic thing about humans, hmm? Showing off with flamboyant physical features."

"I don't think it's animalistic."

"Well. Being attractive isn't going to matter for me here anyway," I said bitterly. When he didn't say anything to dispute it, I felt even worse. "You think they'll laugh?"

"No," he said. "They won't be able to look away."

"If they're anything like you," I pointed out. His eyes widened.

"I'm sorry," he said, and looked down.

"It's okay." Everyone else scoured my appearance like I was a freak, but when Inquieto looked at me, I had to admit that his awe almost made me feel . . . special.

Soon, the glowing fungi fields disappeared, and nothing but the blue, red, and amber lights of the celestial nebula-like city dazzled my eyes.

"So, we got all dressed up," I said. "Is this event only for the wealthy?"

"Not at all," he said, a small crease between his eyebrows. "Government officials from each of the Thousand Regions of Paz and influential people related to the Legacy District were invited first, but the rest of the general public who wanted to attend were chosen through random lots. As for clothing, everyone can afford some level of formal attire. Some higher quality than others," he conceded, "but no one is left without."

"Is your sister considered wealthy? As a high counselor?"

Inquieto rumbled a little in his throat. "Moderately. Her career requires a high level of intelligence, aptitude, time, and responsibility, and so, yes, she is paid proportionately."

"And . . . you're paid less than she is?"

"Yes. All wages for each career path are strictly regulated by the government, and since my career is experimental at this stage, they aren't as willing to devote funding. My salary is adequate, though, and my career is more rewarding than any amount of money it comes with."

"I'm a burden to you," I said. "Can you afford—"

"Do not worry about that, Carmen. I'm glad you're here."

I looked down. It felt weird to be the recipient of Inquieto's nonstop generosity. No matter what he said, I felt too dependent on him, weak and vulnerable. What if something happened to him? What if he stopped caring?

"What about people who don't have skills?" I asked, my voice small. "Or have disabilities?"

He hesitated a small moment, his face guarded, but then he adopted his tone of reading out of a textbook that occasionally came out of him, as if he were reciting an explanation that he couldn't put into his own words.

"Everyone is recognized as having value in the greater whole of Gnosia. In cases of severe disability, people are given a generous stipend so their needs are met and they can live as full a life as anyone else. Is that not how it is on Earth?"

"Well, it depends, but mostly no. A lot of people are left to fend for themselves; many live in awful conditions, homeless, starving. People die of poverty. All the wealth on the planet is owned by less than one percent of the world's population. Some of those people earn it, but they only give a relatively miniscule amount of their wealth to charities. A lot of them inherited their money and hoard it or waste it on extravagance without having earned a penny for themselves. It's disgusting."

"Some humans don't have homes? Food? Are you saying they are left to die?"

"It's bad, I know."

"Everyone here is taken care of. Everyone has a place where they fit, naturally, with contentment. They say everyone has something to offer. Even someone . . ." He winced and looked down, and his voice lowered. "And I don't think it's necessary to be part of Gnosia to have that perspective."

"I don't think it is, either. But I guess other humans think differently."

"Differently," he echoed. He took a breath, and his countenance cleared. "I don't understand this . . . inheriting money. Why?"

"Parents like to pass on their legacy and make sure their children are taken care of after they die."

"That's an interesting way to express the sentiment." His words gleaned a smile, as if he were clinging to some hope that there were good aspects of humanity. I knew the feeling. "It sounds like humans are very close to one another. Family bonds, social groups . . ."

"Something like that," I said, stopping his descent into analyzing humans via animal characteristics.

"Are you close to your family?" he asked, cautious.

"Yes," I answered automatically. But my heart twisted. "Not really. I . . . I haven't visited my grandparents or cousins in Mexico in, god, I guess almost ten years now. My father left when I was a kid, so I haven't seen him or any of his side of the family since."

"And your mother?"

I paused. "She died. Ten years ago." I took a shaky breath. "I don't have any siblings, and I don't . . . I don't really have any close friends. There are people I work with who I like well enough, and there's one who I . . . I miss him. But even we weren't close enough to . . . I never really let him in."

"You'll have a chance to see them all again," Inquieto said after a moment. "Your mother's family. You'll have a chance to . . . let your friend in, as you put it. When you go back."

"Yes, I . . . I guess I will."

My next breath felt like I was straining against a vise. I inhaled through my oxygen mask, but I let it dangle around my neck when our cell slowed. We were stuck in a long line of cells, some individual, some hooked together into suspended trains, all headed toward the enormous, drilled hole in the side of Provenance District's north wall—the Legacy District.

I looked past a couple of enormous stalactites, wrapped in a spiral of glowing red and blue lights. The construction equipment had been moved away in the past two days, allowing the glimmering white banner, with the government symbol of a lower half of a circle under a horizontal line, to be the sole focus of the cavernous entrance. The Legacy District shone with brilliant light beyond, and I caught a glimpse of multistory buildings inside. They were constructed with the familiar pagoda-style architecture of Raíz, but these bore a distinct difference: they didn't touch the ceiling, meaning they had no mirror versions reflected aboveground—striking symbolism for Fortalecen's Isolationist views to remain on Paz and abandon the surface, no mistake.

Our cell tilted down a gentle slope toward a row of docking stations. The cells ahead of us parallel parked into individual stations, so all together they looked like a car-carrier truck on the freeway. I tapped my fingers on the cushion of my seat as we waited our turn. We skipped the first several stations, and when we reached the last station, I knew why. A group of disciplinarians stood waiting, having cleared the way of guests.

"I knew this was a trap," I said, tensing. "If Fortalecen invited us—"

"Carmen, it's all right. I should have told you they would be here."

"You knew?"

"They are keeping others away so we have space to enter the Legacy District."

"Where's Prístina?"

"She doesn't want your arrival to be an obvious political statement; if she were with us, it could be interpreted that way. She's somewhere inside, though."

I felt a thud in my chest as our cell hitched into the docking station, which lowered us down like an elevator straight to the disciplinarians. Most looked as on edge as I felt, but when one of them approached our cell, the others relaxed as if he'd infused them with courage. I recognized the leader as Citizen Sirven, the short, stern disciplinarian who had escorted us from the High Council meeting.

Inquieto opened the door to our cell, and it unfolded into a ramp. I stood right away, wishing I had some way to defend myself, knowing the disciplinarians could stun me at a moment's notice. I should have kept that damn kitchen knife.

"Welcome, Citizen Reúnen," Sirven said with a crisp nod. While his stern frown didn't dissipate, he folded his hands behind his back in a casual pose.

"Thank you, Citizen," Inquieto replied. "Carmen?"

I let out a slow breath and stepped onto the ramp. My next inhale brought the scent of burnt matches into my nostrils, even more potent than in other parts of Raíz I'd visited, no doubt from the recent construction. The lack of good air quality piled yet another stressor onto my already-strained nerves.

Beyond the disciplinarians' circle, people's eyes latched onto me even faster than I would have thought. I bowed my head and took a quick breath through my oxygen concentrator as if I were stealing the air. Everyone of influence was going to be at this event, every prestigious reporter, prominent socialite, elite politician—and Inquieto, a humble animal behaviorist propelled into fame by his association with me, a human among paz.

Knowing that I was putting Inquieto through this horror show was enough to make me stand tall. I would not make a fool out of him. I was here to show these ogling paz how intelligent and classy a human could be, and damned if I couldn't succeed.

My high heels clanged on the ringing metal ramp, drawing more attention. I squirmed away from the embarrassing feeling of being way overdressed. There was no backing out now. I, and my ruby-red dress, were here to stay.

Inquieto took in all the growing stares, a quick pulse at his temple, but when I reached him, he smiled and looked only at me. All uncertainty vanished from his eyes. He gave me a nod of solidarity.

"Are you ready?" he asked.

"As I'll ever be."

Inquieto nodded to the disciplinarians, who escorted us through the crowd. People parted like the Red Sea, so I was able to get as good a look at them as they did me. None of the guests' finery was anywhere near as bright as mine, but that *had* been my intent. They wore a blunted cascade of dim hues, but their materials at least varied. Their robes now had the pearly sheen of silk. Their decorative shawls and sashes were trimmed with glinting silver and gold. Most of the women's necks were wrapped from jaw to collarbone with fabric as detailed as lace, but they left their elegant, flashing shoulder ridges exposed. The men's robes bore long, silky lapels down their fronts from shoulders to floor, though only a few were as dramatically black as Inquieto's.

Everyone wore subtle jewels of pale blue, pearly white, or jade so dark it was nearly black. They glittered on long strands around their necks or waists, or dangled from hooks over the top curves of their ears. No doubt the idea of piercings would seem barbaric, though Inquieto had made no comment on the little empty holes in my earlobes, if he'd even noticed.

We finally passed under the enormous, draping banner and entered the district. The space opened up into a wide street paved with pure white stone flags, giving everyone room to spread out.

"Thank you, Citizens," Inquieto said with a deferent nod to Sirven, yet his tone was surprisingly dismissive.

Sirven nodded in return, though his mouth formed a hard line. "We'll be watching, should you need us."

"Carmen will be well with me," Inquieto said, and just like that, we were walking away.

"We're allowed to wander?" I said, shifting a furtive glance back at the disciplinarians, who had fanned out but weren't following us too closely.

"Yes. Prístina ensured that," Inquieto answered. "Being surrounded by disciplinarians the entire evening wouldn't help people view you as a peaceful, equal being."

"Damn right," I said, looking around with a bit more clarity. The cavern ceiling loomed high overhead, but I felt like the enormous mass of people were walls closing in. I took another deep breath through my oxygen concentrator. Walking slowly, I'd only needed it every few minutes; at our somewhat faster pace, five breaths had done me in. I tried to keep from blinking too much, but my eyes were starting to sting, and my nose itched.

Then I saw something familiar that I prayed would offer salvation.

"Inquieto, what's that?" I pointed to a row of waist-high tables along one side of the street. Countless small glasses that looked like votive candle holders swirled with a honey-hued liquid. People picked up glasses and sipped the beverage as they milled down the street.

I was already walking toward the nearest table while Inquieto answered, "Elua. It has properties that can set people at ease, but I don't think—"

"Is it poisonous for me?" I asked as I swiped two glasses from the table.

"No," he answered, "but I don't think now is—"

"If any party calls for a drink, it's this one." I shoved a glass into his hand and clinked my glass against his. "Cheers."

I took a hefty swallow and chased it down with a swift breath through my oxygen concentrator. I didn't know if this elua would chill me out like it did the paz, but god, I hoped it would.

Inquieto clicked his tongue, but he looked at his glass with a slight shake of his head. "What the hurl." He took a swallow.

I laughed. "That's your attempt at human slang?"

The skin around his golden patterns turned pink, but he rumbled with humor. He set our unfinished glasses on a small table that was already covered with empties.

My next step felt like I was floating on the swell of a cool breeze; someone had taken whitewash to my brain and left it clean and carefree. A dreamy smile drifted onto my face. I ignored the throng for the first time, the elua giving me strength to finally climb the oppressive wall.

My mouth opened as I took in the sheer beauty around me. The completed section of the Legacy District was the size of two city blocks. The buildings lining the main street soared at least ten stories high, with glimmering siding the colors of pearl, copper, jade, and onyx. Their pagoda-style roofs were coated in a material that reflected dim light shining down from a strange ceiling, which looked like the stone had been doused in condensation; broad, shallow bubbles of gray-tinted glass clung to the underside.

The double glow between roofs and bubbles was bright enough to make the entire ceiling shine, and in turn, shed natural light down to the street. The white stone paving reflected the light as well, so I felt like we were inside a giant, glowing prism. The rest of the underground Provenance District of Raíz had the illusion of celestial glimmers in a night sky; the Legacy

District felt as charged and invigorating as daylight, generating hope in an effect I could only view as magical.

Thick stone columns that anchored the corners of the buildings were sculpted with an architectural style different from any I'd seen in Raíz. They were etched with rigid, deep, step-cut bas-reliefs and cage-like grids, all grounded in the bedrock foundations of the street. The extreme lighting defined them with severe shadows, giving them a sense of permanence that was starkly different from the sense of exploration and poetry in Prístina's art. The pagoda roofs were distinctly straight and flat.

People meandered in and out of the buildings like they were touring model homes and explored the streets with expressions of awe and admiration. But many stopped mid-stride when they saw me, either for the first time, or the first time in clothing and outside of a zoo habitat. They exchanged glances with one another as if seeking comfort or spreading wordless gossip. Some seemed curious; others were clearly appalled they had to share breathing room with me and hurried past, a reaction I absorbed in a whole new light after Inquieto's revelation of the collective PTSD that paz suffered from their ancient conflict with los cortados.

My skin crawled as I struggled to ignore them. The last thing my jittering nerves needed was to be reminded of my time in the zoo. The elua kept me from running, though, as strange little thoughts swam through my brain like a lullaby—these people weren't really at fault, were they? They were being confronted by a new idea, a new species they'd never encountered. I couldn't really blame them for staring, could I?

I started to stare back as if they were on display in their natural habitat and I was the guest being entertained. Parents walked with their children, the tiny ones clinging to their mothers' backs, the older ones frolicking like little spotted fawns. Groups of friends rumbled in staccato beats. Obvious couples passed around them within bubbles of absorption, admiring each other as much as the wonderous sights around them, though none touched aside from clasping forearms in a formal way as if they were exchanging a multitude of lovers' secrets in their own private Gnosia frequency.

I wondered if Inquieto had ever enjoyed a stroll down the lane with a paz woman. His dedication to the Curio Life Museum made me doubt it, and that brought me strange relief. I realized that I was terrified of someone else occupying his time. I needed him to be devoted to me and getting me home.

I snuck a glance at him, but cringed when a high, piercing whistle shot through my ears. I waited for it to stop, but it kept wailing like a monotone siren.

"What is *that*?" I asked.

"Music."

"Music?"

Inquieto sent me an apologetic wince. "Most of it is only experienced through Gnosia."

"What, so there are like . . . mental singers somewhere?"

"A group of people have organized their 'voices,' in a way, to accompany the instruments in a public frequency, but it's more than just sound. It's difficult to explain."

The single high note continued. "Well, it sucks for people who aren't in Gnosia," I said. "Human music is audible. I think you'd like it."

"I do," Inquieto said, so soft I could barely hear over the persistent whistle and chatter around us. "You altered your voice's pitch in the museum in a way I've never . . . That was music, wasn't it?"

I raised my eyebrows. "Oh . . . that was just a song my mother used to sing to help me fall asleep. When I was a kid."

"It was beautiful."

I swallowed a small lump in my throat and gave him a wry smile. "Well, a lot of music is more upbeat than that."

I listened to the single monotonous note in the air, and the matching note of a silly pop song, which I'd belted out during many a shower as a teen, popped into my head. I sang a snatch of the chorus through laughter, swaying my hips.

Inquieto smiled in delight. His rumble of amusement sounded like a cat's contented purr, but when I saw his look of fascination move to my hips, I felt a sudden warmth rush through my chest. I stopped singing, feeling dizzy.

"Here," Inquieto said, stepping close. He surprised me by pressing my oxygen mask gently against my mouth. I inhaled.

"Thanks," I said, my cheeks growing hot. What was wrong with me? It had to be the elua.

I jumped when a flying object flitted past my head. My heart sped up as I watched a white spherical object the size of a baseball double back toward us.

"Recorder," Inquieto said, blinking away from me as if he were coming out of a dream. He sounded unfazed by such a troubling concept, wearing a content smile. Clearly, his elua was working. He pointed at two more recorders that were circling the street, and I picked out more of them flying throughout the crowded district, swiveling around like they were on the hunt.

I hunched in on myself at the reminder that I was being watched, not just by passing people, but by cameras that would no doubt broadcast this entire event to the planet on pubcom. I'd been singing and swaying like a complete idiot in front of people who didn't even know what audible singing was. I groaned and looked back at the elua table with longing, but at this point, I had to admit that feeling at ease in this setting might not be a wise idea. I'd have to make do with whatever relaxing chemical was still left in me and hope for the best.

"It's a good thing the recorders are here," Inquieto said. "People will see how wonderful you are."

I tilted my head in frustration, but he was right—maybe not about the wonderful part—but if recorders were here, I had to take advantage of them. I looked around, trying to find something to discuss that would show I wasn't just some silly fool.

"What are those?" I asked, pointing to the glass bubbles on the ceiling. An empty cell track wove between them, but it didn't look functional yet.

We resumed our stroll as he answered, "They're meant to absorb and filter sunlight with greater efficiency than we've ever managed before. Our bioelectricity depends on solar charge. Our bodies can store solar energy for years, but three thousand years underground would be quite a test."

"No doubt," I said.

"The more extravagant technology is beyond the filters, though, on the surface," he said.

"Oh?"

"A generated magnetic field to shield our largest cities from solar storms, and therefore protect Gnosia from being disrupted. A test shield is in place over the Legacy District, but if Fortalecen has his way, more will be built over every major city around the globe. He is very proud of it," he said, sounding bitter, "even though it was Mother's team at the Understand who designed it."

I frowned. "Your mother? Is Marea on the Isolationists' side, then?"

"Yes." He'd gone stiff, staring straight ahead.

I let out a low whistle. "This feces gets better and better. Are Cálido and Tenaz here?"

Inquieto's tense muscles sprang like a plucked guitar string. "They're meeting us down the street."

I quirked my eyebrow at him. He rumbled a little, and his sweet smile became mischievous. "You're not the only one who planned a good surprise for tonight."

"I didn't think paz did good surprises."

"We don't. But you made it sound fun."

CHAPTER THIRTEEN

THE CROWD AHEAD of us thickened. People were all trying to get a look at something in the middle of the street, vying for a place in a circle with such intent, they didn't notice me coming until I was right at their backs. But when one woman glanced over her shoulder and saw me, the domino set was knocked down. Everyone around her scattered out of my way.

"Inquieto! Carmen!" called Cálido from within the circled crowd. Tenaz smiled beside him, and quite a few disciplinarians stood around them doing mild crowd control.

I waved nervously at the pair, but then my eyes widened, and I burst into a huge grin.

"Smita!"

Smita tensed from her place at Cálido's side, analyzing me. Little clear oxygen tubes ran from her nostrils to a small rectangular device strapped behind her ears, but her mouth was left free to yip in a joyful greeting. She darted at me full speed, but stopped a few feet from Cálido, wiggling and jumping in the air as if something invisible was holding her back.

I reached her within seconds and dropped to my knees. I scratched her ears and threw my arms around her neck.

"Smita. You're okay." She licked my chin and kept wagging her whole body with excited whines and barks. I laughed through tears.

Her body stilled and leaned against me as I tightened my hug. My lip trembled against her fur. I sniffled, not letting go as I glanced up at Inquieto.

"Thank you," I said, my voice breaking a little.

I had never seen a paz cry; I didn't know if they could, but Inquieto looked so full of joy and compassion, he might as well have been shedding tears.

"I promised you I'd get her out, didn't I?" he said.

I nodded against Smita's soft fur. I pulled back and looked into her face.

"She gets to stay, doesn't she?"

"Yes, with us," Inquieto said. "She doesn't have to go back to the museum, Carmen. I made sure of that. Good surprise?"

I let out a shaky laugh. "The best."

Smita wiggled backward out of my arms. She whipped her head to the right, and her body stiffened as she jutted her snout forward. Something scuttled along the side of the street. An animal the size of a cat, but looked more like a salamander with rubbery skin and feelers on its back, hunched at the edge of a lustrous garden patch between two buildings. I raised my eyebrows as it performed a little playful spin and darted off, looking like it wanted Smita to play tag.

"An ochassa," Inquieto said.

So, that was the creature Inquieto's mother had compared me with at andalim. I felt a low swell of rumbling anger, but it rolled away under a wave of soothing elua.

"Smita's on some kind of leash?" I asked, eyeing the disciplinarians who were still keeping an eye on us and our growing audience.

Cálido lifted his hand; a small white button was clipped to a ring on his finger.

"Ultrasonic waves," he said with a grin. "She's wearing a corresponding device between her shoulders next to the oxygen concentrator. You just can't see it because of all the . . ."

"Hair," Inquieto supplied.

"Fur," I corrected as I stood up. "On animals, we usually call it fur. Cálido, thank you for bringing her here. I . . ." I looked from him, to Inquieto, and to Tenaz. "Thank you."

Tenaz smiled. "We're happy to help, Carmen."

Though Cálido wore traditional men's robes of dark jade with pearl trim, Tenaz's outfit was markedly different. It was bright cobalt blue, and along with a backward-vest top, he wore loose pants that tied around his waist and stopped several inches above his ankles like Thai fishermen's pants. A pale yellow scarf adorned his neck, and yellow fabric crisscrossed over his back in a pattern of four X's.

Smita barked playfully at the ochassa.

"She hasn't wanted to sit still all afternoon," Cálido said.

"She hated containment as much as Carmen did," Inquieto added.

"Come on." I smiled at Smita. "Let's walk."

I took a step, and she leapt in happy anticipation. We both looked at Cálido.

"Don't let me stop you," he said. He flicked his wrist, I assumed either to widen the ultrasonic restraining field or get rid of it entirely. "Go," he said with an enthusiastic shoo.

"I think we should stick together, Cálido," Tenaz said. He exchanged a simultaneous glance with Inquieto.

I frowned, but Smita eyed me with an insistent growl. The strangers watching us backed away with nervous glances, but they still looked entertained, overall.

I took a step, and Smita burst into a full run but stopped only a few feet away, looking back at me expectantly. I laughed and clicked as quickly in my stilettos as I could to catch up. My entourage followed, including the disciplinarians, though they kept their distance, trying to be unobtrusive and failing due to my hypervigilance. I caught a glimpse of one keeping pace with us above our heads on a pedestrian platform that stretched between two buildings three stories up.

Smita's nostrils were fluttering like butterfly wings, but she didn't glue her nose to the ground as she hunted for the little ochassa, who had darted into an extravagant curbside garden. Smita must have been more overwhelmed than I was by Paz's strong odors.

As we strolled past the garden, I was enamored with the plants on display. Grand flowers exploded like fireworks from short, spiky bushes. Fuzzy gray moss, which I'd seen coating rocks aboveground, now cascaded as flowering vines from high rocks like waterfalls. The grass at my feet, normally stunted and brown, was rich and green, dotted with tiny wildflowers arranged in ornate patterns like a Persian rug.

Nearby, an enormous jade plant was splayed on the ground like a scaly starfish; I realized with wonder that it was one of the tall, twisted treelike plants I'd seen dotting the Paz landscapes like a Van Gogh painting. Now, it was unfurled, soaking up the filtered sunlight from the bubble ceiling.

"On the surface, the heat stops the buds from opening," Inquieto said. "They only unfurl in twilight in nature." He paused, surveying the cultivated garden with an expression of wonder. "I haven't seen plants this lush and green since I was very young."

"They're beautiful," I said.

"These species could die out once Oscuro draws close. Fortalecen is trying to showcase that we won't have to sacrifice the joys of our world by moving underground." He sounded almost sad as he murmured, "This is one of his more compelling arguments."

"Would you miss Paz?" I asked. "If Prístina and the Migrationists get their way, and you leave. Would part of you miss all this?"

His pensive frown persisted. "I have dreamed of so much else, I haven't given much thought to that question. I think I would miss certain things, the glowing fields of yelnuo, the taste of jeshu spice, the countless animals . . . Most are adapted to survive underground, but I'm not sure if we could take any with us. I worry about the fate of the curios." He sighed. "I suppose it's possible that Paz and I have a deeper connection than I'd expect. Maybe I'd only notice once I'm gone." He looked at me with compassion. "I don't know what it's like to be dislocated from home. But"—he ducked his head—"I suppose there's a lot more to miss about Earth for you."

Smita pounced amongst some low-lying bushes, her tail whipping fiercely.

"Come on, Smita," I said, welcoming the distraction from thoughts of Earth, and also slightly worried about what she would do if she found the ochassa.

Smita came to my side and trotted past the parting crowds, panting and looking at everything and everyone in sharp wonder. We were probably getting more attention than any of the magnificent and innovative sights of the Legacy District; Prístina would be thrilled. Among the many whispered, or some outright loud, comments about me and Smita, I also heard the repeated name Tenaz Entienden.

I glanced back. Cálido and Tenaz were smiling and making reassuring gestures to the watching crowd. Tenaz, especially, waved at people with indulgent smiles. Every paz he acknowledged either grinned or blushed or looked with bright eyes to their friends. Flying recorders zoomed around like drones.

It was becoming clear that, somehow, Tenaz was famous, and I had no doubts that my new Migrationist club was using his fame to make me look good on my first day out. My irritation that Prístina had set this up without consulting me blended with my anxious hope that it might actually work.

Never did a singular paz wear an expression all their own as we flowed down the river of reactions. The crowd swirled into currents of fear in places, but then would swell into a flood of curiosity before tumbling down bubbling rapids of rumbles and excitement.

I heard a chorus of sharp little gasps from my right. A group of children bounced on the edge of the street, looking at Smita, me, and *especially* at Tenaz, with pure adoration on their faces.

"Tenaz Entienden!" one cried. Tenaz smiled and pushed a small button on the side of a bronze cuff on his wrist. A little bronze disk, the size of a half-dollar, shot from the cuff and stopped in midair a few inches off the ground, right in front of the children. Then it sprang outward with a click into the size of a dinner plate. The children all gasped. They took turns hopping onto the disk and leaping into the air, what few inches they could. They landed in various states of imbalance, eliciting rumbles of good humor from many watching parents.

The parents looked at Tenaz with grateful smiles, and many looked at me with renewed appraisal, like they were seeing me in an entirely different light now that I was associated with Tenaz. Was he one of the sports players I'd seen on pubcom, flashing through the sky, propelling himself from disk to disk?

After each child had a turn on the disk, Tenaz walked over and spoke to them with an unceasing smile. Cálido lingered nearby, looking at Tenaz with no less admiration than the

children, though his feelings were clearly deeper. I hadn't seen
any paz look at another person that way. Did paz not feel love
as strongly as humans did? Or did they just hide it, embedded
in clandestine frequencies of Gnosia? Whatever the truth, it
was clear Cálido felt love for Tenaz so strong, he *couldn't* hide it.

I smiled. Cálido was true to the Spanish meaning of his
name, *warm*. His quippy humor was as vivacious as fire, but it
never burned. His nurturing spirit was comforting like a mug
of hot chocolate.

I wondered, would anyone ever look at me the way he did
Tenaz? Even Crispin had never matched that level.

I glanced at Inquieto and caught him looking away from
me in a hurry. I felt an unexpected slip of disappointment
that I had missed my chance to see the soft glow of his amber,
corona irises.

"Carmen," Tenaz said, waving me over. A few glances
passed amongst the watching parents. Their subtle expressions
varied, but, one by one, they melded together; frowns lessened,
heads tilted in consideration, and finally, appreciative smiles
spanned the entire group.

Cálido and Tenaz exchanged subtle smiles, but Inquieto
was frowning a little, tightening his arms across his chest and
hunching his shoulders, retreating into himself. I suspected he
would have preferred a menagerie of dangerous beasts to this
crowd of pressing people.

Yet, it seemed the tide had turned in our favor. Gnosia,
along that single stretch of street, had reached a collective
decision.

They liked me.

A weight lifted from my chest, and I inhaled a freeing
breath. I took a step toward the group, and to my surprise, no
one objected to the idea of me interacting with their children.

The kids all huddled together, watching me with wide, sparkling eyes, bouncing with excitement like they had in the zoo. I stopped a few feet away and crouched to their level.

"Hi," I said gently. They all grinned and looked at one another and their parents in quick glances before gluing their eyes back to me. One child—it was hard to tell if they were boys or girls since none had the shoulder ridges that I'd deduced were an adult female feature—took a few bold steps to reach me. I raised my hand in a single wave of greeting. The child smiled and pressed their palm to mine.

My heart swelled. There was no barrier between us. I wasn't throwing rocks or stuttering an apology for yelling in a language the children couldn't understand. No angry parent tried to yank the child away.

"I'm Carmen. What's your name?"

"Meta," said the child with an even bigger smile. Smita came sniffing up to us, led completely by her nose in the air. The child squealed in delight and rubbed their hands in Smita's soft fur. The kid's mother stepped forward with a wary half frown, but Inquieto swept in and crouched next to Smita, wrapping his arm around the dog in a gentle, but firm, hold as the child kept petting. He sent the mother a nod, and she relaxed. Tenaz started talking to our audience, but his words faded into fuzzy beats when my attention locked onto a huge stone sculpture through a parting in the crowd.

I stood, pulled toward the new sight so fiercely that I ignored all else. Everyone in my way slid to the side, but no one tried to stop me, and Inquieto was too occupied with Smita and the children to notice I'd left his side. For that, I was grateful, because I didn't want to have to explain what the hell I was doing.

The sculpture reigned in the center of the street, four huge, round disks standing on end, fused side by side. Each

was wider than my arm span, and they looked ancient, in drastic contrast with the new, innovative technology and architecture around them. Their pale gray stone was weathered, bordered with dark green and blue jewels that were clouded and
chipped. A gold mineral shimmered between the cut gems
like gilding, each jewel's facet precise and sophisticated.

As I drew closer, I saw each disk bore deep petroglyphs of
two overlapping ovals, like abstract flower petals or a Venn diagram. A smaller circle, shimmering with gold, was positioned
along each oval. The panels on the four disks seemed to be
in sequence, showing the little circles' revolutions around the
ovals over time, always in parallel. My lips parted as I remembered Prístina's description of the overlapping, elliptical orbits
of Paz's two suns—Luz and Oscuro.

Within the intertwined center of each set of ovals, detailed
bas-reliefs were carved of people's profiles from the shoulders
up. On either side of each large profile, the full bodies of smaller
people stood or sat in poses of typical daily activities.

My eyes narrowed as I took a closer step to analyze the
nearest art panel. My mind felt numb, and my skin prickled
with goose bumps all the way to my toes, because I had seen
artwork like this before.

On Earth.

In Baja California, the ancient carvings had been etched
into limestone and gilded with volcanic obsidian. They'd been
painted with solidified volcanic ash, crushed lava, black charcoal, and orange and yellow ochre. Yet, they were the same style
as these in the Legacy District—the profile of a person with no
hair, here adorned not with swirling yellow paint but with a
golden mineral that gleamed like the patterns of paz skin.

Yet, the smaller people etched on either side of the paz profiles weren't gilded with golden patterns, and I recalled that the
similar people on the Earth artwork hadn't been painted with

yellow swirls, either. Here, most were worn down even more than the rest of the bas-reliefs, but from what I could make out, several had their arms extended as if in welcome. They were encircled with thin borders, as if they existed on a different plane of existence, separate, but known. A plane that might offer salvation from the looming, dangerous suns of Paz.

Above the artwork, fragments of symbols peeked through the rock's weathered face. Three rows of them, in the same arrangement I'd found on Earth. I stepped closer. The weathering didn't look natural, more like the symbols had been ground down on purpose, and by some completely different tool than what had been used to create the bas-relief below.

I reached out to touch them.

"Captivating, aren't they?"

I jerked back and sliced my fingertip on the rock. I ignored the pain from the small cut when I saw High Counselor Dignidad Fortalecen standing right beside me, closer than anyone else dared to be. He was gazing at the artwork, his long arms folded across his chest, his posture rail-straight. He was dressed in a much finer version of the high counselor uniform; the long, brown lapels were glossier, and the cream fabric of his robe was heavier so that he looked like a solid, immovable statue.

"You're distressed," he remarked, though he still didn't look at me. "Quite acutely. Surely, I am not the cause."

For fuck's sake. I knew paz could detect the presence of other people through electroreception, but did it go further? I didn't think I'd shown any outward signs of my shock at seeing the artwork.

I tried to calm my breathing and steady my heartbeat, but the simple thought that he could probably detect both through electrical pulses only made my adrenaline increase. My cut finger stung, which made me even more pissed.

The corner of his mouth shifted in the shadow of a smile. Could he sense my pain signals, too?

I glowered at him. "What do you want?"

"Tell me," he said, calm and reflective as he kept his eyes on the artwork, "where is your keeper? I could have you placed in containment right now. You are allowed free on the condition that you never leave the noble Inquieto Reúnen's sight."

"I—"

"Ah, there he is," Fortalecen continued, making a smooth show of peering behind us toward the gathering around Tenaz, Cálido, Inquieto, and Smita. Inquieto was still smiling and speaking with the children.

Yet around Fortalecen and me, people weren't staring; they filtered around us and the sculpture like minnows around a river rock. I felt like we had disappeared, out of sight, out of mind. It was eerie enough to raise the hairs on the back of my neck.

"He traded one beast for another," Fortalecen said, but his slight nod to Smita pivoted to me. "I don't see how he can bear the stench."

"That can go both ways," I said, wrinkling my nose. Fortalecen was clearly wearing some kind of cologne, strong enough to overpower the air's constant background odor of burnt matches. In truth, his scent was only unpleasant because of its potency, like many paz artificial scents. To other paz, I assumed his fragrance was tastefully subtle, akin to sage, myrrh, and the salt of an ocean breeze, though each note was twisted by foreign sources.

He didn't deem my insult worthy of a response. He shifted his deep-set eyes back to the artwork.

"Where did these come from?" I asked, my heart thumping as I tried to keep my voice steady.

"We found them during the excavation for this district," he said. "Our forebears made them many years ago, and then hid them away. I placed their work here as a reminder to my people that nothing can stop us from retaining our sophisticated culture during these trying times. We can be better than we've ever been, better than these," he nodded at the artwork, then looked up at the ceiling, "certainly better than *that*." I took *that* as meaning the extravagant Mirror District aboveground. "These are our roots. We are tied to our ancient ancestors, to this planet. And the roots go deep."

"How many years ago were they made?" I asked.

He paused, but it felt deliberate rather than hesitation.

"Twenty-two thousand years ago."

"That long ago?" I said. "This artwork is so similar to modern paz art. The deliberate cut facets of the gems, arranged like puzzles, gilded. Prístina Reúnen uses that style in her artwork, but you haven't used any in your Legacy District. If you're so set on getting in touch with your roots, why avoid this style? Clearly, it's been passed down through millennia, whether consciously or subconsciously—through Gnosia, maybe?"

He finally turned his sharp black eyes to mine. His magma-hued irises smoldered. His voice turned hard and low.

"You know nothing of Gnosia. Do not speak as if you do."

"Paz aren't so high and mighty as you think. Humans may not have Gnosia, but we've passed down art styles and stories through thousands of years, too. Some cultures call it 'dreaming.'"

Dreaming was the English term for a slew of Aboriginal words from Australia, but it barely scraped the full scope of the concept. Still, I tried my best to explain because as soon as I'd mentioned my species as a whole, Fortalecen looked at me like I wasn't just a single pest, but an infestation that needed swift extermination.

"Family members pass down sacred knowledge," I said, "gained from insight from ancestral spirits through dreams, meditation, or exploration through painting, dance, or song. Stories, advice for survival, lays of the land, they're all told using the same methods as their ancestors did thousands of years ago. They use the same mediums of ochre and charcoal, stone, bark, impermanent sand, and the canvases of their bodies that contain their ancestors' genes, to pass down stories. Those stories have been known for so long that no one can say who the original orator may have been in some distant age."

I traced my fingertips down the cheek of the paz woman in profile on the sculpture. A tiny drop of my blood glistened on the gold mineral patterns. "Do you understand the people who made these, Counselor?" I ran my eyes around the circular border of cut gems, and the two elliptical orbits of the golden orbs of Luz and Oscuro. I hovered my hand over one of the worn-down, smaller images of a person who lacked gold patterns, standing within their own individual circle, arms opened in welcome. "Can you feel a true connection?"

Fortalecen was silent. I lowered my hand, shivering. I looked his way.

He was smiling, which took me off guard. But it was a cold smile, and the burn of his eyes felt livid.

"Citizen Reúnen updated his findings of you. He reported that you study ancient humans as a career. How amusing, that I get to hear your interpretations for myself."

"I guess admiring the past is something we have in common," I whispered with a defiant glare.

His lip twitched.

"Carmen!"

I spun as Inquieto rushed to us, but he slowed and nodded to Fortalecen in respect. I glared at him for being so nice, but then I saw the fire kindling in his eyes.

"Citizen Reúnen," Fortalecen said like a sharp slice of a knife. "You must keep better track of your belongings."

"Belongings?" I said. "Like hell am I his 'belonging.'"

"An obsession, then," Fortalecen said with a cruel sneer. He eyed Inquieto. "I would question the company you choose to keep, but the answer is too obvious. You're hardly a paz yourself." He looked over the crowd. "I must prepare for the congregation. Enjoy *watching*, Reúnen."

Inquieto stiffened and clenched his fist at his side, but said nothing. Fortalecen strode away. Passersby immediately started staring at us again as if a dam had been released.

"Carmen, are you all right?" Inquieto asked.

"Fine." I swallowed and squeezed my eyes shut for a second to stop the stinging that the sulfur dioxide–infused air was causing. "How many Earth years are equal to twenty-two thousand Paz years?"

I waited with closed eyes for his answer. He didn't ask the reason for my question. I gave him a moment to calculate.

"Fifteen thousand," he answered.

I felt like I'd fallen off a building and the wind was knocked out of me. I opened my eyes to see the artwork and remembered to take a breath through my oxygen concentrator just in time to stave off a storm of blackness.

"These were all over pubcom after Fortalecen's team found them," Inquieto said. "Nothing like them has ever been unearthed before. It's fascinating to think about what life would have been like so long ago, beyond Gnosia's memory. You see the headdresses they wear?"

"What?"

He pointed to the small, weathered petroglyph of a man, standing with open arms within a circular border, who lacked golden patterns and possessed three-knuckled hands. The man's hair was piled on top of his head. To an unknowing paz eye, a species who—before me and Smita—had never discovered hair before, it could be mistaken for a headdress. Clearly, Inquieto hadn't yet made the connection, but trusted whatever "facts" he had learned from pubcom. He hadn't yet noticed that the man was human.

"Carmen, what's wrong?" he asked with a frown.

I shook my head, and eventually my mouth caught up. "Nothing."

I dragged my gaze away from the artwork. People around us were filing out of the model buildings and congregating in the street in larger groups. My hands grew clammy.

"What's this congregation Fortalecen was talking about?" I asked.

"We can watch from up there." Inquieto pointed to a suspended bridge that linked two pagoda awnings across the main street. He sounded as uneasy as I felt, but I was too distracted to bother asking why.

CHAPTER FOURTEEN

I SCRATCHED BEHIND Smita's soft ears as we stood on the bridge, looking down at the mass of people three stories down. Inquieto stood at my side, and Tenaz had volunteered to accompany us. Children weren't a part of this mysterious event, and many parents were thrilled to have a famous athlete of the sport I'd learned was called tiq to entertain them. Behind us, playful voices and rumbles bounced, with Tenaz's smooth, rich voice interjecting when he could get a word in edgewise.

The street below was a sea of white and gold, glimmering in the prismatic light of the district. About fifty feet from us, Fortalecen stood near the center of the throng, with only a small circle of open space between him and his audience. Baseball-sized recorders buzzed around him and scanned the crowd.

"There's Prístina," I said, pointing down toward the front of the circle around Fortalecen. Cálido stood beside her, and I frowned deeply as I saw the zookeeper, Justo Muestran, with them.

"What's *he* doing here?" I asked.

Inquieto huffed. "He didn't treat you well, Carmen, but he's still part of the Curio Project. Prístina brought everyone she could to bolster the Migrationists' numbers. If she can sway even a small amount of this audience to support our side, on Fortalecen's territory, it could help immensely."

"Then why aren't you down there to help? I can hang out with Tenaz and the kids."

"I like being with you."

I was so caught up in Inquieto's fascinating eyes, I didn't register Fortalecen had begun his speech until Inquieto looked down.

"Time to take shelter as our ancestors did," Fortalecen said. We were within earshot, but there was no way people farther away could hear his moderate volume. "We must trust in their wisdom and move toward our future without fear, without doubt, without regret."

He paused and scanned the crowd. His expression was pointed and meaningful, and even members of the crowd who were too far away to hear his speech reacted as if he were still speaking. Most of their pondering expressions were of approval.

Shit. His spoken words were meant for the recording devices that circled the crowd like vultures; people at home were watching his speech on pubcom. But here, in this massive crowd, he was filling in the gaps of his speech with electromagnetic communication, impressing his meaning upon them not only through words, but through thoughts, visions, memories, the encompassing connection of Gnosia. And I couldn't comprehend a single message.

"I am fulfilling our vision of subterranean expansion," he said aloud. He raised his hands in a grand gesture. "This Legacy District will empower us to dwell in greater comforts and freedom than ever before, and continue to provide ideal life for generations to come. Three thousand years from now, our distant children will look to us, their forbears, and they will thank us for leaving them our legacy."

Smiles and excited murmurs flew through the audience like a racing wind.

"A legacy of darkness," Prístina said, her voice quiet and determined. The entire crowd turned as if they had heard her clearly.

"Counselor Reúnen," Fortalecen said with a cordial nod. "We are pleased to see you at our celebration." He raised his hands to the audience, who all stood straighter and issued a susurrus of approval.

"This is no cause for celebration," Prístina said, striding toward Fortalecen through the parting crowd. "Skulking underground for thousands of years, never seeing the sunlight . . . Sentencing our children, and theirs, and a dozen future generations to an uncertain future, one where they have no guarantee of remembering our high level of civilization. Your protective magnetic shields cannot be tested on a practical scale before the cataclysm strikes. They may not work at all. Why risk repeating this harmful cycle?"

"We share a bond that is unique, known and experienced by none other than us," Fortalecen said. "Gnosia depends on Paz. No other planet would be attuned to our needs. Leaving Paz would strip us of our identity, our purpose, and our way of life. We could become base, helpless, our civilization lost, not due to lack of memory, but from lack of harmony."

"You don't know that. We might find a planet with a similar magnetic field or we could adjust over time to new ways of life, maybe even life without Gnosia." The swift, audible reaction to her final words was palpable. Prístina turned to the crowd. "Are you all willing to trust in Counselor Fortalecen with such unquestionable fervor that you would bet your livelihood, and all our descendants' lives, on his word?"

The crowd grew quiet. I watched as their expressions of hope turned away from Fortalecen and focused on Prístina, slipping into frowns and shifting shoulders of doubt. Some cocked their heads as if considering new information, and their contemplative expressions spread outward like ripples in a pond. But nearer to Fortalecen, an outcrop of mistrust toward Prístina appeared, and spread. Much of the crowd's attention swept back to Fortalecen, the lines of their faces settling into resolute faith.

A silent communion, shifting back and forth like the swells of a deep ocean. A clash of ideals being considered, refuted, and dispelled by the collective consciousness of the paz. Fortalecen and Prístina were waging a battle, with everyone in attendance, their pawns.

The only sound within the entire Legacy District came from the kids playing with Tenaz behind us, but as engrossed as I was in the sight of Gnosia at work, they were like distant echoes in another place and time.

"This is scary," I whispered, gripping the railing of the bridge.

Inquieto looked at me as if he were seeing me for the first time, but his surprise seemed serious, bordering on grim. He took a breath and looked back at the throng, watching the eerie display of undulating postures.

"People at home won't be as affected, at first," he said. "Seeing something on pubcom, from a distance, allows smaller House opinions to arise that might vary a little from the norm, but in a gathering like this . . . Even Prístina could be submerged if the surrounding opinions are strong enough, and she may be no match for Fortalecen's uniquely strong influence. Gnosia is the most powerful force on the planet."

He flexed his right hand, open and closed, open and closed.

"Is it true that Gnosia could disappear if you leave Paz?" I asked. "Or is that just Fortalecen's propaganda?"

"It's a real possibility," Inquieto said. "All procurer ships and pods in the Curio Project are automated for that reason. Everyone's too afraid of what could happen if paz leave our planet's magnetosphere."

A little shriek startled me. I looked behind us and saw a child holding Tenaz's wrist cuff that held the coin-sized tiq disks. The kid wore a telltale "oops" face, and my eyes widened when I saw why. The disk was flying straight toward me.

I dodged in time, but a flash of brown and black fur leapt over the bridge's railing after the disk with an exuberant bark.

"Smita! Dammit!"

I was stunned by how high and far the dog went. The little tiq disk ricocheted off a low-hanging stalactite and soared straight down toward the crowd.

I slammed my palms on the railing and cursed all to hell as I climbed on the edge. If Smita could stick a landing in Paz's lower gravity, then I could, too. I hoped. I kicked off my high heels, took a deep breath through my oxygen concentrator, bunched up my dress in a fist to keep it from billowing out, and prepared to jump.

"Carmen, no!" Inquieto said, but he was too late. Wind blasted my face and rushed through my hair as I fell three stories down. People had already scattered out of the way from Smita's race, so I hit an empty space in the street. Pain blazed through my shins and ankles, but it disappeared in a flash.

"Smita! Stop!" I shouted, but she was already far ahead.

I followed her at full sprint, the extra strength in my legs and spring in my step propelling me faster than ever before. It would have been exhilarating under different circumstances, but now I didn't want to think about what would happen if Smita reached Fortalecen.

"Gaurav trained you better than this!" I berated between heavy pants, though I couldn't blame her. Even a well-trained dog could only be trapped in a cage for so long. Plus, Smita only spoke Hindi, and my translator only spoke Paz.

Prístina and Cálido were already doing crowd control ahead, trying to calm people down and get them out of my way. I felt a spike of dread when the tiq disk shot straight for Justo Muestran nearby. He looked so focused on Fortalecen, he wasn't paying attention to the chaos. The disk smacked him in the shoulder, hard. He jerked in surprise and caught it. He inspected it with a dazed look.

"Let go!" I yelled as Smita latched onto the sight. I didn't think she'd hurt him, but he might get a damn good scare to have a sixty-pound animal with super-strength and a mouthful of sharp teeth knock him over. Even if he deserved it, I doubted the crowd would react well.

"Justo," Prístina said. Justo startled and looked around as if coming out of a dream. He saw Smita and me, and his eyes grew round. He flinched and flung the disk at Smita. She caught it between her jaws and shook it like a T. rex would with a low snarl, ears flapping.

I knew she was playing. The rest of the crowd did not.

I slowed, my last step swaying like a buoy on the ocean as black spots pounded into my vision. I fell to my knees and put my arm around Smita in a firm restraint. I started coughing and had to take a deep, deep breath through my oxygen mask, all while ruffling Smita's ears to distract her from behaving like a complete carnivore.

"It's all right! She won't hurt anyone," I said between breaths of blessed oxygen. I glared at Justo. "I thought you paz were supposed to be able to sense things coming."

I tried to grab the disk from Smita's mouth, but that was a mistake. Her slobber made it slippery, and it shot from my fingers.

Fortalecen caught it.

"We can," he said, cool and calm from only feet away, though he had to be furious.

I held on to Smita as she pranced in anticipation to get the disk back. Cálido pushed a button on his ultrasonic device to lock her restraint into place. She sat down, and I kept my hand on top of her head as I stood. A couple of recording drones caught her eye, but she seemed content in merely watching them for now.

Justo's shoulders relaxed, and he looked toward Fortalecen so calmly, it was as if he'd forgotten I was there.

Prístina surprised me by clasping my forearm in greeting. A domino wave of electricity lapped through my arm.

"Welcome, Carmen," she said, smiling, yet with a tinge of worry in her eyes. Those around us took a collective easing breath.

"Thanks," I said, with a terse nod.

"Welcome?" Fortalecen echoed.

Prístina eyed the recording drones with a calculating expression.

"Yes, Counselor," she said. "We must not judge Carmen or her companion for finding a tiq disk enjoyable, as many of us do." She smiled at the crowd, who rustled in tentative agreement, though tension still charged the air.

"Justo," Prístina continued. It took two more times calling his name to get his attention. "Now would be a good opportunity for you to apologize to Carmen, as we discussed. Your treatment of her in the museum was deplorable, and your words on pubcom were unkind."

Justo looked at me, and again, his eyes grew round with fear.

"Unkind is far fairer a description than I would use," Inquieto said, panting as he finally caught up with me. I inched into his long shadow.

"Justo," Prístina commanded. "Apologize. You work for the Curio Project, not for the opposition."

"Opposition," Justo muttered. The corner of his mouth twitched in an odd spasm. He looked at Fortalecen, shot his eyes at me, then rolled his shoulders and eyed Prístina. "Opposition." He locked onto Fortalecen again in silence. Prístina frowned.

"What's wrong with him?" I whispered to Inquieto. "He never acted that way at the museum."

Inquieto's frown was deeper than his sister's, and his face looked even paler than usual. But all he said was, "I don't know."

I stiffened as I saw the disciplinarians that had been tailing us all evening making their slow, steady way through the crowd. The recording drones kept hovering.

"You speak of the risks we take in returning our society underground," Fortalecen said to Prístina, as if Smita and I had never interrupted their debate, "but what of your risk? Venturing into an unknown galaxy, interacting with dangerous, foreign environments, and worse, other species. Species who are not part of Gnosia, who have proven violence is their way of life, who could degrade us into savagery."

He glowered at me, and the surrounding crowd narrowed their eyes in unison. His next words floated above our tight circle, spanning all of his Legacy District, if not in volume, then in grandeur. "We saw this creature, who the Migrationist movement claims is peaceful, in containment. We saw how violent she was."

The faces around us showed oppressive mistrust. My skin crawled. Inquieto stood taller beside me, staring them down.

"My friends," Fortalecen continued, "our ancestors would be ashamed of what Counselor Reúnen and her subversive following—and House"—he sneered at Inquieto and Cálido—"are suggesting. To leave our planet . . ." He shook his head, as if the concept were unspeakable.

"That idea," he looked at Prístina, "is more dangerous than you know." He approached Justo and placed a hand upon his shoulder. Justo froze under his simple touch, and then trembled.

"Citizen Muestran, you've overseen this curio," Fortalecen said, and though his tone invited Justo's opinion, his sharp eyes stalked like a predator ready to pierce skin. "Surely, you cannot agree with Inquieto Reúnen's assessment of its intelligence, worse, its peaceful, safe demeanor?"

"I . . ." said Justo, flicking his eyes between me, Inquieto, Prístina, and Fortalecen. The flying recorders spun in slow circles to capture the faces of the crowd; they ended their simultaneous twirls on my face, and then turned like indecisive heads between Justo and Inquieto.

Justo seemed shorter and frailer than usual in Fortalecen's shadow, growing jumpy as if he were wanted for some crime. Whenever his sharp beetle eyes shot my way, he would wince, but when he looked at Fortalecen, his distress seemed to increase as if he were caught between a lion and a tiger.

"Can you, Justo?" Fortalecen pressed. He squeezed Justo's shoulder and locked eyes with the man. "Your time around this creature must have convinced a capable, thoughtful man such as yourself that it is a danger to our society."

"Citizen Muestran," Prístina said, frowning with concern. "Speak your thoughts."

Justo didn't, but trembled harder and blinked at the ground, his eyes shifting with rapid, erratic thought.

"I assure you, Counselor Fortalecen," said Prístina, "Citizen Muest—"

"It—" Justo said. I startled as he pointed a long finger at me. His face was twitching in severe spasms. "It is . . . It is . . ."

"What?" I said, heat flushing from my chest outward until I felt it all the way in my toes. So many people were watching,

I could feel every single eye, boring into me. "Say it. Say what I am."

"You—dangerous. You're confusing every—your fault. It's your fault!" Justo stumbled as if he were standing on a fault line. But rather than help him stand, Fortalecen released his shoulder and withdrew a step. I looked from Fortalecen's shrewd, gleaming eyes back to Justo.

"What's my fault?" I said. "Explain it to me. Don't hold back, Justo."

Justo's eyes widened as if he'd been shot. His upper lip rose in a snarl with bared teeth. His nose and eyebrows clenched around his eyes. He let out a howl of rage.

He lunged.

Inquieto pulled me out of the way with lightning reflexes. The crowd scattered, shock on their faces. Smita growled, hackles raised, straining against Cálido's ultrasonic leash.

"Your fault!" Justo yelled, skidding on the street and spinning around. He let out a wild, vengeful screech. The disciplinarians surged through the crowd.

"Fractured," said one woman near me. "He's fractured!"

People yelled in dismay. Overwhelming fear buckled the crowd's faces in an avalanche.

"You see what she's done?" Fortalecen said. "This poor man. A victim to this creature's violent madness and corrupting influence."

Justo panted hard, his body hunched. I pressed my back to Inquieto. I hadn't been on Paz long, whether it felt like an eternity or not, but I had collected a decent amount of observations. I had never seen a paz behave remotely the way Justo was now.

Justo took a jerky step forward. All the people around me spasmed in unison as if stung by a swarm of bees. They started backing away, bumping into each other in their haste.

Citizen Sirven and a fellow disciplinarian ran toward Justo, arms outstretched and ready to stun him into submission. They looked grim.

"No! You don't understand," Justo screeched, raising his fists high. His face contorted into deeper knots of rage as he screamed again with the ferocity of a rabid animal. "No one! The Legacy; we have to follow the Legacy! It can't happen again!"

The disciplinarians slowed, assessing their plan of attack.

"Justo, you must calm yourself," Fortalecen said loudly, though he'd made no objections when Justo had lunged at me.

His words seemed to only make Justo worse.

"It's the creature's fault!" Justo whipped his head back and forth like a cat's agitated tail. His eyes rolled, and his body twitched like a marionette controlled by a drunk puppeteer.

I looked around at the spectators. They had all latched onto one another's horror, including Tenaz, Cálido, and Prístina. Inquieto was pale, but his expression wasn't useless, frozen terror. He eyed the disciplinarians and looked beyond, searching for a way out.

"Your fault!" Justo shouted, ignoring the disciplinarians and swinging both fists at me. I grabbed his hands to stave off his attack, but he was stronger than he looked, like his insane anger had awoken a surge of adrenaline.

"You need soothing," Fortalecen said. A quick glance showed his words were aimed at *both* of us. "Let us help you."

"You'll do it!" Justo screamed, spraying spittle in my face. "You'll do it again!"

I growled and shoved him away. He fell back and hit the ground, hard. Gasps filled the air.

Sirven exchanged a glance with his companion.

"No!" Justo cried. He scrabbled at the floor with his golden nails as he tried to escape. Sirven ran at us, but he passed by me, focusing on Justo. Justo kicked in a mad dance, but the disciplinarians dodged every attempted blow. Within seconds, they grabbed Justo's arms and pulsed electricity into his body. His muscles caved; he dangled limp in the disciplinarians' arms.

They hoisted him off with dire expressions, nodding to the gathered crowd. Everyone maintained their looks of dismay, watching Justo go.

"Carmen," Inquieto said. "Are you all right?"

I nodded. "I think so."

"Justo will be treated and well-cared for," Fortalecen said to the crowd in a commanding voice. "This newcomer, how-ever . . ." He flashed his eyes to me; everyone else's followed. The fear on their faces from Justo morphed into suspicion of me. Then, a flood of enmity pulsed and ran through the crowd as swiftly as the disciplinarians' electricity had knocked the insane Justo unconscious.

The paz's collective mind had surged into a raging sea, with stronger reactions than I'd ever seen before.

They had become a mob.

"We saw how this creature reacted to the attack," Fortalecen said. "With a complete lack of compassion. With retaliation." The flying recording devices flicked around us like flies. "Perhaps the disciplinarians focused on the wrong perpetrator."

"She acted out of defense," Prístina argued.

"Cálido," Tenaz said furtively, drawing my attention as well. Cálido frowned, his usual cheery demeanor tainted as if he, too, were infected with Gnosia's virus of hate. As he met his lover's eyes, he took a breath and seemed to rouse from a nightmare. He nodded and handed Tenaz the ultrasonic device that held Smita at bay.

"I've never seen anyone run that fast, or jump that high," Tenaz said to me with a wry, tense smile. "You'd make a good tiq player." He shoved the ultrasonic device into my hand. "Now use that strength and speed to get out of here."

My eyes widened. I nodded and grabbed Inquieto's arm. "Smita," I hissed, patting my thigh once. Smita stood at attention, and as soon as I started running through a part in the crowd, she took off at my side. Inquieto tried to keep up, but I practically dragged him out of the Legacy District in our escape.

My final glance back showed that no disciplinarians were following. Maybe they were too busy with Justo, or maybe Prístina's defense made them doubt they had legal standing to arrest me. Maybe they just knew they'd never catch me at this speed.

Fortalecen was surveying the crowd in silence, spreading his lies through Gnosia with more power and influence than mere words could match. When people thought I was an animal, my fury was accepted as feral and natural. Now that I was a person, would I be viewed like Justo? Dangerous and criminal? Cold shot through me, and my stomach turned.

I couldn't help but doubt . . . Was Fortalecen right?

Was humanity nothing more than a base, violent species? Was physical retaliation an instinct inside of me that I would never be able to suppress? I had battled my temper for years like the scratch of an addiction. My rage had only increased on Paz, to a level that soured my stomach and pained my heart, but what could humans do to fix me when no one but Mamá had ever done me any good?

Mamá was gone. Without her, would going back to Earth offer salvation?

***

"It's empty?" I gasped, lowering my oxygen concentrator, which I'd strapped around my head during our run through the city. Smita panted beside me, and Inquieto was just as out of breath as he pushed both hands against a wide door to a beautiful building that hung from the ceiling of Provenance District like an inverted pyramid. The building was gunmetal gray, carved with the same gemstone patterns as the Curio Life Museum.

"Yes," he answered, ushering me inside. My heart thudded when I saw nothing but darkness ahead, but I didn't have time to hesitate. We hadn't been chased from the Legacy District, but with my bright red dress and a dog at my heels, I had no doubt we'd been noticed.

Inquieto closed the door behind us. The pungent odor of sulfur dioxide was filtered away by the indoor ventilation system, and the odorless carbon dioxide along with it, giving my itchy nose, stinging eyes, and constricted lungs much-needed reprieve. Smita loped in and shook herself from head to tail, her ears flapping.

"What is this place?" I asked, looking around for predators that might hunt us from the shadows. The room was large and round with a high ceiling, where tiny lights twinkled like a night sky.

"The Curio Mineral Museum," he said.

I tensed. The room did resemble a museum lobby. A few small, indistinct display cases lurked along the walls, containing extraterrestrial rocks rather than animals, I hoped.

"Don't worry, Carmen. It's closed," he said, but his voice was strained. He was braced against the wall, his head bowed and his chest concaved as if a heavy weight pressed down upon his shoulders.

"Inquieto." I rushed to him. He'd had plenty of time to catch his breath by now, but he was still panting. I tilted my head to see his face, which was deeply furrowed.

"Inquieto, what's wrong? Are you hurt?"

"No," he said, short and tight.

"What happened? What was that out there?"

He shuddered. He flicked his eyes at me before looking at the door again. I didn't miss the fear in them.

"What happened to Justo?" I pressed. "Please, tell me."

Inquieto's voice broke. "He fractured."

"What?"

"He fractured from Gnosia. Became separate."

"He seemed . . . insane."

Inquieto nodded once. Every word seemed a struggle. "Thoughts and experiences are meant to be shared in Gnosia. Knowledge, ideas, ambitions . . . All are joined so that any goal can be accomplished by many people. No one is overworked or asked to perform more than they can physically or mentally handle." His voice dropped. "Everyone has their harmonic place.

"But sometimes . . . a person can become obsessed with a single task and allow excitement or devotion to overwhelm them. They isolate themselves and push themselves too hard, becoming angry when others don't share their level of obsession. They become erratic, emotional, even . . . violent."

"Justo seemed torn between two ideas, not just obsessing over one," I said. "Between Prístina and Fortalecen . . ."

"Maybe that's worse," he murmured. His eyes roved the floor as if searching for answers.

"Or maybe that's not all there was to it," I said. "It wasn't until after Fortalecen interrogated him that Justo lost control. He even touched him on his shoulder before Justo attacked me, did you see? Fortalecen is supposed to be really strong in Gnosia, right? Is it possible he could have influenced Justo's state of mind?"

Inquieto shook his head at the floor. "No," he said, though he sounded disturbed. "Or . . . if he could, why would he? No one deserves that. No one." He took another ragged breath.

"What are they going to do to Justo?" I asked, picturing his spasming face and ferocious lunge, still not convinced that Fortalecen hadn't somehow unleashed him like a dog in a pit fight.

Inquieto pushed himself off the wall, but he looked over my head as if he wished I wasn't there.

"There are different levels of behavioral correction," he said. "Some are simple and not intended for the fractured; even normal citizens can experience small discrepancies in behavior. Most of the time, if someone has a negative thought, it can quickly be dispelled by others through bioelectric soothing and Gnosia mediation. However, there are times when two, or several, people have a strong disagreement—for example, if someone resents someone else's salary, they might steal something they believe they are entitled to. In a case like that, the deviator is placed in a rehabilitation facility. Therapists ease them back into a level emotional state. Then they are released and live normal lives."

Inquieto tightened his fist.

"But the fractured . . . They are sentenced to undergo a medical procedure that forces their minds to reintegrate with Gnosia. Some have little trouble doing so, but there are others . . ." A deep, dark hole seemed to open up in his pupils. "There are others who aren't the same after their procedure. Some cases are so extreme that the high level of correction submerges them under Gnosia. Their entire personality is no longer their own, but is created and filled by the thoughts of others to keep them functioning. To the outside world, they behave as any cooperative citizen would. In reality, they are empty vessels, swayed completely by those around them, compliant to Gnosia in every way."

He sighed and bowed his head. "I don't know what level they'll use on Justo, but when violence is involved . . ."

"They lobotomize them," I said. The word came out English, but I was certain its essence applied.

Inquieto grabbed my hand with sudden speed like I was a lifeline. I looked down in surprise. Together, our hands looked like seashells and sand on a sunlit beach at dawn. His long fingers nestled in between each of mine, nearly touching my wrist. My heartbeat slowed as my chest swelled.

"Is this all right?" he asked, meeting my eyes.

"You paid attention when I talked about human touch," I said, a lump forming in my throat as I focused on the smooth, warm comfort of his hand. This was the first time he had touched me in any way that wasn't for some practical purpose, like helping me navigate or to keep from falling, or to soothe me with painless electricity. This simple hand-holding was . . . different.

"I pay attention to everything you say," he said, his voice tender.

I took a small breath but didn't answer. His gaze was direct, and the fascination that never left his eyes when he looked at me was deeper, somehow. But then he winced and looked aside.

"Inquieto, what's wrong? There's something else, isn't there? You can tell me."

His grip tightened to borderline painful force, but I didn't stop him. The slits on his back opened and reflected the twinkling light of the room in a dimmer flash than usual. He looked as if he were standing at the edge of a doorway, terrified to step through. I knew whatever words were coming must be important.

"Carmen, there's something you should know about me. I'm . . . I'm not part of Gnosia."

"What?"

"I was born with a condition . . . My bioelectricity is over-developed. Whenever I try to communicate, the electromagnetic radiation my body emits causes nothing but interference with everyone else's. I suppose, for you, I could describe it as . . ." His eyes flickered as he searched for words.

"Imagine if we were trying to speak, and a loud piercing noise shot through the room, or our voices became mangled and coarse. Or, if you were trying to remember something, and the memories you pictured were overwhelmed by a blinding light, and you were so distracted, you couldn't see them anymore. That's what it feels like when I try to communicate with anyone via Gnosia, for both me and them. It's worse when I touch anyone for direct transfer. Prístina and I both got headaches for days the last time she offered to try. I . . . underwent physical therapy for a while, but . . . I gave up over three years ago."

The gravity of what he was saying hit stronger with every despair-infused sentence, and suddenly, all sorts of little details of our interactions with other paz clicked into place. So many paz spoke aloud around us rather than in telepathic silence because they were doing it for Inquieto's benefit; the High Council had even stated so, though I hadn't gathered the full meaning at the time. I frowned deeper as I recalled Fortalecen's stinging words toward Inquieto in that meeting about not being able to "hear" him, and just now in the Legacy District, about how Inquieto was "hardly a paz" and how he should enjoy "watching" the congregation rather than participating. Could Inquieto contribute to big societal choices, or be involved in government at all if politicians were so deeply embedded in Gnosia?

Inquieto seemed to want to change his world for the better, but he had no voice.

Prístina had told me that Inquieto was different from everyone else, but I hadn't imagined she meant something this extreme. She had spoken of her child's potential differences as well; maybe she feared Inquieto's condition was hereditary. And his mother . . . Marea's accusation of everyone at andalim being "out-thinkers" had struck Inquieto deeply—now I knew why. And I hated her all the more for it.

"On pubcom, Justo mentioned you had past discrepancies of behavior," I said carefully. "Are you . . . Are you considered to be fractured?"

Inquieto loosened his grip on my hand, but I clutched him tighter. He took a shaky breath. I rubbed my thumb over the back of his hand, trying to calm him. He watched and exhaled slowly, I hoped drawing comfort from my touch.

"No, Carmen," he said, his voice a little rough. "You can't be broken if you were never part of the whole. I don't understand any of them. They don't understand me. I'm alone. I'm separate. From *everyone*."

I closed my other hand over our entwined hands. I shook them, garnering his gaze.

"You don't need them," I said. "You don't need some group-think hive to be fulfilled. You are a person in and of yourself. You are more whole than any of them."

Something shimmered in his amber-and-black eyes, vaguely familiar, though I couldn't place where I'd seen it before.

Then I remembered. I'd seen that look in Crispin's eyes whenever he looked at me.

It was hope.

Inquieto tentatively rubbed his thumb across the back of my hand, copying what I had done, learning.

"My past behavior . . ." he said. "Justo must have found it on public record. Or Fortalecen told him before the pubcom segment. I don't discuss it with anyone."

"I'm not just anyone."

A tiny smile tugged the corner of his mouth. "No. You're not."

"So?"

"My father has tended to countless infants throughout his career, and none of them . . ." He sighed, staring at the floor. His free hand flexed at his side. "As an infant, my bioelectricity poured out of me in waves. Whenever I was hungry or needed comfort, I would use it to force the attention of my parents or any caretaker. I began physical therapy from an early age to learn what times were appropriate to use it, how strongly to push against the environment, against people, to sense the world around me.

"I did well, at first, but as I grew, it became more and more apparent that my disability went deeper, that I couldn't communicate through Gnosia, and no amount of therapy was helping in that regard. It was . . . frustrating, but I managed to stay calm, controlled."

He continued to clench his fist and open it again in habitual rhythm.

A therapy exercise.

"When I started school, accommodations were made for me so I could learn as best I could through texts, recordings, and other mediums without Gnosia. Even so, the other children knew I was different. They avoided me. It bothered me, but I kept to myself and didn't cause any trouble."

"But something happened?"

"When Cálido came to school," he said with a heavy nod. "I was so happy to have him there, to finally not be alone, but halfway through that first year, he began to spend more time away from me. After a while, I asked him why, and he wouldn't give me a satisfactory answer. Even at home, he spent more time with the neighbors.

"One day, I heard a boy my age talking in the school hallway. He was the smartest in the class; everyone admired him for it. They took everything he said as truth. He said that I was so . . . *wrong* that even my own brother had renounced me. Cálido was right beside him and didn't contradict him. I decided that the other boy was at fault, that he was turning my brother against me."

His hand clenched into a fist again, and this time stayed that way.

"I lost control. I started yelling in his face. The other children scrambled out of the way, and Cálido just stood there, looking terrified, but all of my anger was for the other boy. I remember how pale he was, how wide his eyes were. But he opened his mouth and told me no one would ever like me now. I was a child, Carmen."

I wasn't sure if he meant his plaintive statement as an appeal for my sympathy—if so, he had it—or as an excuse for his behavior.

"I grabbed his shoulders as tight as I could, and I just—I was so angry." He squinted his eyes shut. "I stunned him. I felt his entire body go slack, and he just . . . fell. I wasn't allowed back to school."

"Oh," I said, feeling a well of pity. The fact that a paz could express as much anger as he had—as I sometimes did—was scary to think about now that I was surrounded by them. But with Inquieto, it wasn't frightening. It was . . . comforting. Like I had a kindred spirit on this planet.

"No one can just . . . do that, Carmen," he continued. "People don't naturally have the ability to stun. It takes years of training to develop the control necessary to elicit such a powerful pulse and just as long to understand how to use it safely. Only animal handlers and disciplinarians are trained to use it. Most others have no desire or need to spend the time."

"But you did it on your own with no training. What happened? After?"

"I was brought before Raíz's Low Council. Terrifying to a first-schooler. They decided I needed psychological therapy for my outburst in addition to physical. They . . . wanted to take me from my family. There is a school for special cases, for children with behavioral problems. Mine was such a severe case that they even considered more extreme levels of revision . . ."

He shuddered with a deep internal pain I was sorry I'd prodded.

"Memoria Levantan stood against them," he said. "You met her at the High Council meeting. She was a member of the Low Council when I was young. She thought, in a case like mine—since there *weren't* any cases like mine, not with stunning involved—that taking me from my family might make things worse. I am grateful to her. She helped my mother procure one of the best tutors for my education and the best therapist in Raíz."

"That's why she called you by your first name in the council meeting when none of the others did."

"She was often at our house. She didn't have to involve herself personally, but . . . she did. By the time I left for career training, I was a capable adult. Without her help, I don't know if I would have reached that point."

"But you did," I said with a small, encouraging smile.

Inquieto's shoulders fell with a shuddering sigh. "I've never told anyone that story . . ." He winced. "Do I frighten you now?"

"No," I said, looking up into his eyes. "No, Inquieto. If anything . . . it makes me like you."

He raised his eyebrows. "I don't understand why."

"I don't feel as alone." I shrugged. "It makes you seem human."

He took a short breath, a little ragged, and I wondered if I had insulted him. But his eyes lingered on mine, and a soft glow appeared in his deep pupils, like I'd put flame to a wick.

"I barely know you," he said, "yet, to have someone to talk to, someone who is not paz, who has independent thought . . . who even *acts* on anger and strong emotions . . . It's freeing."

I looked aside. *Acts on anger.* Weeks ago, I might have laughed and clinked a beer mug against his. Now I felt the sudden urge to hug him and cry. I had long thought my hardened façade would keep these vulnerable emotions far, far away, but the raw fear and crumbling hope I'd felt after Mamá's death now returned in the face of Inquieto's heartbreaking honesty.

I'd never felt like I had someone to talk to, not after Mamá left. I knew how to skate by with confessions—tell Crispin just enough to get through a moment of weakness, to satisfy his worried questions when he'd pick up that something was wrong. A brief catharsis that never went too deep. If I went too deep, I'd drown.

I'd never tried therapy like Inquieto talked about. Not officially. I'd dug myself into a deep enough hole at times to realize I probably needed it, but I'd never followed through. I'd forged my own coping mechanisms because no one knew me better than I did. No one else could tell me how *I* worked. I coached myself constantly, every day, to keep moving forward. I was in tune with every breath and every thought—that was honesty, wasn't it?

But as I looked up into Inquieto's sweet eyes and thought of the remarkable fucking *honest* confession he'd just gifted me, I knew my own was inadequate.

But I could worry about that later, I told myself. This moment wasn't about me. Inquieto needed me. And as I replayed everything he'd just told me, a sudden soft, sad realization pulled at my heart.

"Music," I said. "Without Gnosia, you can't hear paz music."

His eyes looked infinitely sad, but the glimmer of hope remained.

"Only yours," he whispered. Then he smiled, and I felt like he'd lit a candle inside me, pushing my worries away. I heard a small purr, and the soft stroke of his thumb felt charged and warm on my skin. "And when you sang . . ."

I laughed as a blush warmed my cheeks, but then gasped as a static shock sparked between our hands. I jerked mine back. Inquieto inhaled sharply and stared at his before curling it against his side. I felt cold without him.

"What was that?" I asked, an amused smile at my lips.

"Nothing," he answered, not looking at me. "Excess charge."

Smita scratched her side noisily nearby. I took a large breath and shook out my hands, pacing a little around the room. A flash of sparkling light caught my eye from deep within a patch of darkness that I only now realized was a hallway. I approached the arched doorway and peered inside. The small light twinkled far ahead like a child peeking through a cracked door.

"Would you like to look at some of the displays?" Inquieto asked quickly, sounding like he needed a distraction.

"Okay," I agreed. He joined me, and we walked side by side down the hallway. I'd run barefoot through the city, having taken off my heels before my epic jump to the street chasing Smita, but I still had to focus so I wouldn't trip in the dark. The glimmer of light grew closer, and when Inquieto pushed open a glassy door at the hallway's end, blinding light made me stumble over the threshold. He caught me before I face-planted.

"Is it too bright for you?" he asked.

I squinted up at him. "I'm adjusting. Too bad I don't have my sun mask."

"I'm sorry. Though the light contrasts so much here, I'm not sure if it would help. And . . . the green in your eyes is so pretty, it seems a shame to cover them." He released my arm and slipped his hand from my waist. "Your comfort is what matters, though."

"I wasn't sure how well you could see color," I said, feeling my chest grow tight as my heart swelled at the compliment, as rare on Paz as physical affection.

"I can see color well enough to admire . . .." Inquieto's eyes sparkled as he looked at my eyes, and then down to my vibrant dress, lingering on my breasts. His cheeks turned a subtle, blotchy red and he looked aside.

I felt a flutter in my chest as I suppressed a smile at his endearing shyness, but also a squirm in my stomach. My mind seemed to split for a single second before knitting itself back together in an oddly rearranged position, though I couldn't put my finger on exactly what had changed.

I released a soft breath and looked around the room. The sights and sounds of alien beasts didn't surround us in this curio museum, but the subjects on display were no less entrancing. Parts of the room were pits of darkness, so black that I doubted paz could see at all when passing through them, but that didn't matter with electrolocation on their side.

In other places, prismatic colors dazzled my eyes. Multifaceted crystals of all hues, rocks of all shapes, pure extractions of minerals of all sheens and sizes, and smooth cylindrical core samples filled the room. Bright spotlights lit each stone upon tall pedestals or shone upon enormous boulders on the floor. In one corner, a huge array of rainbow crystals reflected the light to cast a polychromatic spectacle upon the ceiling and walls.

The place seemed so sophisticated and the minerals so fragile, I grew anxious that I might break something. Some paz might view me as a literal bull in a china shop if they heard I'd stepped foot into a museum like this. Luckily, Smita seemed content to merely sniff around.

Inquieto passed through a patch of darkness until the edge of a spotlight made his skin's edges glow. He looked around at all the minerals with fond affection, as if they were his best companions.

"How many times have you seen these?" I asked.

"Too many to count," he said, "but I want to see them through your eyes."

I glanced down from his poignant gaze. "Show me," I said.

He smiled and gestured to the nearest display, a lustrous pink core sample, standing a foot high, that ran with deep purple veins.

"This is from Planet 0257. There are shining cliffs of it that overlook a field of black sand. In the summer, a massive tide causes the field to flood with a saltwater sea. The records show the pods that mined this rock nearly didn't get out in time." He shook his head in admiration.

"Really?" I asked. I smiled, imagining the planet and the exciting escape, before the thud in my chest reminded me that a similar pod had taken me in such a careless manner on one of its explorations.

"Yes." Inquieto beamed and approached another lit pedestal. This rock's outer crust was dull and pocketed with holes, but inside was a spiraling, green gem.

"This one is from the third-closest system to our own. It formed when rapidly cooling lava met with a combination of trace elements to tint it green. A pod found this specimen buried in the slopes of the highest volcano on the planet. A worm caused the spirals, see?"

He pointed to the outer crust; a fossilized, segmented body crawled on its surface. "The creature must have been strong enough to burrow through rock, or hardy enough to withstand intense heat. Either way, it's impressive."

We continued our wanderings while I listened to Inquieto's marvelous descriptions of places he had never been. The more I heard, the more enamored I became. The reality of what I was seeing set in.

"All of these are from different planets," I said, feeling the need to whisper in such an awe-inspiring space. "I mean, really, this is incredible. I can't even imagine . . . I could spend all day in here."

"I know what you mean," he said.

I lingered at one display, catching fragmented glimpses of Inquieto as he passed from one lit area, through a patch of darkness, and into another beam of focused spotlight. His smooth movements hummed with life, his quiet joy renewing now that he was away from the world in which he did not fit, now that he could dream of other places filled with living, comforting animals, and perhaps people who would be more like him than his own kind.

But I felt frozen. As much as I tried to focus on moving forward in life and in my career, I wasn't like Inquieto. I didn't focus on hope and life; I focused on people long dead—maybe I'd become as empty and hollow as they were. Sometimes it felt like anger and anxiety were the only emotions my shallow vessel could hold. They consumed me. I couldn't control them. Could I learn?

I twisted my silky dress in my fist near my thigh. I couldn't go there . . . not now. Not with Inquieto watching me as much as he was the crystals and geodes. With my peridot eyes, smoky quartz hair, and ruby dress, I felt more like a mineral on display than a fellow living being.

Perhaps I was. That's what I had told Crispin. That I was made of stone. So, why did I feel more like putty when Inquieto looked at me?

My eyes were soon drawn to a polished oval stone that shimmered like an opal—Mamá's birthstone. I'd given her a necklace once that had both hers and mine, aquamarine, embedded in silver. I felt compelled to walk to its pedestal as if I might find her there, waiting.

I eyed the plaque of information on display. All of the plaques carried far fewer words than Inquieto's tongue, and I suspected his explanations were far more thrilling. I hadn't paid them much attention before, unable to read them myself, but now I narrowed my eyes. Three rows of symbols were arranged at the bottom of the plaque, just like the shorn-off fragments of inscriptions I had seen in the ancient artwork displayed in the Legacy District. Just like the more legible symbols etched on the similar art in Baja California.

"Inquieto, what are these? These rows of writing?"

"Coordinates," he said, "for the planets each mineral came from."

It all hit me at once, puzzle pieces snapping into place. Even through the chaos of Justo's fracture and Inquieto's revelation that he wasn't part of Gnosia, I wondered how in hell I had forgotten the ancient bas-reliefs.

Bas-reliefs that showed humans opening their arms in welcome. Bas-reliefs that might have contained coordinates for Earth before time had worn them away.

Yet the welcoming humans in the Legacy District artwork were usurped by memories of the final panel of art I'd seen in the Earth cave before the root fire blazed through. I'd put that disturbing section of art from my mind ever since my abduction to Paz, focusing instead on the similarities between the artworks' gem-cut styles and gold-patterned paz.

Now I felt sick as I remembered the jagged cuts and cracks in the Earth cave's bas-reliefs that looked like deliberate destruction. Ochre and charcoal paint had been smeared across the face of a docile paz, evidence of cultural superimposition, an erasure, perhaps, of a time of peace, replaced with paintings of an ancient war that followed.

Spears flying between people painted with red and black and others painted yellow and white. People on both sides penetrated with arrows. People fleeing, fighting, wailing. A bird taking flight with a yellow and white corpse inside—an ancient paz spaceship, perhaps, carrying the dead home to a dying planet.

Paz viewed me as a volatile, instinctually violent creature, and perhaps they were right. Ancient humans would have had no idea what to do with an advanced foreign people. Maybe they had relied on instinct.

Inquieto had said the artwork displayed in the Legacy District was dated to fifteen thousand Earth years ago. Gaurav had dated the creation of the nearly identical artwork on Earth to fifteen thousand Earth years ago. And fifteen thousand Earth years ago, a small group of paz explorers had visited a long-since-forgotten planet, trying to find refuge from Paz's destructive climate.

In that long-ago era, paz could have visited Earth as weaponless, peaceful explorers, engaged in unanticipated war with spear- and arrow-armed humans, and returned with a trauma that shook the core of their entire species' collective psyche. When Inquieto had told me of the ancient war, he'd insisted that humans were nothing like los cortados. I'd assumed that meant he was certain that we *looked* nothing like them, that he had other evidence to support his claim, but he'd also said that Gnosia memory had forgotten details from the traumatic event.

The more I thought about it, the more I became convinced of the truth of one of those crucial, missing details.

Humans were los cortados.

"Carmen?"

I took a breath through my oxygen mask to disguise my quaking breaths. I focused again on the opalescent stone.

"What's this one?" I asked.

Inquieto smiled. "This one is my favorite, found in river-beds of Planet 6527. The planet shimmers with countless rivers of running water, with spiraling green continents. Simply seeing an image recorded from the procurer ship's orbit was enough to make me yearn to be there."

I picked up the smooth mineral, warmed by the spotlight. Even though I was swarmed by fresh fears and chilled with dread, I gleaned a little comfort from holding the stone. Though, as I felt Inquieto watching me, I found I yearned for his hand instead.

CHAPTER FIFTEEN

WHAT WOULD INQUIETO do when I was gone?

After the car accident that had killed Mamá in Mexico, I was laid up in a hospital room for two days, spaced out on morphine. I still remember the jarring beep of the heart monitor ransacking my disturbing opioid dreams in a steady rhythm. Each beat had wavered in and out of audible zones, *almost* letting me drift to unconsciousness before the monitor beeped louder than ever.

That's what new thoughts of Inquieto felt like. His sorrow-lined face when his loneliness peeked through—*beep*—his eyes wide when he saw Justo, fractured, taken away, horrified that one day it could be him. *Beep.*

The beep's volume faded into his gentle purr of humor—*beep*—the sweet sparkle in his eyes whenever I told him anything new about me or Earth or humans—*beep*—the warm touch of his hand clasping mine—*beep*—his promise to find a way to get me to Earth.

Beep.

An ache of guilt deep in my stomach.

Beep.

What would he do when I left him behind? All alone again on Paz?

The jarring beeps didn't cease come morning.

Had a lobotomy-esque procedure been on the table after his childhood outburst? *Beep*. Had Counselor Memoria Levantan persuaded the Low Council to spare him? *Beep*.

What would he do if I told him that humanity, I, was los cortados? *Beep*.

Would he view me as violent, fractured, a danger to him and his already-precarious reputation? *Beep*.

I didn't know any answers, but I couldn't ask him. He was smiling when I entered the kitchen for breakfast.

Beep.

* * *

While Inquieto was at work, I huddled in my bedroom with Smita, paced the living room with Smita, sat and stewed in miserable thoughts while Smita chewed on one of Inquieto's sandals that he'd donated to the cause.

By the time he came home that evening, I'd decided I was done hiding. I was done being a victim of my circumstances, and by god, I was done sitting around with nothing to do. That determination latched onto me with such force, I decided on a bold, probably insanely stupid, approach to my problem.

"Inquieto," I said, right after he'd walked into his wing of the house. "Are we alone?"

He raised his eyebrows. "Yes."

"Really alone?"

He frowned and raised his hand a little, cocking his head as he sent out an invisible pulse of electrolocation. He nodded.

"Good. Inquieto . . ."

I suddenly felt feeble and small, my heart seizing in panic, but as I looked at Inquieto, I chose to speak, not for the reasons I'd planned, but for the simple, soft realization that I didn't want to lie to him. He had confessed his most vulnerable secrets to me. It was only fair for me to do the same.

"Inquieto," I said softer, but with no less fortitude. "What did *los* cortados look like?"

He frowned deeply but tilted his head a little, no doubt curious about my out-of-the-blue question.

"No one knows," he said. "Gnosia doesn't remember, or so everyone says."

I nodded and looked aside with a wry grimace, almost ready to break down now that I knew my hypothesis had true weight. I took a deep breath and met his eyes.

"I'm *los* cortados," I said. "Humans are los cortados."

Inquieto's face blanked for a moment. He said nothing and slowly set down his work satchel, not looking at me as he processed my news.

"Why do you think that?" he finally asked.

I told him. I told him about the artwork on Earth, about the matching artwork in the Legacy District. I didn't hold back about the human-painted images of warfare marring the peaceful paz bas-reliefs. I told him my theories. It all tumbled out of me until, when I was finished, I felt like a lump of clay, desperate for him to reshape me into something more useful than a terrified woman trapped on an alien planet.

"The artwork in the Legacy District suggests ancient paz viewed humans as a welcoming species," I said at the end, my eyes unfocused as I stared at the floor. "They thought we could give them hope. But the artwork on Earth . . . It's evidence that we couldn't. We didn't. Our people killed each other."

Inquieto was silent for a long time. At least, it felt that way. I finally dared to look up at him. His face was soft and sad, but not frightened or disgusted like I'd feared.

"What do you think?" I asked.

"I think it makes sense," he said quietly. My heart thudded hard as my stomach tightened. It was one thing to believe a crazy theory in my head; it was a different thing altogether to hear someone else agree it was true.

Inquieto folded his arms across his chest. "I also think it does not help our case."

"Our case? That's your reaction? You still want to help me?"

He let out a breath like I'd slapped him and crossed the room in seconds. "Carmen, I don't care what you are—human, los cortados, paz—I care about you. I promised I would help you, and I will."

My bottom lip trembled. I looked down.

"I was so afraid you'd back out," I said, my voice crumbling.

"No, Carmen, never." He tilted my chin up so I had to face him. He was looking at me with such tenderness, I felt an urge to retreat, yet a desperate need for comfort compelled me to stay close.

"Do you think less of me?" I asked. "Knowing I come from a planet with war?"

"Humans still war? In the present?" He drew a breath, and his eyes grew round and full. "Carmen, is that the kind of planet you come from? Humans hunt animals for meat, they fight one another, they . . . kill?"

"Yes," I whispered. "We do."

"You've seen it." Inquieto searched my eyes. "Haven't you?"

I cleared my throat and stepped back. "Not in person. I can't fathom what some people have to go through every day." I twisted my fingers together, trying to push out violent images swarming into my head.

"Carmen," Inquieto said. He brushed my forehead with his fingers, and a soothing pulse lapped through my body. I closed my eyes. The concept of paz bioelectricity manipulating my body scared the bejesus out of me, but it was hard for me to object when Inquieto made it feel so damn nice.

"I could never think less of you," he said. "Humans might war, but you're not like that. And if you aren't, there must be other humans who are peaceful, too."

My knuckles tingled in mnemonic pain from their collision with Pete Dockson's face, plus the multiple times growing up when I'd hit another kid at school who'd bullied me for my Latina appearance. No matter how good a cause I was standing up for, I'd lost my temper and gotten physical.

"You had a very sharp stick in your museum display, Carmen," Inquieto said, a soft, wry smile at the corner of his mouth. "You could have hurt me when you tried to escape. You didn't."

"I don't want to hurt anyone," I said, almost a pout. But I didn't say I wouldn't, not if I was in danger, not if . . . not if *he* was. I hoped that would be acceptable enough for him to understand.

A tear rolled down my cheek. I backed away and rubbed my face, trying to regain hold of the conversation I'd rehearsed a million times all afternoon.

"No one but you and I know about the artwork on Earth," I said, sniffling. "So, that's to our advantage. But now that I'm here, someone else might notice that some of those worn-down carvings in the Legacy District are of people with three-knuckled hands and hair. Fortalecen was studying those bas-reliefs closely. He—anyone—might start to suspect they show humans. They might make a connection between me and los cortados. I can't wait to be blindsided if someone figures it out. I have to be able to defend myself against any accusations. I *have* to know if I'm right about this. And I can't just sit here and wait for the council to find Earth's coordinates through the curio database or astronomy. I have to find a way to get home before feces hits the fan."

"I understand, Carmen," Inquieto said gently. "What do you propose we do?"

I felt a levee of strengthening calm slow my flood of words. I took a soft breath and continued, "If paz visited Earth in the past, then they had to know Earth's coordinates. Maybe that's what the inscription was on the Legacy District artwork, but it's too worn down to read now. Do you think we could find them by looking at recorded history?"

Inquieto tilted his head in consideration, but then frowned. "I scoured the government archives when I was a child. Even now, I spend a lot of time researching, learning, and I haven't ever seen records that delve more than a few thousand years into history in-depth. With Gnosia memory, recording history isn't as necessary for paz. And the los cortados conflict was before the last magnetic erasure. We have no records from before that time, and everything they once knew is lost to us. I'm sorry, but I don't think finding coordinates through history records is a viable option."

"Goddamn Gnosia," I muttered. "You really think no one ever took the time to write it down?"

"I don't know what to say," Inquieto said. "It's just how paz are."

I shook my head and looked through the translucent doors; the sunlight glinted off the bleak desert landscape.

"Then . . . we go straight to the source," I said.

"What?"

"The Sumergida. The conclave near the equator. They're the ones who sought the truth of the ancient past through Gnosia memories, right? Not everything was lost—they were able to wade through the remnant knowledge to decipher what happened twenty-two thousand Paz years ago. You said they agreed that paz explored another planet, that paz inter-acted with los cortados, and that they may have waged war. The Sumergida know about the past. They might know if I'm los cortados. Or maybe they can prove I'm not and we'll have less to worry about. Either way, maybe they know or can find Earth's coordinates if we ask them."

Inquieto took a hesitant breath.

"Inquieto, please."

"You're right. There is a chance they might know Earth's coordinates, whether because it's the los cortados planet or another planet that ancient paz may have visited that no one else recalls. But if they agree to dive deeper into Gnosia mem-ory to find them for us, they may discover that *you* are los cortados. I don't know what they'll do with that information. It's a dangerous risk."

"Prístina said they're not a political faction," I said. "She said they prefer to hold knowledge, not use it. Even if they find out I'm los cortados, they might not say anything to any-one. It's probably less of a risk than waiting for someone like Fortalecen to find out first."

"I suppose it's possible."

Okay. Time to tip the scale.

"You promised you would help me. Will you?"

Inquieto's brow furrowed, a stronger reaction than I'd expected. Crispin would have smiled and given in with a half-careless shrug. Inquieto's frown made me feel guilty for manipulating his kindness.

"Would you be safe if you went back, Carmen, to a planet with war?" His frown deepened, and I felt a shudder run through me as doubt struck. I fumbled for elusive assurances that everything would be fine, but before I had to answer, he looked down and nodded to himself. "No, it doesn't matter.

If you want to go back, I'll get you to Earth. I do promise, Carmen."

Within the day, travel arrangements to the equator straight north of Raíz were made. Inquieto had debated whether to inform Prístina of our plans, but without her clout as a high counselor, snagging a flight cell so fast and with such subterfuge would have been nigh impossible. She had acquiesced to not knowing our destination, with reluctance. As we were walking in hurried steps through a small, unoccupied hangar on the outskirts of the Mirror District, Inquieto said, "She would never have done something like this as recent as last season. Prístina takes her role as high counselor very seriously."

"You're worried about her going too far like Fortalecen," I said.

He twitched a nod. "It's helping in this case, though," he admitted. "I just hope she's careful. If the High Council finds out she's going against their wishes . . ."

"I'm allowed to be free as long as I'm with you," I reminded him. "We're not breaking any laws. Plus, Prístina's probably glad to get us out of the way while she does damage control for my intercourse-up at the Legacy District."

"That's true," Inquieto said, but he slowed and turned toward me. "Still, this could be dangerous. Going to the Sumergida, finding the truth . . . Carmen, for the first time, I've realized that Paz isn't as safe a place as I've always thought. If you can be in danger here, then . . ." He took my hands. "If anything ever happens to me, if we're ever separated, I don't want you to do anything that could risk your safety. Please tell me you won't ever do anything rash. Don't make things worse for you on my account. If anything happens to me, do not interfere."

"What would happen to you? What are you talking about?"

"I don't know," he said. "Nothing specific, I just . . . Life isn't as predictable as I thought. But you've become *more* predictable for me, and I can imagine you might . . ."

"You're crazy if you're asking me not to do something 'rash' to help you if something happened."

"No, I'm telling you not to. You must think about *you* first. Please."

I looked from one of his eyes to the other, soaking in the warmth of his hands.

"I just want you to understand how I feel," he said.

"Okay," I said, giving him a quick nod, though I avoided his eyes. Before, I'd been worried about what would happen to *my* future on Paz if Inquieto ever stopped caring. I realized I had faith now that he would never stop. But if we were separated by other means? If someone tried to hurt him? No. No, that was something I couldn't deal with. He'd risked so much for me; why wouldn't I risk the same for him? Even imagining someone hurting him made my stomach clench with anger and my pulse race.

Inquieto's face grew more worried, and I realized he might be picking up on my increased pulse or other physical signs of anger; he was hyperaware from his electroreception. Maybe that was why he was so worried about me doing something rash, why he felt like he could predict my actions better than he could before. He could pick up on the warning signs of my temper even better than I could.

He seemed to accept my answer, though, and we continued our walk. We reached an open ramp of the only flight cell in the hangar. The craft looked like a horizontal teardrop frozen into sparkling ice. The exterior was white and reflective, with a few arched, gray-tinted windows along the sides. Two larger windows were propped up in a small hump over the pointed end of the teardrop. Smita sniffed her way up the ramp, attached to the wide rear of the flight cell, and Inquieto and I followed into the dim interior. The decor had the same feel as the train-like cells, with white walls and floors, tinted windows, and beige benches on the perimeter. A section for cargo was roped off near the ramp, and we set our travel bags down inside.

"Prístina's contact already entered our destination's coordinates," Inquieto said as he approached a panel filled with buttons like those in the cells. Going on autopilot would make our clandestine adventure easier, though I tried not to think about what would happen if something went wrong. "This flight cell makes supply runs to the Sumergida on a seasonal basis, transporting items they can't get from closer sources. When we get to the drop point, we'll transfer to a tunnel-based cargo cell to travel the rest of the way. The equatorial regions are too hot to stay on the surface."

"How long will that take?"

"Half a day to get to the drop point, then a full day and night in a cargo cell to reach the Sumergida."

We settled into benches along the sides of the flight cell as the ramp closed behind us. There were no seat belts, so I hung on to a handle on the wall and hugged Smita tight when the flight cell started vibrating toward the edge of the open hangar. Like the curio pod, the craft whooshed into the sky without the need for a runway. I was surprised by how smoothly we flew when we reached a level altitude, and I relaxed a little and scratched Smita's head.

The view through the nearest tinted window was exhilarating. Finally, I was able to see more of Paz than just the immersive city. We passed over sparse forests of tall black spire plants that Inquieto called inashilta, fields that looked empty until Inquieto revealed they were filled with stunted lesh that only unfurled at night, and rocky crags and gorges of purple-and-black-striped strata. We flew over several lakes and a snaking river, and finally over a broad expanse of water that Inquieto said was a gulf of the Campo de Cristal Ocean. There were only three continents on Paz, he said, but they largely outweighed the ocean mass.

All signs of civilization disappeared as we grew closer to the equator, and by the time we reached the drop point late in the evening, I was startled to see a large squat building with a flat roof and what looked like a helicopter landing pad breaking up the wild scenery.

We touched down on the landing pad without trouble, and I jolted as the pad began to descend into the ground. I made sure my oxygen concentrator was accessible around my neck, but also that my hair and face were covered by my shawl and sun mask, and my gloves firmly over my hands, this time as a disguise.

The landing pad took us into a large, dim cavern. The stone walls and floor were straight and smooth, but the ceiling was a forest of stalactites. Big crates, bags, and smooth-sided barrels were stacked high into tall pyramids and decked myriad shelves. A row of tarnished silver vehicles sat along one wall. They each looked like a cross between a beat-up tank and a garbage truck, with crawling caterpillar tracks for going off-terrain, though I imagined with such wide girth, they'd travel at a snail's pace.

Inquieto opened the flight-cell ramp with a hiss and metallic scrape. Oppressive heat hit me; I couldn't imagine how hot it must be on the surface.

"Wait here," he said.

Smita sat down at my feet, and we lingered in the shadow of the ramp as Inquieto crossed the cavernous warehouse toward the row of vehicles. I shrank back farther when I saw a distant person come out to meet him. They spoke for a few minutes, the stranger glancing my way a few times. Then the person nodded and gestured to the vehicle at the end of the line nearest a big, looming tunnel. They left Inquieto's side and disappeared from sight.

Inquieto returned. "That cargo cell is loaded with supplies for the Sumergida," he said. "It'll take us there, and they'll have another one loaded up with the flight cell's cargo by the time we return. We'll take the empty flight cell back to Raíz when we're done."

"Sounds good," I said, shouldering my bag.

The inside of the cargo cell was filled with crates and barrels, only offering a cramped space near the rear door to ride. There were no seats, but three thin pallets were spread out on the floor. I smiled as I realized that Inquieto had probably insisted Smita have one as well.

I pushed my bag against one wall at the head of a pallet and sat down, leaning against it. Smita and Inquieto followed, and the ramp closed behind us, sealing us inside. My heart picked up speed as darkness and heat smothered us and I imagined spending a full day and night in this tight vehicle. A glowing amber orb appeared in Inquieto's hand across from me, lighting up the space and giving his golden patterns a lovely sheen. I felt a little better when I saw his comforting smile.

The ride was rumbling and uneven as we started our journey. There were no windows, but Inquieto said there'd be nothing worth seeing anyhow. Nothing but rocky tunnel and darkness. My stomach clenched and my skin crawled whenever I pictured our surroundings or the possibility of our vehicle breaking down and us having to walk along the sweltering tunnel to escape.

Inquieto must have noticed my distress because he was even more talkative than usual. I was grateful for the distraction but finding it hard to hold up my end of the conversation. He must have picked up on that, too, because after a little while, he asked if I wanted him to read to me.

"I have copies of records from the archives," he said, flicking his wrist so that his tablet projected from his ring. "Nearly a thousand. Each stores around a year's worth of time, if you consumed them without ceasing."

"Wow. Does everyone have so many?"

He rumbled a little. "No."

"You're a bookworm."

"What?"

I laughed. "Never mind."

He half-smiled, as if unsure whether I was making fun of him or not. I smiled and gave his bicep a little squeeze in assurance. He looked down at his arm, and his smile turned true. I'd forgotten what a novelty simple touches like that were to him, but ever since he'd first taken my hand in the Curio Mineral Museum, I'd felt like a floodgate had opened. My instinctual human need for physical affection couldn't be overridden, not even by the self-conscious heat in my cheeks.

"I just mean you enjoy learning," I said.

"I do. Most paz don't need written knowledge. They can learn from other people in far more depth."

"That's why you have so much stored. You can't learn through Gnosia. You have to learn through written records."

He nodded, though he seemed less upset about his disability than he had in previous conversations. "I don't have many concerning ancient history—as I said, there aren't many in existence—but I have one that might give us some clues."

"You do?" I sat up straighter against the wall of the transport, leaving behind slick trails of sweat.

He turned his tablet screen to face me, filled with glowing amber words that I couldn't read.

"This will take forever," I groaned. "We can't even research separately. I'm useless."

"You are not useless. You said your career on Earth focuses on history. You might find something I would otherwise miss."

He sounded so confident in my skills that I didn't argue. Arguing wouldn't get me any closer to Earth, anyway, but diving into these records like I was researching my master's degree thesis might.

"Okay," I said. "Let's get to work." I leaned back against the wall and decided to give in to silence and strap my oxygen concentrator to my mouth and nose. I tried to maintain patience as he read aloud.

The record started by describing the changing climate around twenty-two thousand Paz years ago. A tingling started in my toes until a shudder writhed under every pore. Dangerously high temperatures, boiling rain, drought . . . it was all happening again in present day. It made everything in the record feel real and threatening. But as the subject matter progressed into the ancient paz's culture and technology at the time, its details grew hazy; it read more like a brief encyclopedia entry, only a broad overview of the times.

I lowered my oxygen mask in frustration. "Is this the only history book you have? For this time frame?"

"It is. But don't worry. We'll find something, Carmen. There's still more."

Inquieto's voice was smooth and low as he continued reading. He made every word sound original as if he were inventing the story himself. It lifted my spirits as I watched his lips move and his eyes pace around the circular tablet in a gradual whirlpool toward the center. He didn't ever turn the tablet upside down, so I assumed the words flipped at some point halfway down their spiral trek. I wondered how he didn't get dizzy. Whenever his eyes reached the center of the circle, he would touch a finger to the tablet, and a new set of words would appear.

It was hard for me to concentrate on their meaning every time his voice resumed its gentle cadence.

* * *

I slept fitfully that night, though it was impossible to tell if it really was night in the eerie darkness of the transport and the tunnel outside. I woke when the rumbling of our cargo cell grew more intense. Smita whined on my lap.

"We're almost there," Inquieto said, sitting across from me. He looked far more alert than I felt.

"Have you been up long?" I asked.

"For a while," he said with a gentle smile. I looked down with a blush as I imagined myself sleeping with him watching. Or maybe he hadn't been watching at all. Maybe I was self-centered to think he would.

I pressed my hands hard against the floor as our cell tremored like an earthquake. It stopped with a metallic groan and gave one last shudder before everything stilled. I dug around for mouthwash in my bag and took a swig, then fluffed my hair and hoped I didn't look too harried.

"Are you nervous?" I asked.

Inquieto winced a little. "I admit, I am. But we'll do this together, Carmen." He took my hand, and I held tight. I met his eyes.

"All right," I said. "We can do this. Let's go."

I didn't think it would be possible, but the dim tunnel we found ourselves in was even hotter than the warehouse. I wove a hasty braid in my thick hair, but I didn't have anything to tie it with. I could only hope it would last. Poor Smita was panting nonstop, even with her oxygen concentrator feeding into her nostrils.

I followed Inquieto toward the front of the cargo cell. The only light in the tunnel came from the orb in his hand and some distant source far down the tunnel ahead, which glowed an eerie red. The sulfur dioxide smell of burnt matches was worse here than in Raíz, and my experiences with spelunking told me what the filtered spectrum of red light meant—this tunnel was high in carbon dioxide. I took care to breathe more often through my oxygen mask as we started walking with careful, echoing steps, but I saw no sign of any people.

"Do they know we're here?" I whispered.

"I sent word," Inquieto said, though he sounded as on edge as I felt.

"I ask that you come no closer," a woman's ethereal voice echoed in the empty tunnel. I stepped one foot back, my heart pumping. Maybe the Sumergida *did* know I was los cortados; maybe they were too afraid to help. Maybe they would turn me in to the High Council.

A rail-thin silhouette of a person stepped into the dim red light ahead, thirty or so feet away.

"We must know for certain that you are in control of your senses, Citizen Reúnen," the woman said. "These halls hold those most attuned to Gnosia; we are sensitive to overstimulation. Were you to stray into our multitude of frequencies, you could do us much harm."

A pained expression crossed Inquieto's face, but he nodded once. "I am certain, Citizen. I have long maintained my solitude."

I frowned. The woman, and apparently the Sumergida as a whole, weren't afraid of me, a dangerous alien. They were afraid of Inquieto, afraid of his strong bioelectricity, and that realization made my heart ache.

My thoughts of Earth had become muddled since arriving on Paz. I'd begun to feel a connection with Inquieto, a shared sense of being surrounded by strangers who didn't get me. The feeling that all I did on Earth was wander around, studying ancient people so I didn't have to interact with living ones, had been creeping in.

Was I being selfish in comparing my plight to his? There was nothing stopping me from connecting to other people, no human Gnosia that I couldn't access to obstruct companionship. Yet it still felt like an insurmountable task. I thought again of Crispin. He felt so distant, and as I imagined the possibility of returning to Earth and finally opening my heart to him, the idea shriveled and curled away into dust.

The Sumergida woman was silent for a moment, and then turned so the light could shine upon her expressionless face. Her gold patterns were vertical stripes down her rigid body, her shoulder ridges smaller than most women's I'd seen. She wore a dull white robe, which combined with her white skin to give her a ghostly aura. Her arms hung limp at her sides like she'd lost all use of them.

"Then we welcome you, Citizen Reúnen. Carmen O'Dwyer, our curiosity is great. I am Mediator Descanso, the voice between our order and visitors. Given your conditions, I will be the sole communicator during your stay."

"Why?" I asked.

"Sumergida do not speak aloud," she answered. Her sentences were all slow, like her voice had to swim a long distance to reach us.

"They only communicate through Gnosia? All the time?"

"Correct. Come." She began walking down the tunnel, her posture straight, her arms still dangling at her sides. She faded into the darkness beyond the light, as did we after passing under the source: a single archway of brown vines that glowed with yellow bioluminescent bulbs rather than leaves. I brushed one porous bulb with my fingertips and recoiled when I thought I saw a vine unfurl from the shadows, baring thorns like teeth.

The creepy plant grew farther and farther behind us as its glow faded to red, and then disappeared entirely. I reached out for Inquieto's hand; light static tingled between our palms. He led me at a gentle pace through the consuming darkness.

"We apologize for the lack of light, Carmen O'Dwyer," Mediator Descanso said as we caught up with her slow pace. "We know it can be disconcerting even to some of our paz visitors. We try to provide some lit spaces to ensure comfort."

"Why do you keep it so dark?"

"We deprive ourselves of light so that we may rely solely upon electromagnetic waves," Descanso said. "We have found that we can better access Gnosia if we strengthen and hone our bioelectricity in all respects. To a degree."

I squeezed Inquieto's hand, knowing the last comment was aimed at him. The woman's words had lacked all condescension, but held truth.

"I thought paz need sunlight for solar charge," I said.

"We make periodic pilgrimages to the surface," Descanso answered, "to select locations far from the equator."

The darkness continued. I could feel each bead of sweat roll down the back of my neck under my braid; one trailed all the way down my spine, sand in an hourglass as the minutes flowed by. Smita's nails clicked and clacked on the stone. Inquieto's breathing was heavier than usual.

Red light trickled down the tunnel again from ahead. I imagined a stoplight warning me to go no farther. I squeezed Inquieto's hand tighter. He glanced down at me, but I couldn't see the irises in his black eyes. They only reflected ominous red.

The light shifted to yellow the closer we got, and I saw dozens of yellow bulbs on vines, creeping up the walls to the stalactite ceiling. Though grateful for the light, I shuddered in the glow, wondering if I'd imagined one of the vines moving in the archway in the tunnel far behind us.

The tunnel opened ahead, and I let out a slow breath through pursed lips at the promise of a brighter, wider space.

"As our ancestors did," Descanso said. She gestured to the wall on her left as she passed into the bigger chamber. Her comment seemed out of place, but when I reached the wall she had indicated, I realized she was continuing our last conversation as if no time had passed at all to make us forget.

"Inquieto, look," I whispered, pausing.

On the tunnel wall, just before the opening into the wider room, were petroglyphs made by a sentient hand; that was unmistakable. But they were of a style foreign to anything else I'd seen on Paz. The panel displayed stylistic figures of people, faceless monos, but clearly paz based on the five vertical lines down their backs. Though the art looked ancient, they were far simpler than the elaborate bas-reliefs of the twenty-two-thousand-year-old Legacy District artwork. Perhaps these were even older.

Rudimentary figures of paz stood in a circle, linking hands with bowed heads. A long procession led by an individual wearing a large cloak was carved nearby. The cloak was the only image that bore paint—red, orange, yellow, blue. All the paz raised their hands toward a horizontal line that I realized must represent the barrier between the underground caverns and the surface level of Paz, for two magnificent suns were etched high above. Each sun bore two faces like a Greek theatrical mask; one half was smiling with benevolence, the other distorted by a vengeful leer.

"A pilgrimage to the surface to reach sunlight, like Descanso said," I murmured. "Accompanied by a religious ceremony, perhaps?"

"I don't understand this," Inquieto said, hovering his hand over the stone, tracing the long procession of people all the way to the paz wearing the colorful cloak, still vibrant even with age. "Why does the sun have a face?"

"You have reasons to both revere and fear the suns, right?" I said. "The light and heat are too harsh at the equator for surface-dwelling, but ancient paz needed sunlight to give them their bioelectricity. They felt they had to appease the suns so they would give them blessings instead of destruction."

"They personified the suns?" Inquieto asked.

"They may have *deified* them," I responded. "As powerful beings who had influence over their daily lives."

"You are astute, Carmen O'Dwyer," said Descanso, making me jump. I hesitated to leave the beautiful artwork, but the reminder of her presence drew me away from the panel. I crossed into the wide circular room lit by eerie vines.

My eyes widened when I saw the walls—they were *covered* in layers upon layers of chiseled markings and faded paint that looked ancient. I turned in a slow circle, and my heart drummed a familiar beat of anticipation. This chamber was an archaeologist's treasure trove.

Countless works of art spanned the stone from smooth floor to stalactite ceiling, some overlapping, some panels more worn than others, some partially erased to make way for new art. These caves might have been used for hundreds, if not thousands, of years, painted and repainted, carved and re-carved, by countless generations of paz living far below the harsh light and heat of the burning equatorial surface. A constant dwelling place through the long passage of time.

I felt like I was walking through a disjointed timeline as I wandered the perimeter of the space. Descanso didn't stop me, so I let myself absorb it all, though I stayed far from the columns of vines spread in intervals along the walls. They seemed like foreboding sentinels protecting the art from modern hands.

I approached an enormous tableau that depicted daily life among the ancient paz, etched in a style reminiscent of viewing an ant colony between glass. Paz milled about an incredible host of tunnels and rooms. Faded splashes of paint over vivid depictions of motion made it evident that their lives beneath the earth were rich and vibrant. The images were lit by thousands of painted, sparkling lights, and enormous fires were surrounded by dancing paz with colorful clothing. The ancient paz seemed to flaunt their beautiful golden skin in ways the current paz never did.

There were a few sections that depicted paz hunting large beasts with spears and hammers, all within the natural underground caverns. They shared space with what appeared to be several different animal species, including some cousin of the undullua lizards I had seen scaling the Provenance District's rock walls.

I then let out a soft breath of awe as I saw an entire area, floor to ceiling, covered with faded red handprints, all with four-knuckled fingers. They were true-to-life size, suggesting a paz had dipped their hand in paint and planted their print on the stone, just as countless cave paintings on Earth featured human hands from cultures all over the world, dating as far back as forty thousand Earth years ago. The hands were surrounded with radiating red lines, perhaps depicting paz bioelectricity.

"How old are all these?" I asked, mesmerized as I slowly paced the room.

"Age matters little," Descanso said. "Time is a construct, an illusion. The *meaning* is present, always, and the intent. However, for your purposes, these caves have cradled our species for longer than one thousand lifetimes." She took one step to the side and tilted her head in a slow motion toward the wall that lurked behind her. "Since time immemorial, when paz were hardly paz at all, but a predecessor. Yet, we are one with the past, in the present. One in the future."

I waded through her musings to approach the wall she'd acknowledged. The stone looked porous like pumice, fissured like brain matter, worm-eaten with countless small holes. At first, I thought the weathering was natural, some geological phenomenon. But as I studied further, I saw a pattern. Chevrons rose in peaks and valleys, an ancient cardiogram of living stone. Waves and whirlpools swirled underneath a primordial ocean, all made from individual holes like strokes of a Pointillism painting.

A dark doorway loomed to the right, with a slope leading downward into darkness. The patterns of holes continued into the depths and out of sight. I wondered how deep beneath the surface the paz evolutionary predecessors had dwelled. And how deep did the modern conclave of Sumergida now live? How many members of the mysterious sect surrounded us?

In the immense heat of the earth, I felt like I stood in the cradle of life, as old as the planet itself, a fetus spawned from the warmth and darkness of a womb. Life incarnate.

Inquieto came to stand beside me. His face was unreadable as he took in the display. He slowly raised his palm to the wall, hovering an inch away. He shuddered, his chest concaving as if someone had sucked the breath from his parted lips. His eyes widened.

"What is it?" I asked.

"It's amazing," he whispered, keeping his palm parallel to the stone.

"Inquieto?"

He closed his eyes. After a moment, he opened them, and an awe-filled smile spread on his lips.

"The holes," he said. Excitement replaced his awe as he tried to explain the enigmatic artwork. "They go deep. When I send a pulse of electricity into the wall, I can sense *everything*. The holes twist and turn and connect in patterns past the surface, intricate tunnels my electrolocation can travel, a journey for my senses . . . It's like . . . It's like joining a gust of wind whistling through a mountain pass or lapping across water, sending ripples." His smile broadened. "It's what I imagine music would sound like. *Your* music, but layered, as if countless singers were weaving multiple patterns and pitches in a varied, but unified, song. But instead of sound, it's . . ." He turned to me. "It's something *I* can experience. *My* people made this, different from us, yes, predecessors. A similar species from before. But . . . I can understand it." He took my hands. "I wish you could experience it."

"I'm glad you can," I said. I'd never seen him this happy; maybe it was the first time he'd ever felt a true connection with his own people. He released one of my hands and raised his palm toward the wall again. His hand shook a little, like he was sending out a stronger pulse than before.

"Citizen Reúnen," Descanso said sharply. Inquieto recoiled from the wall, and he clenched his hand into a fist.

"I'm sorry," he whispered.

"It is easy to wish to forge a connection to the past," Descanso said. "However, there are those in the present—"

"I am aware, Mediator," Inquieto said. "It won't happen again."

Inquieto's face was rigid, but he smoothed the hard lines with practiced discipline, no doubt from his years of therapy. I wasn't certain what had happened, but perhaps the artwork had been so enthralling, Inquieto had strayed into the Sumergida's Gnosia frequencies, trying to forge a connection, longing for the missing piece between him and his people, past or present.

But he had promised Descanso he would maintain control, and the tension from his misstep was potent as if he had charged the air itself into a lightning storm between him and our host.

Descanso gestured for us to sit upon a thin rug of faded red and brown in the center of the room. Otherwise, the room was empty of furnishings. I supposed a simple rug and dim light might be the extent of the "comforts" the sensory-deprived Sumergida offered to guests.

I tried to ignore the shaky feeling in my chest and the heat beating in my temples as I sat down and crossed my legs. Smita laid her head on her paws at my side, and Inquieto took a seat on my other. He was tense, his hands gripping his knees, his biceps taut.

"It is a novelty to receive such enigmatic guests," Descanso said, and though she looked at Inquieto, and then me, the peach irises in her black eyes seemed out of focus. "We are accustomed to others only scraping the surface of true Gnosia, but never have we met anyone separate. We are in awe. We are in bewilderment, as well, as to why you are here."

"We're trying to find a way to get me back to my home," I explained. I maintained steady eye contact out of force of will, trying to appear innocent and unaware of my possible connection to los cortados. My voice sounded loud and out of place in the close, ancient darkness of the cavern. I wiped my sweaty hands on my robe. "The High Council appointed a team to try to find my planet's coordinates, but we're not optimistic. We're willing to try every avenue. Ancient paz civilizations had technology for space travel. Do you think your order can dig into the past to find coordinates for planets the ancients may have encountered? Maybe they knew about a lot of planets. Maybe mine was one of them."

Descanso sat still for a moment, her unfocused eyes unreadable.

"Gnosia memory is complicated," she said. "Past and present can weave amongst one another, even confusing themselves with suspicion of what is yet to come. We have memories from the era you reference, but they are not so specific that coordinates would be reachable."

I took a bracing breath, feeling like I was boarding up windows to ready for a storm.

"What about a planet that you already remember?" I said with care. "A planet you *know* that paz visited? Twenty-two thousand years ago."

Descanso's frown was contemplative, but her eyes hollowed into haunted pits. I had no doubt that she knew to what planet I referred. "No," she said. "Not even the child would be able to witness defined details with such clarity."

"The child?"

Her shoulders slumped, her hands like fallen angels on the floor, her fingers tattered wings.

"What child?" I asked. I glanced at Inquieto, but he looked as bemused as I was.

"We asked too much," Descanso said. "And still, the child could not see."

"Couldn't see what?"

She didn't answer. The heat from the room wrapped around me, confining, smothering, as I waited. My lungs felt like bellows in a forge; each breath only stoked the inferno.

"Mediator Descanso?" I pressed.

"A father's father came to us, asking . . . asking the question you ask," she responded. "The child sees much, but not . . ."

"Why would someone else want to know old coordinates?" I asked.

Smita growled, low and steady.

I tensed and looked around for danger, but Smita only perked her ears at an insect the size of my palm side-winding along the floor near the wall. Its feelers tapped a glowing bulb on one of the vine columns, and I gasped when the tip of a vine with barbed thorns opened and clamped onto the insect. The insect wriggled fast for only a few seconds before it stopped. The vine opened its thorny jaw again and slowly sucked the insect into its length, swallowing it like a carnivorous Venus flytrap.

"Carmen O'Dwyer," Descanso said. I peeled my eyes away from the disturbing plant, my skin crawling, but Descanso's eyes were no less unsettling. "We cannot help you. We express our regrets. You may stay here for the night before returning to your city."

"What? That's it? You're not going to even try?"

"We have visitors' quarters near the surface," Descanso said, rising. "You will be comfortable there."

"Talk to your superiors," I said, standing as well. My pulse quickened in my wrists, and my hands felt hot and swollen at my sides. "Let them know we're here. Ask them to help."

"We all know you are here and what you seek," she said, cocking her head. Her eyes widened a little, and I realized that she must have already told her superiors of our quest in a single flash of Gnosia, and she was struck by the novelty that I hadn't automatically understood she'd done so.

"So, you've made your decision," I said. "It took us days to get here, and you're going to turn us away?"

"It is not uncommon," she said. "Many who seek our knowledge leave disappointed. We are not omniscient."

"Mediator Descanso," Inquieto said, "we need to find Carmen a way home. Perhaps we can contact this child, ask them to try again—"

"That is not possible," Descanso said.

"Make it possible," Inquieto said, surprising me with the force behind his demand. He had shown Descanso such politeness before. "We traveled far and risked much to come here, and Carmen has traveled *far* from her true home. We hoped that—"

"Citizen Reúnen, we cannot help you."

Inquieto's back flashed in the light. Descanso remained stoic, but her eyes focused more on him than before, reaching a clarity that betrayed the strength of her anxiety. To her, Inquieto was a bomb that could decimate the Sumergida minds if he lost control. She must have been satisfied by his restraint, however, or perhaps one of her superiors in the bowels of the earth was, because she took a slow breath, and her eyes unfocused slightly again.

"You may stay the night," she offered again, "before your journey back to Raíz."

"God dammit," I cursed under my breath. Inquieto laid a hand on my shoulder. I nudged it with my chin to shove it off, but it turned into more of a nuzzle of thanks. My anger still simmered, but I breathed through my nose, in and out, and stopped myself from yelling at the infuriating, useless Sumergida woman.

I knew that the next step was to reveal to Descanso that I was los cortados. I knew that we'd come here to prove or disprove my theory, that we needed to compile a defense in case someone in Raíz suspected the connection. But the haunted look in her eyes when I'd merely hinted at los cortados made my resolve shrivel into cowardice. She'd given no clues as to whether she knew I was a los cortados or not, but she'd proven she, like everyone else on this planet, was terrified of them.

I kept silent.

"We thank you for your time, Mediator," Inquieto said stiffly. "We would be grateful to stay the night."

Descanso nodded. "Follow me, if you will."

She led us down another natural cave tunnel. My braid started to unravel. I ran my fingers through the sweat-dampened strands in annoyance, but the strings of heavy hair around my face only made me feel hotter and more claustrophobic. I welcomed a distraction when we passed by a room on our left. I peered inside and saw thin streams of glistening glass covering the walls and floor in swirling patterns. Long metal tables and crosshatched metal racks stood throughout.

"What's in there?" I asked.

"The channeling room," Descanso answered, though she didn't pause in her stride toward a second room ahead. "On rare occasions, some of our order glean new perspective from working in light."

"Channeling?"

"We filter Gnosia through physical channels to decipher deeper meanings. This room is devoted to unearthing details through art."

I grabbed Inquieto's arm. "That's the medium you use for your artwork, isn't it? That glass? And Prístina uses it?"

"Nano-glass," Inquieto said, ducking his head with a bashful wince.

We reached the visitors' quarters, which consisted of another round room with shaved-rock walls and a stalactite-dripping, vine-lit ceiling. Bunk-bed shelves were chiseled into the walls, each covered with a thin mattress with no blanket; the heat was so stifling, I doubted I'd ever want one.

Smita hopped onto a bed and sprawled out, trying to cool down. I frowned a little in worry, but she seemed fine otherwise.

"We will send a meal soon," Descanso said. "We will speak before you leave tomorrow morning."

"Thank you," Inquieto said with a deferent nod. I muttered my own thanks, and Descanso left us to our own devices.

"Wow," I said, "that was something. Really impressive."

"I'm sorry," Inquieto said. "I thought they would try harder."

"Who's this child Descanso was talking about? She got weird when she talked about them."

"I don't know. I've heard the Sumergida are strange, but . . ."

The slits on his back twitched with frustration. I was grateful for his support, but I winced and looked down. I was putting him through this infuriating endeavor, and it wasn't getting us anywhere. Seeing him like that, all worked up for me, just made me want to make it stop.

"Hey," I said softly. He met my eyes, and the slits in his back closed. "You think they'll get mad if we use some of their art supplies?"

"What?"

"I want you to show me how you make your artwork," I said. "It'll be a distraction."

"You don't like my art *that* much, do you?" he asked, looking truly perplexed.

I laughed. "I do, Inquieto. I really do. Show me, please?"

He took a slow, deep breath. His tense shoulders eased. He smiled.

"All right."

My cheeks warmed, and I smiled back. If Descanso had been able to tell us Earth's coordinates right when we arrived, would Inquieto have still smiled like that? Would this moment, *this* smile, have never happened?

We headed back down the tunnel toward the channeling room, keeping an ear out for Descanso or any of her peers. When we reached the entryway, I slipped by Inquieto and felt a small crackle of static electricity raise the hair on my arms. I brushed my arm to smooth my shivers.

The rivulets of glass on the walls and floor sparkled like spider threads and roamed like streams through wild green hills. We wandered the room, discussing the unique modern artwork, which, though abstract, looked symmetrical, like pulsing beats of distorted light under tightly closed eyelids. I could make out shapes in them like psychiatric ink blots. I asked Inquieto what he saw in them, and we laughed at our nonsensical answers for a little while.

"Hey," I said, looking at a panel where the glass branched out like tree limbs. "This looks a little like . . ." I turned and grazed the Reúnen House symbol on Inquieto's collar with my fingertips. At my touch, the pulse in his neck quickened, and I became more aware of his body heat than I had been seconds ago. My cheeks flushed.

"Sorry," I said, stepping back. I sneezed, embarrassing myself even more, but the burnt-match smell trapped underground was so irritating, I was caught in a small sneezing fit.

"Carmen?" Inquieto's fingers grazed my arm, and I inhaled a sharp breath through my oxygen concentrator.

"I'm fine, I'm fine," I managed to say, rubbing my nose. I retreated to a table of art supplies in the room's center, trying to suppress my burning blush. The table was set with various tubes and cylinders, all organized in a starburst pattern rather than straight lines. An empty metal rack, crosshatched like a grid, stood propped up on the table like a three-foot-high easel.

"So, how do we use all this?" I asked.

Inquieto kept his distance across the table and picked up a little cylinder filled with clear liquid and a tool that looked like a soldering iron.

"This is a stylus," he said, raising the tool, then the liquid, "and this is nano-glass. We often use it for windows and building materials as well. It's stronger than any other paz-made material, and it contains matter-shifting technology."

"That's how your doors work," I said. "Nanotechnology."

He nodded. "The process is simple." He flipped open the tube's lid. "Making the nano-glass go where you want depends on your talent. As you saw, mine goes everywhere."

I laughed. "That's what I admire about it."

His smile sweetened. He seemed cautious as he stepped around the table to join me in front of the metal rack. He opened a panel on the side of the stylus and filled the hollow space with nano-glass, then hovered the tool over the rack. He pushed a button on the side, and the stylus started buzzing loudly as liquid nano-glass shot out of the stylus. He moved the stylus in a circle, showing me how the liquid hardened into glass the moment it touched the rack. I gained a new respect for Prístina's art, realizing there was zero room for mistakes.

Inquieto didn't even try to control the nano-glass. His gentle movements were mesmerizing, but when his artwork didn't look quite as wild as the hurricane circles I admired, I suspected he was holding back in my presence, endearingly bashful. After a few minutes, though I could have watched him for hours, he handed me the stylus so I could try.

I felt like I was in Mamá's art studio again, laughing with her as she worked, while I played with paint on my own canvas—even as a teenager, I'd viewed it as playing. I'd given up on ever matching her talent, but it wasn't until now, with Inquieto, that I remembered how much I'd enjoyed it despite that. I'd put away *creating* art for so many years now. Why had I stopped?

"I told you I'm no good," I said after a while with chagrin, looking down at the metal rack covered with wayward strokes of hardened glass. "I study it so that I don't have to make it."

"I'm no good, either," he replied. "But it's fun, isn't it?"

"Yeah," I agreed, especially seeing his bright smile and hearing his good-natured, rumbling purrs as he worked. My heartbeat seemed to slow; each pulse reached toward Inquieto with such longing, I pivoted toward him. I set down the stylus on the worktable.

"You are good at it, Inquieto. You're so passionate, not only with your art, but for your curios, how much you care for them. I've never . . . You're really . . ." I shrugged, my confidence retreating. "I just love your artwork. That's all."

"Love," he murmured. His amber irises swirled with just as much power as his artwork. "I've never heard that word spoken aloud; I've only seen it written in records. It's old Paz, outdated for thousands of years. No one . . ."

He lowered his gaze to my chest, right where my heart was thumping like crazy. I looked down to make sure I didn't have some embarrassing stain on my robe but saw nothing. I darted my gaze back up, but he had already looked away. His cheeks took on a ruddy hue.

I looked at his artwork; a sliver of a rainbow danced on one edge.

"This reminds me of my mother's," I said. "One of her paintings in particular was . . . just like this, only in color. Brilliant colors."

"You're not the only human to make art like this?" Inquieto said, softly stunned. I could feel his sense of connection and his yearning for more, as vividly as I'd felt his emotions when looking at his artwork on the curio pod during my last moments on Earth. Part of me wanted to confide in him that his art had been key in leading me to Paz. But I couldn't. It felt like too big a step—a giant leap toward a rock-solid foundation—that I wasn't ready to make.

"Mamá would have liked you," I said. I managed to stem back my tears and swallow the small lump in my throat before it swelled.

"She sounds like a wonderful woman."

"She was. She was everything to me. My dad, my extended family in Mexico, none ever came close to making me feel accepted. Really loved. She was my whole family." My voice dropped. "And then she died. I had no one."

"And then what?"

"What?"

"You said 'had.' Not 'have.' What changed?"

I paused. I hadn't thought about my words before saying them, but he was right. They held more meaning than I'd realized.

"You," I whispered, afraid to look him in the eyes. "I know it's dumb, but when I'm around you, I feel . . . protected, like you really care, but not only that—enlivened, like we could do anything we want if given the chance."

"You can do anything you want on your own, Carmen." He took my hand. "But I do care for you."

I brushed the back of his hand with my thumb. He turned his palm up, and a powerful static shock crackled between us.

I gasped a little and jerked back. He turned to the table and started cleaning up the art supplies so fast, it was alarming.

"What's wrong?" I asked.

"We should get some rest," he said. "We have a long journey home tomorrow."

I ran my fingers along my palm, but the charge was gone. I decided not to argue and helped him clean up the rest of the supplies. He dropped his artwork into a trash receptacle against one wall. I did the same with mine before he could protest, though he looked like he wanted to rescue it.

We left the channeling room behind and approached a set of bunk beds in the visitors' quarters, where Smita snoozed on the bottom mattress. The room felt eerie with its sickly yellow light emanating from the crawling vines along the walls and ceiling. Every small skitter of insects and breath of air echoed in the tunnels. Who knew what the mysterious Sumergida were doing in the depths?

I tried to shiver away my goose bumps and sat down next to Smita. She laid her head in my lap and relaxed so fast, an onlooker might think we'd been cuddling for hours.

Inquieto reached for the top bunk, ready to pull himself up.

"Wait," I said, brushing his arm. "I'm not . . . I don't think I'll be able to sleep yet. This place is creepy. Do you want to read a little?"

He seemed hesitant to meet my eyes, but he took a short breath and nodded. "If you like."

"Well, we don't have to."

"No," he said. "I'm sorry. I would like to."

Smita perked her ears. She whined once and swished her tail, inviting him into our cuddle pile.

He glanced at me with a quick flash of his mesmerizing eyes. "May I?"

I looked at the space in my bed on Smita's other side. "Sure," I said, though my chest tightened and my heart sped up.

Inquieto sat down and rumbled as Smita greeted him with licks and energy. He scratched the top of her head and coaxed her to settle again, her head on my lap and her tail swishing on his thigh. I knew Gaurav must miss his dog terribly, but Smita and Inquieto got along just as well. I was glad she seemed happy here.

Inquieto flipped his hand in the deliberate motion that made his tablet project from his ring. I stroked Smita's head and watched him read, trying to focus on the words he spoke rather than the shape of his lips as they moved, the profile of his nose, and the tablet's glow reflecting in his attentive, earnest eyes.

Not long after, Smita stood up and shook herself. She hopped over my lap, making me grunt as her back paw stabbed my stomach. She wandered the room, investigating the other empty beds.

My thigh brushed Inquieto's knee. I stiffened, hyper-aware of our closeness now that Smita was gone.

Inquieto's muscles were tense as well, and he kept his eyes on Smita as she paced. The silence felt like delicate lace; the longer I felt pulled to say something, the more likely a single tug from either direction could tear this fragile intimacy apart.

The silence might have only lasted a few seconds, but it felt like hours before Inquieto finally said, as if nothing had changed, "Would you like me to keep reading?"

"No," I said softly, and neither one of us moved away.

It was the first time I'd ever been in bed with a man to simply . . . *be.* I'd never been one to linger and cuddle. With Crispin, it was all business. Get in, have fun, get out. But here, with Inquieto, there was no objective, no expected time frame, no limit to my patience. We were just here, close, comforting.

I leaned into him and laid my head on his shoulder. He stiffened. I felt his chin against my hair as he looked down at me. I didn't move, my heartbeat quickening. I wondered if he could sense each anxious pulse.

He let out a gentle breath and wrapped his long arm around me. He squeezed me close, his body trembling a little. I nestled my cheek into his chest, inhaling his warm, familiar scent that melded a sandalwood-like aroma with a clean, citrusy source I couldn't name. His heartbeat was so fast, I smiled. After a moment of silence that felt charged with energy, he said my name. That was all, and that was all it took for me to welcome the soothing vibration of his voice as it resonated through me. Our breaths synced, our bodies relaxed, fitting together like some grand creator had made a mistake in crafting two separate people from a particular ball of clay, rather than one.

I felt a brush of some soft, new feeling I'd never experienced before. I felt whole.

CHAPTER SIXTEEN

WHEN I OPENED my eyes, Inquieto and I were lying down together on the mattress with such ease, it felt like we'd intended to sleep there all along. His head was resting on mine as I lay nuzzled against his chest, his breaths slow. I didn't recall putting my oxygen mask over my mouth, but he must have helped me strap it on after I fell asleep, which also meant he must have consciously chosen not to move to his own bunk. My body flushed when I saw the back of his hand resting on my thigh. I turned my head the tiniest bit to get a peek of his face. His eyelashes fluttered a little, but he still slept.

He was handsome, I couldn't deny it, no matter how different we looked. My secret thoughts scared me, but watching him sleep brought a happy flutter to my chest and a pleasant tingling to my toes. Would it all go away when he awoke? If he ever knew the turn I'd taken, somewhere along the road—I couldn't even pinpoint where—would he stop wanting to be so close?

I heard a light footstep behind us. I gasped and rolled over in Inquieto's arms. A frail old man in a dingy white Sumergida robe stood in the entrance of the visitors' quarters, watching us.

Smita sighed and curled up tighter at our feet. Inquieto didn't stir, and I hesitated to move. The man's face was expressionless for a moment, his eyes unfocused even more than Descanso's had been. His features slowly shifted to a ponderous look as his pupils focused, little by little, his yellow irises starting to twinkle. Then his eyebrows raised and he smiled as if he'd just been reminded of something wonderful. Yet then his smile faded, he tilted his head, and his eyes drifted to the side.

"Ah, that was then," he said lightly, though his speech sounded strange, like a child trying to pronounce new words. "Yes, then. This is now."

His smile widened even more in his wrinkled face as he looked back at me and Inquieto. His expressions looked foolish, in a way, like he'd never looked in a mirror and was oblivious to social perceptions.

"Come," he said, turning around toward the entrance. "Come." He disappeared into the dark.

I frowned. I debated waking Inquieto, but the Sumergida man seemed to only be speaking to me. I carefully lifted Inquieto's arm and slid out from his comforting embrace, though my fingertips caught on his as if they had a mind of their own and protested my retreat.

I crept through the cave tunnel and peered into the channeling room. I raised my eyebrows when I saw the old man seated before an art project on a metal rack that hadn't been there the day before. He was already holding a stylus and putting nano-glass to the rack in slow, upward strokes. His hands shook a little, and his golden patterns were dull with age. He looked so focused, I wondered if he'd forgotten about me. His earlier comments *had* sounded a little addled.

I cleared my throat, but he didn't look up. I couldn't see the details of his project, but he must have been working all night because the glass patterns were so elaborate, and his current strokes were so smooth and slow, there was no way he'd started this morning.

I took slow steps, and when I reached his side, I stared in wonder and confusion at his artwork. The piece shimmered with clear glass and mercurial silver rather than gray stone and clouded gems, gold, or obsidian, but there was no mistaking the art as the ancient paz style with which I was becoming so familiar.

I lowered my oxygen mask. "Wait . . ."

I realized I was staring at an *exact* replica of one of the panels displayed in the Legacy District. A bas-relief of a paz woman's profile was etched in the center of Luz's and Oscuro's elliptical orbits. Within the left oval, a small human man opened his arms wide in welcome, his hair piled on top of his head in the manner Inquieto had mistaken for a paz wearing a headdress.

In the original artwork, the right-hand oval's images had been worn away. Yet here, under the hand of this Sumergida man, the glass replica showed two people in the oval. One was a human man, the other, a paz woman. They were embracing.

"How did you . . . ?" I said. "Have you seen the artwork Fortalecen found? But what is . . . ?"

"Dignidad Fortalecen," the man said with poor pronunciation, his voice low and crooning, laced with sadness. "He found the origin in Raíz, yes. Yet we know." He gazed at his glass artwork as if in a trance. "We know."

My eyes traced the circular border of flat glass, which imitated the three-dimensional, gem-cut bas-reliefs with an optical illusion through silver shading.

"There," I said, pointing to the top of the metal rack where the artwork was unfinished. "Right there. What's supposed to be there? Do you remember? Does Gnosia remember?"

The old man shook his head in one slow motion. His next words were slow and precise, as if he were long out of practice in speaking but wanted to make sure and get it right. "Everything of importance is here."

"No," I said. "It's not. In the Legacy District, the artwork had coordinates here that were worn down. I told Descanso that I need coordinates for my home planet. So where are they? Why didn't you finish this?"

The man was silent, staring at his artwork.

"Please," I said. "Try to remember. For me."

"We tried all night to remember for you. We remember."

His dreamy gaze drifted to the image of the human man and paz woman embracing. Like the coordinates, that image had been too worn down to make out in the Legacy District. The Sumergida had remembered it, though; they'd remembered something lost to time. For me.

"What else do you remember?" I whispered. "Those people . . ." I pointed to the human man whose arms were open in welcome. "Are my people—am I—los cortados?"

The man hummed a single, low note that went on for nearly a minute. The note slid downward and ended in a silent nod.

"Everything of importance is here." He laid a wrinkled hand upon the image of the human man and paz woman.

I looked away and took an oxygen-infused breath through my mask. I felt like my entire world was trapped in an ever-shrinking cube. I was right. I was los cortados. And this man didn't seem to care about the danger that knowledge posed for my life.

"Everything of importance?" I said. "So you don't think me getting home is important? After I was kidnapped? Those missing coordinates aren't important?"

"Their importance is your perception," the man said, "but we cannot see them. Even the child could not see."

"Mediator Descanso mentioned a child, too. What child?"

"The child who can see more than any of us. Further and further and further . . ."

"Can I talk to the child? Can I ask what they can remember?" I said.

The man cocked his head with a frown that looked confused. Then his expression cleared into quaint realization as if he'd handed me a book and remembered I couldn't read.

"The child is unreachable—a place unwise to tread, Carmen O'Dwyer."

"Carmen?"

I jumped at Inquieto's voice from the entrance. He nodded in greeting, and his eyes flicked to the seated man. "Am I interrupting?"

"No," I said. "I was just asking—"

"We are finished," the Sumergida man said, standing on shaky legs. "We wish you well on your journey home."

"But—"

"May we learn more of the present," the man said, drifting off into his ambling speech and vacant gaze. "May we ever learn the future." He toddled off through an exit so dark, I hadn't even noticed it was there.

"What was that?" Inquieto asked.

I shook my head. "Useless. They can't find the coordinates. That man tried all night. And worse . . . I am los cortados. I am."

My shoulders fell, and I took another trembling breath through my concentrator to stave off dizziness from the stifling underground air. Was this my future? If Fortalecen won, if the council couldn't find the coordinates to Earth in time, would I be stuck underground for the rest of my life?

"Carmen. It's all right. We'll figure out what to do."

"Inquieto, I . . ." I couldn't understand how he could be so calm, but unlike the Sumergida man, Inquieto's response was filled with compassion. And god love him, Inquieto hadn't let me down yet. If he said we'd figure it out, well, it gave me real hope that we actually would. Maybe this was just a setback. I shook my head and let out a short breath. "Dammit. Fine, let's just . . . Let's go home."

"The cargo cell should be unloaded by now," Inquieto said. Then he whispered, "We can go home."

It wasn't until we were seated inside the cargo cell, bouncing with the rumbling engine and uneven ground, that I realized what I'd said. I'd called Raíz, Inquieto's house, home.

"I'm sorry," Inquieto said. I looked up at him, seated across from me. His lined face looked tired and defeated. "We came here for nothing."

Everything of importance is here.

I pictured the Sumergida man's artwork sparkling in the dim light of the cavern, showing a human and paz embracing. On Earth, an ancient paz explorer had found peace, maybe more, with an ancient los cortados. And even after a horrific battle, at least one paz had returned home and wished to remember, and to record, the beautiful connection they'd found with a human. War wasn't the whole story. The Sumergida had found the truth.

I met Inquieto's eyes.

The ancients spoke to me through ages, through millennia, across light-years and the gaping expanse between this life and whatever comes after.

They gave me permission to fall.

"Maybe not nothing," I said.

We spent the day and into the night reading more from Inquieto's history record, though neither of us expected anything useful to miraculously appear. We could only hope the High Council's research team would find Earth's coordinates through modern means; perhaps Prístina would have news when we reached Raíz. Inquieto seemed even more fervent in his attempts to help me after the Sumergida visit was such a failure. I tried to match his determination, but despite the importance of our continued quest, my rigid need to find my path home was starting to bend.

At the smallest prompting, I would divert our conversation into tales of our respective planets, our homes. We would discuss our shared interest in art and delve into stories of our childhoods. Curiosity was getting the better of us—perhaps the trait we shared in common the most. And I found I'd never been more curious about any person than I was about Inquieto.

Gradually, in that tight little space between supply crates, our voices mingling with the rumbling engine of the transport, we began to test new ground, voicing our fears and misgivings, our hopes, though we skirted specifics, worried about scraping raw emotions too soon when our futures here were so uncertain.

Late into the night, I finally opened up to him about the full details of Mamá's death, to my surprise. Even more surprising, I didn't stop there. Stories about her left my lips that I hadn't talked about, had tried not to *think* about, for years. Inquieto listened with interest and delight, and with compassion that lacked all pity. I didn't have the urge to rail against him for feeling sorry for me, like I had so many others back home. My memories of Mamá returned to a state of light and fondness, rather than festering in an empty pit in my heart. Every time I looked at Inquieto, it felt as if Mamá were saying, "*Vamos, mijita!*"

Take the next step.

CHAPTER SEVENTEEN

"INQUIETO! CARMEN!" CÁLIDO was beaming when we arrived home the following night. The suns had long set, allowing me to walk freely in the fresh air without my sun mask and shawl, invigorating my spirits.

"Everyone's here," Cálido said. "We have a good surprise for you."

"Oh, yeah?" I said. The human concept of a *good surprise* seemed to be really catching on.

"In the garden," he said, with a beckoning wave. My mind sharpened as I realized *everyone* must include Prístina. She'd been working nonstop for the Migrationist cause and with the High Council—had her efforts paid off? Would a good surprise have to do with my future?

Inquieto and I exchanged confused looks, but followed. Smita trotted along, doing her damnedest to get in my way as we headed around the house toward the back garden. A dry breeze rattled the scrubs and made twigs scuttle across a dusty stone path. The aromas the breeze carried were potent, but all wonderful.

I sighed softly when we turned a corner and entered the garden. Though the lavender and steel hues of dusk shadowed everything, the myriad colors that pushed through were gorgeous. The sheer contrast between the shriveled garden in harsh daylight and the bloom of cool, soft night was awe-inducing. Spherical amber lights lined the stone path, making the gold of Inquieto's skin shine like a sunset on water. The ends of my hair even glowed a little. The whole place felt like a dream.

A large fountain waited at the end of the path, made of spirals of blue glass that glinted through the water. The water wasn't steaming as the lake had in the sun; it babbled in pleasant song and flowed into little rivulets of controlled irrigation to bring life to the unfurled flora.

Prístina sat on the fountain's edge. She wore a cloth sling over her shoulder. Tucked within, cradled against her side, was her orange- and red-marbled egg. She looked up with ease like she'd been expecting us, and Tenaz, standing nearby, perked up with a smile.

"Inquieto," Prístina greeted with a nod, "Carmen. Welcome back. Was your journey a success?"

"We didn't find the answers we were looking for," Inquieto said simply. He nodded at her egg. "Is something wrong with . . ."

"No, not at all." She hugged her egg with one arm. "It was Carmen's idea to keep my little one close."

I raised my eyebrows. "My idea? I didn't ever . . ."

"Human nature, then," Prístina said. "Your biology. It's inspiring, Carmen. Humans must be so close to their children, even before they're fully developed. It's beautiful."

Inquieto frowned slightly. "Humans carry their eggs close?"

I blushed. "We carry them inside of us. Not as eggs with shells. The babies are born from our bodies, not hatched from an egg."

He blinked with raised eyebrows, looking from my face to my stomach. His shoulders fell, and he looked down with a furrowed brow like he was trying to hide disappointment.

"Humans and paz are linked at our core," Prístina said, "but I think our biological differences will work to our advantage. The more different we are, the more our case for peacefully interacting with *separate* species will be highlighted. Humans are better than we could have hoped for, Inquieto."

"Don't assume what I hope for, Prístina," he said softly.

She winced a little. I realized that Inquieto might be the only person alive on Paz who wasn't easy to read. This probably wasn't the first time she, or others, had tried to speak for him.

"Cálido said you have some sort of surprise?" I said.

"Yes," Prístina answered with a smile. "Please, everyone sit down, and I'll explain."

We all crowded in close on the edge of the fountain.

"As you know, the incident at the Legacy District did not go well," she began.

"That's an understatement," I said.

"I've been working to sway the council to continue to allow your freedom. However, we also need to overcome the public's prejudices."

"Explain this to me," I said. "Inquieto said paz don't succumb to their emotions or descend to a mob mentality. But all I've seen since I got here is collective mood swings whenever I'm around."

"It's not your fault," Inquieto said, but he didn't deny the truth of my statement.

"The first proposal for mass migration happened nearly one hundred years ago," Prístina said. "You see how long it took for us to progress to this divided state. Your presence here has . . . aggravated the depth of people's emotions in a way most have never seen before."

She glanced at Inquieto, and then away with a flinch of shame for comparing her brother's strong emotional states to the current havoc of Gnosia. I didn't dare look at Inquieto; I knew by now he'd feel worse if I saw his hurt expression.

"It makes sense that many people are confused," Prístina continued, "looking for guidance from one another. Some are getting caught in the sway."

"Like Justo."

Prístina jolted and clutched her egg tighter. It seemed an unconscious act rather than a calculated ploy of a politician.

"The decision to move forward with Fortalecen's plan of moving underground, or to follow the Migrationist movement toward the stars, happens soon."

"Will the decision be made globally, democratically?" I asked.

"Yes," she said. "The High Council will make the ultimate decision, but we only decree what Gnosia decides. Therefore, we cannot delay in swaying people to our cause." She looked at Cálido and Tenaz. "We've planned a way we can start."

Cálido grinned and handed out clear eye masks for the augmented reality system linked to pubcom. I felt an uneasy twist in my stomach, but they'd said this was a good surprise, so I pressed my mask onto my face. Inquieto slowly did the same.

I waited, looking at the garden around us, listening to the babbling fountain. For a moment, nothing happened. Then a breathy sound brushed my ears through the mask's tiny speakers. When it ended, an echo remained in its wake, and then the sound of a new breeze started, at a slightly different pitch, like someone was blowing across the top of an empty bottle. The sound was so subtle, however, that the note was barely discernable from the wind.

I looked at Prístina in confusion, but she nodded to the space in front of us. My eyes widened as I saw a projected, three-dimensional image of *me*. I was in the Curio Life Museum, wearing palm-frond clothes, squatting down in front of my pile of tinder and lighting a small fire. I smiled up at my zoo audience, excitement and hope written on my every feature. The breathy pitches continued to play in my ears, soothing waves replacing any other sound the recording may have once had.

I knew in reality, I had yelled at my audience soon after that moment, but the recording lingered on my smile, and a new image floated into its place like a dream. I was in my habitat again, drawing with my charcoal stick on the rock wall. I drew straight lines and connected circles that imitated Prístina's artwork, and a quick image of her glimmering art on the museum walls drifted across the recording to show their similarities.

"Is this being broadcast now?" Inquieto asked, making me jump.

"Yes," said Cálido with a grin. "Everyone's watching."

"What?" I scowled and hunched my shoulders. My entire body flamed, while a dead weight solidified in my stomach. I tethered my fingers together and cringed as I kept watching what felt like a cheesy montage sequence of my life.

I was in the Legacy District next, making my grand entrance in my vivid red dress, which contrasted even more with the surrounding paz than I'd thought, now that I could see from an outside perspective. Inquieto and I walked through the district, looking around in wonder. I felt a clinch of dread as I prayed they wouldn't show me singing and swaying my hips like an idiot, but they did. I grunted as I watched, but then they showed Inquieto's entranced smile and I let out a small laugh.

The image of Smita bounded toward me next. The dog looked so happy, I doubted any watching paz could misinterpret her signals. I laughed again as I saw the recording of me hugging her wiggly body while her bushy tail wagged. The camera panned toward Tenaz, who stood nearby wearing his tiq uniform, smiling broadly as he watched us. I recalled the little spherical recording drones that had flitted around us all over the Legacy District, swiveling back and forth to capture everything of interest. There could be no end to all the recordings caught of me since my arrival.

The recording then showed me, still petting Smita, looking up at Inquieto while mouthing the paz word for *thank you*. My heart slowed as I watched Inquieto's face, full of tender care, just as I remembered. I pulled my tight fingers apart and gripped the edge of the fountain. Inquieto's hand was near, and the side of my pinkie touched his.

The sound of a breathy, echoing breeze continued to play in my ears. It wasn't quite music, but it had the effect of softening each recording as if Prístina had infused the entire broadcast with elua. The recording followed me and Inquieto toward the garden of the Legacy District, where my eyes shone with awe as I looked at the extravagant foreign flowers. Then Tenaz was speaking to the group of admiring children, letting them jump on and off the tiq disk.

The camera zoomed in on me, watching, and then on Inquieto, who, though I hadn't realized, was watching me. The camera only stayed on him for a second, but it was enough for me to catch an expression on his face that I'd never seen from him before. I'd seen him look at me with fascination and wonder, with gentle care and sweet hope. But I'd never seen him look at me with such deep affection, melded with powerful longing.

I snuck a glance at him now, sitting beside me. His jaw was clenched, while his eyes focused straight on the recording. I lifted my pinkie and brushed his once, feeling shaky as warmth charged a pinpoint connection between our skin. His chest hitched in a tight breath, but he didn't move his hand away when I laid my pinkie on his. He also didn't take his eyes off the recordings for a single second.

The recording had switched to Tenaz inviting me to interact with the paz children. My chest tightened as I imagined all the people at home right now, judging me for talking to kids, but on the pubcom recording, I smiled at the little child I'd met in the Legacy District, Meta. They touched their palm to mine, and I watched the tentative joy on my face, and theirs, and the tension in my chest loosened. A soft sensation of hope prodded my heart, growing more purposeful with each new heartbeat.

I had never seen myself like this. The *me* I knew avoided children, or anyone else vulnerable, so I wouldn't be tempted to feel vulnerable, too. I never wasted time enjoying the little things when there was so much work to be done. I wore wry smiles lacking true joy. I never looked at anyone with as much gratitude as I had Cálido and Tenaz that day in the Legacy District, and absolutely never with such sweet care as I had with Inquieto.

Tears welled in my eyes, and one drop fell when I blinked in surprise. The recording moved to an unexpected location. It showed me in Inquieto's private living room, wearing paz robes, focused on pubcom with narrowed eyes. A ploy to show off my intelligence to viewers at home, I hoped.

At the time, I hadn't known I was being recorded, and I felt a little unease while I waited for what else this pubcom broadcast might show. Yet, the anger I expected to feel for being recorded without my consent dissolved in a wash of gratitude. The recordings showed only good things that made my heart warm. This was how Prístina, Cálido, Tenaz, and Inquieto saw me. And I thought, in one small, poignant moment, that maybe Mamá had seen me this way, too.

Mamá wouldn't have wanted me to shut people out like I'd been doing for over a decade. She wouldn't have wanted to see me angry and grieving. She'd raised me better than that.

I bit my bottom lip to stem a sob. I stroked Inquieto's finger again with my pinkie. His hand was trembling and pressing down hard as if he were trying to cement himself to the fountain's ledge. He curled his fingers away from mine and clenched his fist, moving his hand to his lap. I was about to ask him if he was all right, but I was distracted when the recordings echoed words for the first time. We, all of us, were sitting around the long table during my first andalim meal in Inquieto's home. A recorder, which must have been hidden at the time, panned around the table, showing everyone in attendance, though it sped over Marea's stiff face and Oyente's reserved frown before it would reveal their displeasure.

"Which one do you like best?" Inquieto's soft recorded voice asked as he gestured to the food on the table.

"This one," I answered with a sad smile. *"It reminds me of something my mother used to make."*

My tears fell in earnest now, plastered under my mask. My recorded self described Earth and humans as best as I could at the time, focusing on good aspects.

"The people of Earth are very much like paz," I finished.

"So similar," Prístina's voice echoed with the soft, breezy sound surrounding the entire broadcast. *"The probability is nearly impossible, yet here you are. A vivid example of what the universe holds. Imagine what else we could find."*

The broadcast ended showing me wearing the sweetest, happiest smile I imagined I'd ever worn in my entire life. The recording didn't show where I was at the time, or what I'd been looking at, but I remembered that moment. Inquieto and I had been packing for our trip to the Sumergida, and he'd handed me my oxygen concentrator. It was a simple gesture, an unremarkable moment, yet my smile . . . that powerful smile was for him.

The breezy sounds ended, and the image of me smiling disappeared. Prístina took off her mask, and Cálido and Tenaz did the same. I pulled mine off; the inside was wet with tears.

"Now people will see *you*, Carmen," Prístina said.

"Thank you," I said. "I . . ."

I looked down, not sure what I could say to encompass the tumultuous feelings within me. Shame crawled in my belly as I thought of all my past behavior on Paz that the pubcom segment had left out, followed by my callous dismissal of Crispin's feelings on Earth and my reckless act of punching Pete. But surpassing all that was hope. I could do better. I could be better. I could be the person Mamá had always wanted me to be, do what she had always wanted me to accomplish, which had nothing to do with my career or how far I could push myself to get on without her. I could live a life she'd be proud of, one that included the love and kindness she had always shown and tried to foster within me.

"It won't be long now," Tenaz said. "House units can think for themselves after seeing this. Paz don't want to be negative. Everyone wants to maintain harmony in all we do. When everyone joins together in public, good views of you will spread faster than any of Fortalecen's negativity."

"Yes," Prístina agreed, "and as soon as we find Earth's coordinates, there will be no obstacles in sending you home."

I felt like the air deflated from my lungs. I swallowed and gave her a short nod.

"Thank you," I said, quieter this time.

In one swift motion, Inquieto tore off his pubcom mask and stood. He flung his mask onto the ledge of the fountain and left without a word. I watched in surprise as he disappeared around a curve in the garden path.

"Inquieto?" I called, but no response came.

"We never know with him," said Cálido. "Nothing we've tried to help works. Soothing's impossible; he won't drink elua whenever I offer."

"He'll be all right, Carmen," Prístina said. "Sometimes he needs to be alone."

"Oh. Yeah, I think . . . I think I might need the same thing," I said. "I might sit out here for a while."

Prístina nodded. "Whatever you need. We'll see you later."

She and Tenaz rose and started down the path, but Cálido lingered. He tapped his thigh a few times, then looked at me.

"Carmen," he said. "I haven't always been understanding of Inquieto's condition, of his experience in the world. Especially when we were children. I was impatient that I couldn't understand his thoughts automatically through Gnosia. I was embarrassed to be related to someone so different. Now that I'm older, I get it, but . . . I need to do something to make up for those early years. No matter how different it makes him seem. It's part of who he is, and I'm proud of who my brother is."

I recalled Inquieto's childhood story, how he'd said that Cálido had done nothing when the bully denounced Inquieto in front of everyone. I had never witnessed Cálido showing embarrassment of his brother, though maybe a little lingering impatience when not allowing Inquieto to finish sentences from time to time.

"That's really sweet, Cálido," I said. "But where are you going with this?"

"I compiled those recordings for pubcom," he said. "I sorted through a lot of recordings that I decided to leave out."

My heart thumped. My mind raced straight to my conversations with Inquieto that included the ominous subject of los cortados.

"Inquieto really likes you, Carmen."

"Well, I would hope so," I said, disguising my immense relief with a wry smile. "He's supposed to be my champion in all this."

"No. I mean, I've seen evidence that he . . ."

"Cálido?" Tenaz said, poking his head around a stand of spiky bushes.

Cálido grinned. He walked to his lover and ran his fingertips down Tenaz's arm. I could hear a crackle of static from ten feet away. Cálido sent me a sly smile, then let Tenaz pull him out of sight.

My heart squeezed. I took a breath and stood up so fast, I swayed on my feet as I considered what Cálido was implying. I had experienced a static charge like that from Inquieto's touch, starting with the first time we'd held hands in the Curio Mineral Museum. More crackles and static pops had startled me ever since when we'd touched and locked eyes. Excess charge, Inquieto had explained, but it always happened whenever I felt the most connected to him, not just physically, but emotionally.

That strong connection now surged in my heart, channeling through me, reaching for the other side. I saw the link I hadn't realized was broken until now. I saw a chance to make it whole.

I had to go find Inquieto.

When I entered the dim, empty living room of Inquieto's wing of the house, a loud buzzing overwhelmed my ears. It seemed to be coming from his bedroom, and as I approached his door, I recognized the sound as that of a nano-glass stylus. I frowned and pressed my hand to the solid door, and it dissolved into vapor. The noise of the stylus buzzed louder, much more intense than when Inquieto and I had been playing with one in the Sumergida's channeling room.

I didn't know if I should bother him. My hands were clammy, and my stomach twisted, but he'd seemed upset when he left the garden, and I couldn't just . . .

I took a breath and peered inside his room.

Inquieto was standing in front of a tall metal rack propped up like an easel. He gripped the nano-glass stylus like a spear, driving it against the metal with a force that made the clear and silver nano-glass spray across the rack like a crashing tidal wave. A red-orange glow flared at the stylus's tip like it was overheating, but Inquieto didn't seem to care. He kept moving his tense arm in a steady, forceful circle around the rack, throwing his entire body into the burning heat and beautiful liquid glass that swirled into a violent hurricane.

His decision to make the art must have been just as torrential and spontaneous, because his black robe hung halfway off his body like he'd considered sleeping and failed. His bare chest glowed in the fiery light of the heated glass, his sharpened tree-ring patterns glinting like molten gold. A light sheen of sweat made his white skin shimmer like ice, his every muscle defined by the play of light and shadow.

I was mesmerized, watching him work with the passion I'd always known he had, that I had sensed he possessed from light-years away when I'd first seen his artwork on the beautiful, ensnaring trap his species had made. But the paz hadn't succeeded in their trap—it was Inquieto who had captivated me, and now with even more rapture than I'd thought possible.

Yet, his face was furrowed as if he were in deep pain. His fervor was tragic and raw. I couldn't stand it.

"Inquieto?"

He jerked and caught himself on the metal rack as if he couldn't stop his own momentum. He dropped the stylus, which ceased its flow of molten glass and rolled away. His chest rose and fell in deep pants. His black eyes were intense as he searched my face, but his jaw tightened, and he flinched as if resisting agonizing torture.

My whole body ached to see him that way. I felt like I was hooked on a line too strong to fight. I strode across the room, grabbed his shoulder, and pulled myself close.

I kissed him.

His lips were warm against mine, but he didn't return my kiss. He didn't embrace me or respond at all. My heart clenched in a mortified knot. I dropped my hand from his shoulder and pulled away.

He looked down at me with round eyes, parted lips, and a crease of blatant confusion between his eyebrows.

"I'm sorry," I said, my throat thickening and my cheeks flushing. "I shouldn't have . . ."

I tried to step back, but he grabbed both my biceps with a static shock that made me gasp. He held on to me in a rigid lock as his eyes searched my hair, my cheeks, my nose, lingering on my lips with an analytical expression. I pressed them together as if I could make them disappear.

His frown faded, and his eyes sharpened with vivid understanding. I recalled with humiliation that I'd told him lipstick was worn to appear attractive. Now did he understand why?

"Carmen." His voice was strained, but my translator allowed his lips to match the word in rare and beautiful synchronicity, and I couldn't look away.

He slid his arm around my waist, his grip soft but immovable. The simple, intimate touch was enough to take my breath away. He lifted his other hand, shaking a little, so that his palm hovered over my heart.

"Carmen," he said. This time, my name on his lips was filled with gentle longing.

He pressed his hand against my chest with a swift force like he'd jumped off a cliff.

A powerful pulse of bioelectricity crashed into my heart and exploded into fireworks of ecstasy. It spread throughout my body, enrapturing every nerve and enveloping every muscle. It pulsed down to my core and made me melt with heat until my toes tingled. All the horrific tension my body had built up in knots since my abduction unraveled, and my doubts and fears retreated in the wake of listless euphoria.

The intense sensation faded. I looked up at him, as mesmerized as I had been at my first kiss, but this was amplified. This feeling was more, and I wanted more.

"What was that?" I asked, breathless.

He drew his hand away, a small flicker of doubt in his eyes, but he held me close, and he whispered, "I think it means what you meant when you pressed your mouth to mine."

A flutter of hope spread from my heart outward. I placed my hand upon his warm cheek and gazed into his beautiful amber and onyx eyes.

"Inquieto," I said, and kissed him again.

He crushed my body to his, and I wrapped my arms around his neck and dove into a deeper kiss, guiding him until he understood how to respond. He was trembling, and static electricity crackled between every place our skin touched; I finally knew what it had meant all along.

He sent another electric pulse of euphoria into my heart, and I lost my feet, falling into his hold. He scooped me up in his long arms, and I wrapped my ankles around his hips and rocked once against him. I smiled against his mouth with relief as I felt a familiar hard heat under his robes.

I broke our kiss to catch my breath. I gave his bottom lip a small lick. He shuddered and looked deep into my eyes, his kindling with a golden flame.

"Can we do this?" he asked. "Carmen. I don't want to hurt you."

I slid my robe higher up my thigh and guided his hand to caress my bare skin. He sighed with longing and squeezed harder than I expected.

"We should do this," I whispered. "I trust you."

He leaned his forehead against mine and ran his strong, warm hand up my thigh and grasped my hip, tingling my skin with static. He spoke against my lips, and I felt him smile.

"We should. I've wanted you for so long, Carmen. All of you. I . . ."

He kissed me, and I was overcome by his intense passion as he roved his hands over every part of my body that he could find. I rocked against him again and slipped my tongue into his mouth. He moaned and tangled his hand in my hair. He cupped my breast and sent a smaller pulse into my heart, this time in a slow, sensual beat that shuddered through my entire body.

He carried me to the bed and laid me down onto the soft blankets, which were rumpled and chaotic from his inability to sleep, and covered me with his heat. His hands were everywhere at first like his torrential passion had finally broken through a dam, but then he slowed, stroking my skin, squeezing my curves, soaking in and memorizing every piece of me as if he might never experience me again.

"You're so soft," he murmured. I kissed his cheek and ran my hands over his firm skin and hard muscles. "Carmen . . . you're so beautiful."

I felt like a needle pierced my heart. I cupped his cheek in one hand and trailed a finger over his smooth head with the other. I lost myself in his deep, beautiful eyes, and smiled.

The more we explored each other, the more our raw instincts took over. My entire world closed in on a single, precious point;

nothing else could ever match this night's intensity, its bliss, its harmony. In my mind, there was only him. Inquieto.

I didn't want to part with him even when our energy was spent and we lay tangled together in sweaty, panting bliss. He rolled onto his back, and I snuggled against him. He didn't seem to mind. He stroked his fingers through my damp hair.

"Thank you," he murmured. I would have laughed if he didn't sound so earnest.

"Thank *you*. That was . . ." I laughed. "I've never felt this damn good."

"Me neither," he murmured, sounding sleepy. He danced his fingertips across my arm, sending residual tingles into my skin. "I'm glad you were available. It would have been difficult to stay patient after feeling how soft and warm you are."

"Available? What do you mean?"

He glanced down at me, nestled on his shoulder. "For this . . . Physically available."

I crinkled my eyebrows. "Are paz women not always 'available'?"

"Are humans?" His head perked up.

"Yes . . ."

"You can have intercourse when you're not ovulating? You're not . . . inaccessible the rest of your cycle?"

I raised my eyebrows. "No. I can have sex whenever I want."

Inquieto's eyes widened. He grew a smile like he'd won the lottery.

I giggled. "Oh, you have been missing out." I pecked a kiss on his cheek.

He turned a little red, tugging on a strand of my hair absently and looking at the ceiling.

I rubbed my hand in circles across his smooth chest, fighting another laugh that wanted to come out. But in the small silence, thoughts about Inquieto with paz women tied a little knot in my chest.

"I . . . I wouldn't know," he said in delayed reply. "Not through experience. I've only heard . . ."

I rose up on one elbow. "You're—were—a virgin." The word *virgin* came out English. "You've never had sex before?" I clarified.

"There's a lot of . . . touching involved."

"Yes, there is." I fought another smile, but then Inquieto's frown drew one of my own. "Oh." An ache of pity overwhelmed me. "You can't be that close to other paz. Your bioelectricity is too strong."

Inquieto's jaw tightened. He nodded once.

I had never seen Inquieto greet another paz by clasping forearms. I had never seen him touch another paz at all.

"In theory I can, physically," he said in halting words. "But any intimate connection involves immersion in Gnosia. Anyone who . . . might . . . want to be close to me would relinquish that deeper connection, and we would both have to actively try to stay on different frequencies so I wouldn't make them uncomfortable, and . . . it's difficult to think with any restraint when . . ."

"Having an orgasm."

He rumbled with humor despite the sad conversation. I smiled, glad I could cheer him at least a little.

"It's even more intense when a couple decides to join Houses," he said softly. "People join with partners who can deepen their connection to Gnosia. It doesn't work as well when more than two people try to join so deeply; the greater whole of Gnosia would dilute the partnership and make the bond irrelevant. Partners are meant to become, in essence, a single person."

"So based on society's opinion, you have no reason to join Houses with anyone."

He didn't answer, his frown despondent.

I squeezed his hand and nestled into him again. I didn't know what else to say. Sex was one thing, but our discussion of the paz version of marriage made me uncomfortable. Or maybe my discomfort stemmed from my desire to kiss Inquieto again right this minute. Maybe the two were tied.

"You don't have bioelectricity," he murmured, stroking my hair again between his long fingers. "You aren't part of Gnosia, either. So . . ."

I let out a shaky sigh and ran my fingertips down his chest until I reached the scarred line that was his belly button. Hatched from an egg. My mouth curved in a half smile.

"I'm glad we could do this." I met his eyes. "I like being close to you, Inquieto."

He rolled onto his side to face me. He met my eyes, his gaze direct, intense, and filled with deep pain.

"I will miss you so much when you're gone, Carmen. I didn't want to say anything because I don't want you to feel guilt for leaving. But I will miss you."

I drank in his every feature—the small, endearing crease between his eyebrows, the polished layers of gold on his skin, the diamond shape of his marble cheekbones and chin, and his full lips, bent in a troubled frown that I would do anything to turn into a smile.

"What if . . ." I said, clinging to his hand. "If Prístina's plan works, if they convince paz that I'm peaceful and won't hurt anyone, what if I . . . if we . . ."

His eyes traced every small line and curve of my face as if looking for answers. He finally opened his mouth to speak, but then he pulled me close and kissed me instead.

CHAPTER EIGHTEEN

INQUIETO FELL ASLEEP first. I stayed wrapped in his arms, feeling a soft, fuzzy joy that brought irrepressible smiles to my face and the constant, spontaneous urge to plant kisses on his skin in arbitrary places. I memorized every inch of his body with both eyes and hands, trying to imprint this moment in stone so I would never forget it. It was a good thing I did, because when I awoke in the morning, he was gone.

I felt a spasm of worry in my chest as I remembered what we'd done, what we'd shared. I dressed and left his bedroom, only to find an empty living room, and my worry gnawed its way into a pit of deep fear.

He regretted it.

Had I taken a step too far?

I swallowed a lump in my throat and folded my arms tight against me, feeling small. I took a deep breath and tried to talk myself down. He'd given me no reason last night to doubt his happiness. His absence was probably for some brief, harmless reason. Maybe he was in the kitchen making breakfast.

I walked through the house and frowned when I heard Smita barking from one of the underground stories. I neared the round foyer, but stopped in the shadow of an archway when

I heard voices, arguing. They sounded like they were near the front door.

"It's dangerous, Inquieto."

It took me a second to place the voice. When I did, my stomach sank.

Marea Reúnen.

"Mother, you don't need to act this way," Inquieto said.

"I stood by when you began this project, despite my concerns for your well-being. But that creature's behavior has escalated to an unfathomable degree. You *cannot* continue to associate with it."

My face furrowed.

"Carmen is not an 'it,' Mother," Inquieto bit out. His voice wavered as if his muscles were shaking. "She is a person like us."

"It is nothing like us. I don't understand how you can't see that. That creature shoved Justo Muestran to the ground." Marea's voice was quiet, but her horror unmistakable. "It caused the poor man to *fracture*. What will it do to you? When will that animal hurt you?"

"She brings me closer, Mother!" Inquieto said in a raw explosion of passion. I jolted in surprise. I wanted to run to him to help, but I wasn't sure if the conversation was too personal for me to be involved.

For a moment, there was nothing but austere silence. Then Marea spoke, her voice low and trembling, revulsion dripping from every word.

"It is a different species, Inquieto."

"That doesn't matter," Inquieto said, quieter, but no less intense. "Sometimes I feel like *I'm* a different species. But Carmen—I'm like her. She brings me closer to the one place I can belong—closer to *myself*—in a way no one else ever has. Like no one else ever could. We are close to each other."

He said the word *close* with obvious weight, and Marea Reúnen's revulsion made it clear he'd said something important. My lips parted, and I leaned against the wall. Paz couples deepened each other's connection to Gnosia. Their bond brought them closer to the whole.

I understood. *Brings me closer* was the paz equivalent to saying he was in love with me.

"Inquieto," Marea said, softening a little. It sounded like a deliberate switch in tactics. "Please, you need to listen to what I'm saying. You have been spending too much time with . . . her. You know your emotions are susceptible to your own mind's focal points, your solitary—"

"*My* emotions are susceptible?" he said. "Look at how all of you have treated Carmen. The waves of mistrust, Gnosia storming back and forth, something everyone says isn't supposed to happen. If you could see it from the outside, Mother, you would understand, but you don't. You can't. No one understands what I see, what I experience, except for Carmen."

I finally dared to peek around the corner. I could see both of them in profile, facing off.

"You *have* to take this opportunity to separate yourself from her," Marea said, glaring, "and spend time with us. Your own kind, your family."

"Maybe I should separate myself from *you*." Inquieto stood taller, widening his shoulders, instinctually taking the dominant stance meant for the predatory animals he cared for in the curio museum.

Marea took one step back.

"You need to control yourself," she said.

"I don't want to control myself anymore," Inquieto said, with such solid defiance, I would have cheered if I wasn't worried about interrupting.

"After all the work I've done," Marea said. "All of the years of therapy and private tutors and the patience I have shown you? You choose to cast all that aside for this—" She shook her head, and her face hardened. "Clearly, nothing I have done, or can do, will help you anymore. Nothing except *this*."

"Mother—"

"Shouldn't she be the one to decide, Inquieto? Regardless of your . . . *feelings*, isn't what I have to offer her choice? If you insist she's equal to us, then she deserves that, doesn't she?"

Inquieto stared his mother down, shaking with emotion, clenching his teeth together. His face furrowed into deep lines of anger.

Then his expression crumbled. He growled like a wounded animal and yanked the front door to the side. He left the house with a blinding flash of sunlight off his back.

A storm had just blown through Reúnen House and left tragic disaster in its wake, and I didn't even know why.

Marea faced the door, watching him go. Her breaths were quick, but otherwise, she maintained her straight posture and silent composure.

I took a breath and stepped into the foyer, avoiding the splash of raw sunlight cast from the doorway.

"What choice are you talking about?" I asked.

Marea startled and turned around. Nervousness flickered through her eyes, no doubt because of how "dangerous" she believed I was, but she kept her head held high.

"One that should be simple," she said. "I am offering you the choice to leave Paz and return to the planet you came from."

I blinked, the rest of me frozen. "They found Earth's coordinates."

"*I* found the coordinates," she said, a sneer curling her lip. "I volunteered for the team as soon as I discovered you entered my son's life. And now . . ." Residual revulsion crossed her face.

"I am grateful that I did. It's time to fix the Curio Project's drastic mistake in bringing you here."

"Wait," I said, still processing. "I can go home?"

"Yes. And for Inquieto's sake, for *everyone's* sake, it is best you do so as soon as possible. You can come with me right now, and you will be on your way to Planet 0916 in the morning."

I felt like I was swimming through liquid lead, my heart weighing me down; I was drowning. "You don't even want me to say goodbye to Inquieto?"

"You don't know my son," she said. "You can't possibly understand the harm you have done to him. *Are* doing to him. He is fragile and always has been. I have spent years trying to help him. I succeeded. He became a sound adult, but then you came. You have undone *years* of work I did to stabilize him. I need you gone, *he* needs you gone, before he gets worse."

"He is not fragile," I said, incredulous as my mind snapped awake. "He is strong and passionate and loving. He stood up for me when no one else did, and you want me to just sit by and let you—let this whole messed-up society—destroy all that beauty inside him? You have suppressed him for years. You weren't helping him. *You* were the one hurting him!"

Her black eyes flashed, but paz as she was, she didn't express her temper any more than that.

"Isn't going home what you've wanted all this time? To go back to your own planet with your own kind to be as damaging to them as you want? You don't belong here. You know that as well as I do. Come with me and *go home*."

I winced and looked down. A dry wind blew up dust from the cracked dirt outside and whisked the tops of my bare feet.

I wanted grass again. I wanted to hike through green forests and cross running rivers and touch the petals of familiar flowers. I wanted the light of a single sun on my face and the sweet smell of cool rain. I wanted to reread my favorite books and eat a cheeseburger and fresh tamales and hear Crispin's—*any* human's—laugh. I wanted to see Mamá's paintings again.

The vibrant colors of her paintings swirled into Inquieto's brilliant artwork in my mind. Powerful longing flooded in, combined with memories of Inquieto's sweet smile, his intense eyes and even more passionate touch, the warmth of his arms around me, the endless sacrifices and risks he had taken to protect me when no one else would.

I heard the gentle brush of Mamá's voice, as if in a dream, "*Quédate, mijita*." *Stay.*

I knew then that this deep connection that had been building inside of me since I didn't even know when, but that felt like always, would make it impossible for me to take Marea Reúnen's offer. Nothing, *nothing* about Earth, or any other place in the universe, was worth the painful imaginings of a life without Inquieto. I felt a growing knot in my chest as if my heart were being tied up and bound, and I welcomed it.

"No," I said.

Marea's eyes narrowed. "What?"

"I'm not going with you. I'm not going back to Earth."

"Carmen," she said, trying to placate me by using my name, "it is time for you to go home."

I looked straight into her eyes and said, "Inquieto is my home."

She glared at me, but a small sliver of heartache pierced her frown. She looked like she was fighting, god forbid, a singular *emotion*.

"You foolish creature." Her lip twitched like she wanted to say more, but she held her tongue. Her eyes hardened with determination. She turned on her heel and left through the open door in a smooth, swift stride, her golden back flashing in the sunlight.

I leaned against the wall, breathless.

My stomach fluttered, and my heart felt like it would burst, but not out of anxiety for what had just happened, or the knowledge of the opportunity I had just turned down.

My face exploded into a smile.

When Inquieto got home, whenever he got home, I would tell him how much I loved him.

* * *

I found Smita in the kitchen, scarfing down a breakfast laid out on the table, which Inquieto must have made for us. He also must have shut Smita inside when he went to answer the door, thinking he'd be right back. Maybe he would have come to the bedroom and woken me up softly, smiling.

But Marea had shown up and ruined it all. I couldn't imagine what he was going through.

I spent the day with Smita, throwing a tiq disk for her in the living room, watching the suns' light progress through the tinted windows, lower and lower in the sky.

I was sitting cross-legged on a cushion when I heard the low whine of a cell engine outside. I perked up, my knees bouncing and toes fidgeting as I listened for a clue that it was Inquieto. I got one when the house's front door slammed open even louder than when he had left that morning.

Excitement thrummed in my chest as I stood, but I froze when a series of mismatched footsteps stomped through the house. Smita bounded in front of me and barked, hackles raised.

I scrambled back when no fewer than six disciplinarians flooded the room. They took positions at the door and around the walls with trained, tactical speed. I didn't recognize any of them.

One plunged straight toward Smita.

"No!" I yelled, but before I could stop him, he clamped his hand around the back of Smita's neck and stunned her to the ground. Then the disciplinarian stepped over her still body, leering at me.

I ducked away and reared back for a punch, but he had no trouble sensing my imminent attack and dodged. I gasped in surprise as someone else's hand grabbed the back of my hair and yanked on my scalp so hard my eyes watered. The disciplinarian who had come in for the sneak attack pulled my hands against my chest and pinned my back to their body in a fierce lock.

I kicked and fought, and almost got loose when the disciplinarian seemed to forget how much stronger I was than I looked. But their partner stopped my kicking by slamming his foot on mine so hard, I wondered if it was broken.

Through my haze of pain and panic, I managed to wonder, why hadn't they stunned me?

I found out when someone new entered the room.

"You," I snarled, locking eyes with High Counselor Dignidad Fortalecen. He wore his traditional High Council uniform and looked as stiff and refined as always. His thin, bronze patterns, following his bone structure to a fault, glinted in the light of the setting suns through the tinted doors. He slipped a single glance at Smita's out-cold body with what I thought was a subtle breath of relief, and then turned all his attention to me.

"I couldn't thank you more for what you've done, Curio 0924," he said, dispassionate and collected. He linked his hands behind his back and strode forward, smooth and menacing.

"What do you want?" I said.

"As I said, to thank you. I thought I already had enough knowledge against you to solidify my people's decision to remain safely on Paz forever, but now"—a low rumble, sinister as thunder, sounded from his throat—"you've secured my success. And my power. I'm here to make sure you are taken out of society, permanently." His voice then dropped, and he prowled another step. "Perhaps, you'd rather be in a cage, away from fractured, depraved Inquieto Reúnen. Tell me, did he get too close to you in the dark?"

I bit my tongue in surprise. What was he implying? Had Marea told him about us? I swallowed, unable to utter a single syllable for fear I would condemn us prematurely.

Fortalecen took a final step that put his face only inches from mine. My nostrils were filled with his foreign scent, like twisted versions of myrrh, sage, and sea salt.

"Did he invade your territory?" he hissed. "Rile your base, animal instincts?" He leaned in and brought his lips to the cold metal of my translator behind my ear. His words seethed with hatred, "But you're not truly an animal at all, are you?"

My heart skipped a beat as he drew away. His icy stare filled me with dread that I tried to mask.

Why would he choose now to finally admit my intelligence? He couldn't mean . . . He couldn't know that I was los cortados. Had my fears come true? Had he studied the artwork in his Legacy District? Had he made the connection?

My tongue felt too dry to move, my mind numb. I was on the sidelines of my own life, watching a train wreck in slow motion.

"Where's Inquieto?" I whispered. "What did you do to him?"

Fortalecen smiled. "Don't worry, Curio 0924, I won't let him touch you anymore. Stun her."

"No!" But my protests were useless. A pulse shot into my spine. I crashed into the dark.

* * *

I awoke lying on a cold floor. I jerked in panic and scrambled to sit up. I shot my eyes around and saw I was inside a small white room with one clear wall straight ahead. A bigger room was beyond, white-walled and sterile. A long table near the center sat under a white spotlight from a round fixture on the ceiling. The table was surrounded by glowing screens and a wicked set of strange, pointy metal torture devices disguised as medical equipment. Someone had dressed me in a thin, gray shift that had the aura of a prison uniform.

Higher panic seared through me. My pulse pounded in fuzzy beats in my ears, so it took me a few seconds to realize that a voice was chattering, and it wasn't my own anxious thoughts. Only when I heard Inquieto's name did I force myself to slow down and pay attention.

"Taken you and Inquieto to the therapeutic center," the voice said, sounding distant and small. Relief flooded my body when I realized it belonged to Cálido, but where was it coming from?

"Cálido, what's happening?" I whispered, my mouth dry.

He spoke over my words as if he hadn't heard me, and his voice sounded like it was inside my head rather than coming from an outside source. It had the same distinct, intangible feeling of my translator. Had he tampered with the device to get me a recorded message? He was its inventor, after all.

"Prístina's still pleading with the council, but we can't wait for her. Fortalecen moved too fast; the council was appalled at how close you and Inquieto have become, and with Inquieto's childhood history, Fortalecen swayed them to agree with whatever he wanted. He convinced them that Inquieto fractured. They sentenced him to a level-six behavioral revision procedure. That's the highest level there is. People aren't the same after a level six, Carmen. The procedure isn't as perfect as the council pretends."

"No," I whispered. "Inquieto . . ."

"You're in a viewing room right now, not the curio museum," Cálido continued. "That window isn't made to keep strong animals inside. It's not nano-glass, Carmen. You can break it. Do whatever you have to do to get Inquieto out. Please. But know that there's a recorder in the room, so don't—just . . ." He sighed. "Be careful."

I frowned at his troubled tone. What did I care if there was a recording device when Inquieto was in danger?

"Tenaz is waiting for you in a cell outside the back entrance. After you rescue Inquieto, go—"

The door to the outer room opened with a hiss, and I missed the last of Cálido's instructions before his voice ended, and my head was empty again.

"Inquieto!" I shouted.

Inquieto was being escorted into the room by two strong-looking disciplinarians on either side. He wore a simple white robe with no shoes, and he stumbled a little as they led him toward the medical table, his head swaying like he'd been drugged.

I jumped to my feet and pressed both hands against the glass window.

"Inquieto!"

He looked at me. He was deathly pale, his face paralyzed with fear. His eyes seemed out of focus, but then his consciousness slowly swam toward me.

"Carmen," he said.

A disciplinarian gripped the back of his neck.

"No," Inquieto shouted, struggling, but clumsy from the drugs. "No! Let her go!"

He fell and hung limp in the disciplinarian's hold, his eyes vacant.

"No!" Angry tears stung my eyes. "Don't hurt him!"

They threw Inquieto onto the table. They strapped him down, wrists, ankles, and neck.

One of them sent me a contemptuous look of disgust as they left the room.

On the table, Inquieto didn't move. What would he be like when he woke up? Would the man I'd come to love—*deeply*—really be gone? I reared back my fist to punch the glass but froze when the outer door hissed again.

Fortalecen entered the room. The door closed behind him, and he pressed his hand against the surface. It shuddered into place, locking it from the inside.

He was alone.

He eyed Inquieto, his expression stoic, without pity. Then he turned toward me, and his sleek bronze eyebrows raised in surprise as he saw my poised fist. His eyes glinted with hardened delight, yet then, his expression changed so swiftly, I was caught off guard. His hard edges disappeared, and he shook his head in a great show of compassion.

I narrowed my eyes.

"Carmen," he said, using my name for the first time, and it sounded foul from his lips. "I should have known you would do anything to *fight* for your savior, but even I underestimated the force of your erratic emotions. I should have known that you wouldn't be able to comprehend that this procedure is for Inquieto's benefit."

"Benefit?" My throat felt raw, and my voice broke. "You're going to hurt him!"

"No," Fortalecen said, not abandoning his sickening compassion. "I am doing you a kindness, Carmen. I am allowing you to witness the change in him. You can take comfort when he's free of your menacing influence and can return to society as a stable paz. Under careful watch, of course."

I slammed my fist against the glass. It creaked, and hairline cracks radiated outward. I growled and almost hit it again, but Fortalecen's burnt-orange irises glowed with anticipation. He hadn't moved away from my aggression at all, despite the touch of wariness peeking through his sympathy that I was convinced was feigned.

I frowned deeper and flicked my eyes around the room. A white spherical recording drone was mounted on the ceiling in a corner. Its little blue indicator light showed it was on and functioning, just as Cálido had warned, capturing everything we were doing.

If Cálido had known a simple viewing window in a medical facility couldn't hold me, why wouldn't Fortalecen know the same? Even if he hadn't, the high counselor had disciplinarians at his beck and call. As soon as he saw the glass could shatter after one more blow, why was he still putting himself at risk?

Had he expected my reaction? Was this a setup? Was he hoping to catch my outrage on camera?

I steadied my haggard breaths. If I lashed out, Fortalecen would get what he wanted. A violent display from a wild animal. A final nail in the Migrationist movement's coffin, the final brick that would seal all paz underground for millennia.

"You can't sentence him to this," I said, my voice and muscles trembling as I struggled to maintain my rage. "Inquieto isn't like other paz. He's not part of Gnosia. He can't be. If you take away his identity, other people can't fill the gaps in his mind with theirs, do you understand? He'll be even more cut off than before. He'll be alone and empty! He'll be gone!"

Fortalecen returned a single nod. "And you will leave his side knowing that all the harm you've done to our society, and to *him*, will soon fade away."

"He loves me," I said, tears watering my eyes. "You can't take that away."

"Love," Fortalecen said, and I was surprised that his cocky demeanor turned ice cold. "Even the shadow of such raw emotions are dangerous and unstable and *must* be corrected. I viewed you as a feral animal, come to protect what it perceives as its carnal mate, but the fact that you can succumb to such a primal condition as 'love' makes you even more threatening, curio. *Los cortados*," he then said, with far more contempt and at a volume that the camera could capture as a powerful revelation.

Shit. If he hadn't already told the High Council that I was los cortados, and if the public didn't already know, I had a feeling they did now. Whether that recorder was broadcasting live or not, I had to assume it was and take advantage of that assumption if I had any hope of coming out of this in a good light.

"We're not the first ones," I said, raising my chin in defiance and locking into Fortalecen's gaze. "Inquieto and I aren't the first paz and los cortados to fall in love. That ancient artwork you so proudly display in your Legacy District—the Sumergida showed me what it used to look like. It used to show a paz woman and a human man embracing. They lived peacefully."

I choked back a sob and looked at Inquieto. His round eyes, so often filled with wonder and love that Fortalecen wanted to take away, remained closed.

"The Sumergida cannot see the full truth. They never have," Fortalecen said. His face was hard, and I thought I heard contempt in his voice, though I couldn't fathom why. He revered Gnosia. Why would he disapprove of those most connected?

"The Sumergida remember the artwork through Gnosia," I argued, and my mind started to piece past observations together. "But when you found the real stonework, you ground down those etchings of love and peace so you could use the rest of the art for your political agenda, didn't you? I *knew* they were shorn off by a different tool than the ancients used. You did it!"

Fortalecen glanced up at the recording device with his eyes only, almost too fast to see, and I knew I was right.

"Foolish logic from a lesser species," he said, taking two bold steps to the glass. He looked down into my eyes. I had never seen so much vile hatred course through a person in the single second it took for him to transform from feigned compassion to a low, seething taunt.

"I can see the violence in your eyes, los cortados," he said. "An evil mind, bent on war."

My heart railed harder, familiar rage boiling inside me like a geyser.

"You're a monster," I said.

"No, Carmen. You and your kind, *any* species that are not part of Gnosia, are the monsters."

My whole body shook. The glass creaked under my tense hand. "Say what you want about me, Fortalecen. Say I'm a monster. But Inquieto is not. Let him go."

Fortalecen's cruel humor was a low growl in his throat. He turned away and strode to the table where Inquieto lay, helpless. He opened a rectangular panel on the wall. The interior displayed a glowing screen filled with complicated symbols that I couldn't understand. But I understood the wickedness in Fortalecen's eyes as he pressed his hand upon the screen.

A boxy, white machine, which took up half the wall across the room, hummed to life, with multiple rows of lights flashing. Several flexible clear tubes, all roped together, rose out of the machine's side. They stretched to the ceiling and across the room, all the way to Inquieto's medical table. The tubes fed into the device on the ceiling that resembled a metal halo, each tube connected to a different syringe-like needle around its edges.

The wicked halo was positioned right over Inquieto's head. It started to lower.

"No!" I yelled. "Turn it off!"

Fortalecen eyed me, but he didn't move from his place in front of the table. He also didn't say a word. All he had to do was wait.

If I wanted to save Inquieto, I'd have to go through him. Even if I got the satisfaction of giving Fortalecen what he had coming, disciplinarians would probably surge into the room to arrest me or worse. Inquieto would be put through the procedure anyway. Fortalecen would win.

If anything happens to me, do not interfere, Inquieto's past words swam through my head. *Please, tell me you won't do anything rash. Don't make things worse for you on my account.*

Like hell would I have listened to his advice before, but now I focused on the true depth of his words. I *would* interfere—I would save him. But he was right. I shouldn't do anything rash. I had to dig deeper. I had to uproot my thriving rage that threatened to strangle my every thought. I had to plant stronger emotions, steady, lasting, and unyielding, filled with purpose, fueled not by grief, but by hope.

This was my chance to prove, not only to the paz watching, but to *myself*, that I was different. I was better. I closed my eyes.

Temper, querida.

Thanks, Mamá. This time, I had my temper under control.

No matter what, I wouldn't fulfill my role as a violent los cortados to save Inquieto unless I had no other choice. But I also couldn't let those needles get a single inch closer to his head. I darted my eyes around the room, searching for *any* other way that wouldn't lead to a hopeless conclusion.

The hum from the machine across the room quickened into a whir. Liquids of varying foul-looking shades shot into the tubes, ready to feed some horrendous cocktail of chemicals into Inquieto's brain.

"You can't stop it," Fortalecen said. "Your brute strength is useless here."

"Is it?"

I slammed my fist into the glass, feeling an exhilarating rush of release, but the superficial flash didn't overwhelm my senses. I kept control as the glass splintered and shattered under my blow.

Then I lunged toward Fortalecen.

His muscles jolted, but his eyes were alight with excitement. He took a bracing breath, and I knew my suspicions were true—he wasn't planning to dodge. He'd prepared himself to take this blow when planning his charade.

I didn't give him the satisfaction. I blew past him in a single leap and slammed into the vile machine across the room. The metal crunched under my weight, sparks flying. Fortalecen snarled, but I grabbed the rope of liquid-filled tubes and yanked them off the machine before he could even think to stop me. The tubes split, and acidic-smelling liquid sprayed everywhere. I let them go and shielded my face. The machine sparked even more, with violent pops wherever the liquid touched. The whirring heightened to a shrill whistle, and white vapor started hissing from the machine. I took a step back and glanced at Fortalecen. His eyes were trained on the vapor. Fear flickered on his face.

Then the whole thing blew.

The force of the explosion felt like I'd slammed into a wall, or rather, that a wall slammed into *me*. My ears rang, and then sound cut out completely as my back and skull hit the floor. Debris blasted across my body as sparks crackled and dust rained down from the ceiling. The overpowering smell of smoke and freshly struck matches assaulted my nose. The spotlight on the ceiling dimmed and flickered in chaotic spasms. I rolled over and covered my head, cowering for a moment of blind fear. I was back in Mexico, a car horn blaring, crushed by metal, Mamá's single scream echoing in my ears before she went silent forever.

The falling debris settled. I gasped, but my chest felt tight. I wanted to stay huddled there, wait for a paramedic to save me from the car crash and take me to a hospital . . . where I would learn Mamá hadn't made it. All-consuming fear hit me, more charged than that devastating, hole-creating moment. There'd been no saving my mother by the time we each reached the hospital. But I could save Inquieto now. There was still time.

I ground my teeth and forced myself back to reality. I coughed dust and pushed myself up on wavering arms.

My stinging, watery eyes widened when I saw that the entire wall that had supported the boxy machine was gone. The recording device dangled from the ceiling by a thread, swaying in the open space. Its indicator light was dark and useless. I was inches away from the floor's broken edge, and a simple look down was enough to send me reeling back.

I'd had no concept of where the therapeutic center was within the city. I hadn't given it a thought until now, when it was thrust in my face, that we were suspended from the high cavern ceiling of Provenance District. The relatively small explosion hadn't damaged the rest of the building, which stretched vertically under me as a long, white cylinder, but people on the street far below had scattered around the mangled machine and the wall's debris. The machine looked like a speck on the street; the people were grains of salt. Even with Paz's lesser gravity, there was no chance I'd survive that fall.

My next breath was tighter than the last, and the one after, painful, as I realized that my dizziness wasn't only due to fear. The building's oxygen circulation was thinning from the wall-sized hole in the room, and the high level of carbon dioxide and sulfur dioxide underground was sweeping inside. At this height, lightweight carbon monoxide might even be a possibility. The paz were evolved to handle all that; I was not. And I didn't have my oxygen concentrator.

I clutched my chest and forced myself to take slower breaths, fighting my inner scream of panic.

Inquieto stirred with a small groan. I twisted around and stumbled to my feet. I didn't see Fortalecen anywhere through the debris, but Inquieto still lay on the table, far enough away from the explosion to be spared. The halo full of needles had stopped in midair over his head. His eyes were closed, and he didn't move or make another sound.

I rushed to him and ripped the cuff around his neck loose. I checked for a pulse and let out a breath of relief, but I regretted the unnecessary exhale when my next breath sent a swarm of black spots into my vision. I braced myself on the table, noticing the alarming sight of my fingernails turning slightly blue, but I managed to wrench the other cuffs around his wrists and ankles free.

"Inquieto." I put both hands on his cheeks and shook him lightly. "Inquieto!"

He didn't move. I wrapped my arms around him and cradled him against my chest, tears filling my eyes. I looked around for the faint outline of the door. When I saw it through the falling dust, I slid Inquieto off the table, thankful now more than ever for my extra strength on Paz, but his weight didn't help my short breaths get any deeper. I shuffled to the door, knowing how unlikely it was that my palm's low level of electricity could open it, but hoping I could smash it open before I fainted. I laid Inquieto down and propped him against the wall.

I slapped my palm against the door, but it didn't dissolve into vapor. I stepped back, took a breath, and ran at the door full force. My shoulder hit, but the door didn't even tremble. I cringed and slumped against its hard surface to the floor.

I tensed when I heard heavy footsteps behind me. I looked over my shoulder. Fortalecen stood underneath the dangling recording device near the corner of the blasted wall, his expression dark and menacing. Without a word, he slammed his palm against the adjoining wall and sent out a shuddering electric pulse.

Everything went dark.

The only lights were distant pinpricks from the city below, too weak to penetrate the upper reaches of the cavern where we stood. No twinkling cell tracks snaked nearby. I was blind.

I strove to calm my breathing as I crouched over Inquieto. Fortalecen had gone silent—and suddenly, I knew what he was doing.

I couldn't see in the dark. Neither could Fortalecen.

But he had other ways to navigate the blackness.

I took as deep a breath as I could, and held it. Breaking down the door fast enough to escape didn't look like an option, not when I couldn't see Fortalecen or how he might try to stop me—or from what angle he might attack Inquieto if I was distracted.

Hammers pounded at the edges of my brain, but I pushed them back, trying to think of solutions. Fortalecen knew I would stay by Inquieto, unless he thought my drive for survival was too base. But I thought, deep down, he recognized how truly paz-like I was.

For once, that was a detriment.

I ran my trembling hands along the floor, searching for anything I could use as a weapon. I hadn't wanted it to come to violence, but I wouldn't hesitate if there were no alternatives.

I heard a metallic scrape on the floor ahead. It sounded like Fortalecen had the same idea, and my panic forced me to exhale and take another quick breath.

My skin tingled as I imagined, possibly even sensed, the electrical pulses Fortalecen was sending into the room. Paz may have sugarcoated their uses for electrolocation, with talk of soothing and innocent navigation, but some Earth animal species shared that ability for a much more dangerous purpose. My guess was that the paz's bioelectricity had evolved for the same reason, and Fortalecen knew it well.

To hunt.

He could sense the walls, the equipment, the table. It was all coming to him through bioelectric feedback. How soon would he find my beating heart, my twitching muscles, the shape of my crouching body?

I stopped my silent search for a weapon, afraid that any movement, however small, could alert him to where I was. I balled myself up as small as possible, coiling my muscles to either pounce or roll out of the way.

I heard a light footstep, a brush of his robe's hem. He was getting closer.

I closed my eyes. I would need to take another breath soon. When I did, he would find me.

Fortalecen had stopped making any sounds at all. I couldn't even hear him breathing; with his ability to withstand less oxygen, maybe he wasn't. Maybe he could hold his breath longer than I could.

But then I caught a faint whiff of his familiar scent. The notes akin to sage and sea salt had faded, so only myrrh remained, barely there. Fortalecen probably had no idea it could give him away. An enhanced sense of smell might be a small thing compared to paz electrolocation, but it was enough.

The scent was coming from my left, so I rolled right.

He spun, sharply aware of my presence as I'd predicted. But I had surprised him; I barreled into his legs and knocked him over before he could react. I grabbed his arm and yanked him away from Inquieto, dragging him across the floor in the only direction I could—toward the wide opening of the broken wall.

My shortness of breath made my legs feel weak, my brain dizzier with each passing second. Light flashed once from the ceiling before us plunging into darkness again, and I stumbled, my grip loosening.

I yelled in surprise when Fortalecen broke free and twisted, grabbing my calf and pulling me to the ground. I fell flat on my back and tried to crawl backward, but Fortalecen climbed up my body, crushing me. Strobing electric lights flashed and flickered, while sparks sprayed from the broken wall, blinding me, not stopping. The light exposed his face with shocking definition, deepening shadows, reflecting off the shimmering bronze so his monstrous skeletal patterns were all I could see. I was being assaulted by death itself. His breath was hot on my face as he grasped my hair, my scalp burning.

"I have to enforce the security of this world," he hissed, pinning me down. I tried to shout, but he slapped his other hand across my mouth. "You—and every other inferior, *violent* species in this universe—will ravage our peace and destroy our people."

My eyes widened. The lights blacked out again, crawling, oppressive darkness. He pulled his hand from my mouth, and I heard another loud metallic scrape on the floor beside us.

I screamed as piercing pain ruptured my side.

Fortalecen inhaled a seething breath of triumph. "Do you know how long I've waited for this?" He drove whatever make-shift weapon he had found deeper into my body. "To face one of you in person. Not as an illusion from the past, but here, now. Subject to my mercy. But you didn't give us mercy, did you, los cortados?"

I gasped for air. "I don't know!"

White light flashed again like magnesium sparks, burning all thoughts away, highlighting my excruciating pain.

Fortalecen twisted the weapon with another sharp shoot of pain. He was *enjoying* this.

I looked away from his horrifying magma eyes. Through the strobing light, I saw that the little blue light on the recorder, dangling from the ceiling, had turned on. I heard a commotion through the closed door, muffled bangs and voices of people who might offer rescue, but they sounded distant.

"Help," I called, but if their yells weren't pushing through, then there was no chance my weak voice would make it. Fortalecen had locked the door from the inside before the explosion. How long would it take them to get it open?

I inhaled sharply through my teeth when Fortalecen pushed off my body and stood. Light crashed into darkness again. I tried to find the object still piercing my side, but my hand shook so much, all I could do was flounder in the dark. All I could feel was slick, hot blood.

"I didn't plan on seeing you die like this," Fortalecen said, his voice heavy and coarse. "I was so careful, planned with such meticulous attention. When I *suggested* to Justo Muestran that he program the wrong coordinates into the procurer ship to make it look like you hailed from Planet 0916, I planned to persuade my fellow counselors to return you there once my purpose for you was finished. They would view me as a compassionate leader, and you would perish as soon as your automated ship landed on that truly inhospitable planet."

I inhaled wheezy breaths, trying to fight through the pain to process what he was saying. Because he *couldn't* be saying . . .

"You were supposed to remain in containment," he continued, his voice lowering to a simmering hiss. "People were supposed to see your true, feral, violent inclinations, so when I'd reveal you were a los cortados monster, they would see for themselves how terrifying other intelligent species are. But Inquieto Reúnen gave you a translator. To speak, to *explain* your thought processes and behaviors, to awaken sympathy and *empathy* with my fellow paz . . . I knew I had no choice but to wait for a new, opportune moment to prove how dangerous you are. I had to give my people enough time to recognize firsthand that you are intelligent, enthrall them into thinking you could be like one of us, then show them how even the most innocent species, the most *like us*, still cannot be trusted—sapient and violent make a threatening combination, indeed.

"Never did I imagine that you and Inquieto's relations would devolve into such a disgusting and—useful—arrangement. Your obscene devotion to him bolstered my confidence that this outcome, *this* moment, would bring out your worst. Even better, Inquieto Reúnen has proven to be a disturbed, fractured man. His foul behavior with you proves it. I must thank you, truly. You *handed* me the opportunity to easily dispose of you both."

"What?" I said, struggling to stay conscious. My shaky fingers found the piece of scrap metal embedded in my side, slick with blood. I wrapped my hand around it but stopped. I didn't know what would help more—yanking it out, or letting it plug the hole in my flesh.

The lights flickered back on. Fortalecen wasn't wearing the gloating smile I'd imagined in the dark. His eyes grew haunted, his voice hollowing.

"Do you know what it's like to be immersed in the memories of a dying people?" he asked.

The lights turned back off.

"My grandfather showed me what the Curio Project could awaken," Fortalecen continued. "He took me to the hollows of the equator; the Sumergida guided me to the past, to reaches of Gnosia no one else can touch. No one was as attuned or as powerful as me, they said."

I heard him take a step toward me.

"Do you know what that's like?" he whispered, but his voice grew in volume with every new word. "Seeing, feeling the horror of war firsthand, as if I were *there*. As a child! Standing with ancient paz on the blood-drenched soil of your planet. Watching visions of my people bleed out at the hands of yours—from the weapons of los cortados. *Humans. Your* ancestors. No, you can't know what I've gone through; you're not part of us. You can't understand, and that is why I had to bring you here to show your threat to my people. *That* is why I cannot let you live."

"You!" I screamed, finally making sense of everything he was saying. "You were the child the Sumergida talked about. They said you couldn't find the coordinates for Earth, but you saw visions of los cortados when you were a kid and—"

"They told you correctly. As a child, I couldn't find the coordinates," he said. "No matter how hard I tried, they eluded me for years—until I discovered them at last, etched in the ancient artwork in my Legacy District. You wondered if I could feel a connection to my ancestors, do you recall?" A low rumble prowled in his throat, but there was no mirth in the sound.

"You scraped the coordinates off the stone so no one else would know," I said. "But you used them. You used them to find me. You took me to Paz on purpose. To prove a *point*?"

"Inquieto's charity only postponed the inevitable," he said. The lights flashed so I could see a fracture of his cruel smile, right above me. "The moment I planned is finally here. Everyone will know that you attacked me and that I was forced to defend myself. Sympathy for me will meld with abhorrence of you. You *will* fulfill your purpose."

He planted his foot on my neck, poised to finish his kill. "The chaos and violence you have brought to our world will cease. People will be terrified to ever leave the safety of our home lest this happen again. We will thrive underground, and Gnosia will always remain."

I felt hard pressure on my throat. I couldn't scream; I couldn't move. Fortalecen was going to win.

Inquieto . . .

Tears filled my eyes. *Mamá, te veo . . .*

I almost didn't realize it when the lights flickered back on through my blackened vision, but the sight of Inquieto, standing over Fortalecen with a glower of rage on his face, jerked me back to lucidity.

Fortalecen looked up. His mouth gaped in fear. I didn't blame him. Inquieto's black eyes raged, his amber irises alight with flames. His golden skin flashed and his back reflected the light above, making him shine in a holy glow like a vengeful angel.

He grabbed Fortalecen by the shoulders and dragged him away from me. I took a huge gasp for air, one that blazed pain through my side.

Fortalecen recovered quickly from his dismay. He broke free of Inquieto's hold.

"She was dangerous," Fortalecen said as if I were already dead. "She tried to kill me! She would have killed *you*, Reúnen. You couldn't see how dangerous she was."

Inquieto took a step toward him. Fortalecen backed up toward the broken wall.

"I'm trying to help you, Inquieto."

Inquieto took one more solid step.

"I'm helping our people," Fortalecen said. "Can't you see that?"

"No," Inquieto said. He reached out and placed a hand, almost in a brotherly way, on Fortalecen's shoulder.

Fortalecen dropped like a stone.

He collapsed in a heap on the floor, one hand dangling off the broken edge of the building, hundreds of feet above the cavern streets. Inquieto's rage blinked into surprise as he looked at his own hand, like he was waking from a dream in which his fury had eclipsed his waking mind.

"You stunned him," I said.

He looked down at Fortalecen's body. The counselor's eyes were glassy and vacant like two obsidian orbs. For a second, I thought Inquieto's horror and guilt from his childhood trauma would hit him, but his expression hardened.

"I did," he said.

I smiled, but each of my breaths crackled and wheezed. Hot blood pooled under me.

"Carmen," he said, his voice shaky with shock as he noticed my injury. He rushed over and scooped me into his arms. I screamed, and he held me close against his solid, warm chest. He touched his fingers to my forehead, but instead of a soothing wave, my body snapped awake. But it wasn't enough. I was only vaguely aware of him carrying me across the bloody floor and into the hallway.

"You're safe, Carmen. Stay conscious. Please." His voice brushed my ear.

"I'm . . . sorry, Inquieto," I said between ragged breaths. "I can't."

CHAPTER NINETEEN

I NEVER EXPECTED to wake up. When I did, I wished I hadn't. My head hurt, my lungs hurt, my right side *really* hurt . . .

"Carmen?"

I winced and looked up to see Inquieto's anxious face. I didn't know where we were, but we were somewhere bright. Too bright to be the dim interior of the therapeutic center.

"Carmen," he said, smoothing hair from my face and cupping my cheeks in his warm hands. "She's awake, Pensadora."

High-pitched whines made me look to my left. I smiled. Smita was right at eye level. Inquieto put his hand on her head to keep her from jumping onto the cushioned medical table I was lying on, but she didn't hesitate to lick my cheek.

I laughed and regretted it, grunting in pain. I jumped when someone approached from my right, and I saw the very first paz I had ever laid eyes on, a familiar woman doctor—Curio Lifeist Pensadora.

"It's all right, Carmen," Inquieto said. "You're not in Curio Medical. We brought Pensadora here to the hospital. She does know your body best." He gave me an apologetic smile.

Pensadora's frown looked apologetic, too. I felt a small surge of victory knowing she felt guilty over her treatment of me in the Curio Life Museum.

"Carmen," she said, my name even sounding like an apology. "I am going to show you your injury so that you will understand what happened and the treatment I have administered. But I don't want you to move." She gave me a stern look. "If you put too much pressure on your wound, it will not heal properly. Do you understand?"

"Yes," I said with a premature grimace. I wasn't sure if I wanted to see my side or not, with the way she was preparing me.

She nodded and folded back a thin white blanket from my waist.

"Whoa," I said, staring. A bright orange and red blob covered the entire right side of my torso, the same kind of rubbery eggshell bandage I was used to, but huge.

"How long will it take to heal?" I asked with a nervous swallow.

"At least seventy days. It was a very deep and jagged puncture wound"—she paused, steadying herself against the horrors Fortalecen had committed—"caused by a non-sterile implement which contributed to infection. I will discharge you from the hospital in two days, if all goes well, but *only* if you have the self-restraint to rest until it heals."

She eyed us both like she would personally make our lives miserable if we disobeyed. I nodded.

"Good. I will speak to the other lifeists on the ward. If they do not alert me to any complications, I will come back to check on you tomorrow."

"Thank you, Pensadora," Inquieto said, more earnestly than I would have. Then again, she did save my life, even if I couldn't forget all the poking and prodding she had administered in the museum. I managed a grateful nod as she left.

I gasped as Inquieto bowed over me and pressed his forehead against mine with desperate speed. He spoke against my lips, too distraught to kiss them, too anxious to pull away.

"I thought you were going to die," he said.

"I love you," I said, fast and breathless and unexpected. But true. Truer than any words I'd ever spoken. "I feel *close* to you."

Inquieto's eyes grew round with wonder, the same as the first time we'd met eyes through the wall of my museum habitat. He stroked his fingers through my hair.

"I didn't have a word for this feeling before I met you," he said. "But I love you, Carmen. I have loved you for a long time."

I kissed him, joy floating through me. When we parted, I had a million questions on my tongue.

"What happened?" I asked. "Are you all right? The procedure—"

"The procedure never started," he said. "You stopped it, Carmen. You shouldn't have risked your life, though. I—"

"I wasn't going to let them hurt you," I said, but the exertion of speaking, let alone with any force, put unwelcome pressure on my lungs. I sighed and ran a tired hand over Smita's soft fur. Inquieto sat down near my thigh.

"Fortalecen," I said. "You stunned him."

Inquieto gave me a slow nod.

"Thank you," I said. "I know that must have been hard for you."

He shook his head once. "You taught me not to fear my emotions. I used my anger against Fortalecen and stunned him to protect you. I don't regret what I did."

I brushed his hand with a single finger. "What's going to happen now? The council . . ."

"Lifeists and disciplinarians arrived by the time I carried you through the therapeutic center. Some accompanied us to the hospital. Others retrieved Fortalecen. I was too worried about you to answer their questions, and my stunning of Fortalecen was . . . powerful. He was asleep for a long time."

He paused with a heavy, pensive frown before he continued.

"Without any coherent witnesses, they turned to the recording device in the room."

"I thought that was destroyed."

"Those recorders are built for any environment. They're hardy. Cálido had infiltrated the system and was working to disable it from the beginning, but when he saw that recording the events was in your favor, he got it working again after the explosion. The recorder caught Fortalecen hurting you. The High Council wanted to analyze the recording right away. It was . . . telling. Your motives and actions were clear, as were his. *You* were the peaceful one, Carmen. Everyone saw it. Once Fortalecen woke up and was deemed medically sound, he was arrested. His trial has lasted for days."

"Days? Is that how long I've been asleep?"

He nodded.

"What about us?" I asked. "What are they going to do? That recording showed Fortalecen saying I was los cortados. Everyone must think—"

"Fortalecen tried to ensnare you in a trap, but he caught himself instead. He broadcasted the recording to pubcom as it was happening. The public saw everything. Cálido says Gnosia is responding well to your innocence. Prístina's sway with the council is stronger now with Fortalecen gone, and Memoria Levantan, the longest-serving member, was sympathetic to you from the beginning. Considering all that, and Fortalecen's crimes, I'd predict we have a good chance of coming out of this okay."

I smiled at his use of my common phrase that my translator had never quite figured out. *Okay.* I hoped with all my heart it was true.

"And if they decide we're in the wrong anyway?" I said.

"I'll keep you safe," he said, taking my hand, "and clearly, you're even better at protecting me. We'll find your way home."

"Inquieto, when your mother came by, when she offered to send me back to Earth . . . I said no. Before any of this happened. I didn't want to go. I didn't want to leave you."

His round eyes searched my face as if he were testing his footing on a high bridge, terrified it might break, praying for courage to cross.

"Carmen . . ."

I opened my arm wide, beckoning him closer. He smiled, the sweetest smile I'd ever seen, and wrapped his long, comforting arms around me. He rested his chin on top of my head, and I felt his trembling sigh. I cried happy tears and nuzzled close, listening to his strong heartbeat that matched mine.

***

The High Council chamber in the Egalitarian looked exactly how I remembered. The domed ceiling of tinted, crystal-faceted glass welcomed sunlight into the round sepia-hued room. The obsidian symbol of Paz government, a half-circle under a horizontal line, loomed over the circle of seated high counselors.

There were two differences, however. One, I wasn't as frightened as the first time, when I'd had no clue of my surroundings or fate, when I'd depended solely on Inquieto, who'd been a mere stranger to me.

The second difference was that instead of eleven counselors, only ten sat behind their individual desks. The eleventh stood near the edge of the room near the prisoner's door, flanked by five disciplinarians. Fortalecen's hands were bound together in white cuffs. I knew exactly how those restraints felt, and I hoped they chafed his wrists as much as they had mine. Instead of his fine counselor robes, he wore a plain gray, floor-length shift. He had neglected to look at me since I entered the room through the larger, ornate door a few moments ago.

"Carmen O'Dwyer," said Counselor Memoria Levantan. "We, as the High Council, would like to formally thank you for your assistance in apprehending the criminal Dignidad Fortalecen and bringing his injustices to our attention. Paz is grateful to you. We cannot have this kind of behavior in our society."

She spoke stiffly about Fortalecen and his crimes. I could only imagine the personal shock the High Council had to deal with during his trial.

"We are in favor of sentencing him to the highest level of behavior revision," Memoria continued, "but, as you are his primary victim, and . . . being able to offer an outside perspective from Gnosia, we would like your opinion before we make a decision."

"Behavior revision? Like what he wanted to do to Inquieto?"

"That is correct," Memoria said. "We are undecided as to whether his extreme actions were due to fracture or not. His crime was based on detailed, premeditated, long-term plans." All ten counselors experienced a domino wave of subtle shudders. "Fractures are sudden occurrences. Citizen Fortalecen's situation is unique, but we think a soothing immersion into Gnosia will help him, regardless."

"No," I said.

She lifted her eyebrows.

"He deserves a punishment," I said. "A strict one. He doesn't belong in society." I glared at him. He wore a hard frown, but a crease of confusion formed between his eyebrows.

I took a step forward and regretted it when my side panged. I had been offered a chair for the hearing, but I'd wanted the satisfaction of showing Fortalecen that his attempt to kill me hadn't come close. I fought my pain as I continued.

"You can't keep correcting people's behavior artificially. Treating mental illnesses through medical means can be helpful, yes. Crucial, even. But going so far as to making Fortalecen a compliant slave to your society's every whim isn't going to help anyone. Is the revision really intended to help the patient? Or to placate them for society's sake? Put him in prison and get him therapy to deal with whatever messed-up stuff his grandfather put him through with the Sumergida as a kid. Try medicine other than behavior revision so he can heal, and maybe, eventually, he'll figure out how to be a decent person on his own. That's my advice."

Counselor Levantan's thoughtful frown spread around the circle of counselors. I snuck another glance at Fortalecen.

He hadn't shown me any anger since I'd walked in the council chamber for getting him arrested, but now he glowered at me with fury. His expression was more pointed than his looks of hatred before when he'd acted like my entire species was crawling in my single body. I suspected his enmity had now become far more personal. He was furious because he didn't understand why I was showing him mercy. He was furious about being in my debt.

"Carmen is showing wisdom in this," High Counselor Prístina Reúnen said. The others looked her way. "There are many changes we need to implement in our society as we progress toward the future. Citizen Fortalecen's sentence can be the beginning of those changes."

Counselor Levantan and several others nodded in sync.

"We will confer and decide on an appropriate sentence at a later time," Counselor Levantan said.

The disciplinarians surrounding Fortalecen gave her curt nods. They took Fortalecen by the elbows. He shrugged them off with a stiff jerk and walked with them on his own, his head held high. The humble side door to the chamber opened, and Fortalecen disappeared.

"Although our attention has been focused on Fortalecen's trial," Levantan said, "we did take the time to address other issues. Carmen O'Dwyer, you have shown us that we cannot blame other species for our own inadequacies, or allow fear to prevent us from seeking an avenue toward the next phase of our existence, a phase that may include migrating to other worlds.

"As you know, we now have the coordinates to send you home to your planet. We hope you can understand why we are not yet ready to interact with your people, but we will send you home, discreetly. We offer that chance to you, and you may take it now or at any point in the future you decide. However, you have shown great worth and have proven your civility to us. If you wish to remain on Paz, we will grant you full citizenship, and you will be treated as an equal in every respect. The choice is yours."

I looked up at Inquieto. He kept his gaze on Levantan, and other than a subtle tightening of his jaw, wore a complete poker face. I felt a soft swell of gratitude. He didn't want to influence my decision. He didn't want to stop me from leaving him if I wanted to.

I took Inquieto's hand, intertwining my fingers with his. He released a small breath and squeezed back.

"I have another idea," I told the council. Memoria raised her eyebrows, and Prístina leaned forward with curiosity.

I fought a smile.

* * *

I once traveled across a galaxy, but I had never witnessed space.

Now, through a window on the wide bridge of a paz space-ship, I soaked in the deep blackness and pinpoint stars, feeling smaller and less significant than I ever had. Yet, with Inquieto in my life, I felt important. It was a strange experience, to have my mind blown away by how small I felt, while my heart knew how big I was. Yet, even with the disconnect, it felt right. I felt whole.

The shriek of the lluthian shook me out of my reverie.

"Cálido looked her in the eye," Inquieto said as I heard his footsteps from behind me. Smita's clicking nails trotted behind him.

"Aw," I said, imagining the poor yellow-and-red-spined creature leaping into its cage's glass wall.

"I can't count the amount of times I've reminded him not to," Inquieto continued. "He's in the cargo hold with her now. You can hear how well their interaction is going."

I stifled a laugh. "You think he's cut out for this job?"

"He'll have to adapt," Inquieto said. "Just like the animals."

"True," I said, still staring, literally, into space.

Inquieto and I were alone on the bridge, which, other than the enormous nano-glass window, was lined with panels containing more buttons and translucent blue screens than I could count. The ship was on autopilot for the moment, leaving Paz's gravity well before it could perform a jump to the nearest solar system via something akin to a real-life warp drive. Cálido had offered to explain the technology in more detail, as well as the ship's artificial gravity system, even though Tenaz assured me it would be a boring lesson. I was glad they were both accompanying us on this extraordinary journey. It was a comfort, having people around me who I'd begun to think of as family.

"You think the lluthian will do okay on her home world?" I asked. "After all this time away?"

"We'll stay long enough to make sure she does," Inquieto said. "We will with all of the curios, and we'll take care of any who can't readapt to the wild. We'll make your idea a reality, Carmen." His voice lowered. "I should have tried to get them home long ago, no matter how fascinated I was, no matter the connection I felt. Thank you for showing me that, Carmen."

"You would have asked the council, eventually," I said. "You're sweet and thoughtful. I know you would have reached that idea on your own at some point in life. Don't be hard on yourself." I turned and saw my words had drawn a sweet smile through his words of guilt, but my smile faded a little. "How's the rest of the team?"

His eyes flicked down, but he nodded. "Gnosia is still intact, for now. We'll know for certain when we clear Paz's magnetosphere."

I extended my hand. He drew close and took it.

"You're going to do great," I said. "If Gnosia disappears, they'll have you. You'll guide them to understand they can be happy as individuals."

"And we'll teach them that separate doesn't mean alone," he said. He brushed my cheek, and I closed my eyes and leaned into his warmth.

Over a Paz year had passed since my abduction, and that year was a whirlwind. After the events revealing Fortalecen's treachery, Gnosia swung toward the ideals of migration, and official plans were decreed not long after. Prístina said it was the fastest decision Gnosia had made in known memory, though from the sound of their one-hundred-year debate before my arrival, I told her it had been a long time coming.

There were outliers from the decision, however, also a largely unprecedented situation. A significant few still argued against migration and loudly expressed their hatred of me and Inquieto. I suspected, even if we could succeed in our hasty plans to take shelter on another world, some people would remain on Paz, hiding in the dark, hoping the few magnetic shields still being built would protect their bond of Gnosia. The Sumergida had yet to voice their stance on the matter; as deeply tied to Gnosia as they were, I couldn't imagine they'd be keen on leaving Paz. We could only hope that, if paz descendants returned in three thousand years to check on their peers, they'd be all right.

The early plans for migration quickly turned to action. Marea Reúnen surprised us all by joining forces with others at the Understand to develop necessary technologies for the enormous undertaking. Perhaps it was part of her personal penance for outing my and Inquieto's relationship to Fortalecen. We'd both had been loath to forgive his mother's betrayal, but she had convinced us that she never would have told Fortalecen if she'd known he was going to sentence Inquieto to behavioral revision. She'd even thanked me for saving her son. Profusely. I had to admit, I'd enjoyed having the high ground in that conversation.

Meanwhile, Prístina had begun the task of organizing the populace. I didn't envy her, especially since her egg hatched midwinter. She named the beautiful baby girl Esperanza—*hope*—and carried her around wherever she went, Esperanza clutching her shoulder ridges with tiny hands.

Esperanza wasn't born with Inquieto's disability like Prístina once feared, but connecting to Gnosia might not matter for her generation, regardless, or future generations. The strongest quandary concerning migration remained to be tested—would Gnosia survive away from Paz's signature magnetic field?

We were about to find out.

Thirty intrepid paz, all supporters of the Migrationist movement, volunteered to come with us on this first manned exploratory mission. Half were House partners, like Cálido and Tenaz, with hopes that the person who brought them closer to Gnosia, who knew them best, would also be the most effective person to keep them sane once Gnosia disappeared. The other half were un-partnered, to see how they would fare. Inquieto had been given the profound responsibility, along with a paz psychologist, to aid their transition into individuality should the need arise. Hopefully, they'd find distraction in the momentous task before us. They were all scientists, ready to aid our common goal of returning curios to their home planets, while assessing each planet for migration potential, not just from an orbital view, but by standing on firm ground.

I wished I could have stayed on Paz longer to spend time with Esperanza, and even to get to know Marea and Oyente better now that they finally accepted me, but there would be time for that later. We only had the equivalent of four more Earth years to find a place for the paz species to settle. There was no time to waste. As I'd told Inquieto, it was time to be fearless.

Still, I felt a nervous jitter in my stomach at the idea of more extraterrestrial encounters when Paz had been such a mixed bag. I'd never been content to stay in one place for long, though, racing from wildfire to wildfire, traveling Earth with fervor. My wanderlust and Inquieto's vibrant sense of curiosity and adventure were too strong for us to contain. And why should we?

I met Inquieto's gaze. He started to lower his hand from my cheek, but I pinned it there.

"What's wrong?" I asked.

"Are you sure you don't want to go back to Earth?" he said softly.

I frowned. He'd asked me that countless times over the past year. I thought I'd finally convinced him that he was stuck with me, but maybe actually being on a spaceship, where a push of a button could take me away in moments, had reawakened his fears.

"Paz was dangerous for me at first," I said, stroking the back of his hand with my thumb. "Earth would be dangerous for you. People wouldn't trust you. We don't know what happened between paz and humans in the ancient past, not everything. But it looks like there really was a war."

"We shouldn't dwell on what happened in the past," he said. "People can change. We are here, alive, now. That's what matters."

"You're right," I said with a soft smile. Mamá would have said something like that.

I'd been caught up in the past too long, focusing on expressionless people on stone walls, struggling to take any step toward a future without her. Now the future seemed easy with Inquieto, no matter how far we might venture into the unknown.

"Still," I said, "it would take a lot of groundwork for interaction between our species to be peaceful."

"You wouldn't have to bring me."

"We talked about this."

"I know. But you always have the option, Carmen. Like the council said."

"Not as long as I'm in love with you, I don't." I kissed his palm, and then twisted in his arms so he could wrap them around me while I looked at the magnificent view outside the window. He rested his chin on top of my head. Smita trotted over from the corner and sat on my feet.

"Though," I said, "Smita probably misses Gaurav. And . . . I would love to show you Mamá's paintings."

Inquieto squeezed me tight. "I would love to see them."

I nestled against him, happy and content, listening to his heartbeat. A growing thrill ran through me with imaginings of the exhilarating explorations our new future together might hold, and not just of the planets on our otherworldly itinerary. I wanted to explore Inquieto and to let him explore me. I wasn't afraid to show him everything, to let him in.

He pressed his hand against my heart, sending electric bliss into every new beat. I relaxed against him, and everything else drifted away.

"One step at a time," I said.

I found I was content to linger on this one.

THE END

GRAND PATRONS

Richard Szambelak

INKSHARES

INKSHARES is a community, publisher, and producer for debut writers. Our books are selected not just by a group of editors, but also by readers worldwide. Our aim is to find and develop the most captivating and intelligent new voices in fiction. We have no genre—our genre is debut.

Previously unknown Inkshares authors have received starred reviews in every trade publication. They have been featured in every major review, including on the front page of the *New York Times*. Their books are on the front tables of booksellers worldwide, topping bestseller lists. They have been translated in major markets by the world's biggest publishers. And they are being adapted at the biggest studios and networks.

Interested in making your own story a reality? Visit Inkshares.com to start your own project, connect with other writers, and find other great books.